Z i f f :

A Life?

Ziff:

A Life?

a novel by
ALAN LELCHUK

CARROLL & GRAF PUBLISHERS
NEW YORK

ZIFF: A LIFE?

Carroll & Graf Publishers
An Imprint of Avalon Publishing Group Inc.
161 William St., 16th Floor
New York, NY 10038

Copyright © 2003 by Alan Lelchuk

First Carroll & Graf edition 2003

Library of Congress Cataloging-in-Publication Data is available.

This is a work of fiction. Any resemblance to actual persons, living or dead, events, or locales, is entirely conicidental.

ISBN: 0-7867-1115-9

Book design by Shona McCarthy

Printed in the United States of America
Distributed by Publishers Group West

To Saul and Daniel

Also by Alan Lelchuk

American Mischief

Miriam at Thirty-four

Shrinking

Miriam in Her Forties

Brooklyn Boy

Playing the Game

8 Great Hebrew Short Novels (as co-editor)

On Home Ground (for young readers)

Contents

A Brief Word
from *Ziff: A Life,* a biography by Daniel Levitan

With some reluctance, the author has decided to publish here a brief private correspondence, actually two letters, that were sent between the subject of this biography and the writer. Though the notes might have been relegated to the end of the book, as part of the appendix, I thought, out of fairness to everyone concerned—reader, writer, subject, book—to place them up front. Hopefully the reader will understand why this unusual course of action was chosen after reading the exchange of letters, and I hope Mr. Ziff will forgive this modest trespass.

D. L.
Mascoma, N.H.

Aug. 15, 2001

Dear Arthur,

Would you be interested in writing a personal note at the beginning of my biography in which you can lay out your own thoughts on the whole matter, and speak frankly? If you wish to disassociate yourself totally, in print, from my project, you are welcome to. Or if you prefer, you may want to speak aloud to me some or all of the critical comments you've said to me privately; please feel free to. Naturally, you will have the manuscript in hand (which I've almost finished revising), so you can see for yourself what I've been up to, and whether I've done you any possible harm or rather, measured you and your career fairly, with utmost care and respect.

It goes without saying that I'd be open to your thoughts and criticisms of my work, should you care to offer them.

Though it's not been easy, to say the least, these past three years of writing your literary biography have been a labor of passion, a journey of unforeseen turns and pleasures. In part, I've learned the lesson that in fact your recent novels have sought to instruct in, namely, how tricky and elusive the notion of a writer's identity, and how striking the gap between the limited living self and the fluid literary character. Further, how very confrontational, dramatically so, the two can be at times, in opposing each other. Yet whether I've been able to convey this intimate ironic drama with the appropriate delicacy and judicial integrity in my small book is another question, of course. But I've tried, believe me, I've tried.

I look forward to hearing from you, and meanwhile wish you a happy new year for 5762.

Danny

Aug. 22, 2001

Dear Danny,

Your kind but cunning offer for me to write a prefatory note of disclaimer in your book on me is not without its charm, perhaps all the more so because of its apparent sincerity. Is it more of your beguiling but dangerous innocence that is prompting this offer? Or a rush of late season guilt? Surely not thinly disguised guile or perverse malice? Whatever, I shall decline.

As I've said before, your book is your book, and I have had, and continue to have, nothing to do with it.

Also, as I have warned you earlier, more than once, be prepared for all sorts of unsightly blemishes to surface in your work that will no doubt embarrass you, and injure your reputation—is there any left of it?—much more than it will affect me. I refer to your built-in arrogance, broad literary disdain, barely suppressed anger, humiliating envy (of me), that will show through and seriously disfigure your so-called objective biography. (Why not simply call it a novel and go scot-free? Because you'd have to return the $ advance?) The results will not be pretty, pal; I mean the blood spilled and bones broken on the literary battlefields will be yours, all yours. You may not believe me, but even as I write this, I cannot but help feel a certain sympathy in advance for you, stemming from our old friendship. You always were blindly dogged, wrongheaded, dangerously impulsive, your own worst enemy, and the paths you've chosen, often adventurous, were often marred by wrong turns at crucial junctures. This current path was dead wrong from the start, however. You're in over your head, Dan.

Naturally I will have my lawyer look at the manuscript (directly from the publisher), as a necessary precaution, though I don't think you'd be foolish enough to manufacture incidents or embroider conversations, or attempt to recapture (and thereby reinvent) old mutual scenes that might in any way invade my privacy or injure me personally. *(And as you know, I get injured very easily.)* My compulsive habit of notetaking, which you may remember, could come in very handy here.

Yours,
Arthur

Since a life has to begin with birth and to continue through the years these facts must be introduced in order. But have they anything to do with him [the subject of the biography]? That is where doubt begins; the pen trembles; the biography swells into the familiar fungoid growth. . . . Facts have their importance.

—But that is where the biography comes to grief. The biographer cannot extract the atom. He gives us the husk. Therefore as things are, the best method would be to separate the two kinds of truth. Let the biographer print fully, completely, accurately, the known facts without comment; Then let him write the life as fiction.

Virginia Woolf
Epigraph from *Ziff: A Life* by Daniel Levitan
(as cited by Hermione Lee, *Virginia Woolf*)

Ziff:

A Life?

PART ONE

one

I TOOK MY LAST NEWSPAPER OF THE MORNING INTO THE STUDY, IN ORDER to read the car ads of the *Union Leader,* New Hampshire's yellow rag that might have supported Hitler on a No Tax pledge. As I sat down in the leather lounger, I noticed an early morning fax had arrived. More bad news? I mused. Yet another overnight rejection by a European publisher of the new novel? If I read it now, my morning of writing would be ruined. No way. I turned off the receptive fax machine and sat back with the safe ads for four-wheel-drive trucks. I wanted a Toyota 1986–87, with an extra cab, for about $3,500. The only one I found had "the usual bed/body rust," so I stood up, stretched, and went to pee before starting to work. The awful daily grind; was Sisyphus an obscure novelist?

Moving back into the study, I saw the fax had slipped to the rug, so I was forced to bend and pick it up; any sign of disorder in the room—a book dislodged, the postage scale moved—and I couldn't begin. (Even though the entire room was a mad clutter, as Becka never failed to note, with piles of papers and notes burying other papers and notes, and books strewn everywhere; but it was a mess, a puzzle that I understood, meaning no one else could tidy it up.) Setting the page down, I decided what the hell, get it over with, and suffer the first hour or two of minor depression. Minor, because I had gotten so inured to literary snubs of one sort or another that the dejection was familiar by now. Being down and out as a writer had its own neurotic comforts.

The fax read, in caps: AN INTERESTING IDEA HAS COME UP HERE. SOMEONE HAS POINTED OUT THERE'S BEEN NO BIOGRAPHY OF ARTHUR ZIFF,

THE PERFECT AUTHOR WOULD BE D. LEVITAN. INTERESTED? SERIOUS MONEY. LET'S DISCUSS. PATRICK

I read it twice, seeing the publisher's letterhead, my head swirled, and I sank down. A slow smile spread across my face—a grimace in disguise?—and after a minute or two I actually laughed aloud, the whole thing was so preposterous! A good joke, all right. I sipped my coffee and cackled.

"Hey, what the hell is going on in there?" called out Becka, in passing to the stairway.

"Oh, just something funny, very funny, if it's not a hoax actually. I'll show you later."

Why bother now, right? Well, I'd fax back. But what could I say? Simple enough.

In caps I typed: VERY FUNNY. Switched the fax back on, and sent it off.

Turned on the radio, WOKO, country music from Burlington, Vermont, to hear the repetitive boring music and the disc jockey's dulcet-voiced knowledge of trivia and gossip. Wearily, I sat down to the day's work of three to four pages, opening my ancient laptop and pressing the keys to enter the new novel file. I stared out at the gray day, the tall pines in the bluish distance, the flag-less flagpole (left by the old owner) in the meadow. Thoughts of Ziff drifted vaguely across my mind. One of the two or three most famous (serious) writers in the country, maybe in the world. A writer whose books about himself, through ingenious disguises and deliberately slippery masks, had created an aura of mystery about his true self and real adventures, especially sexual ones. Arthur Ziff, the great demon of Jewish orthodoxy and conventionalism, the *dybbuk* enemy of the rabbis and suburbanites who, nevertheless, bought his books with a relish bordering on fanaticism. Arthur Ziff, poor boy from Dorchester, Mass., who had wound up cohabiting with and eventually marrying Jeanne L., France's most acclaimed actress, in a marriage that was second only to Marilyn M. and Arthur M. in celebrity prominence. (What *was* the full truth about their relationship, breakup, other partners?)

Arthur Ziff had been my best pal for ten rich years, during which we had exchanged manuscripts, stories, secrets, adventures. And now, after a hiatus of five years over a literary double-cross—against yours truly, Danny Levitan—we were friends again, albeit a bit shakily.

A pair of barn swallows soared onto the outside porch, checking out their winter nest. The simple and obvious truth dawned on me: of course, a book on the real Ziff would be worth every penny of forty or fifty grand in this era of financial literary inflation, of public relations hype and decadent culture. (Just fifty? Wouldn't it be a great coup to have an up-close portrait of this bad boy of American literature, this sexual outlaw? Maybe even be that rare book: sensational and literary at the same time?)

For me, some useful money, too, what with the various debts I had accumulated these days, not to mention the items I had wanted but couldn't quite afford: a good used van for Becka, the four-by-four truck for myself, a small redwood deck out front (in place of the concrete stoop), an expansion of my cramped study. And why not some future college tuition for the boys? . . . More. The book itself might even put Danny Levitan back on the literary map, after I'd disappeared for nearly a decade.

Only problem was, there was no way I would stoop to write it. Let them get the usual sort of hack, academic or journalist, like those who usually wrote the modern literary bios. Some hack who, posing as a critic and biographer, would get it all wrong, straight down the line wrong about the life and the books, either smothering the life with deadly academic detailing, or, seeking to juice it up, missing it completely with a self-preening self-referential style of journalism. In a curious way Ziff would love just that sort of treatment, as Bellow had in his own way, to get his real life off the hook, you might say. No one messing seriously with the real, sometimes hot-potato facts, no serious interpretation, no separating the real from the fabricated in the Ziff fiction—those novels that had been honed so carefully in order to tease and to obfuscate, to tease and to manipulate, to entice and to mislead, to win readers and to create a moving, elusive target. Named "postmodern" by the sly academicians and mandarin aesthetes (watch your biases, Danny-boy), those works had succeeded thoroughly, of course.

Yet no one knew who Ziff really was, what he was up to or wanted, what the facts of his erotic life were, how he measured himself in literary terms (or was to be measured), and so on. The brilliantly crafted novels, the wily ingenuity of Ziff's promotional campaigns about the self, even the two autobiographies and National Book Award–winning book about the mother (just missing the Pulitzer), all that was not only brilliantly "managed" but also succeeded famously. Without appearing on any of the vulgar TV shows, without huckstering around the country to promote the books, without pretending to be a Dickens and giving ridiculous national readings, Arthur Ziff had become a grand celebrity who was also a serious writer, the very funny and very obscene novelist who was on most short lists of the top American writers.

And yet, forgotten Danny Levitan sitting here in the woods writing yet another novel that only a select few read anymore, might say a useful word or two about the giant bad-boy figure, and a smart word or two about his books, too. Was Ziff really that good after all? Or was he really that *bad,* and therefore very good, like Céline, driven by crazy, malevolent impulses? Or rather driven by other, more practical drives, let us say? I walked to my stand-up desk and saw my framed old photo of Ziff, myself, and a good mutual friend, at a pickup football game during a 1968 Thanksgiving. Lean, youthful, playful. Yes, I could write a pretty fair literary biography; at least sort out the dross from the valuable. Avoid squeamish Puritanism and awed pyrotechnical wonder while complimenting the wild imagination. And . . .

The whole idea was preposterous, I conceded. Never in a hundred years would I write such a thing, and betray confidences, loyalties. Besides, I was a novelist, not a biographer.

The fax machine beeped, and the thin, shiny sheet began its grunting creep upward until it was finally snipped at the end.

Message read: OF COURSE WE'RE SERIOUS AND YOU'D WRITE A SPLENDID BOOK. THINK IT OVER. WE HAVE TALKED IT OVER HERE AND ARE EXCITED. LETTER WITH TERMS TO FOLLOW (SEND TO AGENT?).

Just what I needed, right? Well, I had thought it over, so I typed out another note and faxed it off. GOOD IDEA, WRONG WRITER. LUNCH ON THE 2ND STILL ON, 1PM AT JOY WAH?

Relieved, I put the episode out of mind and settled down to the work of the day. Now 11:00 A.M., only two hours to lunch, and mail; and later maybe an hour or two more of the forced labor camp. ("Levitan Gulag" was posted on the door.) Then pick up one of the superb sons and maybe manage to get a tennis match in. If not, rake up more leaves, change screens for storms, take down snap pea fences for winter. The play, the work, that I had come to look forward to, now that the literary world no longer called, up here in the rugged New Hampshire granite and countryside; beautiful, boring, beloved, lonely. A perfect place to write, to stay obscure, to go crazy.

That night on my answering machine there was a message from Ziff—on cue?—asking if I had seen the letter from L. Postman in the *Times* yesterday. If not, take a look at it, it was something else. I made a mental note to look it up in the library, and figured I owed Arthur a call anyway. This weekend for sure, since the evenings seemed consumed by dinner and boy caring. A letter of interest from the old punch-drunk writer/journalist? What the hell could that mean, mention of me, or Ziff? Sometime I'd have to polish that rough account I wrote up, some twenty years ago, of my skirmish with the Great Postman, who had tried his best to bully the novice (me) into dropping a chapter from my first novel that included a character modeled on the real Postman, demanding my presence in a four-hour meeting with my lawyer, my gutless editor (and publisher), and when that didn't work, threatening me with dark alley retaliation sometime in the future. Ziff had been right there by my side, my best ally.

"Why do you always have to listen to that machine first thing when we enter the house instead of helping to get us settled?" protested Becka, in a usual indictment.

"Yeah, you have a point." Turning to my son of seven, I said, "Gaby, let that go immediately!" referring to the improvised stringwhip he was twirling menacingly in his older brother's direction. "Do it once more and you've lost it!"

"Dad, you always say that to him," Jonathan chided, "but you never actually punish him."

And so the evening commenced with its two to three hours of refereeing, controlling, cajoling, and, finally, reading and story-telling for a delicious half hour.

That night, before falling off to sleep, I thought how the smartest thing to do would be to inform Arthur of the ludicrous proposal, and get his views. It would be amusing to the wise fox, why not? Or would it raise the level of friction once again?

Ziff didn't seem very amused when I told him about the offer two evenings later on the telephone.

"And what do you think about it?" asked Arthur in his sly, testing voice before planning any course of attack, seated—I pictured—on one of his deep, cushiony couches.

"Oh, I think it's pretty funny, which is how I replied."

Seeing that there was no need now for attack or defense, Arthur loosened up. "Pretty funny—you mean like Tom chasing Jerry and winding up with his own tail? All for the fun and pleasure of the *Times* reviewer, maybe? Yes, that would be funny, I suppose."

I was slightly perplexed. Whose tail? "So what you're saying is, it's not enough money, right?"

"You got it, pal. Take a million, not a penny less. And use my agent if you need him—he's nasty, but that's why he gets the best deal. Anyway, did you get to see the Postman letter? If not, and I still have it around, I'll fax it on up to you."

We chatted on a bit, with Arthur telling me about the fake new novel of the hyped Brit. "Read just two pages in a bookstore and you'll see how phony it is. Just two pages, here and there, any-where in the book."

"I thought so, from the review in the *Times*. Did you see it? They gave it to Roger Hackley, one of the standard *New Yorker* wise guys, who sucked up to it petty good. The language of praise was just right for a high school review."

Ziff laughed. "Oh, the *Times*. They'll never change, you know that. What was it Flaubert said, how he'd crawl on his knees from

Rouen to Paris if the newspapers gave up reviewing books? Well, I'd walk from Berkshire County to Manhattan if the *Times* gave it up. My Long March for literature." A final joke, and we hung up.

The phone call made me feel loose and even relieved, having gotten it all out in the air and being upfront about it. Arthur Ziff was a good pal, I felt again, who, despite our more recent differences, had once helped me and my career enormously. It would be insane to write something that might crush the friendship once and for all. Relieved, I toasted my decision with a grape juice.

And yet, as I watched a World Series game on TV, I wondered if the crushing of a friendship was also the right grounds for ruling material "inadmissible" for fiction. After all, wasn't it precisely when Ziff had used me, Levitan, in a novel that the friendship had suffered a somewhat crushing blow? Especially since the portrait was a cartoonish distortion, and since we had agreed, years before, not to use each other in our work? (Just now the center fielder played a fly ball casually, and it glanced off his glove, the kind of sloppy error that never happened with the center fielders of my day, Mays, Mantle, and Snider. . . . *Remember the baseball catches and chatter with southpaw Ziff up at Yaddo?*)

In fact it was Ziff himself who had taught me to use everything at my disposal, all the material of my life, in one way or another; Ziff who had used mother and father and ex-wife and old friends for his material; Ziff who had constantly pointed to Updike as the best example of a writer writing from the latest experience of his life; how even the great one, Bellow, excluded nothing and no one. So, as grounds of literary judgment, injury to a friendship did not require mandatory exclusion. (Especially if the book you wrote was not written with malice intended.)

Consider those first meetings at Yaddo back in the late sixties, in the late fall. He had just come off his first real blockbuster, and came up to the retreat to get away from the publicity and commotion. I was a very young writer, an apprentice who had published but one long story in a national magazine, and I was there for three months to work on a long "Dostoevskian" novel. (Ha.) At dinner, dressed casually, he was amusing and intelligent, exchanging banter and wit with Elizabeth, the wonderful midwestern lady who hosted us, and the other five members at the table. Afterward, an old writer friend of his, up from Pennsylvania for a ten-day stay, took Arthur off for a private drink. Too bad, I thought, since his relaxed manner and witty intelligence made me want to have that drink, though I rather doubted it would happen.

I found out soon enough that I was quite wrong. Sometime in the next day or two, walking away from the breakfast table, Arthur asked if I wanted to join him for a four-o'clock walk, after our day's work schedule. So at four we met up, and walked from Yaddo to the town of Saratoga Springs, about an hour away. Under the low, dark sky, we talked about literature, and a little about my background, from Brooklyn to Cambridge; Arthur was curious, friendly, funny. At a store he picked up a few toiletries, and on the way back he queried me about my writing, what I was working on, what I had published, and asked to see something, either published or not. I was flattered. Walking at a good pace, we made it back in time to each get a shower before our six-thirty dinner—revved up by Arthur's wit—and then the after-dinner sit and chat (thirty minutes of solid boredom) in the adjoining music room. After the whole hour-and-a-half ritual, we made our way to West House, our residence, and Arthur reminded me to give him some stuff to read for the evening.

Unsure whether to give him my long published story or a recently written rejected piece I had mentioned on the walk, I decided to give him both, since the total came to about seventy-five pages.

In West House we played a game of Ping-Pong, joined by a small circle, talked a bit more, and then adjourned for the evening. On the way to his room he picked up his reading homework from me.

The next morning at breakfast Arthur told me he had read both pieces, and why didn't we talk about them later on, on another four-o'clock walk? No more than that. All through the day, while scribbling two to three pages of my *Possessed* on my Olivetti portable, I wondered nervously what the verdict would be.

On a brisk late-afternoon walk around the Yaddo loop, the

news surprised me. "Your story in the *New American Review* is okay, but doesn't really interest me. But the rejected piece, that's something else. Who rejected it, *Commentary*? that's always a good sign. Well, it's a terrific piece, but it's not finished, not nearly. It needs to be fleshed out, made double the length or more, at least. Put down what you're working on and pick this up again. It'll be terrific."

Stunned, I told him I couldn't really do that, I had almost 350 pages of my novel, and—

"Look, you know how I wrote *Dorchester Boy*? I was in Ann Arbor working on a novel and my friend Dan Meyerson and I were having a beer, and I began telling this story of the Jewish boy from Mattapan and the *shiksa* from Wellesley, and halfway through he said to me, 'Put down what you're working on and write this story now, immediately. Do it.' Well, I did what he said, though it was difficult to drop the other piece, and that's how *Dorchester Boy* was written. Understand? I know it'll be tough to drop your book, but you can always go back to it. Just work on 'Polymorphous Play' for now, and give it its full due. Take it all the way. You won't regret it. Now we better hustle, or we'll miss our opening course and then we'll be up shit's creek with Elizabeth and Polly, and you know what will happen tomorrow with our carrot sticks for lunch!"

It took me nearly a week to follow Arthur's prescription, so reluctant was I to drop the work in progress. At last I began to dip into the material again, gradually immersing myself in it and slowly fleshing it out, and all the while I imagined Arthur looking over my shoulder, encouraging me. After about three to four weeks I was as convinced as he had been, and showed him another section, maybe twenty-five to thirty more pages.

Handing it back to me after the reading he said, "It's terrific, you're doing it, kid. It's going to be a memorable book, and you're going to be rich and famous. Just keep going."

Just like that I was on a new mission, guided by Arthur's critical sense and bedrock belief; as I worked on it with steady day-in, day-out regularity, I saw how right he had been, how I had shortchanged the material, and how rich was the vein—the vein of my own Cambridge life during those hot days of the sixties. Every day two or three pages, and at the end of a section or two, I'd show it to Arthur, and he'd be a serious critic, smart, specific, nonsentimental, constructive. As Virginia Woolf had once opined, I was getting the best criticism a writer could have, a series of private hours with an honest and intelligent literary person.

Moreover, through the next weeks of regular walks and chats and evening discussions, it became clear that we were on the same page regarding literary matters, and so Arthur asked one day if I would want to read the manuscript he was working on, and see what I thought. Presently I was reading his work—what was to turn into *Mendelsohn's Meditations*—and commenting. It was an intense and wonderful exchange, a habit that was to extend beyond that winter.

And socially, Arthur again rather amazed me. No matter what famous guest arrived, fellow novelists, a drama critic, a poet, a playwright, I was always invited to join in the company, for a drink and conversation. No matter that I was a 28–29 year-old fledgling, a beginner in the writing trade, an anonymous soul, I was Arthur's friend and therefore a welcome guest. I felt privileged and flattered to be around those bright and opinionated people of national interest and soon discovered that I could hold my own, on literary grounds. So far as New York or publishing gossip, of course, I was out of my element, and merely listened. When it came time to talk about Babel or Maupassant, Melville or Chekhov, however, I would speak my mind. Many of those discussions were stimulating, but I was especially gratified by Arthur's wholehearted welcome into his circles of friends and admirers.

Still, the most important fact of the friendship, then and over the next four years at least, was the seriousness with which the writing was taken. That's what counted the most, and demanded the most immediate and lucid attention. Dinner parties, books to read, articles to write, girlfriends, events to attend, important deadlines, none of those took precedence over him reading my manuscript (and vice versa). Within a week of my handing over a forty-to-fifty-page section there was a reading and a literary judgment, and though most of it was strongly positive, there were also times when judgment meant weeks and months back to the grinding wheel of revision. But it was all okay, since I had a concerned, remarkably intelligent reader who was on my wavelength completely. An open reader and tasteful judge—where were you going to find that?

Gradually my name and novel were being leaked around New York, and I was beginning to hear from an editor here or there. "Just concentrate on the work" was the steady refrain I heard from Arthur. "The money and other stuff will come. Get it right first on paper." That was always the mission, the priority. Nothing about agents, money, editors, houses. The work.

On the same track for literary matters, we found soon enough that we were on the same track regarding women. This meant we were free-and-easy bachelors, with little interest in marriage or monogamy and less interest in moralistic homilies about how to live. (When Lou Roderowitz, the celebrated magazine editor and self-appointed Jewish pope came up for several days and began to pronounce his dogma against sixties' fornication and leftist politics, it was clear to both of us what we were escaping from: Jewish ownership, superego tyranny.) Observing and discussing women, thinking of play and sex, we were imaginative rivals, you might say, playful/serious boys interested in the whole mysterious game of sinful pleasure.

Our frankness about sex and sexual experience was mutual and refreshing. Nothing was off-limits—talking about capacity and desire, morning versus night fucking and erotic positions, dynamo women and perverse habits, attractive (or repellent) odors and growing fondness for cunnilingus, our own weaknesses and limitations (duration of erection, declining number of orgasms), unwanted boundaries. Coming to the territory from different paths, with a variety of spices, both of us were crazy about pussy—as well as very fond of females as friends—and the pleasure to talk openly about sex was exhilarating, freeing.

As that fall turned to winter, Arthur decided to return from

Manhattan to Yaddo, where I had gotten another three-month stay, and our special friendship blossomed. One day Arthur, opening his mail, came across a large check from the publisher, and asked me what I thought he should do with his money from his recent book, "a lot of money." Since I was still wearing my two-dollar thrift-store winter coat, I felt assured of my answer: "Put it in the bank for a year and forget about it. Next year, you can decide." Well, it was a good solution, and Arthur decided it was a better solution than that given by accountants and friends, tax shelters with oil or cattle, real-estate investments, stocks and bonds, etc. So he did just that, put it into a bank CD for a year, and the problem was solved. "You're a smart boy," he said, and I accepted that, though I had spoken out of a pauperish innocence, not having the faintest idea what options there might be other than a bank. And when he told me the sum of money, I shook my head, figuring that a million bucks was a Monopoly number, not real.

Our high time lasted through the snowy winter and spring, where we walked, talked literature, read manuscripts, watched the revolving writers and artists come and go. Breakfasts at eight, black lunch-pail pickups up for our studio lunches, rendezvous at four for long walks around the six-hundred-acre estate, dinners with Elizabeth and the crew of four other inmates, evenings reading, occasionally a visit to Lena's in Saratoga to eye the outside world. It was a ritual fit for a boxer or monk in training. Occasionally a visitor from the outside appeared, to visit Arthur, and he'd go out for dinner. As far as women, his slim, curvy girlfriend came up for an occasional weekend. (Sleepovers at Yaddo were not allowed or even desired.) At times I, too, saw a pal, a Skidmore coed I had met, a robust, spirited English major. But those were occasional diversions, not regular habits. The chief focus remained writing, reading, talking. Gradually my pages accumulated. Arthur would read them and offer, the next day, his shrewd, unsentimental commentary.

Our conversations about literature were inspiring, and radically different from the academic life, where you talked about careers, scholarship, teaching. Ours reminded me of why I had gone to an English Department grad school in the first place, because I loved books and wanted to talk about them. And now here, on our Saratoga Springs magic hillside, Arthur and I were doing it, all kinds of talk about all kinds of writers; the moral freedom of Colette, the compression of Babel, the slickness of Hemingway, the genius of Chekhov, the richness of Bellow. And we'd argue, too, over the value of a magnificent ox like Dreiser, the mannered elegance of Fitzgerald, the qualities of several modern writers. On critics, too: Was Howe really literary, or political? Was Trilling as deep as his difficult surfaces? Was Rahv as good on the Americans as the Russians? Although taste was subjective, we both understood that the common denominator of criticism was taste, and if you didn't have that, the rest of your argument was not very interesting, even if you could write. Not to mention discussions of style and voice in modern writers, or narrative flow and character development in our own work. I was a literary boy, he was a literary boy, and it was exhilarating, like when you were kids on the streets and talking, arguing baseball teams and players. Too bad we didn't tape those discussions, I thought later, for pleasure and instruction. Who knows? We could have marketed them years later for my kids' college education fund.

So, in virtual isolation, fed, clothed, and protected by Yaddo from outside intrusions such as phone calls, drop-ins, or practical breakdowns, we stuck to our duty, behaved like loyal seamen or devoted schoolboys, attending to the task at hand. Time was suspended. Life was sweet.

This clockwork literary life, sustained by friendship and personal affinity, continued after we left the retreat and reentered ordinary (real) life. Arthur returned to his rental home in Woodstock, New York, and I to my rented apartment in Cambridge. I visited there semiregularly, for a week or a long weekend, while he came to Cambridge to see my turf—"It's like Ann Arbor was, when I was in grad school," he nodded approvingly, having a lunch in "The Plow"—and we even discussed my renting a place in upstate New York while I finished my book. But we stayed put, and talked on the telephone daily. Also, by that time, one of Arthur's friends and editors had become seriously interested in my novel, having heard about it from Arthur. He started calling me at Yaddo, and then in Cambridge, but I wasn't yet ready to show anything.

Sharing a literary passion was at the center of other shared interests, as I said, like baseball, reading, friends, gossip, women, sex, and the literary life over the next months (and years). And after I had purchased a home in New Hampshire, and he one in the Berkshires, we continued in the same singular vein of intimate friendship, meeting up here or there or in New York. In the meantime an event had occurred. Some four years down the road, I finished the novel that Arthur had spurred me on to write, and by that time, five publishers were after it. Guided by Arthur in artistic matters, I also was guided by him in practical matters; soon the flow of adoration, and the promise of money, were rather overwhelming. But he kept me straight and true, focused on the book. Indeed, after I had signed with one of the five publishers, FSG, and they were very excited about delivery and a fall publication, I called Arthur from the gas station in "downtown" Mascoma (my country phone being knocked out) to check on a final reading he had given the book. His response was: "I got bad news for you: It's not ready, at least the second part is not ready. You need to take this back, and spend some real time going over it, and I don't mean a few weeks, I mean a few months at least. It's just too doctrinaire, and the voice of your protagonist needs real refining and bringing out. I know it's a drag, a real drag, but you have to give it another shot. The first half—well, the first half and the middle section— are wonderful, but the last half or so needs real revision. You take it, look it over, and see what you think. I know they're waiting for it down in New York, but so what? Let them wait another three or four months. Just get it right first, this is the only shot you have at it. Okay?"

"Okay," I replied, crestfallen, having gone downtown in a rush and feeling like a ton of bricks fell on me. When I got home later, I looked at the manuscript, slowly started reading, and saw for myself the rather stiff quality of the voice and prose, compared to the energy and relaxed power of the earlier half. And the next day, when I called down to my New York publisher and gave them the news, my editor groaned and pleaded, saying arrangements had been made, publicity was all ready, etc. Oh, it would have been so easy to give in and send it on down, collect the second half of my advance money; the publisher was very eager, having already lined up five mass-market paperback reprint houses for an auction, but Arthur had been right, as usual. Part Two did need more revising. He called again to shore me up. So I stayed firm, telling my much-chagrined editor to hold off. And four months later, reasonably satisfied, emotionally drained, I handed in a final manuscript, knowing that I'd get yet another shot at rewrite after copyediting. So, in sum, I had one more Ziffian lesson in writerly patience, and resistance against the wheels of publishing.

Now what, on the other hand, had Arthur seen in Danny Levitan? A literary boy with taste and strong opinions, willing to voice a dissenting view. A young writer who, along with his self-belief and determination, was eager to learn and was a good student. An American lad with a *Yiddishe kup* and a poor boy's hunger. Out in the world, a street-smart fellow, bold with the women, quick with the wit. Temperamentally, a fearless Brooklyn boy with a sense of humor and strong emotions, though more "primitive" and less worldly than the boy from Dorchester. Someone who could talk baseball, books, and the ladies for hours and hours, feasting on the delicious specifics. A protégé, a rookie, a friendly younger rival by six or seven years.

At the same time that Ziff was my mentor in literary matters, he became my guide—a Beatrice-like guide—in personal affairs. At the next retreat stop for me after Yaddo, at the McDowell Colony, I met a Manhattan journalist, well known in New York social circles, and we began a summer romance. As it heated into an affair more serious, and I worried about moving in together, with the pressure of the book and her social background, Arthur tutored me anew, saying she'd be a "great challenge" for me. Joey Parnell was a lovely, willowy blonde, near thirty, descendant on one side of Mayflower English who became New England bishops and governors, and on the other of the famous Irish rebel-hero.

Those credentials were reinforced by a mother who had been high up in the Democratic Party and a close pal of Edward R. Murrow, and a father who had been head of the CIA; Joey P. came from higher stock than my Brownsville Russian-Jewish roots.

While I was drawn by Joey's attractive looks, her emotional fragility, and solid intelligence, I felt nervous over the pedigree, the phone calls from celebrity names, the social circle in Manhattan, the Episcopalian spirits hovering in the background. "Do it, it'll be good for you," Arthur persisted, about whether to have her move in with me up in Cambridge. Knowing Joey himself, he was bemused, let's say, by the incongruous pairing of us, and added to my tacit fears by stating them and others aloud. "How is she in bed? Can you get it up with her? If you can do that, and handle the mother, who knows what the future might bring? A little Levitan, maybe? You could do worse, you know." For me, a true blue multimistress man, adhering to monogamy would be a daunting feat.

And all through the next four years of our working romance, Arthur was there as a guide and friend if things got tight. While Joey wrote her book on Vietnam in one study of my seedy railroad flat near the Orson Welles Cinema, I toiled on my novel in the smaller study, facing Centre Street. When Kissinger called from Washington, D.C., to invite her down for a "useful chat" about the "Phoenix Program"; when Mom came for dinner bringing a well-known liberal president of an Ivy university, and I was checked out; when we went down to Ames, Massachusetts, to spend a weekend with the Plimptons, and some Boston Celtics dropped over for a little lunch; or when I trekked down to St. Barts to spend a week on the oceanside estate of Joey's stepfather—(he a former head of the British Tories and Churchill's buddy), such events and such figures needed a certain amount of humorous vetting and conversation, let's say, and Arthur was right there with me, to ease me through, before, and to humor us both, after. Those "operating room" socials needed my later accounts aloud for clarity and comedy, and our postop chats did just that.

For four years I read every word of Joey's fine manuscript,

making suggestions everywhere, always bolstering her confidence against her publisher's stupidity and her editor's poor guidance, and admiring aloud her lucid prose style and narrative ability. Later, when Joey's book won every prize around, including the Pulitzer, and she was celebrated as a new role model intellectual, I felt delighted for her, not minding just then her odd omission of my role publicly while thanking instead the wrongheaded arrogant editor and others. On the other hand, when my novel came out, it was knocked silly by practically every roving shotgun reviewer who had been fired up by my early success, my friendship with Arthur, my rebellious subject matter. (The book had its share of admirers, too, but won no prizes.) The disparity was sharp and wounding. There was Arthur, playing nurse and doctor, describing his past wounds and injuries from reviews, and reminding me that it was the book that counted in the long run, just the book.

And when Joey and I broke up soon afterward, for a variety of reasons, I split with sadness, fond memories, and a social education. It had been the challenge that Arthur had predicted, worth the years. I had learned a good deal about class and society in America, a great deal about myself—my haughtiness, my weaknesses, my follies. (Was I wearing the right boxer shorts? Why'd I waste my youth on basketball and baseball when I could have hit tennis balls? Was I induced to wear red pants to dinner in the Caribbean and escape lasting shame? Was pâté de foie gras really better than chopped liver? Oh, it was useful to get that education in person—from life, not James or Dostoevsky—but far more painful and humiliating.)

So Arthur was helping me understand myself, I knew, as well as persuading me in writing about myself, in transferring my own experience into text, and employing my chaos as a trump card of exuberance. I was alert, grateful. At that time, too, I was close with Philip Rahv, the renowned literary critic whom I had met while teaching at Brandeis, and who had asked me to join him in a new *Partisan Review*-style cultural journal. Enjoying it at first, I gradually became disenchanted with the demands of magazine editing and left-wing politics. Not to mention the tyrannical demands of Ely himself, a Russian bear who was a better man, and a better friend, at a distance. Once more it was conversations with Arthur, who also admired Ely's superior literary capacities, that clarified matters, and enabled me to break from Ely and stay with fiction.

And in the years following, nearly ten years, Arthur stood for those same qualities—clarity, honesty, generosity, artistic truth. What a powerful friendship—writer to writer, friend to friend, lasting through three or four novels, several girlfriends. So what if later on it started to fray and break down over long-distance mis-readings, some thinly veiled Ziff satiric portraits, subject matter overlapping. . . . Hadn't we had our ten years of trust, truth, reciprocity? Hadn't Arthur proved to be a literary comrade, wit par excellence, tutor, therapist, patron? Hadn't he raised me from a wild boy to a reasonable man—without abandoning my sense of mischief—from an apprentice to a writer, so that when I looked back, it could only be with pleasure?

(Or was all this a bit too rosy, a bit too innocent? Was "older brother" Arthur already understanding that "kid brother" Danny could become, eventually, a real rival? Was it not reasonable to wonder about budding conflicts and competitive anxieties, if not in the first months, then later, down the road? Well, maybe, but not now. . . . For now, look back in pleasure.)

Those fond memories lingered the next day, Friday, when I went back to my novel in progress with a clear resolve of No, and I felt a surprising sense of virtue; I was doing the right thing by not writing the wrong book. Clearly, biography was not my thing. (Though, even as I said this, I countered with: Did you ever know beforehand what was the right or the wrong thing in writing? Until you got into a work and saw how it was shaking out, what sort of prose and imaginative energy it was generating, what sudden crazy path it was leading you on and, if you let it, taking you to a new, unforeseen world, how could you tell right from wrong in art? Oh, the critic might proclaim confidently right from wrong, but not the creating artist who wandered lost in the forest, searching for that untrod path, compass gone, surviving by his wits, his guts.)

I settled in to my command post for the morning, radio on VPR (classical music), newspaper sports scanned entirely (with the Sunday football picks), dog walked, mug of coffee on the desk. I turned on the laptop—which I worked on despite its tiny screen, and despite the larger, new Dell sitting on the computer table. Why? Out of habit and my affectionate memory for its double, my old portable Olivetti typewriter; and clicked on REALLY, my novel file. Called REALLY, WHAT CAN A MAN DO?, it was the long, sad tale of the life of an ex-bachelor, ex-ladies' man, ex-playboy of the academic world, living in an era of women's power and now domestically indentured, and behaving well; in other words, the full, comic tale of D. L.'s life. Into it about 135 pages, I was having a good time, with myself as the chief comic target, and it didn't matter much what would happen to it later, who would take it or who would back off of it for politically correct reasons.

After some two and a half hours and three decent pages, I figured it was time to print them, and see how they shaped up, before taking the pencil and marking it up. I flicked the switch on the miniature Canon printer, waited for the green light and health-sign beeping, slipped in the page, typed in the "P" for the computer to signal its gray partner, and observed the new-world elves go to work making a page at a time; those chip-controlled elves had become a writer's best ally in mutual productivity.

Just then the fax beeped on the next desk, and grunting and creeping began there, too—a duet of beeps and little rings.

Fax read: CONCERNING YOUR PROPOSED ARTHUR ZIFF BIOGRAPHY: GREAT IDEA! WE ARE VERY INTERESTED IN COMPETING IN THE BIDDING. OUR BASE IS SIX FIGURES. SHALL I SPEAK DIRECTLY TO GERARD B.?
MARK MILGRAM, CHAIRMAN
VIKING PENGUIN

Shazaam! I pulled back from the sheet. Stunned. Amazed. Bewildered. My chest heaved, my heart started beating fast. I stood up and walked about the small study, in a daze. M.M. was the same fellow who, through underlings at his office, had turned down my last few books, including reprints of two he had loved in the past, offering various excuses, when the real reason was that

Danny Levitan was down and out on the glamour scale, maybe a 3.0 out of 10. A fellow whom Danny had liked, too, with his own real wounds and tribulations. And now, turning around like this. Why? How? And the dough! Maybe double the money of Pat and Emerson House. In a week. How? And how the hell had Mark M. heard about this at all, let alone describing it as the biography that I "proposed," rather than a proposal made to me? Was it publisher ESP? Were all the literary computer and fax lines tapped, and funneled into one mainline New York computer, for a Publishers' Intelligence Agency?

After a fresh coffee I called my agent, but as I began to inform him of the latest twist, Gerard told me that Mark had already called, and offered "a six-figure base" in any bidding. Nearly swooning, I said, "Really?" He laughed and chatted. "I told you that these things, once they get going, do not make much sense. Anyway, let's wait and see what happens. Go back to work!"

I was so confused that I stopped at my stand-up desk, took up a pen and a small spiral pad, and wrote the number out: $100,000. For a book that I had not yet written a word of, or barely considered! . . . Wake up, Danny boy, that's the way things are done nowadays. You've been out of the literary loop for so long really that you haven't the foggiest about: (a) the money that's tossed around in inverse ratio to what's been written; (b) the commanding presence of Arthur Ziff as a subject of biography. He was a hot item, a glamorous subject. More so perhaps than any other American writer. But that's what literary culture in America in the late 1990s had become: glamour, style. Not any substance of emotional depth or new serious truth, but the surface of things (coded as "craft"), a variant of the recent Style emphasis in the *Times*. (Watch your bias, Danny boy, go easy now.) What made Rushdie so coveted was the glamour of an author on the hit list; no matter that his last books had been deadly dull, unreadable bores. (Or that seven of ten impoverished writers would trade places tomorrow with the PEN martyr, trade in their obscurity for his notoriety, his millions, his artistic sainthood, his chauffeurs and security guards.) The aura of glamour counted: who was hot for the *New Yorker,* say, for the *New York*

Review of Books, the *New York Times;* Arthur Ziff fit the bill. He passed the test of all three, serious enough and sexy enough to be the lead man of all the magazines and journals, a kind of Clark Gable of the modern—oops, postmodern—lit. cult.

Now, if you mixed in handsome Clark with a brainy general, why, you had a pretty stylish figure, all told a rather unusual act—a triple-threat writer, you might say.

"You all right?" asked Becka. "You've been standing there for quite a while now." She smiled. "Have you had an epiphany?" An old joke, dating back to her Russell Sage pals who had loved Joyce.

I nodded dumbly, still bewildered. Finally I left the study, got on my old wool jacket, and leashed the dog for a walk in the woods. A clear, cool day, and the autumnal air was scenting the forest. The walk through the birch and pine, and deeper, the beech and maple, would clear my head and maybe determine a direction.

I crunched along on the old logging path, which had been bulldozed anew last fall and was now laced with leaves, twigs, pine needles, and cones. "Well, Hobbes, girl, what do you think? Is it crazy, or is it crazy?" The golden Lab looked up at me, her soulful brown eyes trying to figure out my unlikely talk. "Yeah, you're right, it is perplexing. And you know what?" Hobbes paused at the question and waited. "I should judge it by the feel of the writing, by the intellectual challenge. And if it doesn't challenge me or stimulate the juices, forget it, right?"

I leaned down, petted her lovely head and soft ears, unclipped the leash, and let her run freely in the woods. Why not? And isn't that the way I should treat the matter and myself, too? Take the leash off and run free with the material? . . . Friction with Ziff? So what? And legal friction, Dan?

I wound the logging loop swiftly, up, down, and around in twenty-five minutes, seeing the outline of nearby Cardigan Mountain and the bluish landscape of hills through the leafless trees. In the low sky I could make out thick cumulus clouds moving slowly, a bit like a herd of buffalo forming for a stampede. . . . toward me?

Near the end of the canopied trail, Hobbes returned to my side, and to her leash. Good girl. Somehow I felt better, surer.

Alan Lelchuk

Back in the study I found a manila file of old Ziff notes and soon clicked open an old file on my hard disk; I also browsed through old letters, notes. Give it a shot, right then and there. Why not? So I opened a new file, naming it GENERAL Z for amusement, and tried out a few lines, a rough draft of an opening:

> In constructing a life of the writer Arthur Ziff, a writer I have admired and a man who has been my good friend, my aim will be to tell only a version of the truth. By that I mean I will have few illusions that I am seeking the whole truth, or *the truth;* I have known him as well as I have known anyone in my adult life. And what is obvious is that the so-called facts are colored if not distorted by one's perception; that memory plays havoc—lies, dilutes, and expands the real, so that the final picture it produces is frequently not to be trusted; that what makes a certain sense to me, moral or aesthetic, may make a wholly different impression on a general reader, who will draw other conclusions.
>
> If I start with the unlikely conceit of Arthur Ziff as the literary doppelgänger of Erwin Rommel, the great German field marshal of World War II, the reader will forgive me.* But it strikes me that certain startling affinities in dissimilar characters can frequently serve to illuminate and to edify in ways hitherto unforeseen. Furthermore, it will help me to locate certain traits, habits of mind, ways of seeing, strategic plans, that otherwise may be missed. We all remember Rommel, the brilliant German tank commander who, after helping in the French campaign of 1940, was promoted to the chief general of the Afrika Korps Panzer Division and nearly made it to victory in Alexandria, Egypt before his defeat at the hands of the British at El Alamein. By the time he was recalled to Germany, he had lost all military respect for Hitler—he had never been a Nazi—was wounded in an airplane crash, and then, when he apparently participated in the

---

*General Patton was a braggart and nasty, Montgomery was ascetic and insufferable, Zhukov was a great strategist but not the dashing Romantic; and Lord Monash, the Australian general from WWI, who was Jewish, was a tempting candidate, but also not the ladies' man that Rommel was.

assassination attempt on the dictator, was forced to take poison, in 1944. As a man he was handsome and smart, with a playboy style and a blond elegance that matched his brilliant capacities as a tank strategist and field marshal; his nickname, The Desert Fox, was most apt.

With Arthur Ziff you have certain similar characteristics. A prodigy at twenty-five, he won a National Book Award with his first novel, *Dorchester Boy,* which launched his meteoric career. Slender, medium-sized, strong-boned, with the famous fierce stare and dark, curly hair, he was quick-witted and conversation-charming; his work was known early on for its hard, stylish prose and for its tough, trenchant observations about Jews, class, and women. (He was never one to suffer fools or frauds for pious or clannish reasons.) But he also has been a master strategist of his books and career, surveying the field before him as well as the books and writers who went ahead of him. This was no innocent swallow flying about on mere impulse and instinct, but a purposeful, shrewd hawk, searching here, scrutinizing there for prey. And prey once found, he darted down and attacked with an efficiency bordering on beauty, so much so that the onlooker was confused as to what he was supposed to be focusing on—an act of lyrical art, or a feral, predatory kill?

Indeed, nearly all his books were aimed to track and hit specific targets, including the infamous and hilarious *The Carnal Confessions of Rabbi Shmulewitz,* which sold in the millions and which earned him the permanent enmity of the Jewish Establishment. (The literary one as well, with Nuremberg trials judge Irving Rose accusing him of being "the number one defiler of our traditions, customs, and beliefs, an aberrant descendant of the great Jewish writers of this century.") After his enormous success he was a bona fide star on the literary field, a familiar face in all the national magazines, and a common name in all the college canons; and yet he did not go vulgar into Hollywood, television, talk shows, but kept his elegant distance, hiding raffishly behind stylish personas of invented self and protagonists, emerging now and then for well-placed interviews and appearances. Moreover, the fictional protagonists served to create mask after mask, just as the interviews and so-called autobiographies provided just enough fact and information to entice readers while at the same time casting everything about that life—foes, friends, affairs, facts—in shadow, doubt, and mystery.

Yes, there was a life to lead, but one in accordance with a true literary superstar. Here, too, as in literature, it was Rommel directing and planning with a sly masterly hand, not some MGM or pulp vulgarian. For example, the affair with Mme. Jeanne Lemaire drove the French intellectuals into a tizzy: How could the dark-haired Joan of Arc of the French left, the ex-Catholic girl from the Brittany countryside, spend the best years of her life with the obscene Jewish writer whose chief point of reference was a place named "Dorchester, Mass."? Is that what French culture had cultivated, its finest movie actress and bravest political soul, to skip town for the sake of *une vulgarité absolue*? It was none other than the cultural czar Jack Lang who noted, when Jeanne went to live with Ziff in Manhattan, "This is one of the lowest points of French culture since Jean-Paul Sartre went on the streets of Paris on behalf of Chairman Mao." (Even old buddy Godard deserted her on that one, saying, "You leave us for a Ziff?") One can imagine how Mr. Lang felt when Mme. Jeanne Lemaire was sent packing, her child in hand and career in shambles, back to her native country.

Sending women packing, in shambles, seemed to be a specialty of the House of Arthur Ziff. This was the third well-publicized affair in which the lady had suffered such a fate. What can one say about this pattern? One explanation might be a psychoanalytical one: the excessive love of the mother created an inability in Ziff to love any other woman, and to react with a sharp disappointment when the cohabitant turned out to be not Mother but (just) another woman. But that is a little too easy of course. . . . (And maybe not, if we consider the famous book devoted to his mother, *Judith: Dying Days.*) And yet is it not a fact that one of the unique things about the fiction is the lack of guilt or remorse in the protagonists? This attribute, or lack thereof, also can be seen in the life as well. Guilt and/or remorse is not an emotion that can easily be associated with the man, or with his chief characters. For example—

The phone rang, interrupting me; a question about a home oil delivery. I turned back to my pages, and realized how swiftly and how many I had written, and with what compelling interest. Reviewing the three-plus pages, I saw the obvious: The pages were draft material, with much of it notes to myself rather than finished stuff for a book. The prose needed polishing, the material needed shaping, the "facts" needed deeper interpreting; and crucially, my own participation as witness needed insertion and examining. Yes, Danny Levitan needed to be there himself, exposed and vulnerable, for the "veracity" of the evidence to be apparent, at least to myself. But I was satisfied, leaning back, with the main feeling: There was a real book here, wasn't there? Whether it would fit into the tight confines of a biography rather than a freer, looser form would be one challenge perhaps. . . .

On Thursday I drove down Interstate 91 to Bellows Falls to my lunch appointment with Pat at the Joy Wah. Now a Chinese restaurant, it had gone through several evolutions since my old editor pal and I first started meeting there nearly a dozen years ago. Joy Wah was situated on the Connecticut River in Vermont, approximately halfway between our two homes, Pat's in western Massachusetts and mine on the Vermont edge of New Hampshire. Seedy Chinese, with special $8.95 luncheons and a good view of the river, Joy Wah had served us through three of my novels, and a couple of rejected mss. as well, not to mention dozens of other book and life talks.

Patrick Rohmer was a ruddy-faced Irish rebel in worn tweeds, originally from upstate New York, who had dropped out of graduate school and become an acute social and literary critic before turning to editing (and part-time farming). Smart, witty, prudent, yet with a quietly adventurous side, he was a perfect complement to a Jewish renegade from Brooklyn like myself, who could run off a bit wild. After humorous opening banter, beers were brought and orders taken. And Pat said, "Well, have you thought it over? What do you think?"

I sipped my beer and replied, "On Friday I got another offer, from Viking Penguin. Six figures."

Patrick's handsome pink face reddened, then he laughed merrily. At last he said, "You are serious, aren't you?"

"Very."

"How the hell did they hear of it—my God! . . . So you're going to do it? *With them?*"

I shook my head. "Half right. I'm going to do it, but not with them. With you, once you match the offer."

Pat looked at me, saw I was serious, and nodded. Measuring.

"This is not just loyalty," I said. "But I think I'll need you on this one, to keep me on the right track and off the easy, sensational track."

He nodded again, his light eyes intensely curious. "When do you want to know?"

"How about . . . now?"

Patrick smiled, checked his watch, said, "Sure. Why not? Let's give it a shot, *if* the right person is in." He stood up and left the table.

My heart revved a bit. I took up Pat's *New York Times* and opened to Sports. Wished it was the *Globe*, but . . . I couldn't help musing again about the project, wondering it if would be a literary betrayal; but then, instinctively, I found myself focusing on the most recent novel of Ziff's, where, not for the first time, the Master had used materials of my life—my journeys as a young seaman *(dekksgutt)* of sixteen and seventeen on Norwegian ships—for his protagonist's youthful background. Betrayal. But who was betraying whom?! And yet, this biography was not to be an act of revenge; it was to be—no, it *had* to be—a work of serious challenge and literary inquiry. A journey for myself, like a novel. Nothing less. And Pat would see to that because, in his bones, he was a literary boy.

Pat returned. "Nothing final until my Thursday editorial board meeting, but it looks pretty good. The marketing guy is actually doing cartwheels. I'd say you're . . . on." He held out his hand.

Accepting it, I said, *"We're on."*

Pat ordered another beer for himself.

"Remember," I said, "I need you around to keep looking over my shoulder, something like Samuel Johnson writing on his friend Richard Savage."

Pat laughed. "Yes, that was a piece of writing, wasn't it? Except that Savage was down and out, a drunk, and forgotten, as I recall. Does Arthur drink secretly?"

I smiled. "No matter. Johnson on Savage, Levitan on Ziff, okay?"

The waiter brought over our luncheon specials, "Crab ranggoon" for Pat and chicken with bamboo shoots for me.

"Can you finish it while Ziff is still alive?" Pat asked.

"Oh, I should hope so." I smiled. The question is whether *I'll* still be alive!"

"Once word gets out, you know, there might be some . . . pressure on you, from Ziff."

"Oh, of course, but he'll hear about it from me first."

Pat roared. "Oh, that should be interesting. Very."

"By the way, when I mentioned it to him, in a kind of humorous vein, Arthur thought I should get a million."

Pat stared at me, not knowing how to take my words.

"Don't worry, I've already made my deal, I won't hold you fellows up. Unless I take his infamous agent, of course."

His eyes grew wide in astonishment, and he really almost choked on his food.

two

Rewind to a scene from the past: a small town in southern Vermont; the time, fall 1968 or '69. Ziff and I are having a lunch at a local restaurant, and while eating, we've been having a playful time with the long-haired waitress, and at one point I throw out for fun that we are movie people, in town for a short time to look for some talent for a rural-setting movie. Mary Jean brings us coffee, a check, and adds that she would like very much to "audition" for us if we'd be interested.

"You understand," I reply immediately, "there are absolutely no promises that anything will come of this."

"I understand."

"And there may be some risqué or earthy scenes, you know?"

Mary Jean lets her thick hair fall over half her face, à la Veronica Lake. "You mean, can I do nudity? No prob at all."

"Are you over twenty-one?" Arthur asks.

She smiles widely, showing an upper row of uneven teeth, and swings her long brunette hair away from her hazel eyes. "I'll be twenty-four in March, thanks." She jokes, "Shall I bring my ID?"

"Yes, why don't you actually, Mary Jane," I return, savoring her name and playing the role.

"Mary *Jean*. Well, what's the address? I get off here about eight depending on the traffic, and can be there at nine o'clock, say?"

"Tonight, you mean?"

"Yeah, why not?"

"Where you from, by the way, young lady?" asks Arthur.

A snide laugh. "Buffalo. Well, a little suburban dump just outside, Lackawanna."

Ziff nods approvingly, and I give her our aliases, Max Carey and Vince Scully.

On the drive home, Arthur says we never should have done it, it's way too chancy, crazy. "She'll probably bring her brother or stepfather with her, and he'll have a shotgun!"

"*If* we don't give her the part, you mean," I retorted.

At nine precisely, at Ziff's rented house, a car turns into the driveway, and Arthur sternly cautions us both to go easy. "Sure, *Max*," I agree. When she comes in, I take her jacket, and Arthur asks, "You did bring your ID, yes?" She smiles, a cozy, crooked-tooth smile, and produces a driver's license from her shoulder bag. Detective Ziff looks it over, checking the picture and the date of expiration, and hands it to his partner, me, who nods assent.

"You guys act like CIA," she says, taking off her vinyl car jacket and entering the living room. She's dressed modestly, in a midlength skirt and a canary yellow sweater, with a bright blue headband holding back her long hair.

"My, you look a little like a native squaw."

She laughs, lightening her demeanor. "Yeah, I know what you mean. Actually, I'm supposed to be a quarter Mohawk."

Ziff asks, "Would you like a drink, beer, soda, water?"

"Sure. Beer would be nice."

I go to the kitchen and open one of the six-packs I've bought for the occasion.

"Hey, thanks. I like Coronas, but they're too expensive for me." She points to a stuffed chair. "May I?"

"Please, by all means."

She sits and crosses her legs demurely. My fluttering heart steadies, and I feel relieved. She seems well behaved, decent. I look over at Arthur, who is sitting drumming his fingers, every now and then listening for a noise, expecting disaster.

Small talk, with the boys (us) asking her questions about who she is, where she lives, boyfriends, etc. The answers prove out okay; she's broken up from her "old man" of two years; she's lived in this town for two years but wants out; she's never "really acted" except in high school, when she was in two plays, but she loves the movies; she knows clearly that "you guys have promised me nothing."

Nervously alert, I say casually, "Well, why don't you get out of your outer garments, and let's see your figure, if you don't mind."

"Sure," says Mary Jean, standing up and proceeding eagerly to remove her blouse and skirt. In bra and half slip she is really rather nicely put together, trim, firm, smooth-skinned, with good legs. "Would you like this off, too?" She indicates her half slip, and one of us nods slightly, as at an auction.

I ask Arthur, "What do you think, Max?"

Ziff says, "I think Miss—uh—what's your last name again?"

"Bourbeau."

"I think Miss Bourbeau has a very nice figure."

She nods in appreciation, and asks if we would like her to remove her underwear, too.

I say sure, if she doesn't mind. "I'll get you a bathrobe—in case you get chilly."

I go out, return with a beige terry bathrobe, and hand it to her. She turns about, with modesty, it seems, puts on the robe, and steps out of her bra and panties. Turning back to us, she slowly, surely, opens the robe to expose herself. Her breasts are firm, her skin smooth, and her black triangle is neat. "No tattoos, in case you're wondering," she notes.

Then, unsmiling, she takes two steps forward and asks cordially, "Is there anything you'd like me to do now?"

I sense the sentence has hit Arthur like a rod, as he sits upright suddenly; his or my nerves? I get up, go to a shelf, bring down a paperback, and hand it to her. "Why don't you sit down and read from that play, at the yellow marker? You read the Hedda part, and Max here will read the Mrs. Elvsted part." I hand over another old copy to Arthur, who accepts it warily. Another trick?

Mary Jean takes the book and looks over the lines while I pull up a straight-backed chair for her, some eight to ten feet across from us. She sits down and, crossing her legs—but not bothering to close the robe about her—she commences to read, at the yellow marker. Cars from the highway speed by in the lull.

"'What sort of man is your husband, Thea?'" Mary Jean reads, making a face at her botched pronunciation of the name. I signal her onward. "'I mean—you know—to be with. Is he good to you?'"

Ziff is still staring at her exposed position, and I have to cue him to read.

He reads: "'Mrs. Elvsted [evasively]. He believes he does everything for the best.'"

Mary Jean reads, in a stagy voice: "'I only think he must be much too old for you. More than twenty years older, isn't he?'"

I intercede. "Don't try too hard. Just speak normally."

Ziff takes his turn now, slightly more relaxed. They go on for a page or so before the young woman stands up, stretches wide, and struts casually up and back in front of the directors, half smiling. Spotting something, she walks across the room to a coat rack, takes off her robe, puts on my royal blue warm-up jacket and baseball cap, and returns. Now she promenades again back and forth, the jacket reaching only her waist, with her good legs and firm hips and pubic area revealed fully. She is smiling differently and eyeing us, like a sly, sensual lynx who knows its prey well and is emitting its hunting scent.

"You're innovative, aren't you?" I offer.

"I've seen a lot of movies."

"Enough! That's enough!" declares Arthur. "We've seen quite enough, Miss Mary Jo or Jane. You can dress now."

I look over at my friend and perceive the mix of fear and growing anxiety tightening his face.

The young woman stands sideways, in surprise, for a full minute or so, not quite believing what she hears. Then, with poise, she looks over to me for another direction, but I simply nod, in confirmation of the demand.

She turns about, but changes her mind and returns, comes up to Arthur, close enough to kneel down just in front of him—you can feel him stiffen up—whereupon she reaches down and carefully turns down the cuffs on his blue jeans, performing this tailor's gesture as though she is committing an indecent act. Looking up, her face close to his leg, she whispers, "I hope you don't mind," and she sits on her haunches for a long minute, looking up at him radiantly.

Mute at first, Ziff then says, in a heavy voice, "That's enough, young lady. Please, enough."

She nods; obeys him, stands, and goes off to dress. The room is redolent still from her inventive gesture. Arthur, sitting and drumming his fingers on the broad arm of a morris chair, says, "This was the greatest mistake since I married Joanna Lyons from Terra Haute. We'll pay for this, wait and see."

I shake my head in dismay. "She has her . . . qualities, you know. More than we had imagined."

"Yeah. And boyfriends or brothers, too, I bet."

Presently, escorting the young woman to her compact Nova, I say, "We have your number, you'll hear from us soon, And thank you. You were *very . . . intriguing.*"

"I enjoyed it," she rejoins, leaving her hair over one side of her face, "and look forward to hearing from you both."

Immediately inside, Ziff pours a Jack Daniels for each of us, and expounds on his earlier line, the idiocy of what we've done. "This was not smart. If we don't get killed or beaten up, we'll be held up, blackmailed, sued. At least *I* will. You watch. The best thing is to get out of town, fast." He drank his drink.

"Hey, take it easy. We didn't do anything evil, not a single thing. She's over twenty-one, we read her driving license, it was up to date, and we fibbed a little, playacted, that's all. She wanted more, much more!"

"Oh, yeah, she wanted more all right." But Arthur, walking up and back, would not be dislodged from his firm ground of fear and calamity. "You watch. Maybe even tonight. Sure, why not tonight? We're in for it. Either it'll be the cops, or the old boyfriend and friends. Or some local lawyer—a smart Yid to boot! Oh, Christ, why'd I ever listen to you! You know what the payoff will be for me? Maybe I'll get out of it lucky, five thousand—no, ten, maybe?"

I couldn't resist saying, "You won't get off that cheap."

"Yeah, you're right. Twenty at least, huh?"

Oh, he was lovely in vulnerability! "Well, the *National Enquirer* might up it, you know."

The doors were locked securely, the worrying aloud went on till 1:00 A.M., with every sort of possible threat and legal charge explored, and finally, in exhaustion, I called it a night.

"I'm gonna stay up a bit and try to figure this whole thing out," Ziff said. "Although I don't see any way out."

In departing, I put, "She was pretty sexy in that jacket and cap you know. And she does have a superb Jane Fonda ass."

"Probably a hooker on the side, huh?" Arthur queried.

"Actually, just a waitress, which is what made her so sexy. And she has a way of arranging cuffs, doesn't she? . . . See you in the morning."

"Yeah, if we make it through to the morning."

At ten to eight, when I came down, Ziff was already there, coffee brewed, pacing.

"You're up early," I said. "Sleep well?"

"Are you kidding? Waiting for the shit to fly, that's all. Have your bagel while your jaw is still working. Any hour now, and it'll all come down—either the call from the lawyer or the knock on the door from the 'old man' with the shotgun. Or fist."

"Pass the cream cheese and stop worrying. Any lox?"

Handing it over, Arthur noted, "Boy, we're smart, oh, are we smart. Two smart Jewish writers, real smart, *oy vey*."

The next few hours were more of the same, and even a trip to get the morning newspapers did nothing to allay his anxiety. But at noon a call did come through, and Arthur told me to field it.

"Yes, I see," I said, nodding, listening, and holding off Ziff with my hand. "I see. Well, that's rather interesting. I'm not sure that'll work out just now, though, as we have to leave town for a few weeks. But I have your number, and we'll call you when we return. Okay? Thanks a lot, and you did fine, by the way, really just fine."

I set the portable phone back in its cradle and looked up at the eagerly awaiting Ziff, who said, "How much?"

I deliberately took a sip of coffee before answering. "It seems as though Mary Jean had such a good experience that she'd like to bring her sister along for the second audition, if that's okay with us? 'Connie' is visiting, from Lackawanna, and when she heard about it, well, she wanted a shot. She's a bit younger, actually, far 'bustier' and she 'begged' Mary Jean to ask us to give her an opportunity, too."

Ziff stared at me open-mouthed, his black, curly hair disheveled, taking the words in and figuring it all out. Nodding, he said, "That's when they spring the trap, huh?"

I suppressed my laughter and nodded solemnly. "Yeah, just about then. Right then, when she brings Connie around."

Exhausted, from my trance-like writing, I pulled back from my laptop and wondered how I would ever manage to insinuate that little scene into a biography. Through a dry paragraph of expository narrative? Or . . . was it not possible? I got up and went to the kitchen, where I poured myself another mugful of coffee. The old memory had purged me somehow.

Becka said, "I'm off to the college. Anything you need?"

I shook my head and thanked her.

"Would you pick up one of the kids? Gaby? Remember the bus can get there at ten to three, so please don't be late for him."

"Have I ever been?"

"God, you should hear the gears when I switch gears in the van. Sounds like something stuck in the washing machine."

"Well, you'll be getting your Odyssey soon enough, one way or another."

Actually, Becka had never been a very materialistic young woman, and that was one of her virtues. She had others, too—a literary sense, an interior life, a lucid prose style, a sense of honor. And when her checking account didn't balance at the end of the month, she'd close the account and move to another bank, an eccentricity that charmed me. But she loved virtue a little too much, and Jewish tradition, and also family, her family. Decent human impulses, but not for a renegade like me, for all this went contrary to my natural sandpaperish grain against all well-meaning pieties and niceties—my sense of mischief and waywardness, my hostilities against family mush and religion, my difficult narcissism. So really we had long differed on fundamentals. But once upon a time she had been my smart graduate student, a sexy and skilled Jewish seductress, and later we shared a deep love for our boys. Altogether, she had made the marriage work, taking care of the proper ameliorating mechanisms to keep a freewheeling fellow like myself in check. And allowing me my rebellions, logical and illogical. Thus we had held together, making it through, glued by the boys, the garden, the country life, the friends. It could have been worse, far worse.

Back in my study, I sat back down and reread the scene—real for the most part, with touches of embroidery. Should I try it on Pat? Of course the main problem was rather obvious: Who was going to believe that *that was all that happened* and that Arthur Ziff, that fearless sexual trailblazer of the American novel, had acted with such fear and timidity in his life? No, that was hard to believe, and harder to sell. (Henry James, yes; but Arthur Ziff? no.) Or that Arthur and Danny had next passed up the opportunity to meet the bold woman and her eager 'sister,' in the future? No—that, too, was unlikely, and would not sound credible. Check with Pat, I thought. Standing, I strolled the length of the house, got my jacket and some mail, walked down the bluestone driveway to the mailbox, set in the mail, and raised the red flag. Sunny, cold, lucid day.

Walking back, I realized the obvious: *I would have to invent something happening to buy credibility with the reader.* No Ziff fan was going to buy the "real" version of events—too dull, too pedestrian. (And maybe not even Pat would buy it, for other reasons—like the practical need for something to happen, to warrant the planned campaign for the book? But I could deal with that matter. The practical or the commercial ends were not going to shape this content.)

So I'd invent just a bit, and give Arthur a little more . . . bite, vivacity, daring. Just a little, say, so as not to really cheat. Just tinker with, perhaps. Yes. (Besides, hadn't I already tinkered, to some extent, with the original?) Was a little fiction spliced onto biography so terrible, for the sake of truth? Consider all the unconscious "made up" inserted into autobiography, or the unacknowledged fiction—memory astray, say—in biography.

But, then, what was truth? Where was it? And what percentage of memory was to be trusted—70 percent, 80, or maybe 90? . . . How could you verify this? These were questions, problems. Was there any real book without those?

I sat down and typed off a note to Arthur, saying I was coming down to New York the week after next. Was he going to be in town or in the country? Could we get together for dinner? . . .

Furthermore, in seeking *the truth,* would I not also have to deal with the literary self or persona in the novels? Of course. Could you discuss Conrad without speaking of Marlowe? Obviously this would have to entail some literary criticism, and judgment; was I up to that sort of truth, maybe the highest? Because of the frequent sensationalism of Ziff's content, his novels were often misread, displaced by the controversial; and because of the slippery and crafty nature of the protagonists (and author), the critics were led astray, trailing down false paths marked by catchy signposts such as "postmodern." Easy enough. Could Danny Levitan do better? (Better than Gass, Bloom, Kermode, et al.? Well . . . maybe.) Being a writer helped; and being in tune with Ziff's fiction helped, too. Also, running around on much of the same turf, same experience, didn't hurt. On the other hand, maybe being down and out and semiobscure—why the 'semi'?—led to an inevitable envy, unconscious, perhaps, that would tarnish clear judgment? A subject to consider: my writer envy.

three

Three days later something else flew in, bearing surprise. Not entirely a surprise—except its swiftness—since I had written her a note. A letter came, postmarked Paris, from Jeanne L., the former wife of Arthur Ziff. It was very simple:

> *My dear Dan,*
>
> *Thank you for your letter of the 14th—as I was about to write you—I am very glad that you are embarked on the project of a biography of our mutual friend A. Z. I believe that I can contribute something of interest to this project, having lived fifteen some years with the man. Perhaps we can meet, in Paris (preferably) or in New York (if necessary), to discuss the matter?*
>
> *Please give my warmest regards to Rebecca, and those excellent boys of yours.*
>
> *Your friend, Jeanne L.*

My, oh, my, things were beginning to heat up. A gambit tossed out, and already the prospect of a major opening. . . . I had heard all about the affair and the marriage breakup from Arthur's point of view, but what was her side of things? A great actress on the silver screen and stage, was she also one in life, as Ziff had claimed? And if that were the case, it may be asked who was the greater actor, Jeanne in life or Arthur in his fiction? What were the consequences of such theater, and where were the boundaries to be drawn between life and art? Well, I'd first have to see and weigh all the evidence. And see her soon, somewhere or other. Maybe gay—or gloomy?—Paris was the place to meet after all? Or neutral territory, like Amsterdam or Havana?

Pat called to ask how things were going, and I said they were moving along. When I told him of the lead from the famous French lady, Pat raised his eyebrows across the telephone and said, "Word moves fast, doesn't it? Of course she has her own self-interests, remember."

"Without a doubt," I replied.

He laughed. "By the way, we've already gotten calls from the *New Yorker* and *Vanity Fair*, asking—or begging—for first serial rights. With a floor bid of thirty thousand dollars."

"Maybe I should stop now, while I'm ahead of the game?"

"You mean and write nothing?"

"No; hand in my ten or fifteen pages, and call it quits." I scratched my beard. "I'll let you know what happens in the meeting with Ziff. We're on for dinner next week."

"Well, that should be interesting. Very interesting."

"You mean, will I be 'persuaded' to pull out? Could be; anything's possible."

"Well, don't—you'll write a good book."

"Oh, yeah? How do you know?"

" 'Cause you're smart and tough, like Ziff; you won't be intimidated by him, or fall into adulation. So, good luck."

"Thanks; I'll need it, especially by dessert time. By then this tough guy might be flat on the canvas, or if he's lucky, TKO'd."

The next week, on a cold Thursday night in December, we met

at Florentine's in Manhattan, a swanky Italian restaurant on the Upper East Side.

Ziff was already seated, in the raised platform area by the window, looking smart in his muted tweed jacket and soft beige turtleneck. He greeted me warmly: "Sshh. I've saved you this seat so you can *gib a kuk* across from you, over my shoulder."

Handing my coat over to the waiter, I settled into my cane seat and glanced over. A smashing young blonde seemed to be poured into a skimpy black dress, and seated between two dark, handsome, Italian-looking men, the older one sporting an open-necked shirt to reveal bare chest and large crucifix, and the younger one a two-tone shirt and handpainted silk tie.

"Well, am I a loyal friend or not?" Arthur murmured. "Like the tits?"

I nodded slowly, eyeing closely the full weighty ripeness of those breasts, half emerging from the low neckline.

"Wait till she gets up and you see the rest. But if you look too hard"—he leaned just a bit—"the young guy will hold you down while the old boy cuts your cock off. That's why there're two of them."

A waiter appeared. "Can I bring you a drink, sir?"

"Uh, a glass of white wine, thanks."

"Sure, why not? Make it two. And can we get our salads now?"

The waiter nodded. "The usual romaine, sir?" and went off.

"So how you doing, kid? What's happening up in the north country? Geese flying? Snow falling?"

"And trees squeaking."

"Ohh," Ziff roared, "those trees. Then it's busy this year!"

"And don't forget the academicians. They're squeaking, too."

Arthur laughed. "Oh, they're right there, in on the action. Any sexual harassment case put on you yet? How'd you escape thus far? Don't worry, they'll get you, kid. Maybe Gloria will come up in person for your case. Are you fucking any of the students? If you fuck the boys, they don't come after you so fast, you know."

I shook my head. "Not anymore, pal. It's not worth it."

He nodded. "That's why I stopped teaching—the feminists."

"More powerful than the Communists ever were, huh."

"Are you kidding? They've not only ruined English departments for at least twenty years, but they've ruined the universities, taken the fun out of teaching. Thought control everywhere, class tape recorders, blacklists, bulletin boards, literary canons. Do you see what gets tenure these days? And just flirt with the wrong girl, or she with you, and you'll be turned in. Exposed. Taken to trial." He shook his head. "Look: Since no one reads anymore, and you're not allowed to fuck anymore, what's the point of teaching at all?"

The waiter set down our glasses of wine and salads. "The bread will be right here, sir."

Ziff nodded. "Speaking of Gloria, did you see where the old Stalinist has put her STOP sign on the Freud exhibit down at the Smithsonian? It seems that Freud condescended to women, and therefore, No Go. You did know that that's what Freud's best known for, 'condescending to women,' right? Can you imagine the intellectual level down there, sacrificing Freud for Mannheim's wishes? It gets worse and worse. *Oy,* look, *she's* standing; now, take it easy when you look over; you don't want to get us blown away before we get our linguini."

I dipped my bread in the olive oil, glanced slyly, and followed the young woman walking. Well, strutting slowly, the black sheath covering about half of her, the bulging treasure chest and the emphatic high ass redirecting patrons' willpower and concentration.

"Enough, enough," Ziff whispered.

"Hey, the whole restaurant is watching her."

"Yeah, but they'll take it out on us 'cause we're closest and we're Jewish."

"Ready to order, sir?"

"*Her,*" I murmured.

"Excuse me?"

"The young lamb," Ziff interpreted for the waiter. "Good choice. I'll go with the salmon. Thanks."

"Thank you, sir."

"So, how's married life?"

"Oh, the boys are pretty good. Little one plays cello, and the older one reads and reads, occasionally looking up to be witty and literary."

Ziff laughed. "Oh, sounds like they'll be quite ready for our America, don't you think? Reading books and playing the cello, yeah, just about right. I think I can get you the address of a good monastery on the Canadian border."

"I may need it first."

Arthur smiled. "Always the clever one. And Rebecca, how's she? Do you fuck her once a month? Once a quarter, like a dividend? Come on, give her a break. Really. It's not such a terrible thing to fuck your wife now and then. Twice a year is not a crime, really."

Someone had sidled up quietly, a well-dressed paunchy man in his fifties, and he said, "Excuse me, Mr. Ziff, but I couldn't resist coming over to you and saying how much your books have meant to me. Especially *Judith*. It just knocked me out."

Arthur froze, then said, "Thank you."

"My own mother died under similar circumstances, and your descriptions of the medical ordeal, and the personal anguish, were so right on target that I . . . I just broke down. I bawled for two straight days."

Arthur appreciated that and said, "What's your name?"

"Harold, Harold Grossman. I'm a C.P.A. here in town." He handed Arthur his card. "Do you think I might send you the book for you to autograph it?"

"Sure. Why not? Send it to me in care of the publisher. Thanks for stopping by, Harold."

" 'Heshy,' " Harold winked. As he turned to go, he added, "Pulitzer? It should have won the Nobel, if you ask me."

"Thanks, Harold. But it didn't win the prize, you know." After he departed, Ziff said, "The Yids are sentimental. They loved that book. Not the Pulitzer committee, of course. Although the big cheese from Columbia wrote me a note to tell me how honored I should feel that I had made the short list. Can you believe the prick? I wrote him a note back, asking him if they wanted to send me a Benrus wristwatch for making the short list. He never answered."

The waiter brought the dinners and set them down. "Please be careful, sir, these plates are very hot. Some cheese? Pepper?"

He ground both for me, and a shake of pepper for Ziff.

The young blonde returned, and we sneaked in glances.

"Who gets her first—the old man or the stud, do you think?"

"Equal time, equal opportunity."

"Smart boy. How's your chop? God, to be young with open arteries so you can eat those. How old are you now, kid, fifty-five yet?"

"Yeah, plus a little."

"Oh, boy, wait till you hit sixty, when everything starts falling to pieces. Bit by bit. Do you still get the morning hard-ons?"

I nodded, enjoying the tasty lamb and the fine linguini.

Ziff shook his head. "At about sixty, the morning erection goes. So you still have a few more years. Enjoy it while you can. Now all you need is someone to fuck at that hour, right?"

"Right."

"So what are you writing these days?" Arthur asked. "The buzz around town," he mocked, "is that you're still thinking about doing my 'biography.' What do you say?"

Here it was, a moment of truth, just as I twirled my pasta on my big spoon. I tasted the perfect al dente and answered, "Well, actually, yes, I am still thinking of it."

Ziff took a bite, wiped his mouth with the cloth napkin, then patted it delicately.

I asked, "What do you think about such a project?"

"Oh, it's your choice, entirely." He spoke coolly and evenly. "But I certainly wouldn't cooperate, you know, and it would undoubtedly affect our relationship, as you can imagine."

"I see."

"And there could be other complications in the end. Legal ones, perhaps. But we wouldn't want it to reach that stage, I would hope."

"So," I tried to sum it up, with cordiality, "just the end of the friendship and the possible grounding of the book—before it's airborne."

"It's your choice, as I said earlier."

"But you know," I pursued, "I might be able to write something of real interest about you *and* the novels, don't you think?

"About my work, yes, in all probability." His sharp brown eyes fixed mine, revealing, in their intensity, a touch of yellow in the iris. "But about my life, probably not—not as far as I'm concerned."

"Do you think I'd say something intentionally harmful or . . . malicious?"

"Necessarily intentional, no. But . . . let's say inadvertently harmful, or unpleasant. Without your fully realizing it even."

"You mean . . . just how unpleasant?"

Ziff nodded, his firm chin protruded forward.

"But perhaps you can save me there. I mean, if I were to show you the manuscript, say, and have you comment on it."

Arthur gave off a little laugh, in a gesture of scornful appreciation. "That would be very clever. Showing me the manuscript, having me comment, and then going on to say and do as you wish. Why, you'd have it both ways then, wouldn't you?"

"I hadn't meant it that way."

" 'Bye, Mr. Ziff," called out Harold Grossman, pointing to his wife alongside, who waved. "Remember, *Heshy.*"

People turned, to look over. Politely, Arthur waved back.

Then, turning back to me, he spoke more leniently. "Why are you doing it, Danny? For the money? Do you need it that bad? Or is it for your career, to pick it up after the . . . long decline? A decline that's been unfair to you and your books, as I've written you."

I took my last bite of the lamb but was hardly tasting it now. "Well, maybe for both reasons, I'm not sure. But maybe I just want to write a good book."

"But you're not a biographer; you've never touched the stuff."

I nodded. "True. But a good book is a good book, and maybe my not being a biographer will turn out in my favor. I mean, what I write will have a more unique, serious interest." I shrugged and came up with an example: "Sartre on Genet."

He leaped on that. "So you have me as Genet now, huh? Do I get to take it up the ass, too? Or just blow jobs?" He laughed, then shifted tone: "I think you're climbing up the wrong tree, my friend. And maybe a dangerous one for you to be climbing."

" 'Dangerous'? How?"

"Oh, I wouldn't want to define that just now. Once again, it's your choice. Though I'd add only one other thing: If it's really the money you want, or need, I'll loan it to you. Interest-free. Pay it back when and how you can. Why am I offering this? To bribe you? No. Because you've been a good friend in the past, because you're still an interesting writer who's had his share of unlucky and unjust times, and because I have plenty of money, and it's no hardship on me at all. So if you need fifty thousand, even a hundred grand, maybe to send the older boy to a private school or to make a jazzy bar mitzvah, as well as to give yourself a writing fellowship for a year or two, go ahead and borrow it. No strings attached. Pay it back when you can. Think it over."

"That's a . . . very generous offer."

"As I said, I can afford to be generous. And I'd be pleased to do it for you. You can give me an *aliyah* at the bar mitzvah, and I'll accept it with honor. When's the date again?"

"May eleventh."

Arthur nodded. "Think it over and let me know. We better get going. I'm in bed by nine, you know."

He waved two fingers only slightly, but, like a prince signaling his servant amid a crowd, it was enough for the waiter to come hurrying over. Arthur gave him the credit card, saying to me, "This one's on me." His long face, usually so full of mirth and mischief, was now calm, sober, imperturbable.

four

On the flight to New Hampshire and drive home, I thought the matter over. And one of the things that crossed my mind was why there had been no such literary discussion with Ziff when he had chosen to write about D. L. in a novel of his, especially when the portrait was cartoonish and cutting. (I had unfortunately memorized a few lines: "A writer of some talent, he had lost his edge when he deserted his mischievous angry self. As a man, he was at his best when prowling the streets of coed Cambridge, an old-fashioned masher on the loose, exuding a certain crude charm, it may be said.") Oh, that still cut! No need for talk then, was there? Just the book in the mail, the pain of the mean paragraphs, the follow-up comments of shock and surprise from mutual friends. No consultation then, just the verbal fist in the solar plexus.

Oh, well, what's past is past, I told myself. Really, Daniel, you're not going to act out of that old pain. And his present offer was generous, no doubt. But you're not going to write, or *not write* a book because of the dough. For the tenth time, Danny boy, judge it by the feel of the writing, the pleasure of the journey. Was it likely to be a journey of true literary interest?

Of course, I had to take into account the cautions and warnings of Arthur, especially since he always knew best when it came to the pragmatic. He was well grounded in the high cost of imprudent acts, and expert in the art of counterpunching, whereas I acted too often on emotion and gut feeling, frequently becoming my own worst enemy and only having to face the consequences. Ziff was a man who often beat the consequences to the punch, sizing them up beforehand and heading them off with a shrewd word (inside the text) or a clever interview. Oh, he'd know precisely the most effective way to break me. If he might be Rommel, I might be a *schlemielish* Don Quixote—not the romantic anti-heroic hero but a bumbling writer, tilting at windmills of delusion.

Snow fell lightly as I crept through Andover and turned right for Route 4, northwest for Mascoma. My old Saab 900 knew the road by heart, and I trusted it like a loyal Rocinante. Becka enjoyed mocking the mess inside, the litter of books, hats, bars of old chocolate, spare necktie, sweaters, papers; the trunk piled with tennis rackets, balls, sneakers, ragged workout bags, a bat and baseball glove; the old Saab was a snug, second home. Or better, a portable study for thinking, remembering, clarifying.

Clarifying, that's what a book on Ziff would be for me, I now understood. Writing it, I would have to figure out what the complex friendship of years and years had meant for me. A biography of Ziff would be an emotional experience, not merely an academic, cerebral exercise. Indeed, it might raise all sorts of discomforting questions, such as repressed jealousy, envy, betrayal, but those were worth examining, studying. (After all, might not undesirable qualities produce intriguing results?) And what of the beguiling situation itself—a down-and-out writer writing a book on a hugely successful one, his old pal? If nothing else, I'd be purging the situation once and for all; that was a mission of many fine books. Further: In pursuing that elusive persona of Arthur's, wouldn't I also be pursuing my own self? I mean, seeking a firmer sense of who I might have turned into, here in late midlife. Was I still that tough guy of my salad days, as Pat had cited, that rebellious boy in fiction and life who could run quite well with bad-boy Arthur, making us such good friends? . . . Or someone new?

No, my book couldn't—and wouldn't—be an act of revenge. It would be an act of clarification, a journey of the self, a work of seriousness. That's why Patrick Rohmer was the right editor on the job. Like M. Perkins or R. Giroux, he knew the difference between the serious and the commercial, a book to read or a package of schlock. Pat would keep me on the literary, exploratory path, should I come in danger of veering off without knowing it. The achievement of a noble end was up to me, of course, and my talent; but at least I wouldn't be tricked or detoured by an editor's lust for commercial success or mere popularity.

So, I thought, driving through my familiar hills, a serious biography for me would have to be something like a novel, a personal testing, as well as a traditional work; only then could I enter into other general territories with some truthfulness—maybe learn more about the makeup of a contemporary artist in our climate of chaos and decadence, the jagged narcissism of the modern literary ego (including its own delusions and illusions), the double-edged environment of financial success and celebrityhood. (Maybe use my own experience of obscurity and irrelevance, after my bright start, as a useful contrast? . . . Oh, Danny, don't flatter yourself;

even your obscurity is irrelevant.) Not to disregard the other big questions: What did the sum of Arthur's work add up to? Did the vast array of invented selves aid or impede the art? What might his *oeuvre* look like twenty years after his death?

When I got home, I was greeted warmly by the family, and sprung the presents for the boys: a set of matchbox cars for the little guy, and the board game Stratego for the thirteen-year-old. And that evening I raced cars back and forth on the wooden floor with my little-car junkie Gaby, and then engaged the older boy in a losing effort on the board. Indeed, Jonathan was a better board strategist than his dad; should I use him on the Ziff book?

The next evening Becka's sister and brother-in-law, in from Toronto, came around, and the four of us went out to dinner. At Sweet Tomatoes in Lebanon, the best local eatery, we dined on antipasto, veal, and linguini, and discussed the history and fortunes of Canada. I had grown fond of the odd pair, the witty, irreverent sister Janie and the big-bellied, scraggly bearded Jake, smart, windy, awkward. A former high school teacher, Jake knew about lots of things, from computer chips to Jewish laws (his father had been a *cheder* teacher), and this evening he discoursed, by way of talking about the possibility of a national breakup, on the history of Canada.

"Look, the British created modern Canada only as a wall of resistance to the expansion of America into the north country. That was their main purpose. In 1923 at Westminster, for example . . ."

Think it over repeated itself in my brain and heart. But again I countered with the same reasoning: I couldn't reject a book project out of hand, a priori, rather than waiting to get on the inside of it. No way. What exactly did Arthur mean by saying that this "would undoubtedly affect our relationship"? Wasn't that affected years before, by Ziff himself, in two of his novels? And should I allow an implied threat of legal action to inhibit my aims or censor my work? Hadn't that been tried before, in vain, some twenty-seven years before, which Ziff knew well, when the neo-Hemingway New York bully had threatened me if I didn't censor a chapter in my first novel, which concerned a character modeled on the Great Novelist; and hadn't Arthur Ziff been right there—as I've mentioned—a shrewd pal and a loyal witness to the whole stressful spectacle?

"You see, the crucial battle for influence in Canada and maybe all of North America took place at the Plains of Abraham, just outside Québec, between the French and the English. You've heard of Montcalm and Wolfe, the two great generals, right? Both killed there. Well, if the English hadn't won that, then the French would have dominated the whole continent. Establishing the English language, laws, and liberties of this fair dominion and ending the threat of Froggy despotism and food. . . ."

Yes, I'd have to assemble a list of people to talk to, those "formidable individuals," pro and con. Start there perhaps, and see what I'd come up with. (Run an ad in the *NY Review*?) And scribble some fifty pages, of course. Oh, the project was audacious and intriguing: the forms of narcissism and the carefully wrought sentences, the riotous comic scenes and the precise, hard judgments, the relentless if charmless sexuality alongside the high wit and personal charm; these were among the Ziff pairings and paradoxes to be explored, examined.

From the battles of Frontenac and Fort Ticonderoga Jake had leaped forward: "And now look at the recent decade or so. Do you think the American influence has waned or increased?"

I didn't know what to say, so I bet on waned.

He shook his head and smiled. "Wrong! What with the new trade laws that have eliminated as illegal various measures that were designed to ensure Canadian cultural autonomy, and the fluidity of the electronic frontier, it's worse than ever."

I caught up with him. "You mean the madhouse is coming to the sanitarium?"

"Well, not quite that bad, not yet, anyway."

"Try Newfoundland or Nova Scotia," advised Janie, "You'll be safe there."

Two days later I received an interesting note from one of those formidable individuals. It read:

My dear Dan,

I had forgotten that I am due to receive some sort of award by Harvard and the American Repertoire Theater (and the French cultural attaché) in Cambridge. On the chance to see you at our mutual convenience, I've accepted. You will come down and see me, no doubt. The dates are the weekend of the ninth of February, and they have booked me into the Charles Hotel. Telephone me on Friday and leave a return number, so we can have our meeting.

I will also leave a ticket for you, in case you wish to witness the theater ceremony nonsense.

Warmest regards to Rebecca.

Yours faithfully, J. L.

Well. . . . I decided to take advantage of my trip down to Cambridge to make one other stop. After a few phone calls I had discovered the whereabouts of a retired history teacher from Boston Latin School, and met him at his Dana Street home. In his book-lined study Roland McLaughlin, a white-haired octogenarian, was delighted to meet me over tea and fresh scones. Coughing intermittently, he proceeded to talk about young "Mr. Ziff" at the prestigious public school in the 1950s. "Oh, he was a firecracker! We had a lot of bright boys pass through our portals in those days, but Arthur could hold his own with any of 'em, and then some. Yes, sir, he loved the power of words even then. Know what he did on Bloomsday? Recited aloud *by heart* the first five to ten pages of Molly Bloom's monologue, giving each line its proper weight, so you *heard* Joyce's genius all anew! Well, that was something. And boy, could he shake things up with his sharp, mordant wit!" He edged forward. "At eighty-five, I can speak candidly, son: Arthur was the first Hebrew lad who persuaded me of their real contribution to BLS. You know who you might speak to, that classics legend uh . . . Marnell, if he's alive. And Joe O'Connell from—nah, he's gone. Here, write down your name and address, nice and large, and I'll put you in touch with a few who knew him, if they're not *in extremis.* Hey, Jan, can you bring us some more tea and"—he winked at me—"spike this one with a little rum, huh?" He slapped his knee in delight. "You know, we imparted to young Ziff the two qualities necessary to give a talented lad: discipline and confidence. Cocksure confidence! And he sure has that, eh? Get that in youth, son, and you can take your life to the bank. Hey, Jan, get a go on it!"

I wrote down my name large and clear before the tea went to his head. And jotted down "Boston Latin" for further research.

That night, February 9, I attended the celebration in honor of J. L. at the Loeb Theater. It was grandly attended, from the Harvard literati (Galbraith, Daniel Aaron, Richard Goodwin and Doris Kearns, etc.) to Boston theater luminaries to the French cultural attaché and entourage. At fifty bucks a seat, the fifteen hundred or so seats were filled, and the master of ceremonies, Robert Korngold, who dressed for the occasion in a black tuxedo, delivered a warm and enthusiastic introduction to the woman and the evening.

Next came clips from her most entertaining movies, starting early, with Gerard Philippe and Simone Signoret, moving on through the Truffaut, Godard, and Gerard Dupardieu films, and concluding with her powerful performance as Madame Bovary. Next, testimonials from René Clair, J. L. Godard, Jack Lang, Louis Malle, and a most poignant one from the late François Truffaut, were flashed on a giant videoscreen. High praise about this woman, her acting, her moral courage, her political good sense. Topping off the evening was a personal appearance by Catherine Camus, the writer's daughter, who spoke of Jeanne L.'s incredible fortitude in standing up for her father against the onslaught by the Sartre and de Bouvoir crowd in 1950s Paris. "She is a woman for all seasons, all political weathers, if I can say this." A standing ovation.

And then entered the grand woman herself, a modest, trim brunette, with sensual mouth and almond-shaped eyes, as striking in her aging as she was beautiful in youth, maybe more so. "I am a simple woman, from country peasant stock," she began in her inimitable voice," and I believe this has always helped me. I have changed my convictions only once, when I left the convent because my individual freedom was threatened. I have been very lucky, living and working in the two societies, your country and mine, where such freedom is most cherished. I thank you for this evening and this special honor." She nodded and threw a kiss to Mr. Korngold.

"And now, if you will allow me, instead of speaking to you in *my* voice, you will permit me, I hope, to speak through another voice, a dear old friend of mine. Please." The lights went dark, and a spotlight focused on her as she seated herself with a book; and she began, in her low, husky voice flecked with her charming French accent: "Our friend Emma has grown desperate, the tax authorities have come around to seize her and Charles's property, she has just been humiliated by the accountant, who has asked for her body in exchange for money, and, with nowhere to turn, she has returned to the house of her lover, Rodolphe, to ask him for the necessary three thousand francs. Permit me, tonight, to read this in Emma's—and my—native language." She paused, and turned the pages to find her markers in the novel.

A wave of light applause started in recognition of one of her great cinematic roles, but she silenced the audience with a wave of her long white hand. Still, small, serene, she sat at the edge of her straight-backed chair, firm and erect like the schoolgirl of some fifty years ago, I imagined. And commenced reading:

"Elle se demandait tout en marchant: 'Que vais-je dire? Par où commencerai-je?' Et à mesure qu'elle avançait, elle reconnaissait les buissons, les arbres, les joncs marins sur la colline, le château là-bas. Elles se retrouvit dans les sensation de sa première tendresse, et son pauvre coeur comprimé s'y dilatait amoureusement. Un vent tiède lui soufflait au visage; la neige, se fondant, tombeit goutte à goutte des bourgeons sur l'herbe. . . . ' "

She read in a flat, somber voice, with her signature touch of husky bass, a French version of Glynnis Johns, only here and there suggesting emotion. Looking up every few sentences, she read for the next twenty to thirty minutes, gradually transporting the packed audience back in time, to the last century and provincial Younville, back to the intense scene of poor Emma having to grovel before the dandy lover, and failing, going to the apothecary and, from the third shelf, taking down the blue jar, and, hopeless and tragic, taking a fistful of white powder and swallowing it. Then, returning home to her bed, to Charles, and to waiting for the effects of the poison to take hold.

(I was aided with the whispered translation by my neighbor, a Harvard professor of French.)

She read the ordeal of Emma's end slowly, with satisfying pauses and unyielding dignity. It was as though she were gradually mutating away from Jeanne and back into Emma, as though the voices and the experiences were exchanging, the present modern actress fading out entirely as the fictional literary ghost gathered herself up into her real life, here now onstage. *"Et elle se coucha tout du long sur son lit.*

"Une saveur âcre qu'elle sentait dans sa bouche la réveilla. Elle entrevit Charles et referma les yeux.

"Elle s'épiait curieusement, pour discerner si elle ne souffrait pas. Mais non! Rien encore. Elle entendait le battement de la pendule, le bruit du feu, et Charles, debout près de sa couche, qui respirait.

"Ah! c'est bien peu de chose, la mort! Pensait-elle; je vais m'endormir, et tout sera fini! . . ."

Jeanne was erased and had become Emma now, Emma wounded and helpless, accepting of her physical pain and impending doom. The audience was filling with her pain, too, wincing with each sentence, so perfect in pitch and tuned in emotion was the interpretation. The brilliant reading had denuded the melodrama and lifted the event into tragedy.

At the end, with Emma gone, all was still; not a wave of applause, not a thunderous ovation, just the sporadic sobbing and muffled crying that broke the grave stillness. The master had worked her spellbinding charm on present time and physical theater—Emma had given in, death suffused the air with its unspeakable aroma; some fifteen hundred souls had given in, too, were lost in collective awe and melancholic wonder.

I watched her, unmoving still, sagging dramatically, drawing the last bits of drenching emotion from her captive crowd, at the same time gathering herself for one more molting of skin and self. At last she moved, clapping the book shut!, and parting her parched lips, she reached for her glass of water.

That was the signal for the crowd, her enslaved prisoner, to awaken from their spell and start applauding, slowly at first, but increasing, until it grew steadily and became a crescendo; then the audience stood, almost in unison, clapping and yelling out "Bravo!" and "Long live Emma!" And Mme. Jeanne stood and bowed again, set her hand over her heart, and exited. Applause, calls! She allowed herself to be called back once, twice, for more bows, while bouquet after bouquet of flowers were brought, and set at her feet. Along with half a dozen bottles of champagne.

"This is why we need theater, and need her, so we can forget the dirty-word playwrights and the Hollywood movies," declared my professor/translator, wiping her wet eyes and nodding at me. "She is a marvel, a winged angel, a unique creature, is she not?"

I nodded assent and looked on as a band of admirers encircled the stage, devotees of this actress angel—like Russian ballet fans devoted to their Plestiskaya at the Bolshoi—and wouldn't leave until she had reappeared and blown them kisses. Two and three times, this coronation.

The next morning I was invited to see up close the unique creature, for breakfast. She was radiant, modest, and charming in angora sweater and dark skirt, her hair tied up girlishly in a French twist. At sixty she exuded more sensual appeal than most women at thirty. We chatted small talk, Jeanne evincing great interest in Rebecca and the boys and the book I was writing; and then, breaking in on my answer, she said, "But please, Daniel, come upstairs with me for a moment. I want to have a few words, and also show you something." And locking my arm in hers, she proceeded with me toward the elevator, making me her possession and therefore a person of importance. I felt flattered!

Holding me securely in the elevator, she remarked, "I am grateful more than you know for your note of inquiry about my years with Arthur. For you see, I am basically a shy person, and would never be able to make public . . . certain things."

"But the rumor is that you are writing your own memoir."

"Ah," she tossed her hand, "a memoir! That is obligatory, you may say. For necessary money. After a lifetime of serious acting and over a decade with Arthur, I am nearly impoverished, you must know."

Did I? No. I knew she owned an apartment in Paris and . . .

In her well-appointed room she sat me down, went to a worn black Gladstone bag, and brought out an old cardboard box tied with two strands of white rope. For a moment her calm demeanor changed. "You must tell the truth, please, the whole truth!" Her eyes grew wild, and her face tightened. "This has been my salvation, just this, and nothing else: a journal of my private life with The Monster! When things were impossible, when demands and cruelties were put upon me and I had no recourse, no friend to turn to, I took these notes, meticulously, regularly. You see, you understand?" She held the box in her lap. "My salvation."

As I moved over to reach for the treasure, however, she set it back into the black bag, blocking me, saying, "The truth, you must tell the whole truth and nothing but!—but can you, Daniel, can you?" She leaned into my arms for sudden support, as though the intense heat of that trove was so great her proximity to it was interfering with her balance, threatening to topple her, us!

I caught myself and comforted her, and after I had settled her into an upholstered club chair she said, "Now sit please and let us talk."

Amazed at the turn of events, the tantalizing box—real or fraudulent?—offered and withdrawn, I sat down in the chair opposite her, some six feet away. "But I don't understand. Are you giving that journal to me, or not?"

She lifted a strand of hair from her eyes, smiled, crossed her girlish legs, took up a cup of coffee. "For now I am showing it to you. It remains for you to prove to me that you are to be trusted enough to see it. That is what I want to say to you."

Stymied, frustrated, teased, I offered, "But how can I prove my, my, trustworthiness? What do you mean?"

"Please, drink your Perrier, yes? Or coffee, if you wish."

I looked to my end table, lifted the small carafe of coffee, and poured myself a cup.

"Would you like a bagel, too?"

I shook my head.

She leaned forward, spoke low. "Daniel, why do you want to write this book? And do you think you can be objective in it? And withstand the pressures put upon you by our mutual friend? By the American publishers?" She smiled softly.

I took a breath and prepared to answer. My eye focused on the Gladstone bag, and I had an urge to grab it and run! Should I? Could I make it?

"I want to write a book about a very interesting life, in the world and in his fiction. About Arthur Ziff and his many masks, Ziff and the Anti-Ziffs. I believe there is no one like him."

"You mean the Arthur Ziff that he has created, self-fabricated? Or the real person that he is after all?"

I considered. "Both, I assume."

She nodded, sipped coffee. "It is a very tricky business, I agree. And it will be easy for you to be . . . seduced, let us say, manipulated, into taking a favorable view. Of him, against me."

"Why? Why should I be seduced into that position?"

She shook her head at my innocence. "Because he has many more weapons than I. He has your old friendship, he has his books and stories, he has the friends and the literary fame. He is 'riding high' nowadays, I think you say."

I tried to digest all this, like trying to understand a wave of fog wafting my way.

"And I? I have only myself and this . . ." she indicated the hot stuff in the bag. "This week-by-week journal of what it was like together. The simple truth, not the artfully made up, the clever fiction. If I were younger, perhaps I could seduce you myself"—she smiled playfully—"but as it is, I am almost an old woman." With a certain shyness she smoothed her skirt; studied or natural?

"Oh, you are anything but that, anything," and I meant it, as I saw her fine legs and trim waist, the large, dark eyes. Was I being . . . tempted? I wouldn't mind, as I looked at her and that bag.

"I am human, too, Daniel, please remember. I have my faults, my share of mistakes, yes, but I also have my accomplishments, my pride. Do you think I'd like to look foolish in a book by you, too? Is it not enough to be trashed by him in his books? No, my friend, no. I need to assure myself at least that I will have a fair chance."

Impulsively, I went to her, took her hands—was she already seducing me into an acting performance?—and pleaded heartfully: "I promise you a fair chance, as you put it, an honest appraisal. I will not be swayed by others, or by pressures. And I shall always remember what you are saying, about being human, too, with flaws and mistakes as well as great work."

She held my hands, and fixed my gaze with hers. I was most moved; she was not merely a legend but also a very frail human being. As well as a woman of parts.

She pecked both my cheeks and whispered, "I like you, Daniel, and I am beginning to trust you. Thank you, my friend, thank you."

As she backed me off now, I waited on my haunches, even perhaps trembled, with eagerness and hope. Might I now—

"So Daniel, we shall continue this dialogue, yes? By letter, by telephone, by meeting. No, I do not do e-mail, my friend, no."

"You mean you will not allow me to look at the journal yet?"

"Daniel, please, you must be patient. The least I can do is guard my soul, protect my salvation, until I am sure, quite sure. You won't deny me that, will you?" Her hands were open, palms out, a French saint pleading with a young sinner. "Full trust is coming, I know, I feel."

Presently, walking out of the hotel lobby, I was awash in different emotions. I felt on the one hand that I had come very close to securing a major booty early in the game and had missed out. And that I had been toyed with, teased, like a kind of frustrating foreplay, and now had a case of literary blueballs. I was confused also by what had fully gone on: *What* indeed had I been shown and offered? Intoxicated still by the intense, mystifying scene, I got into my Saab to drive somewhere—home or . . .

Thoughts swirled in my head. Of course, she had probably

invented much of that journal, right? Why not? But was that any different really from Arthur's inventions in his fiction, of her, and others? He called his inventions fiction; she would call hers a journal. Was there a great difference, except perhaps he had a more legal (literary) license? But it was a nice parallel irony, wasn't it? The curving tracks of subjective perspective and cold revenge. I'd have to try to dig down and figure out the truthful bits from the imagined dross.

Before I quite know where I was going, I was heading there—out on the Mass. Pike over to Brandeis, Arthur's alma mater, to visit one of his favored old professors, now retired. Professor Milton Goldmark, probably eightyish now, had told me he still worked there every day, in an office the English Department had furnished him on his retirement, and I didn't need to call, just come on over any day of the week. So I drove out, hoping to get a miniportrait of the young wunderkind in college and also to take my mind off my near-miss with Mme. Jeanne's manuscript. For that hot booty had stayed with me, laying itself upon my consciousness, along with the upcoming bewildering test of trust to see and savor it.

I found the three modern Humanities buildings on a tree-lined hill and wandered over to Rabb, home of the English Department. There, tucked away in a corner office, I found Professor Milt Goldmark, round-faced and wearing plain spectacles, who greeted me warmly and invited me to sit down. Clad in a sport jacket and tie, he wore a big smile, spoke in a kind of squeaky voice, and appeared to be spry, in good shape, still going strong. He told me how delighted he was that I had come by, and began chatting about his old student from the late fifties.

"You know, a lot has been made lately about ADD in kids, but I always thought young Ziff had a RRD syndrome, Relentless Retention Disorder!" He laughed at his artful phrase. "I mean, there never was a fellow who would focus on an object or target the way he did, who remembered everything, but especially if you had wronged him in any way. Then his full brilliance, a merciless brilliance, would emerge in the most devilish way!"

I asked for an example, and he warmed to the occasion, telling me of a certain English prof. who didn't—or wouldn't—appreciate Arthur's wit or talent, and deliberately tried to show him up in class, using remarks like "How's our young Goethe doing today?" "Well, Arthur sized up his man and planned his revenge." Here Professor Goldmark sat back in his swivel chair, pulled one knee over the other and cupped it with his hands, and brimmed with delight. "He discovered that the sadistic anglophile professor had written an unpublished novel several years before, called him up and in his best British voice Arthur said he had heard of it and asked to have a look at it, gave him a London address (a friend of Arthur's), and after a month, wrote the professor on a fraudulent publisher's stationery, saying how much he had admired the novel and wanted to publish it, a contract would be following. Well, Professor X took the bait and bit hard, not able to resist informing his class while teaching D. H. Lawrence how his own novel would be published soon enough, and probably create another Lawrentian storm over in England, including Leavis. Colleagues, too, were soon alerted to the matter, in sly asides, with the same smug superiority. Poor fellow. As the months passed, Arthur would send a letter every four weeks or so, announcing one delay after another, driving Professor X into increasing frenzy, despair. And finally, some three or four months later, just before the end of the semester, a letter was sent announcing the unfortunate news that the novel wouldn't be published after all, as Mr. Haymes's colleagues, who had come to read the manuscript, had found it, and I quote from memory, 'pompously jejune, clumsily written, ridiculous in content.' The professor sank into a serious depression, and was pressed to take a sick leave from the college. When he returned in the fall he was a shell of his old self, now a feeble stutterer who never recovered fully. Those few who knew about the clever hoax and witnessed the subsequent collapse—I myself only learned a few years later—grew in awe of young Ziff's ingenuity and power. Come, I'll show you where he used to hang out, a sanctuary I actually found for him."

Still somewhat reeling from the tale, I followed Milton G. down and across the hilly campus, past the library, and headed for a massive fortress of a building, which I had encountered on first driving in the place.

"This was the original campus, all of it, dating back to when it was the Middlesex Nursing School," Milt explained mirthfully, "always known as The Castle, and you can see why."

Massive stone walls, turrets, portholes—yes, I could see why.

"Used to be our dining room in the old days, then a snack bar. Come on." He led me down a stone staircase to a dark corridor and on to a corner room, where he knocked, got no answer, opened the door, and showed me in. A small office fitted out with a desk, chair, computer, armchair, steam radiator. The bulletin board with pinned notes indicated a campus club.

Milt hit me on the arm. "How do you like it, eh? The first office of young Ziff, where he wrote his early stories and essays. Nicknamed 'Ziff's Castle' by pals. Two doors beyond the boiler room. This was his private studio and central command post, all at once. Not bad, hey? And no one, but no one, was allowed down here, just to pop in. Strictly off-limits. Of course, if the administrators had known about it, they would have blown their stacks. But no one ever came down here—too grim, grimy. But for Arthur, our budding literary star and *enfant terrible,* it was perfect."

I looked around at the windowless cubicle and imagined the young man working away in underground solitariness, serenaded by the clanging of the radiator pipes. A very nice biographical touch, I thought, taking a note.

"Is the room just the way it was when Arthur had it?"

"More or less. Well, I seem to recall that he had a cot of some sort put in, I think for occasional naps."

Oh, for naps, I mused privately—not for nips of mischief?

I thanked the professor and we made our way up and outside, to the welcome blast of fresh air. Hiking back up the steep hill toward our starting point, Professor G. began to chat again about the marvels of young Ziff. "Oh, we had a bunch of brilliant young men and women here in the early days, people like Walzer and Larner, Judy Borodovko, Safran, Marsha Warfield, and Peretz, students who turned down Harvard, Yale, and Princeton to come here. Ziff was right up there among that bunch, and as a literary student, probably the most outstanding. Hey, one other place I should show you, another of his haunts," and he laughed oddly, "his 'special reading room.' " Suddenly he was veering down a small side path, leading down a very steep hill, and I began to see this Goldmark as an ancient mountain goat, not a mere academician.

Presently we were approaching three unusual buildings, starkly concrete verticals soaring skyward. "The Three Chapels—have you heard of them? One of our earliest architectural sites, still rather impressive, don't you think? His favorite was the Protestant, for the light, I think, or maybe because it was the least populated! And he'd come down here, hide out, and read. He had his ways, didn't he? Let's see if we can walk in." We entered, and the high, vaulted ceiling, rows of dark, silent pews, the vast organ and afternoon light slanting down in strips of shadow, gave off a pronounced sacred feeling, as right for literature as for religion. Suddenly a line came back to me, from one of Ziff's late novels, about "books as prayers." Was this its original source?

We returned uphill. I told him how useful the visit had been, and the beaming professor told me to come back anytime. And meanwhile he'd be on the lookout for anything new he might remember.

five

Back home, I had an awful lot to take in. I took copious notes of my interviews and discussions. I wrote up several pages alone on young Ziff at Brandeis, and his youthful literary mischief. (Had he been that way at BLS? To be checked and confirmed; ditto Professor Goldmark's memory. And would I ever get to see those mystery/apocryphal pages of Mme. Jeanne's diary? Doubtful, from that French tease. Besides, how would I ever corroborate the truth of those pages? Ask Arthur? He'd laugh sarcastically, say "no comment," and tell me to write what I wanted. (Ask a mutual friend? What could he or she know about intimacy? But then how did you ever confirm things in biography? Fiction was easier.)

"Dad, Dad!" called out little Gaby. "Come and hear the tarantella I started today! Come on, now, please!?"

"Of course!" I lifted the boy up and whirled him into the living room, where I set him down by his small chair and his one-half-size cello, and he got his music ready.

He proceeded to play, his tongue forming a half moon between his lips in rapt concentration, never looking up at me, and I sat quietly in the Canadian rocker, pleasuring in his sweet sounds as much as the boy delighted in the playing. The small fingers moved swiftly through the different positions, while he pulled the bow across the strings with the other hand; I marveled at the deft skill of the seven-year-old. And his musical ear: He would go around the house humming sweetly the new Bach or Mozart he had just learned. He was a natural, a little country-raised Yo Yo Ma, maybe.

"All right, first class!" I clapped for the grinning, prideful boy, relishing the solitary clapping as though it were a small recital hall, and wondering what it was like to be a natural. Was Ziff a natural? What I did know was that this little boy was devoted to his craft, practicing on his own in the morning, evening, or whenever he needed to relax totally—even though it took all his focus and energy. A lot like writing.

Later, in the car on my way to indoor tennis, I turned on the radio and listened to Freddie Flynn, the host of *Bright Morning,* interviewing the younger brother of the Dalai Lama. Half amused, half serious, the campy lady pursued the odd man with her usual blend of giggling banality and coy pretentiousness, trying her best to trespass on his Buddhism and at the same time to be native-cute. (*"You mean* giving up your vows to be a monk didn't violate any of your Buddhist or Tibetan principles?") And ending with, "Well, for those of us who have not yet found spiritual enlightenment, here's a song from a group called The Rosebuds. . . . " For me, it was instructive to see how easy it was to be trite and gossipy while pretending to be serious. A lesson. Driving, distracted by the familiar gobbledygook, I scribbled down a few lines on my long journalist pad . . . ("Develop Writer Envy; check out Steegmuller's *Flaubert & uncensored Egypt Journal;* reread *Aspern Papers.*")

On the indoor court, I rallied against my opponent, swinging out nice and easy, warming up, emptying the mind. I cautioned myself to play this way in the game, hitting out rather than swinging conservatively. I'd do it in the early going, but then fatigue would take over, and I'd hit to survive only. It was a bit of heaven out there, the soft overhead lights, the whir of the heating system, the huge green netting separating the two courts, the thick dark tarps draping down behind the baselines, catching the balls silently when they flew back there. Hitting the ball, running around, playing a game, blew in breezes of youth, when I'd play a sport every day, many a night. Come home, eat ravenously, and sleep deeply, body and mind tuned, at one with myself. Different from nowadays.

I hit well in the first set, moving Steve around from one side to the other, or pulling him up to the net and passing him nicely. Since my strokes were steady and accurate, I loved playing the passing game, crouching, shoulders turned, head down, disguising where I was going to hit—crosscourt or up the line—and watching the ball hit the strings, not my opponent. Tiring out the young doctor by jerking him from side to side or up and back was a sweet satisfaction. So, too, was advancing to the net after a well-placed sliced approach shot, and settling the drop shot or hitting the overhead. Each well-executed shot, each correct positioning, gave me a discreet pleasure. And when the whole sum added up to a 6–2 set win, I felt swell.

Then, my legs fatigued somewhat from being out of tennis shape, I was less crisp, less focused in the second set and allowed Steve to make it a close set; we had to stop for the time limit with him leading, 4–3. "Good playing, guy," he said, this sweet-tempered pediatrician from Philly, "you were really on with your strokes in that first set."

"Yeah, it felt good there. Before age set in. And you. You came on strong."

The shower was just right, and I dressed slowly, feeling my body toned and relaxed, like my old yoga workouts. We made an arrangement for the next week and exchanged good-byes.

Back in the car, driving the thirty minutes home from White River Junction, my mind was cleared, ready and alert for the intellectual game. Gyms and sports were my regular jump starts, I felt, driving over the frozen Connecticut River. A small passenger jet dipped down through the darkening blue-black sky, heading into tiny Lebanon Airport, just beyond the low mountain. Suddenly I had the idea of dropping Arthur a note, asking him about those early Brandeis days, and then slyly mentioning that apocryphal diary—to see how he'd respond, if at all.

When I got home, I decided to fax a note right then. I rewrote the note three or four times and wired it down. Over dinner I listened to the boys jabber on about their school days, Gaby causing havoc over his macaroni and cheese, Jon scolding him several times, and thought my life wasn't too bad. Did I really need to write this book? A book of such sure turbulence and controversy? Was it going to further my education, add to my ego? Or tear both to shreds?

Afterward, not finding a suitable detective film, I read some Chandler, *The Lady in the Lake,* and smoothed away my skeptical thoughts with his fluent cynicism and dark Los Angeles.

At noon the next day I received an answer from Arthur:

Dear Danny,

The lady in question is a pathological liar, and whatever she may have written, during our years together or afterward, is the fabrication of a sad, sick, and vengeful soul. IF she wrote it at all, and didn't have "help" from one of her renowned cronies.

As for my old Judge days, I have nothing but fond memories of the place, its hallowed halls, and professors like Dr. Goldmark.

Finally, I have no doubt that you'd try to write a good and honest book, with serious insights into literary culture and my own books. But I also think you'd be tricked (a) by the nature

*of the beast to say foolish things; (b) to offer up regrettable, idi-
otic things (such as the journal notes of a raving neurotic bent
on vengeance); (c) to make public judgments that you should
make to me privately and, in the end, (d) wind up producing a
sensational and wayward NYT "best-seller" rather than a
good and serious book. And why in the world spend two to
three years of your time working in a genre that is not yours,
neither in practice nor in desire? Inevitably you'll wind up
writing fiction where there should be fact, and producing semi-
fact where there should be uncertainty and ignorance.*

*Think about it. Choosing to write or not write this book
may be the most important decision of your late writing life.
To quote your line from Branch Rickey, "The best deals are
the ones you don't make." Not exactly Kierkegaard, but a
pretty smart fellow.*

Yours, Arthur

*P.S.: When I first met you, up at Yaddo, you were wearing
a $2.00 coat from a Cambridge thrift shop, you were hungry
to write great novels, and only literature and women
counted. I believe I gave you some good advice in those days,
remember?*

My offer still stands, to loan you a $sum if you need it.

I put down the letter. Was "late writing life" a slip? I wondered, half amused. Was I already done and finished? Or was that
to be my fate if I went ahead and wrote the book?

Arthur Ziff was smart, shrewd, self-protective, literary, and
very clever. He also was vulnerable, blind, narcissistic, missing in
certain emotions, a man of rich paradoxes. A wonderful character
for a complex book, to be sure.

Looking out at the snow-covered Mount Tug, I recalled the
days of my two-dollar thrift coat, and the splendid intimacy that
had developed between the famous writer and the young novice.
Special days, those months at the writers' retreat, in which the

older writer, just coming off his greatest success, nurtured the young apprentice, and helped transform his raw talent into professional accomplishment, like a veteran trainer turning an energetic Thoroughbred into a Derby contender. Those days and nights of training under tutelage were not to be forgotten. . . .

And I was glad to do things for him, too. Disregarding his financial advisers and their tax shelters, Ziff heeded that. And regarding the manuscript that Arthur was working on, I read that and offered my literary opinion; Ziff took that, too. So it was indeed a kind of writer's *Magic Mountain* for both of us, reading each other's work and giving impartial literary judgments, with no hidden agenda, while discussing the strategies of Chekhov, the surfaces of Updike, the style of Bellow. Subsequently, when Arthur went back to Manhattan, he stayed only two weeks before deciding to return, so wonderful was the artists' retreat with D. L. around for friendship. And when I met the midnight bus in Saratoga Springs, surprising Ziff, we had a reunion celebration at the local deli. Arthur kicked in with much Gotham gossip, and I returned with the latest Yaddo news (Polly had cheated me of my three carrot sticks in my lunch bucket; and Elizabeth had written Hal a note about chewing his food too quickly.) On the women front, there was a new sexy undergrad pal from Skidmore. In the next few weeks, besides the usual routine of writing and walking, there were the hilarious hours of looking through Ziff's enormous pile of mail, which he had retrieved in New York and saved, mostly from female admirers and solicitors, with offers, hopes, invitations, several photos. Oh, the literary life was fun again, and richer with two, a little like a double-play combo back together again.

I looked up now, away from the mountains and the reverie of that long-ago poignant past. Remarkably, those ten months lasted for ten years, in which the same exchange of literary opinions and readings, girlfriend and women talk, big-city gossip, academic send-up (Ziff was teaching at Columbia, and I was at Brandeis), and manuscript dissections, still went on. That rare human interchange, intelligent conversation on books as well as people, was conducted for more than a decade in person, by mail, on the phone. A mutual treat for our thirties. And recalling the drift of it just now, a few decades later, caused waves of nostalgia, sentiment, yearning.

Suddenly I was assaulted by pricks of guilt once again: Was I doing the right thing, going ahead this way? And going against Arthur's wishes, advice, red flag of warning? My superego pricked.

The truth was, I didn't know, I really didn't know. The one thing I did know was that I trusted smart, honest Patrick to tell me how the book was going during the work. Not for the commercial marketplace, but for literary sake. *That quality was to be the chief—and only—criterion for judgment.* (But what if Pat got it wrong or became victim of his own pressures? . . . I'd be on my own alert.)

A telephone call, a dinner, a bedtime reading later (*Little House on the Prairie*, volume 4, *The Long Winter*, where a blizzard goes on for four days).

The next day, over at Ledyard College, I met with my two grad students doing independents with me, and we discussed Chekhov's invisible craft, and craftiness. Afterward, packing up my briefcase to go home, I was startled by a strange woman standing at the door. She asked if I was Danny Levitan. Might she come in for a minute? Reluctantly, I asked her to take a seat. Leaning down, I made sure that I had taken the two student papers just left with me. "Yes, what can I do for you?" I said, turning back to see the thirtyish woman still standing, impassive, large-boned, in a raincoat, and a maroon beret. Growing nervous, I again asked her to sit, but instead she reached into her pocketbook. Suddenly I had a flashback to the Phillies' Eddie Waitkus being shot in his hotel room by a fan!

Speaking in a quiet, accented voice, she introduced herself, Helen St. Jean, an assistant to Jeanne L., who had asked her to deliver this package to me. Nodding, she handed me an envelope, and while I opened it, she shifted a bag from behind her.

A note read:

My dear Daniel,
    After talking with several persons who know you, I

believe it is time to hand over to you this partial record of my life with Arthur Ziff. I trust now that you will read the material with full integrity, and, should you choose to use any of it, discuss it with me and use it with taste and delicacy. Naturally, I wrote the original in my French, but have had it translated for you, and am depositing that English version with you, with my growing confidence and highest hopes.

Your friend, Jeanne

When I looked up, the woman was holding a piece of paper, asked me to check the package, and, if satisfied, please sign my receipt of it. Then I saw the Gladstone bag, causing my heart to leap, and I nervously removed the same cardboard carton tied with yellow rope as I had seen in the Charles Hotel. Dumbly I nodded, signed the sheet blindly, and handed it to Ms. St. Jean, who left.

Perplexity gave way to amazement and eagerness. I locked the door, and, too excited to leave for home now, settled in with the surprise delivery. From Chekhov and students to this sudden prize of a package was confusing, overwhelming. (And why had she left that bag as well?) I took out a small flask that I kept for emergencies, called home, and left a message on the machine that I'd be late for dinner, start without me, and sipped Jack Daniels while biting into a granola bar. Was this my lucky day, or? . . . I gazed out at the lush green, the Baker Library tower, and the new rare-books library. . . . Perhaps that new Rauner Library was the right place to donate this rare manuscript after I was through with it?

I opened the package carefully, untying the hemp rope, and discovered a soft vertical file pocket holding a packet of nearly a hundred pages, tied with a rubber band and supported by a cardboard—the manuscript typed in English. How thoughtful. Tilting my chair back, I undid the rubber band and eyed the mystery text, realizing that verifying any of this stuff would not be easy. Meaning, even if the material were revealing about

Arthur, stunningly revealing, what could I do about it in the end? Certainly not legitimately use it in a biography. . . . Send it to Ziff for his next birthday? (Sixty-seven?) Auction it at Sotheby's?

Savoring the jolt of Jack Daniels, I sat back in my cockpit, ready.

Attached inside the first page, I saw, was another note, in small, clear handwriting. I skimmed it. "These pages are for your eyes only, Daniel, and I trust you will tell me honestly what you think of them, as I have little idea of their true worth. Perhaps I am trusting in you to protect me—from myself as much as from A. Z.'s version of me, which will surely appear one day in a contemptuous novel. For as I told you, *I will never allow myself to publish such material.*" Hmm . . . weighty responsibility. Was I up to it?

(Or was I being set up somehow, a woman with her own agenda?)

Certain entries she had marked off in red brackets, and I turned to these first. They were weeks of particular stress and/or crisis, it seemed. I started at a date in a red week, specifically June 4, 1985:

> Once again A. insists that we smoke a joint for our sex. . . .
> I protested, to no use. . . . A Gregorian Chant on the
> machine, turned up loud—for deviltry? . . . Soon, one of
> his usual games . . . tied me to the bed by the ankles and
> arms, using a new soft yellow plastic rope that leaves few
> marks . . . "you'll enjoy it this way, you always do," in his
> patronizing tone . . . and tried to penetrate me from
> behind, using some force, until I cried out! . . . afterward
> asking me if his "cock" was large enough for me? . . . .
> Always the same schoolboy's anxiety about his size, and
> machismo strutting. . . . Crude man, how do I put up
> with it? . . .

> June 7, Friday
> Insisted on going on, and on, about my father, and his
> lusting for me . . . what a mistake to have told him how
> once, when Papa was drunk, he flirted with me; and now,

always, the lust/incest of Papa is his tiresome theme . . . a relentless man! . . .

"Why do you deny it?" he asks, and when I say "I am not, but you are simply wrong," he says, "It's your *resistance* to the idea of his prurience. It upsets your virtuous idea about him. Because he was a doctor. But he wanted to fuck you, didn't he?" . . . His raw ways and vile language, the results of his sordid imagination. . . .

Later, in bed, he spends what seems like hours sucking me, making occasional comments about my clitoris or labia majora, giving me more than one orgasm, only to ask afterward, "Is it as good as when the women suck you off?" And when I tell him I have never experienced that, he laughs scornfully, and wonders why I have to hide that, why cannot I speak the truth? Horrible man, ruining my fun and pleasure always with his perverse propositions!

His aim, I believe: to bring me down to a low level, his idea of a low, crude level, so he can feel justified in treating me like a slut. . . . Only his saintly mother was pure, and not a slut. (I could tell stories about her.) A tired, familiar male tale.

June 9, Sunday

Encouraged me to take him to St. Mary's Church in this Berkshire town, and listen to Mass. Surprisingly, the priest was not at all awful. His sermon on "levels of forgiveness" was moving. . . . Afterward, when we were alone, he dragged me to the apse and wanted me to perform fellatio! . . . Asked if "your Jesus" would mind. Or perhaps Miss Mary would like some, too?' I felt dirty. "So that's why you had us come here in the first place, you bastard!" Denying it at first, he admitted, "Well, perhaps it did strike my mind, but only to experience the full, intoxicating powers of Sunday Mass." His sublime wit. His desire to humiliate me soils my will.

June 12, Wednesday

Conversation at dinner for the 1,000th time about France and its role in WWII. Why? So he could deliver this lecture on French cowardice and incompetence for the 1,000th time: "Tell me about the Maginot Line again. Or was that the Margarine Line? How long did it take to fold, twenty-four or forty-eight hours? And the great General DeGaulle—he should have had a talk show in London for all the fighting that he did. But then again, with the three to five minutes a day broadcast time that England allowed him, he probably didn't have the audience ratings. But can you imagine the size of his balls, wanting to ride into Paris first with his Free French fakes, when it was our boys, along with British lads, who fought and liberated France? Yeah, the Americans do the fighting and dying, and the good old Free French generals show up to claim the fucking glory! You know what? He probably would have been Vichy himself if he thought they would have won and preserved France; good old General Hypocrite, with the usual anti-Semitism later emerging. And where was the Great Man when *The Sorrow and the Pity* was being made, or later when it came out, and you couldn't see the fucking movie in Paris? Yeah, General, tell me what you did to save the thirty thousand Jewish children from being deported to the camps? . . ." When convenient, they're Arthur's Jewish children! As though he'd ever have any of his own, or deign to marry a Jewish woman! Yes, dead Holocaust Jews are fine for my hero, but living Jews, either in the in United States or Israel, are a nuisance. Except naturally in his novels, when they are most useful as ever-present targets! Who is the bigger hypocrite, General DeG. or Arthur Z.???

Re *The Sorrow and the Pity:* No matter that I'm the one who pointed out to him how few theaters in Paris would show the documentary. Or that I am my country's most constant critic. He still needs me to be the target for his French vilification and calumny. (An example of this Francophobic humor: "You have a wonderful Frog pussy—they should bottle that smell for the perfumes. 'Jeanne's Scent,' how's that? Whoa, don't look so hurt.")

Now, why does he really hate the French? Because his books don't sell there anymore, and he's no longer popular! (Unlike the other younger American, whom he therefore despises.) That is the real basis for all his judgments and standards.

18 June Saturday

For my deepest therapy and reading pleasure, there is always my Pascal. Naturally, Z. has always mocked him, calling him "the philosopher of failed Catholics," as though Z. knows anything of Pascal or Catholics. But a few months ago he asked me to show him a passage I had read to him, from my sacred one. Oh, the one you scorned? I thought privately. So I did. This no. 167 from the *Pensées:*

What Is the Self?

Suppose a man goes and stands at a window to see the passersby. If I am one of these, can I say he is standing there in order to see me? No; for he is not thinking of me in particular. But does a man who loves someone on account of his beauty love that individual? No; for the smallpox, which can destroy beauty without destroying the person, will put an end to love.

If I am loved on account of my judgment or memory, is it I who am loved? No, for I can lose those qualities without losing my self. Where, then, is this self, if it is neither in the body nor in the soul? And how can the body or the soul be loved, except for those qualities that do not constitute me, since they are perishable? For it is impossible and would be wrong to love the substance of someone's soul, abstractly, and whatever qualities it may contain. So we never love a person but only qualities.

Let us then not ridicule those who are honored on account of rank and office, for we love no one except for borrowed qualities.

Today my ingenious friend comes by to ask, how do I like the title *Borrowed Qualities* for his new novel? Naturally, the epigraph will be from Pascal, he says, and explains, "It's a story in the Pascalian vein, actually. I'm glad you showed it to me."

This is not the first instance of his *borrowing*, actually. There is more serious "borrowing." But this would take a longer, more detailed, and separate entry.

But to have him steal my beloved Pascal makes me feel like a stupid traitor! And dirty, like in the church, when something sacred of mine has been blackened by a cynical hand. Z. revels in such betrayals, like a perverse monster from a Jacobean play.

I took a break, put the manuscript down, and mused idly, listening to a radio Chopin piece. I felt frustrated by the eclipsed entry on the tender subject of A. Z.'s borrowings. But that was another matter.

The important thing now was how to handle this material, both within the biography and outside. What sort of permission might I actually obtain from Madame, in the end? *(Better get a note from her at the start.)* And didn't Ziff get a shot at challenging the accuracy or refuting the charges? After all, how much of this was true, how much fantasy? And yet, hadn't Arthur suggested to me in the past some of the same facts about this erotic life with J.? But how exactly would I do this, while being protective of Jeanne? Sure, I could ask her if I might show Arthur a piece of the journal; the idea would not only scandalize her, but she might even take the stuff back! Well . . . as for asking Arthur again if he wished to say anything about their long relationship, he'd laugh sardonically and say "No comment." But still, I'd have to ask. (Of course, he'd know then that I was going through with the project, but that was inevitable, wasn't it? . . . Was it?)

Driving home, I listened to sultry Sheryl Crow sing about having fun until the sun came up on Santa Monica Boulevard, and tried to imagine what that might entail.

At home I saw to the boys, Jon playing his jazz trumpet and Gaby racing his assortment of cars, and listened to Rebecca talk about her day. After half an hour I went to my study and impulsively faxed a few J. entries down to Ziff, explaining in a note that he could respond or not, but that it was a delicate and tough situation for both of us, and my work would benefit from his commentary. Yes, I was betraying Jeanne, but I was playing the biographer now, not the friend. *(And what was she playing?)* Naturally, I also wanted to see if I could draw Arthur out, and thereby put together a version of the truth.

"Let me add," I closed, "I am trying, and shall try, to write something of literary interest about you, your career, and your place in American letters. Otherwise, I assure you, I would not dream of undertaking this complicated project. I would have been happier writing another novel. But I do think I can say some things of serious literary value, for now and for later.

P.S.: At the least any future feminist tract called biography that might seek to injure you and traduce your reputation will have to pass through yours truly's book to do it. Yours, Danny."

I returned to read two pages of *The Silver Chalice* to Gaby.

Finally, near ten, I retired to the study, picked up my biographies of Genet by Sartre, Melville by Newton Arvin, V. Woolf by Lee and commenced adding to my notes. Nineteen years of toiling in the New York customs house, a Herman solitary and obscure; a mirror of my own fate to be? Substitute some junior college for the lonely Battery Park residence?

"Hey, want to take a break and see some *Law and Order*?" Becka offered, knowing my fondness for detective triviality.

"Sure," I acceded, paying her attention, and maybe needing

the break. I schlepped the old bios of interest into my Indian Room den—named by me for my Edward Curtis prints—and settled in, half watching, half perusing. And wondering every so often if I had done the right thing. Or had once again scalded myself with my red-hot impulses?

"This new assistant DA sure is angry," Becka noted of the new actress.

I looked up. "And they play to that a lot, don't they? Skewing the script, I think." Was I staying calm in my own? I worried.

I saw her reading and asked her what she was teaching the next day.

"Freya Stark. *Valleys of the Assassins.*"

"Does it hold up?"

"Oh, very much. She may have been anti-Semitic, as Bellow once said, but she was a first-class writer. And very gutsy."

I admired Becka's passion for literary travel writing, and the writers she read and taught, such as Stark and D. H. Lawrence, Alexander Kinglake and Bruce Chatwin, John Lloyd Stephens and Charles Doughty, Eric Hansen and Henry James, among others. And I loved the titles *Seven Years in Tibet, Travels in Arabia Deserta, Stranger in the Forest: On Foot across Borneo, Eothen, A Little Tour of France, Incidents of Travel in Egypt, Arabia, Petrea, and the Holy Land, Personal Narrative of a Pilgrimage to Al-Medinah and Meccah.* At the university she was underrated and underpaid, since she dealt with wonderful literature, not theory or ideology, and, being not on the tenure track but an adjunct in the English Department, treated like a marginal subject by certain important professors. Was that because she had published more than many of them?

"So, I bet the husband did it," she observed.

"Yeah, you're probably right," I agreed, figuring aloud that "maybe if I headed up north one day, to hide out, I, too, could get into the travel writing trade. You know, *Late Life with the Inuit: Fishing for Arctic Char in Fort Chimo.*"

A little laugh. "You can still be amusing."

I liked the "still." "You should write a book about Freya one day, a literary appreciation."

"Yes, one day. Remember, I did an essay once. But for now, let me just finish the current project before I hit old age."

The next morning, before work, I checked my e-mail and discovered a new name, from abroad. (E-mail: Where the modern world of people-hunters, far and wide, hunt down their prey, especially any loner who seeks a private, hermetic life. Yes, poor Melville would have been tracked down in his customs house obscurity and e-mailed, too.)

On my college electronic mailbox on Wednesday I opened it to read this, from Budapest, Hungary:

> *Dear Professor Levitan,*
>
> *You will know me, perhaps? I have been a longtime friend of Arthur Ziff, serving as informal guide to Eastern Europe when he used to come around. But he no longer journeys here, our loss. For many he was a great hero during Iron Curtain days. But now I have gone to understand that you are writing his book; his personal biography. You will want to speak with me, I believe. I know much, on this side of the border, about his secret goings and comings during the long nights of the Communist soul (my weak reference to Rilke).*
>
> *Éva Kertész*
>
> *P.S.: I know your books from Arthur, who once brought me a copy of* Helen at 34. *I found it very emotional, very provocative.*
> *Return address: Éva.S.Kertész.@ELTE.edu*

Frankly, I was pleased by the blissful comedy of this modern missive. I thought of Tertullian's *Credo quia absurdum*. Two cheers, yes.

Who was the lady from Budapest? A Hedy Lamarr double? (Was Hedy Hungarian or Austrian?) And what, indeed, did she know? Did Ziff act differently over there, in secret? How? And did she mean that his heroic deeds differed from his secret comings and goings?

I typed in an answer:

> *Very pleased to hear from you, Éva. I am very interested in speaking with you. You sound like a strong and serious contributor. Let us arrange a meeting somewhere. In America? Perhaps Europe?*
>
> *And thank you for remembering, fondly, my novel H-34. Please call me Daniel. I'm only a "prof" part of the year.*

> *D. Levitan*

No need to tell Éva that she is one of the few to remember my book. Leaning back in my chair, I thought how quickly my world was expanding on rumors alone!

An expanded world just now was pleasing and therapeutic, too, since I had come to feel more and more isolated in my country reretreat of twenty-five years. Local friends had dropped off to one couple, and the few academic friends were spread out some thirty miles away in the spacious Upper Connecticut Valley. Compounding matters, marriage had fallen into an occasional black hole, sending me into a spin of confusion. Rebecca, once upon a time my beautiful grad student, had now, after some twenty years, grown into a willful woman, warm and appealing to her family and friends, but a part-time tiger at home with me. And a good part of it was my fault, no doubt; when I had left the bedroom for a year over her decision to go ahead with having the second child, I had wounded her sharply. But I couldn't help that; a decision like that was not to be made alone. (Despite the fact that I loved the boy dearly, as infant and little cub.) Out of fury, I would act extremely; and I had paid for it, in many a cold hour.

But that was in character for me; I often acted precipitously, extremely, and stubbornly, and it would turn out against my own best interests. Too late to change. That I was my own worst enemy half the time, I had little doubt. Too bad for me. Was I acting that way now, in seeking to write the Ziff book?

An answer came from Arthur quicker than I had anticipated. By the end of the next day, I received a fax, which I waited to read until the evening.

Dear Danny,

Everything I write to you in this letter is private, for your consumption only. Should you use any of this, mild as it is, in a book or otherwise, you will have my lawyer to answer to.

And yet, I write this letter in friendship still.

The J. entries you sent confirm my earlier remark: The woman is a pathological liar, who conveniently omits and/or forgets pertinent facts in her description of matters. Yes, indeed, there were ropes administered and joints smoked; these habits were courtesy of Madame's addictions dating from her last husband the movie director. (Other of his habits I could not deliver, I confess.) Yes, I made cracks about the French and her beloved DeGaulle; she agreed with most of them. Those two societies she "cherished" the most, French and American, she constantly decried and scorned. And why? For two solid reasons: One, they taxed her monies too heavily, and second, they were not Communist or authoritarian Socialist. Individual freedom? Ha. The argument about capitalism and its horrors versus communism and its horrors was one we had for 365 nights a year. She never got over her bouts of 1950s-60s Soviet Comm. mixed in with Sartre-Maoism; if it were up to her, France and the United States would be run by totalitarian chairmen. (Ask Yves Montand, her ex-lover, who broke with her over that. But he's dead. So go see ancient de Beauvoir, if she's alive, and ask her.) Her friendship with Camus I'll tell you about one day, over croissants. As for Pascal, I thought he was terrific, a kind of Catholic Freud (whom she hated); we didn't fight about Pascal as much as discuss him, analyze him. Now, what haven't I covered?

On the French: I have always admired their fries, blow jobs, charlotte russes (were they French?), Proust, Colette, Ophuls, some old movies. See?

As for my obsession with Bruno Schulz, I tried hard to get J. to appreciate his genius but never could. Too Jewish, probably. She always claimed she preferred Maupassant.

Her lines about me and the Jews I'll pass over. I will only add that the probability of Jewishness on one side of her family drove her wild with fear.

There, that should cover most of the bases. Tell me if I'm missing anything. (Does she go into her penchant for vibrator toys in some of the entries? Or is she too modest?)

The life of a biographer is not for you, Danny. Stick to fiction. Leave the biographies to the likes of J. Thurman or Hermione Lee; they know the territory, and, these days, they're the right gender. Hey, do you think one of them might take on our mutual friend in a little bio?

Yours, Arthur

Maybe he was right, in the end. Stick to fiction, Danny boy. On the other hand, maybe you were touching the right nerve, the right button, to inquire into and open up the secretive, clever, many-sided Ziff, who had eluded pinning down with his huge bag of tricks holding fiction and fact?

I went back and picked up the journal again, just to feel out its authenticity, you might say, alongside Arthur's rebuttal. . . .

December 10, 1987

Tonight he asks me to masturbate for him. I resist. He insists, pointing out my Catholic Puritanism, French uptightness, my unsatisfying orgasms. Humiliating me, on regular schedule every few days. At last, sobbing, I give in. He arranges me on the single bed in the small guest room—a reminder of my convent days—and he sits down on the chair opposite, playing a Bach suite.

Helpless, I reluctantly perform for him, while he observes closely. (I know that immediately afterward he will take notes for another scene or book. *There* is his experience.) Eyes closed, I hurry to orgasm, but he tells me to slow down, open my eyes. . . . I stare at my Manet poster "Street Singer," on the wall, and focus inwardly on harvesting garden greens. Before I know it, he's fallen to his knees in order to observe me close up, clinically; every now and then glancing up to look at me. I feel cheap, violated, abused. At last I come, and still he sits there, observing, while I do my best to suppress my moans and tears.

When all is complete, he stands, hands me a towel, and kisses me on the cheek, said I did well, and excuses himself. For what? I ask, trembling, ashamed. Longing for him to touch me now, he shakes his head and moves off. I am left to wonder: Was it all for his voyeuristic notes, for a new book (as everything is)? For his own masturbation? For my humiliation alone? . . .

Absorbed and moved, I nevertheless put the journal down, and recognize again how offbeat and curious these entries were, like the curious piano minuets of Ravel, perhaps. And how much there was to speculate about, to fit together. If the Ziff story was a teasing puzzle before, it was getting richer now. And human puzzles made for good plots, strong protagonists, especially if you let them play themselves out and did not try to tidy them up too neatly.

Did that little scene happen, for example, or was it imagined? Invented by spite, a great motivator? If it happened, it meant one thing, and concerned Ziff; if imagined/invented, quite another, referring to J. L. obviously. Either way, however, the problem remained of how to interpret it, organize it, integrate it in a text. True, the subject itself was one that Arthur took zealously and wrote about at length. Was Jeanne therefore a most useful model?

Indeed, was that the way Mme. L. was to be treated altogether in a Ziff biography—like a Louise Colet to Master

Flaubert-Ziff? A bit more updated, and more detailed in descriptions of graphic intimacy, but essentially the same. (Furthermore, wasn't the history of the twentieth-century novel a tale of the intensive detailing of the intimate, especially the sexual? And Arthur Ziff's *oeuvre* to be looked at as an integral line in that development? A literary tradition that included Joyce, Lawrence, Miller, and the Japanese eroticists Kawabata, Tanizaki? I scribbled down a reminder note.)

One thing was acutely clear to me now as I stood up and poked the fire a bit: this book would be a prodigious challenge, a provocative project. It would take much effort, much stamina, literary acumen, and moral delicacy, to make it worthy of its whole subject. Just as importantly, it would take steely resistance, psychological and mental, to go forward in the first place, and later on, to see it through to its tough end. Furious gossip, nasty rumors, widespread calumny, plus ten minutes of hot-klieg-light fame, all would pour down on me; not to mention A. Z. himself, and the possibility—no, Danny, the probability—of his blowgun darts, dipped in poison and delivered with accuracy like a Jivaro. Was I really self-armored enough to see the job through?

Once again I recalled Arthur's mantra from Yaddo: "If it comes into your life, use it, no matter what; you must, it's what's yours. Otherwise you will be cheating yourself of your own best material and subject."

About ten days later I had a surprise call and visit from a curious stranger—though a familiar name—an editor who, in British accent, said she was up to ski for a week in Woodstock and did I "mind awfully" if she came over for an hour's chat?

I said I could meet her over in Hanover if she wished, but she said, "No, really, I don't want to bother you to come out just for me, and besides, I can simply jump on over from you to Waterville Valley. On the map it looks quite close."

I gave her the complicated directions to my dirt road and secluded house and in an hour she turned up, in cobalt blue parka and a Liberty scarf, admiring my "charming retreat."

"Who plays that darling cello?" she asked on the way in to my study, jacket off. "Is it a quarter size?"

"My son. It's a half size."

"It's my absolute favorite instrument. I played it as a child, and had to lug it around everywhere. How old is he?"

"Seven," I said, offering her the leather lounge chair while I took the straight-backed seat by my desk.

"Is that he, the smaller one?" She jumped up, looking at a school snapshot. I nodded. Pixie-faced and short-haired, she smiled widely, saying, "You're a lucky man. And look, you have *two* of them, don't you." She took the snap of the second, older boy. "Sorry for going on this way, I'm a bit crazy about children, having none myself."

While she sat back down, and listened, I found myself telling her that I didn't come to children until very late myself, in my mid-forties.

"Then there's hope for me, good!" She laughed, sitting at the end of the chair, upright, knees together primly. A pretty schoolgirl, you might say, pale in complexion, clear-skinned, short-curly-haired, a touch of pink bloom on the cheeks; a Julie Andrews type.

"Well, let me come to the point, I mustn't waste all your precious morning," she began, smiling with good teeth and high forehead. "I know that you are embarking on a great project, the biography of Arthur Ziff, and I want you to know that we at the *New Yorker* would love exclusive serial rights. We have published a good deal of Mr. Ziff's recent fiction, as you know, and I myself happen to be an ardent admirer of his, and a fan of yours, I might add. I read your *Polymorphous Play* years ago, when it first came out, and only last year read it through again. It's a terrific book! Which is why I believe that this project is so special; it's been such a long time in literary history since we've had this sort of intriguing situation, where one writer takes on the life and work of another, a living friend to boot, perhaps a mentor. Oh, there have been distant examples, like Nabokov writing on Gogol or Gissing on Dickens; but this is quite different."

"More like ex-friends," I said and reminded her of Melville and Hawthorne.

She smiled, blushed. "I forgot, of course. But a contemporary writing on a contemporary great, that's fascinating enough. What with Arthur Ziff's personal life, of course, it becomes intriguing—in a serious fashion, of course. Like Dreiser maybe taking it upon himself to interpret the life of Hemingway? Now, that would be a match, wouldn't it? The big, tough, machismo male observed unsentimentally by the other, gruff Midwesterner, one the toast of literary America with short, clean sentences and stylish ways while the other, whom I happen to think the superior, is disregarded as the clumsy oaf who can't write a clear sentence to save himself!" She laughed, festively. "You see, yours is a unique situation in modern-day letters, one of historical importance, and we at the *New Yorker* want to be part of it—the long friendship between 'bad boys,' the use of each other in the fiction, the trust you've earned from mutual friends—such as Jeanne L.—the like interest in transgressing boundaries of taste and politeness—why, it's a match made in literary heaven, for godsakes!"

I was flattered and flabbergasted. Yet what and how did she know of Jeanne's trust in me? And had *I* used Ziff in any novel?

She beamed and went on. "As an Englishwoman, I can truly appreciate what this could mean for literary history. That's why I want to offer you the full cooperation of the magazine when you are ready. If we need to take up the whole issue, we will, I assure you. And as for money"—she leaned the slightest bit forward, brown eyes dancing—"it must not be an issue in any way. Whatever six figures it takes to sign your project up for a *New Yorker* exclusive, it will be done. You see, I know that what you will produce will not only be riveting, it also will change the way we view Arthur Ziff, and hence the American cultural and literary scene."

She paused while I tried to digest all that she was saying. But abruptly she stood up, put out her hand, and said, "I want to *thank you so much* for letting me meet with you. Don't worry about the arrangements, I can discuss all that with Gerard. Just set me out on the road to Waterville Valley, and I'm on my way. And one day, if you'll allow me, I'd love to return to hear that darling little boy play his cello!"

In the driveway I gave her the directions: two miles up my dirt road to Route 118; north to Rumney and Route 25; then east over to Plymouth and Route 93 north.

Taking my hand, she murmured, "Keep the aspidistra flying! Hey?" Laughing, she waved and headed off in her blue Honda. Had I missed her skis? I wondered vaguely.

Inside, I was stunned, not knowing what had happened. I put on my country music station and listened dumbly to "What a Woman Needs." The female DJ from Burlington announced that the singer Naomi Judd had just opened a fancy restaurant in Nashville, named Trilogy, which she had renovated for a million and a half but you could still get a full dinner for eighteen dollars, and wouldn't it be "a great place to go for a honeymoon!"

Ah, America, I thought, I understand you less and less as I go on. . . .

But maybe that was a clue as to how to approach my subject?

SIX

II. At the end of Henry James's suggestive short story 'The Middle Years,' I wrote, the artist-hero cries out, 'It *is* glory—to have been tested, to have had our little quality, and cast our little spell. . . . A second chance—*that's* the delusion. There never was to be but one. We work in the dark—we do what we can—we give what we have. Our doubt is our passion, and our passion is our task. The rest is the madness of art.' This grand statement served as one of the impressive epigraphs that hung over Arthur Ziff's desk, and it has a certain accuracy insofar as his life has been lived. For indeed it has been the religion of High Art, according to Ziff's perception, that has guided his life, and acted as his morals and ethics, for better and worse.

Of course, an art for art's sake credo has not been all that unusual for a number of artists; many have lived this way, beyond or outside the realm of traditional morals and civic standards. (A classic fictional example is the artist protagonist of Thomas Mann, *Tonio Kruger,* while an infamous real-life case was that of Oscar Wilde.) In other words, what might be considered offensive and immoral by society's standards may be viewed as no more than the artist's obligation to follow his own path, a sometimes tortuous path far from the beaten one. Forget the extreme Wilde. Did not conservative Henry James live this way?, or Flaubert?, to name two of Arthur's masters. So now, in our age, why not Ziff?

Has it not been true that of all our major writers, Bellow, Updike, Ellison, Kundera, the one figure who has taken his own private path and lived the truly 'elusive life,' let us name it, has been Arthur Ziff? Has it not been a life, furthermore, that has offended many groups and violated most norms and boundaries? And a life that, in the fiction, has been made into a fable, an obsessive fable— perhaps a 'postmodern fable'—centered on that elusive life, that movable self. (Sometimes James, sometimes Genet?) All the more reason, then, for us to try to discover and define that life.

Where and how shall we attempt to draw the line, especially in the modern era, between an underlying philosophy of aesthetics and the personality of narcissism? And may there not be significant consequences resulting from that borderline of difference, consequences of moral, ethical, and aesthetic responsibility? As for the magnetic field of literary persona: How much attraction is due to the myth of the real life, and how much convenient cover is created by the shifting disguises? Convenient for the man, for the writer, for the protagonist? These thorny questions form an important part of this book, and I shall do my best to disentangle the strands and take on the hard questions.

I cited here the incongruous pair of masks of Henry James and Jean Genet, the refined cosmopolitan American aesthete and the very bad boy French criminal homosexual; suppose this indeed were the Dr. Jekyll and Mr. Hyde of Ziff's opposing selves. And suppose, too, that pulling the strings of this incongruous pair was a supercunning marionette manager, a Field Marshal

Rommel returned to life as an American writer planning and conducting literary campaigns with self-conscious élan and brilliance. We are speaking then of a very complicated soul, one that may indeed be a life not easily defined or firmly placed, and one that warrants our most detailed attention.

I paused and stretched wide, looking up at a solitary hawk flying overhead, circling in the blue sky of late March. To paraphrase Chekhov, that's why you lived the country life.

That bit about Genet. Was I implying homosexuality? I'd have to be careful there. And was "refined aesthete" a little much for Ziff? Maybe. Maybe not. And where was Ziff emotionally in all this? I'd have to figure that out. Of use here perhaps the Wilde line "The advantage of emotions is that they lead us astray."

The fax beeped, and I read: LET'S HAVE DINNER. COME DOWN TO THE BERKSHIRES FOR A DAY AND NIGHT. Z." . . . Amazing, just as amazing as that hawk. . . . As attractive, persuasive, and dangerous?

After one week more of increasing nervousness and fear, I was sitting in Ziff's octagonal living room, in his splendid country house, or gentleman's estate. Bookshelves lined the room, tables were laden with newly received books (for blurbs) and magazines, the fire was leaping; we sat opposite each other on thick, downy couches, drinks in hand. The rugs were Oriental, subdued on the hardwood floors; no pretense here, just good, subtle taste. After a warm greeting by Arthur, I was drinking a scotch and water while he sipped a dry vermouth. He looked younger than his sixty-seven or so, in vigorous shape, his newfound, carefully trimmed beard very becoming.

"You're getting to look a little like Max von Sydow in a Bergman film," I noted.

"You mean on the verge of cracking up? Nah, I did that a few years ago," he replied. "But maybe you're suggesting that I try Stockholm after you're finished with me? And the film business?"

"Yeah, something like that," I smiled and sipped.

"A touch more scotch?"

"No, I'm fine."

"Not quite ready for AA yet, huh? Suit yourself. Anyway," he continued, "let me read you something," drawing a card from his shirt pocket. 'Libel: a. Any written, printed, or pictorial statement that damages a person by defaming his character or exposing him to ridicule. b. The act of presenting such a statement to the public.' Now, all I'm reading from is the simplest dictionary definitions, not any of the more complicated legal paragraphs. I've already checked with Larry Tendler, who specializes in that stuff, as you know, and he said this is good enough for us, here, informally. By the way, Larry said you could call him to check any of this out, what I'm saying to you now. You realize what this means? Anything in your book that would appear to defame my character would come under the definition of libel. *Anything.* Now, you understand, Danny, that you may not *intentionally wish to defame me,* but in my eyes, you will do so; and therefore, you—and the publisher who is foolish enough to take this on—will have to go to court to defend yourself. This will cost money, regardless of outcome. Now, have you read the indemnity clause in a publishing house contract recently? What precisely the publisher accepts legal responsibility for, and what he intends you to take responsibility for? No, eh? Well, you should, you know; I think you'll be surprised. The bottom line, as they say, is that they're signed off in case of libel, and you're signed on. Meaning you're at risk, not your publisher."

The scotch was going down slowly and warmly, smoothing the words. Arthur was sitting quietly, speaking cordially; he wore a soft beige sweater and button-down shirt. The trim, gray-flecked beard added a . . . patrician elegance. (I felt like a peasant in my jeans and flannel shirt.) The whole room was larger and more glorious than I had remembered, the late-afternoon light slanted in through the assemblage of mullioned windows, the rows of bookshelves were orderly, and there was little sense of any office mess on the oak tables. The feeling was of muted grandeur. The drawing room of a European writer or statesman, I figured, not one of our posing-tough-guy writers.

"What do you think?" he was asking.

"I think that I shall never have your taste in living," I wanted to say. "Oh, I'm listening, and mulling over your words."

"Truthfully, I don't think your project, after all your hard work, maybe two or three years' worth, say, would ever get off the ground. I imagine that the publisher would pull out, once the suits are filed and the first injunction comes in, on the advice of the lawyers, no matter what your editor wants, or what the early legal advice was. Tough. And you'd be left holding the bag, in more ways than one. Meaning, you'd be stuck with a manuscript that no one in his right legal mind would touch. And on top of everything, they'd ask you for your advance money back. Think of that day, if you can. No book. In debt. Years of work down the drain." He shook his head in sympathy. "Would you like a bit more scotch now?"

I did, actually, but shook my head.

"We'll be eating soon anyway. I've made a six-thirty reservation." He shifted his legs and went on. "You see, if you depicted real conversations of ours that touched on anything controversial, such as other writers, relationships, friends of mine, intimate anecdotes, reputations, racial matters, what else might there be? I'd naturally deny totally what you've written, and claim that you made that material up to injure me; I would have to do that, of course, since you have violated my privacy. And if indeed you made things up, conversations or scenes, as you inevitably would, well, that would be rather easy to put down, unless, of course, you chose to lie on the stand, and then you'd have a different kind of problem, called perjury. Oh, by the way, Larry Tendler will probably represent me in this case, much as he hates to be on the other side against you, since he feels warmly toward you. In fact, he'd like to talk to you about this whole matter, sometime soon, and give you his view of things, including why he felt he has to represent me."

This was a stunner, since I had counted on old pal and old lawyer Larry to be in my corner. As he always had been in the past. But in truth, it was Ziff who had introduced him to me in the first place.

"There's another point, of course, a kind of psychological one: It would look in the literary world as though you're ratting on me; you know, trying to make a fast buck, get a flashy book done to bolster your sagging fortunes. The result, I've sensed already, would be disastrous for you in every way, a kind of unofficial blackballing and unremitting hostility. It wouldn't be pleasant for you. And the very last thing you need these days. You'd end your writing days on a very sad and very dark note, I'm afraid. An outcast in your own field."

He paused, and wondered if I wanted "a bit of brie" before we took off. I shook my head.

The pale light had diminished by now. In the shadows I saw the grim truth of his last remarks, and figured that a Bartleby decade in a customs house was cordial compared to the hole I might be sunk in.

"I know some of this may sound unpleasant, but better now than later, don't you think?" He checked his wristwatch. "Hey, look at the time! We better get a move on. Our veal and fresh asparagus are waiting! Come on, we can continue this while you're eating your prosciutto and melon."

Continue this inquisition? Over food? I stood slowly, knees weak, feeling something like a Soviet prisoner in a KGB sweep, being transferred to the next station of interrogation. Leading, of course, to the final confession.

In the car I had an impulse to ask him where I might sign and get this over with. Instead I watched the wipers slam the light rain back and forth.

At the Colonial Country Inn, Ziff was greeted with zeal and warmth by the stout hostess/owner, Mrs. Tomassi, and we were seated at a quiet table in an alcove. Water, bread with olive oil, and two glasses of chardonnay were brought. I observed the WASPy guests in jackets and ties, and thought how I wouldn't mind joining them for dinner tonight, to chat about the weather, the stock market. The flowered wallpaper was in a pale violet and off-white pattern, and it was lit indirectly. A fresh rose was set in a crystal vase on each table. My interrogation chamber was different indeed from those in the Kremlin.

"Have you heard the one about the old Jew who wakes up in the morning and is sure he's dead? 'Ida, I'm dying, or 'I'm already dead.' 'Don't be silly, Morris,' she responds, 'you're right here in bed.' 'No, I'm sure I'm dead!' 'Moishe, why do you say such a thing, why?' 'Because nothing hurts me, Ida—I must be dead, *oy!*' "

I laughed, despite my sense of foreboding. His prosciutto and melon was brought, along with my appetizer of artichoke hearts.

I said, "You remember Herb Gold's novella set in Cleveland, *The Heart of the Artichoke.* Best thing he ever wrote."

"Old Herb Gold. Years ago, when I went to San Francisco with Baldwin and Cheever, he went out of his way to snub me. Poor devil, he never came back up, did he? Here, take a taste."

Delicious, the artichoke, like the melon and prosciutto. We ordered our entrées, I sipped my wine, and thought that perhaps I'd be spared, through the dinner, at least.

I started to say something about his smart mock turtleneck ("Merino wool?"), but he interceded. "You see, Daniel, anything you might want to discuss, of real interest, about my books, you can discuss in an essay or two—for a good magazine, too. Have your say by all means, I'm a big boy, I can take it. And as I told you, you'd say things of real literary interest, for me as well. But set aside the legal issue for a minute and let's look at something else. Like your life. What I mean is, consider the situation of your *own* biography, some rather touchy facts from the past that could get leaked out. And might embarrass you, don't you think? . . . Take the case of your visit to that English governess in London. Do you recall? . . ."

So began, for a good part of the evening, a litany of sordid events about my life, which impressed me as much for Ziff's memory as for my shameful part in it all. Had he taken his own notes on me? My, oh, my, I had done some foolish and misshapen things, hadn't I! Especially the way Arthur recalled the incidents. And during his lengthy recitation, broken up with bits of sardonic humor, I found myself staring at him, trying to see if his physiognomy was matching up with the words in some way. His long face glistened as he went on, the list of my sins animating him, it seemed; the horn-rimmed reading glasses he had put on refracted bits of odd light at certain angles; the dark, graying hair was clipped short and neatly arranged; the carefully shaped strip of beard afforded a new sophisticated European look; more and more he took on the demeanor of a cultured but severe interrogator, a kind of relentless prosecutor playing cat and mouse with his victim; my first thought was of Porfiry, drawing out Raskolnikov into full confession. . . . But was I in the right Russian realm? I wondered, frightened, fascinated. (Or was the questioner here more political than literary, like a higher-up spook handler?) In either case, Arthur seemed to grow harder as he went on, the flesh of his face being transformed itself into a more opaque element (titanium?) as he continued the long list of my foolish transgressions—with women, with writing, even with my dear old mother, whom I hadn't visited in such long time! Oh, yes, I began to think, he should be doing the book on me! No mercy, just fact.

"Your veal. Something's wrong with it, huh?"

"Uh, no, no," I said, putting a bite to my lips. "It's fine, really." But actually my taste buds had deserted me, and I found it hard to revive them, so dazed was I by the relentless turn of the conversation.

He shook his head slowly, and laughed raucously at the situation he was describing. "Oh, that would go over great if that story got out—you know, Yaddo might even be able to go back and file charges against you for taking a 16-year-old—into your room, I mean—and conducting lascivious activities right in their guest room. Wasn't it the Pink Room, in fact? Weren't they paying your way just then, as I recall?" He lit up again with merriment, patting his mouth with his linen napkin. "Or, at least, that girl, probably now divorced with two kids in some backwater town, if she was to hear of the situation, she could probably go back, with the help of some good-hearted feminist lawyer, and do a very nice and rewarding number on you, huh? For good money, too. The statute on such harassment cases—well, it could be considered statutory rape, actually—has been extended now, you know. Your personal umbrella insurance is paid up fully, right? What's it for, one million bucks? Better up it, actually. What the hell was her name again, Kopinsky, or Irene Shapinsky? . . .

The memory of that young, agile high school senior with the Veronica Lake hair falling over her angular face now floated in quietly as Arthur spoke, warming me, scaring me. . . . Afraid of intercourse, my Catholic high schooler had opted for fellatio, performing with a sweet competence way beyond her years. . . . Oh, I recalled Mary K. and our rich spring together with great fondness. . . . Rimbaud had taken his dangerous trips to African Aden; I had taken mine to Yaddo Eden.

Soon, by dessert time, he had moved on to another line of questioning. "You know, Dan, we haven't yet discussed your envy in all this. The role of it in your motivation. You have considered your *envy*, of course?"

I blinked and scratched at my scraggly beard, tugging my throat. Had I considered my envy fully?

The waitress brought over the dessert tray, and Arthur urged me to have either the chocolate torte or the crème de carmel. "Go on, you're still young. You won't need your triple bypass for a few years yet."

I took the torte, and hoped for the bypass right then.

"You were saying, about your thoughts on your envy of me?" His smile was open and cordial.

"Yes, I'm sure that has been a part of the motivation."

He waited, and I waited.

"Well, go on, tell me about it. I know full well how you've been treated and cheated. Your career trashed and ignored. I think it's been very unfair to you, in all seriousness."

What could I say? I uttered a thanks.

My torte and his fruit cup arrived, along with the two decaf espressos. "Water processed, yes?" He checked with the waitress, who was well trained. "Absolutely, Mr. Ziff."

He nodded and turned back. "So tell me about it. What's the green stuff like? Living with the envy? Is it really green? Look, even I at times have found myself envious—of scenes or passages in Updike or Kundera. Not to mention Bellow. It's natural. Though in your case it's probably harder, envious of the whole career, all the work."

He said this with such apparent understanding and sympathy that it almost pained me to have to disagree with him. "Arthur, I've never envied you your work, believe me. I've . . .

admired your work, yes; enjoyed a good deal of it, of course; but what you do, *you* do. True, sometimes we write in the same area or territory, but I think we do it differently." I saw his long face trying to assess how to take that; then it settled into a look of wry bemusement.

"Sure," he said, "go ahead. And don't forget your torte."

Go where? I wondered. I ate a bite and proceeded. "Yes, I'm sure I've envied your career, no doubt. Who wouldn't?" I tried here to add up the sum of items to envy, not caring too much about my percentages in each. "The immediate success, the international status, the money, the enormous attention paid to every new book—even the reprints—the level of literary respect. Oh, yes, I'm sure there's envy."

He eyed me peculiarly, trying, I thought, to categorize my guilt, search for shame. "How's the torte?"

I could barely taste it. I nodded, and gazed beyond his fixed stare at the small-flowered wallpaper. It was very hot in the small dining room, but I said nothing.

"So you want to get back at me, is that it?"

"No," I said slowly, "I don't think so, as I already told you."

He clasped his hands. "Then perhaps *it's simply to use me, use our friendship,* to resurrect what's left of your career?"

Yes, a nice twist there.

"Hey, watch your fork, no need to mash the torte."

"No, no." I swallowed. "You're right. About the torte, I mean."

"And the other—the exploitation of the friendship? Forgive me for saying so, but that may be even lower than honest-to-goodness envy."

I didn't—couldn't—bother just then to go into defense or attack modes of any sort. Like bring up the numbers of familiar souls who had figured in his books, his "use" or "exploitation" of friendships, his freedom in hammering up friend-target after friend-target and firing away in the sacred name of art. Not then.

"Yes," I admitted, "I see what you mean. It is low, I guess."

He shook his head. Smiled oddly. "You have no shame whatsoever, do you?"

Brilliant judgment! It would be the gulag, for me, I sensed, an American version and for a long stay—the woods of New Hampshire for life? The obscure life. Vaguely I shook my head in compliance.

The shameless executioner/judge eyed me closely for a blink of the eye, a cowardly turn of my head. I chewed slowly, periodically facing his stern stare and considering my ultimate sentence.

Later, back at his house, we took a half-hour walk about the spacious grounds, the full moon illuminating the neat series of stonewalled meadows. We wound up standing by the long swimming pool, shimmering beautifully in the night air. Surprisingly mild.

"Want to go for a dip?" he offered. "It's heated."

"Too late," I said.

"Best thing I ever did, putting this pool in, against Jeanne's vehement protests about my American bougeoisedom! She swam every day, of course. Oh, the French left! I'm gonna call it a night soon. Why don't you stay out here and think things over. It's rather pretty out here on a night like this."

I agreed.

He began to circle around the long rectangle of water, and I followed. Like promenading in the grand ballroom of the Bolshoi Theater in Moscow 1982, during intermission, when the oval center was roped off and you walked around at the perimeter and chatted.

"I don't think you should do this to yourself, Danny. Give it up. This sort of betrayal won't sit well—with the critics, with mutual friends, with yourself. That's what you'll get in the end—not literary talk about the book, but shit about betrayal. And the worst part of it will be that it'll be true, and that will hurt, pal; you might not be able to take it. Maybe even, and I mean this with sincerity, *maybe even not be able to live with it.* And remember, you have two boys to bring up; you don't want to leave them fatherless." He glanced over at me and nodded. "Especially since Rebecca will marry again, and those wonderful boys will grow up with some other fellow for a dad."

My chest heaved as he strung out his late-night scenario. Then, squeezing my arm, he said, "Betrayal is the last thing you need now, in your life. See you in the morning." He winked. "If you need jerk-off magazines, there should be a few at the bottom of the Danish armoire—a private stash for select friends."

I said good night and walked around the lovely pool, half thinking that maybe I'd go in after all. But I wasn't that good a swimmer, and would hate to get a cramp suddenly. The night air was soft and embracing.

What was there to think over? *Betrayal?*

Maybe to jump in, with my clothes on, and see if sinking to the bottom was the right solution to my Ziff dilemma? Was that what he had wanted me to think over, actually? Why, I bet he'd write a very sympathetic eulogy for the *Times!* ("Daniel Levitan was a serious and devoted writer who authored at least half of an American masterpiece, in his very first novel. And although, in subsequent books, Mr. Levitan's work and fortunes seemed to decline, he worked steadfastly and bravely at his craft. . . .") Otherwise it would go unnoticed completely there. Indeed, that appreciation might be the best attention I'd ever get from them, right? A fitting occasion for everyone, yes?

That night as I lay in the thick, cushy bed, I felt a muscle twitching in my hip and knew my body was reacting. But perhaps I was overreacting. Cool down, get away. I couldn't take much more of the powerful Ziff pressure. Why hadn't I laid it on the line about his using me in his fiction? Could I add my peculiar tale to those apostate confessions of pressure in Koestler's *The God Who Failed?*

I left after an early breakfast and knew what I had to do. No doubt now, I figured, driving back.

seven

After I got home and greeted the family, I called Pat and left an urgent message on his answering machine.

That evening, at eight-thirty, he did call and I told him I couldn't go on, explaining the brief weekend at Ziff's, his intimidating interrogation, his unique torturing.

"Perfect, it's perfect," Pat said, laughing. "Use it if you have to. All that little scene means is that you're on target. What you're working on has some real meaning."

Bewildered, flustered, I murmured, "Really?"

"*Really.* You sleep on it, and tomorrow go back to the grindstone. Okay?"

"Okay. And betrayal—is it 'betrayal'?"

"Sure—as much betrayal as any writer who's ever used his life experience in art. You know, Proust, Kafka, Melville, Dostoevsky. All the Great Betrayers. And Arthur Ziff."

Good, smart Patrick. "All right. Just remember, when and if the story gets uninteresting or the writing goes flat, you'll tell me. That's the deal, Mr. Perkins."

"That's the deal. I'll be the first one to tell you. Get some sleep, and get back to work tomorrow."

So ordered, so freed, the next day I wrote:

Judging Arthur Ziff's place in American literature will not be easy. His productivity is impressive; his conceits and obsessions audacious; his prose honed, hard, in control. He is a writer of style, of intelligence, of humor and wit, of force and purpose. A consummate craftsman and skillful professional, he was a natural with his first book and has evolved into a kind of master. His nearly twenty books—14 or 15 novels, one memoir (and one antimemoir), and a book of essays have created for him an undisputed high place in the contemporary literary landscape.

His versatility especially is worth citing. Is there a writer more flexible, more versatile, on the scene today? From early social and psychological realism to performances of wild, raucous humor, and recent forays into the wide-open territory of postmodern elusiveness, Ziff has shown an uncanny ability to traverse closed boundaries and leave readers gasping. Just when you think you have his direction mapped and tracked, he zigzags away, laughing mockingly at your naïveté. He knows how to feint, to bob and weave, to counterpunch, and then to vanish; he is a literary Willie Pep, or to shift metaphors, a Houdini, escaping from every room of sealed-off interpretation.

His forays into postmodernism have impressed many of our most notable modern critics, like Gass, Bloom, Kermode. Certainly, Bellow has not ventured out there; nor Coetzee, Gordimer, or Marquez. Kundera, yes. But for a hard-core social realist like Ziff to enter that territory of deception, that is a tectonic shift. Playing hide-and-seek with the reader, turning critical interpretations upside down, creating provisional narrators and slippery authorial personas, subjecting conventional reading to textual upheavals and moral assumptions to violent dissolution, these habits have become the staples of recent Ziff fiction. Who would have thought it of the accomplished realist? It has been a triumph of bold technique and stylistic intelligence, no doubt.

And yet the smart and skeptical reader may want to pose a few hard questions. Perhaps the chief one is: Have the gains justified the losses? Has the clever, even brilliant play of the cerebral author given us more emotional depth or serious quality than the younger, more conventional psychological realist? Has the current cast of cunning narrator-characters proven to be more substantial or more interesting than the earlier figures? Have the so-called postmodernist themes—like the vanishing and reinvented self, the self-consciousness of the author, the novel-as-a-puzzle text for the reader to figure out—been more emotionally powerful or genuinely interesting than the traditional moral and social themes he attacked earlier in his career?

I paused, reread the paragraphs, and decided to stretch my legs on a short walk up the dirt road. Strolling with the dog, I knew I had to fill in a few gaps there; return, first of all, to the question of where exactly to place Ziff in American literary history. Another point: If I were to challenge Arthur's recent works, I should get into the whole matter of the true worth of postmodern fiction. Was it really a new and valuable genre of literature and guide to the chaos of our lives? Or was it something of a literary scam, a technical sleight-of-hand employed by the thin-of-talent writer for the career uses of the thin-of-talent critic? Furthermore, were there not splendid writers of the past, such as L. Sterne or Dostoevsky (esp. *Notes from Underground*), or even Joyce, who were postmodernist (and far more interesting) some 75, 135, and 175 years ago? If that was the case, what was the real truthfulness or usefulness of the current category?

I stopped at the mailbox, found it empty, and proceeded inside. At my wife's computer I clicked into the other mailbox, and there, on e-mail, I found a new missive from my Hungarian friend:

> *My dear Doctor Levitan,*
>
> *You will perhaps please be good enough to meet me in Rome during April when I come to teach there? I will have much liberty there to discuss matters with you regarding our mutual friend/subject, and can guide you in many interesting things, I believe. Did you know that Arthur came to Rome often on his route back from Eastern Europe, for ten to fourteen days of retreat? His "work" and pleasures there were of significance, in "modes" more than you can imagine. I will be pleased to accept you at my apartment at Corso Vittorio 187, near the Compo de Fiori. Tel. 6874875.*
>
> *Sincerely, with devotion, Éva K.*

I nodded dumbly at the small black-and-white message on the right side of the page, sent from Budapest that morning. I clicked on reply to sender and answered.

> *Dear Professor Kertész,*
>
> *Yes, I shall meet you there, and you can be my guide to Arthur Ziff's Rome. Thank you for your willingness to help out my project.*
>
> *D. L.*

I had erased my playful "Emperor Ziff's Rome." And I decided to break the news diplomatically to Becka; offer her the time for a trip to her beloved Jerusalem in return. Why not? A call came in from a Ledyard student, seeking a writing Independent in the summer. Did I have time? No, but I'd do it. I called my travel agent and asked for a flight from Boston to Rome nonstop. Next was to tell my sons, especially the elder boy, whose bar mitzvah was in May. No sweat, I'd be back in plenty of time to prepare for that. A week or ten days in Rome should do it.

Things were going full steam ahead once again, I sensed. Was I ready yet to try my hand at a little biographical writing?

Sitting down by my laptop, I saw that it had begun to rain outside. Of course, I might be going on a wild goose chase, but so what? I had chased many such geese in my life, even caught one or two. A few nipped, but a few honked, pleased. . . . And on the trip, I might look at a few of the bios I was hoping to read—maybe Arvin on Melville? Matthewson on Dreiser? Troyat on Tolstoy? Ellmann on Joyce? Were the old ones not superior to the contemporary ones? But what about Hermione Lee on V. Woolf? And Judith Thurman on Isak Dinesen. What else? Look back at the broken friendships among literary men, writers, right? (For solace, say.) Start with Hawthorne and Melville. . . .

Before departing, I recalled an old girlfriend of Arthur's—who had served a few memorable roles in his fiction—still living in the Boston area, got in touch with her (at Fidelity Investments), and she agreed to a meeting. At her fourteenth-floor apartment in the Prudential Center, Michelle Kathleen Farrell made us drinks, and we sat on her L-shaped couch in the living room.

I started by asking what she thought of the firing of a famous fund manager, but she cut me short. "We've got an hour or so before my daughter arrives, and we have an engagement, so we'd better get to our chat right off." A very attractive lady in her midyears, she had short auburn hair, red cheeks, and deep dimples. Attired in a striped business suit, she crossed her good legs politely and asked, "Now, what is it you'd like to know?"

With my time allotted precisely, and my role as biographer still strange to me, I stammered, "Well, I wonder about your memories of Mr. Ziff from high school days, and beyond, when you were at Radcliffe?"

She sipped her martini and paused to reflect, her nostrils flaring slightly; excitement or restrained ire? "Oh, Arthur was Arthur—meaning, he had two sides to him, the studious and intellectual side, and the . . . playful. Socially he was great company, always keeping us in stitches. And the few times he came over to meet my parents, out in Wellesley, well, he behaved very well, let's say."

I nodded, appreciating that pat on his poor-Jewish-boy back. Eyeing her cool demeanor, I wondered how to break through that and get to the sex angel in *Dorchester Boy* or the photographic star of Heshy M.'s fantasy in *Mendelsohn's Meditations*. But was I confusing a character with the real person?

"When you said he 'behaved well,' did you mean that he was usually wild, ill-mannered, out of control?"

She half smiled. "I see you listen carefully. No, he could be most cordial in manners, actually."

I ventured forth. "You meant in passion, then?"

She smiled vaguely. "If you're asking *how he fucked*"—she paused and scraped her lips with her teeth—"I could say a lot, quite a lot. But my answer is, *No comment*."

Put on the defensive, I backed off for the moment, shifted course. "Were you able to imagine back then 'the future writer' in the young man? Were there any small, telltale signs?"

Finishing her martini, she stood and went to pour herself another at the portable bar. "Can you use a refill?"

I shook my head, nursing my light scotch and water.

"Sure, you could see back then that he had a keen eye for details, for the way people spoke. He was a great mimic, you know—Groucho, MacArthur, Ed Sullivan. And he was sharp as a tack about reading people, too." Her smile was relaxed for the first time. "Would have made a great D.A. Or better yet, defense attorney."

I got up and walked to the far wall, passing an aggressive modern painting of grim colors and little dark bubbles.

"Early Olitski," she informed me.

I nodded, and stopped at a group of family photographs, including herself, a lithe twenty(?) sprawled, in pleated skirt, on a lawn; yes, she was a young beauty back then. I turned and sat, on her side of the L. "Tell me, do you think you were the model for Colleen in *Dorchester Boy*? Or 'Mish' in *Mendelsohn's Meditations*?"

Her face stiffened and she drank slowly, debating matters. "I only read the first book, and I don't think there's any real resemblance."

I sipped. "What do you mean 'real'?"

"That girl, and their affair, have certain familiar external characteristics, you might say. Buckingham Day, then the 'Cliff. But who she is, and those 'sex acts' she commits with the hero, have little to do with who I was, or my actual relationship with Arthur." A gulp of martini. Breezily she added, "Though I'm flattered that you even presumed that Arthur would want to remember me in his work. Fondly, as I recall, though I read it ages ago."

The lies, and the haughty disingenuousness, were kind of charming, I found—especially the hissed "sex acts"—and wondered what she actually thought. And wouldn't it take a very gutsy honesty to admit here and now that you were a great fellatio artist at age sixteen or seventeen, like the Colleen character in *DB*? No way this cool manager at Fidelity was going to jump that respectability hurdle. Why should she, and to me, no less?

Nearly an hour passed. Feeling baffled and stymied, I was about to call it quits when the door handle jiggled and the door opened.

She was about twenty-five, dirty blond hair, small-faced, quietly pretty. Setting down an overnight bag and a large sketchpad, she removed her jacket and entered the living room. She was wearing a Nordic ski sweater and a simple skirt.

Her mother pecked her cheek. "Dear, I want you to meet Mr. Lavidus. He's writing a biography of Arthur Ziff."

"*Levitan*," I corrected. "Danny," and took her hand.

She smiled a shy, friendly hello, and pronounced, "I think he's a wonderful writer."

"Now, dear, don't go overboard. Can I get you a drink, Saby?"

"Sure. Club soda with lemon? Or ginger ale."

Getting it, the wide-hipped mother joked, "She can't be a real daughter of mine, no vices."

As the young woman sat down on the couch, she proceeded to curl her legs under her and shake her long hair out. I saw immediately the resemblance to her mother; in fact, I saw the mother of years ago, when Arthur knew her, and now I wondered whether the photograph on the wall was of the mother or the daughter. Either way, I saw the good Irish looks and the attractive portrait in *DB*.

"What's Saby stand for?" I asked, preferring a real name.

"Sabrina. Mom and Dad were enraptured by the movie."

The mother handed her her drink, and I asked what she did.

"Grad school, at RISD."

"So you're a budding artist?"

Soft smile. "Emphasis on budding."

"Don't be modest, dear; she's already had a one-woman exhibition. Anyway, is there anything else Mr., uh, Levitan?"

Disoriented by the appearance of this younger look-alike, I asked, "Yes. How long did your romance with the young Ziff go on? And how serious was it?"

Drinking, she ran her hand through her short hair. "Oh, we had a romance, yes, but it was puppy stuff, that's all. I was his first *shiksa*."

The daughter reflexively glanced over at the mother before suddenly remembering my presence and returning to her soda.

"Oh?" I put. "I, *and your daughter,* seem to think otherwise."

Betrayed, the girl shot me a look!

And I felt badly, too, exploiting her glance that way.

But Michelle, after freezing hard for a moment, responded with, "Yes, perhaps you could say that Arthur and I were close friends for a while, through those years. And that maybe he broke my heart at one point. But we all have our . . . trials and adventures, especially at that vulnerable age."

She eyed her watch, signaling me.

"I see." I sipped, and set the earlier question in a new way, "One last point: Did you think the portrait of the young woman Colleen in *Dorchester Boy* was a fair one—to you?"

Her eyes narrowed, and she rattled off, "Turning me into a *teenage nympho,* with all sorts of sex tricks? What do you think?"

Sabrina answered softly, "Hey, Mom, that's not really fair to that portrait, there's more to her than *that.* And the boy is crazy for her—"

"Will you please, young lady? I still have my wits about me, and can speak for myself." She nodded forcefully and added, "He jerked my innocence around pretty good. And to think that he did it again, years later, in yet another book . . ." her voice trailed off, and to my amazement, a few tears rolled down her cheeks.

Confused myself by the nerve I'd struck, I stood up.

She stood, too, and firmed herself up. Imposing again, the handsome money manager put out her hand and said, "But I didn't see you take any notes." She looked at me. "Why? Are you wired?"

Was she serious or teasing? "Uh, yes, you're right. I mean, I forgot, and will have to jot down my notes immediately."

Sabrina was standing, too, blinking shyly. "I wish you luck, Mr. Levitan. And look forward to reading your biography about Mr. Ziff. If it's half as interesting as his novels, it'll be a hit for sure."

I thanked her and bid good-bye to the mother and daughter, wondering if Arthur knew what he was missing nowadays. The pair would make an interesting scene for some future protagonist. . . .

In my car, I made a note to reread the portrait of "jerked-around innocence" in *Dorchester Boy,* and pondered how the biographer kept from being trapped by his own role of genre innocent. (Did he get help from the subject? Should I call Arthur to verify matters?) Maybe what the biographer needed was a good novelist for his protection, someone to keep things honest? A masked-rider protagonist who could drive beyond artificial factual boundaries and interpret lawlessly the selective facts and subjective memories of a real interviewee. For biography, the question seemed to be who was "realer" or "truer" (more trustworthy)—the living woman I had spoken to, or the "made-up" character of the author?

Or was it more profitable to ask who was the more memorable and striking figure, the young real Michelle K. Farrell or the fictional Colleen?

Heading across the Longfellow Bridge back to Cambridge, I sensed the hazards of narrow biographical certainty, and yearned for the wide-open fields and thick, bewildering woods of novelizing.

On the Alitalia jet, staffed (oddly) by an Australian and English crew, I thought for a bit about my envy of Ziff. Yes, I did envy him, but chiefly in one area: literary respect. That, yes. The money and the celebrityhood would be nice, sure, though pleasures from my boys made up for all that. But I was still hooked, unfortunately, on wanting the respect of the literary crowd. That lack of respect hurt, especially when I thought that my books—characters, scenes, situations, rather than the individual sentences or paragraphs—were as genuinely inventive as Ziff's. (Watch the self-pity, pal. Let the critics do their job, you do yours.) So he was right, then? Wrong. Envy wasn't my motive for writing on Ziff. Might it be an element in the mix? Maybe. But if so, what of it? . . . The irony was large: If I wrote a good book on Arthur, I'd get the respect I had been missing. If the book was shallow or cheap, because of my envy, I'd be back to square one or worse. (On the other hand, wasn't it about time to give up that yearning for genteel literary respect?)

"I don't get it," I said to the genial stewardess asking me about drinks. "Why are you guys running an Italian jet?"

She put her hand on my shoulder and laughed. "Things are dizzy these days, aren't they? Qantas has leased these 767s to Alitalia for two years, so the Italians could see if they wished to buy them. Then they asked for Australian crews, too. I know, it doesn't make sense to us, either!"

eight

Unlike the cold and wet spring in New England, April in Rome was warm, blue, and sunny. I found a small hotel just off the Compo de Fiori, and though the room was a shoebox, it had a small but workable writing desk. When I called Éva Kertész at 5:00 P.M., she replied, without missing a beat, "We may begin our work tomorrow morning, yes?" I agreed.

We met at 10:00 A.M. for coffee at one of the outdoor cafés in the sun-splashed square of the Compo. Surrounding the central statue (and fountain) of Giordano Bruno—the philosopher who was burned at the stake here four hundred years before—was a lively marketplace of vegetable stalls and vendors loudly hawking fresh produce and bouquets of flowers, arugula, nuts, bananas, and melons.

"It reminds me of my childhood in Brooklyn," I said to the dark-haired, slim woman, watching the flow of shoppers and merchants.

"Really?" She smiled, interested, behind her sunglasses.

I nodded. "Every morning I went downstairs to Sutter Avenue for my mother and shopped—fresh white fish from the Great Lakes, bagels and bialys from the bakery, lox and cream cheese."

A youthful laugh. "Well, there in the corner is your bakery, the *forno*. And over here you can buy your fish. And smoked salmon from Norway fish farms, I believe."

"Thanks. I'll try it out. Who knows? Maybe I can try out old age here, too."

"Yes," she said, drinking her caffè latte, and lowering her sunglasses momentarily. "Arthur often joked the same way. Maybe you are alike in temperament?"

"Maybe."

Once again she lowered her shades, her dark eyes checking me out. "And maybe you have the same odd tastes and habits as the great man?"

I looked at her to gauge her tone and meaning. Was she being serious? "I guess we'll have to see about those, yes?"

She nodded. "I must tell you, immediately, that we are speaking about a great man. To us in Budapest he was a god. Like Lieutenant Jim in Conrad's novel, who becomes *Lord* Jim after leaving England in disgrace. We would joke, 'Lord Arthur' is coming next week, you know. But it was a serious joke."

Should I take notes now? "You're serious, aren't you?"

"Most definitely, Daniel. If someone was sick and we could not get the proper drugs, he brought them. If something had to be managed through the American embassy, he arranged a friend to help out. If a writer or a professor needed money because his writing was banned or he was dropped from university, 'Lord Arthur' gave him the necessary funds—either American dollars or an account in forints at the Magyar Nemzeti Bank. And always there was a present for a child, a family in need. A casual gift." She shook her head slowly in recalling. "He never failed us."

"My, oh my," I marveled. "Could he do miracles, too?"

She laughed. "Why not? Yes. On occasion."

"Such as?"

"Such as making for sure that certain Communist officials looked the other way when clear rules were broken or violated. To us those bribes were miracles. If you chose wrong officials, you could be shot."

She had a mature, attractive face, with dark, curly hair, small nose, and big brown eyes; beneath the thick makeup you could see that ten, maybe even five years ago, she had been a brunette beauty. I mused, "So he was really Lord Arthur?"

"By all means." She nodded soberly. "To me personally, too, I may add."

Should I pursue that? "Oh? How do you mean?"

She paused, and drained her small cup. "Another time."

I wondered aloud, "Why, if I may ask, Éva, did you want to participate in my project?"

She removed her sunglasses to answer me. "Because the world needs to know the whole Arthur Ziff, not the narrow one I read about too often."

I nodded. "Which narrow one do you have in mind?"

"The selfish man, the narcissist writer, the novelist of sex and dirt."

"I see," I said, seeing little. "I shall keep that in mind."

"I believe I will open your eyes wide, Daniel, and the rest is up to you—your honesty, your perceptiveness, your fairness."

I was uneasy with the burden of virtue she was placing upon me. "You may be overestimating me, Éva. I'm sure I have other qualities, such as self-interest, envy, maybe my *own* narcissistic needs." She shook her head slowly. "You are admirable for such confession, but not very honest. No, you will write the truth, I know that, you know that. Now, I must go and teach a class, that's why I am here, you know. Let us meet for dinner. Come by, please, at six-thirty, and I shall take you to my favorite café first. Come to me at Corso Vittorio 187, just across the street, yes?" She stood and leaned her cheek across for me to peck her. "It is good you are here. And maybe important, eh? *Ciao!*" And dashed off.

I stood up myself and wandered through the market, dazed by the sun, the bright fruit and parade of shoppers, and the new view of Arthur Ziff. Or was that Lord Ziff of Budapest?

A wizened little man called me over to his stall, where he had spread out a collection of old French postcards in sepia and black and white, of ladies from the fin de siècle or the 1920s in various poses and degrees of undress. He offered me a packet of twenty for twenty thousand lire. I was tempted, for souvenirs in New Hampshire, but declined, and he threw his hands up in disgust. Who could blame him? I walked off and bought some oranges and, at the tiny, busy Farno bakery, some breakfast rolls. Feeling virtuous and schoolboyish.

My host, Professor Kertész, led me to the Café viala Pace, a corner cafe set on a small street just a few blocks off of the Piazza Navona. We sat outside in the soft air, beneath an awning, and she ordered two glasses of Prescor. "You try it yes and tell me what you think."

The stucco building, like the others on the narrow, dead-end street, was curiously alive with green vines like an Ivy League college. The old buildings in faded pastels leaned together—a Renaissance theater set. At the end of the street sat an intricate onion-domed church, which Éva explained had a magnificent ceiling, "but it is closed for restoration. A pity. The work is Boronini, I believe."

A family of three, speaking German—older teenage daughter, big shy brother, and mother—took a table next to us.

The waitress, a woman wearing a string of white pearls and leather motorcycle jacket, brought us our goblets of drinks.

Sipping, I said, "White wine and fizzy soda water. We call it a spritzer."

"You like?"

"Not bad," I fibbed.

We sipped quietly for a minute or two, and when Éva got up to use the toilet, I saw how stylish she looked. Tight French blue jeans hugged her trim form, a rust suede vest was set over a white silk blouse, and a pastel silk scarf was tied at her throat; a light jacket was for later. High heels, too. Her hair was very curly, even frizzy, and her face touched up with lipstick, mascara. A mature version of sultry Gene Tierney, from the forties movie "Tobacco Road" say. Focus on your work, I reminded myself.

When she had settled back in, she told me how much she loved this café, this street. She added, "I took Arthur here, and he got to like it so much, he conducted some of his interviews here."

Huh? "What interviews?"

She sipped her Prescor. "His special interviews. Which no one knows of, of course."

"Of course."

"Never the opening interview. Only the second or third. If he was fascinated, you may say."

I nodded, trying to block out the rough German talk next to me.

"This Rome has become my second city. Maybe my first. I come to teach here now for more than ten years."

"I see."

"The Romans. They are very open to foreigners, strangers. Not like the French or the English, you know."

Her eyes were brown and flecked slightly with yellow bits in the iris; was she part Gypsy? . . . Alongside the faded beauty in her face, I observed, there was the lure of the past, of history.

"What interviews?"

"You do not mind if I smoke?" she asked, and I shook my head.

"I smoke only two or three a day." She took out a gold cigarette holder and a Marlboro Light. "I know Americans think it is a crime, soon worthy of prison." I lit it for her using her silver lighter.

"He would put an advertisement in the *International Herald Tribune*, a modest one, asking for people who had fabulous stories of crisis or turmoil, to come and tell him about it. If the stories were good, he had them continue for another hour or two. He paid them well. Very well. Even those he couldn't really use, for one reason or another, he gave something to."

I tried to digest this curious news. "Where did they come to?"

"At first the hotels; he stayed first at the Ritz. Then at the Bernini. I will show you them if you like." I nodded and she went on. "Then there were so many who started coming that he took an apartment—in fact, right next to the one I stay in now, and the 'pilgrims' came there." She smiled. "His name for them." She nodded, remembering. "You see, I preinterviewed them. To make sure there was something of interest. And authentic. And to check the language. My Italian is good, but some Sicilian is difficult; and Sardinian, well, forget it."

"But you mean they were all Italian? From the *Tribune*?"

"Of course not. But word got around quickly through the local population. Also, I had to have them sign a permission sheet—which meant nothing legally, of course, but it frightened them a bit and made everything look official." She inhaled and I kept silent, reveling in the medieval street and glimpsing anew Ziff's audacious imagination.

"Who came?" I asked.

She nodded with increasing vigor. "That was the great surprise. Everyone. People of all classes. All types."

"Such as?"

"Yes," she nodded. "Just like Arthur. Details always." She inhaled deeply and blew smoke out. "An engineer from Milan, whose brother stole their father's business from him and his wife, and disallowed him from setting foot on the property again. A priest who fell in love with the Jewish girl he was hiding, and then turned her over to the Nazis. An American navy officer who came to Naples, fell in love with his young cleaning woman, abandoned his family in Indiana, and never overcame the guilt. A shepherd from Umbria who had murdered his sister for sleeping with his close friend. These are examples."

"Murdered? Did . . . did Ziff turn him in?"

She laughed. "You are naive. These conversations are sacred. They happened only in private, and, for the public, not at all."

"But you remember them?"

A sardonic look. "I have it all on computer file, and disk, for a printout whenever. Everything neat and in order. For 'the master' to study."

I nodded, truly impressed by his ingenuity and audacity.

I wanted to ask for more cases but thought of something else. "But why, what did he do with the material? I don't remember these stories appearing in the fiction."

"Not yet, perhaps," she said, taking a last puff from her cigarette. "But he had other purposes than literal translation. He wanted to find out how far human beings would go, could go. In betrayal. In poison. In lowness. In 'perfidy'—one of his favorite words. To research, to prove, his own . . . thoughts and ideas."

I sipped my drink. "A full professor in betrayal and pain?"

"Perhaps that is one way of putting things. Come, we should go to dinner now. You are hungry?"

I nodded, paid the bill, and we got up to go. Oh, it was not food that I had an appetite for, I knew, but more of the rich Ziff store from his private Mediterranean stock. Here, in the boot of Italy, Arthur lived; or, at least, prepared, researched, planned. . . . Was this land something like my son's Narnia, a place of fantasy?

At Pallaro's, a family-style restaurant tucked away in an alley just off the Compo, we ate from a fixed-dinner menu, a homestyle fish soup, gnocchi, and a veal shank entrée. Too much, of course. But I was so spellbound by the tales of more interviews and cases that I went on eating like an enchanted fool. The dull accountant from the Trestevere section of Rome who was having a long, unhappy affair with his glamorous client's (and friend's) wife. ("The master loved that story, of paradoxes, and never tired of hearing it over and over, with others.") The older painter from Ostia who, as a Brown Shirt, turned in his Jewish friend and never saw him again, but then spent his life secretly aiding the widow and children, and received a Yad Vashem award. The wife of a high government tax official who ran a secret bordello for years and was now in trouble with the tax people. The strong-willed Catholic woman from Bologna who had murdered her lover and buried him under the cellar floor, to keep her children safe from the illicit news, once he threatened to run off with her.

"You see, these are narratives that could not be delivered to the priests at confession," Éva explained, "but had to be told or confessed anyway."

I sat back, not knowing where to start, and asked, "But how much would he give for a story like that?"

She smiled oddly and took a bite. "One thousand five hundred for that tale, I believe. It took two interviews, you see."

I was getting to be a part believer. Arthur Ziff, in the land of the Medici, was indeed a Fellow of the creative arts.

I half laughed and said, "He must have spent a good deal of money on all the . . . research."

"Tax write-off in your country, I am sure. That is why I kept all the papers and records, very precise."

I kept from whistling. "So he's a genius," I figured aloud.

"A very American and modern genius, yes. Which is why I've asked you here—to understand this."

I nodded. "I'm getting to understand."

"Good. We leave soon and take a walk, yes?"

"Yes. But you know, I am not sure I can believe all this, if you will forgive me, *by words alone*. Is it possible to see any actual evidence? Maybe those papers, or that disk you mentioned?"

She looked at me and gave off a little laugh. Devilish, I thought. "We are not in a court of law, Daniel. Or a KGB or CIA chamber. We are literary people, and trust in the words of friends, don't you think?"

Shrewd, to test me. "In ordinary circumstances, yes. But when it comes to a book, with certain facts alleged . . . "

She stood up, said, teasingly, "Let us see what happens," and proceeded to walk, waiting a moment for me to catch up and escort her. She asked if I knew the city and I said not really, having been there only once.

"Come, I'll show you a wonderful building and square; it is a short distance away."

Through the narrow, snaking street, back through the busy Compo de Fiori, we strolled, Éva on my arm; pedestrians were parading, sitting, chatting, eating. Rome at nine-thirty on a spring evening was open and easy and spirited, an ongoing pageant; any minute I expected to see Mastroianni or Giueletta Massina.

"Look, this is the Piazza Farnesi, my favorite square. And the building across the way, with the French flag flying, that is the original palazzo designed by San Gallo and then worked on by Michelangelo. Now look up at the third floor, the windows, and the courtyard. . . . "

And while she admired those old masters, I thought of another, closer one.

Thus we spent the next few days, circling in the same pattern of Roman evening touring and Ziff cataloging. One afternoon we marched down the Corso toward the Largo Argentina, and the old palazzo where Arthur worked when he was in town. On the way Éva stopped at a massive church. "This is where the original Tosca was set, the San Andrea del Valle. Come inside, take a look."

Though I was not there for my purposes, I accompanied Éva into the vast cathedral and was drawn by its cavernous quiet, the muted frescoes on the vaulted ceiling, the intricate niches and fine apse.

"Arthur would stop here occasionally, on the way to his morning work at the center where I am taking you, and I thought you should see it therefore."

"You mean he liked the churches?"

"Yes. Why not? He said it reminded him of the synagogues in Dorchester, Mattapan, and Roxbury." She smiled at the names, at the irony. "Truthfully, he tried to learn about them."

Soon we proceeded on the noisy main thoroughfare of Corso Vittorio, to the Largo Argentina, a traffic center of two islands where orange buses thundered in and out. Éva pointed out a large Fetrinelli bookstore on one corner and, as we turned on Arenula, the Theatre Argentina, playing *Uncle Vanya*. We curved around a small park, filled with ruins, onto Via Boetegghe Obscura.

"Hey," I exclaimed, "I always wondered where that funny-sounding, oddly papered literary magazine got its name from."

"You are learning many things. Good."

The personal architectural tour continued at the narrow Via Caetani as we turned right and marched three hundred yards to number 32. There we proceeded through the archway of an old, decaying building and passed inside, along a courtyard filled with bruised statues and ancient sculptures. "All original, from the Roman period," Éva noted, walking on, taking me along.

We walked up the wide stone stairway of the wondrous palazzo and entered through a modern double doorway into a huge room of thick worn Persian carpet and a handsomely ornate ceiling.

"This was, some four hundred years ago, the grand palazzo of Prince Antici Mattei Caetani. And, if you recall, it is where Henry James placed Isabel Archer when she came over to Rome." I nodded, trying to remember that fact in *Portrait of a Lady*. "Lately it is the home of CISA, or Centro di Studi Americani, which brought American studies to Italy first," Éva explained, as the woman at the desk greeted her warmly. We went into the next room, equally large and of voluptuous decay, where several students sat at a huge, oblong reading table. Worn, sagging bookshelves, old books, musty smells. "Quaint, aren't they?" she said, pointing to a few old-fashioned library card catalogs set in wooden cabinets.

"When Arthur comes to Rome, this is his working ground; come, I'll show you." Vaguely puzzled, I followed her into the next vast chamber lined with books, and yet another, with Éva greeting a few librarians and introducing me. Thick carpets; old writing desks; worn, upholstered chairs; antiquarian smells of old books. And ornate touches everywhere—on the plaster ceilings and faded walls—of ancient glory gone to seed. I continued to follow her through the maze of rooms and corridors of the sixteenth-century palace.

"Here, the Ziff sanctuary," she nodded, arriving at a seedy but gracious ancient room, modest in size, with a desk, high window, reading chair, and daybed. "The prince's old study, in fact." She smiled, with a certain indulgence.

I looked about, again amazed at what I was hearing, observing.

"So Arthur writes here," I repeated, gazing at a small row of reference books, a photograph of an Italian family, and another one of a faintly familiar gentleman.

"The family descendants of the prince," she said, noticing what I was looking at. "And the other is a youthful photo of Henry James, when he visited here early in the century."

"Oh?"

Éva smiled. "Yes, I believe Arthur sees himself as an . . . heir, a spiritual and literary heir, of that unique writer, and therefore also as a protector of this grand house."

"Protector? How?"

She stood with her arms akimbo, appealing in her stance of authentic, helpless admiration. "This center has been in severe financial trouble for a while, and Mr. Ziff has been most helpful. Personally generous, but also raising money through his influence with the American embassy. And," she stumbled a bit—why?— "he has given . . . private grants, you may say, to young students wanting to pursue American literature and history."

"Here? At Italian universities?"

"Here and abroad. At your schools, too."

I nodded in bewildered appreciation.

"Do they do anything in return?"

"Oh, they do some research—for him, occasionally, yes. And perhaps . . . other work." She shrugged. "He has been their 'mentor,' you say? Even the savior of the place, I must admit. Not only when he is here, but in the States, too. He has required only one condition: total privacy for his contributions." She smiled. An idea from Maimonides? I mused.

"I see," I said, once again understanding little, but admiring the Jewish philosopher touch.

She sat down on the daybed and lit a cigarette. I took the chair. Chipped walls; an old, decayed map; Old World vibrations. What the hell was all this?

"But then why inform me, and show me all this if it's privacy he asked for?" I paused, smiled. "Are you an agent for Ziff?"

She shot me a look. "I believe yours will be the one book that truly counts, that remembers him with faith and truth. I have a longing that you know all sides of him, as I told you. Also, yes," she acknowledged, semireluctantly, "I probably have my own personal debts to him."

I eyed the filigreed ceiling and measured her words. "You can tell me what sort of debt if you wish to."

She inhaled deeply. "He has helped me through the years. Found me work here and there. A regular one semester of teaching here at Tor Vergata University, and a part-time job here at the center. In Budapest, translations, a research center connection." She moved an ashtray closer. "And helped my son when he had his school troubles at the gymnasia."

"Oh, I didn't know there was a son."

She nodded. "There is much that you may not know yet."

"Yes, of course. . . . Does that include your own . . . romance with Arthur?"

A slow, troubled look spread across her veteran face. "Why not? It is no great secret back home, and I am very proud of our special friendship."

"Why not? as you say," I seconded. "Do you wish me to keep silent on this subject by the way, later, in the biography?"

"There is no need for that." She smiled with appreciation. "You must write what your heart and mind tell you to write. I will not act as your censor, Daniel. I have felt censorship up close all my life, so I am a maximalist about writing freedom."

I admired her words but tried to read the fuller meaning. And I got the sense that it was quite the contrary she wanted, a visibility in my book, a proof of her existence in his life. She sat there, looking up at me, her dark-eyed gaze mournful, elegiac. I felt a new curious feeling for her.

"He worked here regularly, you say?" I asked. "For the few weeks that he was here?"

"Yes. Mornings. Every morning he writes here. After his early swim, of course."

"Oh? Where?"

"At the sports club. I show you if you wish."

"Sure. And then what, in the afternoons?"

"Much else, besides the late-afternoon walk. Sometimes the interviews, outside. On occasion the students here, meeting. Sometimes direction and counsel to the librarians and director. Also, some personal matters."

"It sounds very intensive."

"Intensive?" She smiled. "Perhaps. He is very well organized, you know. One of the secrets of genius, I am convinced."

I tried to take it all in. "But why has no one known this about him before? Suspected something? No word leaking out? I don't understand it."

"Do you forget his condition of privacy? And that this is Europe. If you betrayed his wishes, you lose his trust. *You have only one chance for the trust.* Then . . ." She made a guillotine cut.

I saw again an opening and raced in. "But are you not betraying that confidence right now, here, and these days with me?"

She shook her head. "I don't think so. It is important *for you* to recognize him, to understand his whole accomplishments. I know that others, such as the magazine journalists, cheap biographers, the ex-wife, will portray him otherwise."

Aha! "Oh, did you know her?"

She shook her head slowly. "I have never known the woman, though I met her once, briefly. Of course I saw her act, in Paris and in the movies. A bit too melodramatic for my tastes." She paused. "She will throw her poison at you about Arthur, I know."

I nodded and accepted that, as a motive (for Éva).

"Other enemies will try to influence you too, naturally. Like Mr. Mike Rossner, his former publisher. Or Chauncey Ames, over in London. Have you talked to them yet? You see, there will be enough poison thrown at him so that it is very important for me to show you see his true work here. And in Budapest."

I stood up, said I could use a drink of some sort, and Éva escorted me.

"Do you still love him?" I asked.

She looked at me with her dark, liquid eyes. "I am still committed to him, and always will be, Daniel. But in love with him now? I don't think so, no. Come this way, please."

We began to rewind our route, through the maze of glamorous faded rooms, and then back into the main library. Éva stopped for a minute to chat with the librarian.

I lingered by a young student studying at the grand table and asked her what she was reading? *"The Grapes of Wrath,"* she said in fairly good English. "I am doing my thesis on Steinbeck." I asked her her name, and where she was from: Suzanne Ohmann from a small village in northern Sweden, completing her studies here.

I talked to her a bit about Steinbeck and the difficulty of trying to write a thesis at an Italian university ("It is impossible to see or find your professor"), and then casually asked her if she had had any dealings with Mr. Ziff. She lit up. "Oh, he has read an essay of mine and advised me about my themes. And when I have finished my studies here, he will try to help me get into an American university for graduate studies. He is very helpful, very special."

Did that include bed, too? I wondered. But I couldn't pursue my questioning, because Éva was back at my side.

Soon Éva and I were having a sandwich at a nearby shop.

"I must tell you, my friend, that the Ziff I am hearing about today is very different from the one that I, and everyone else back home, knows. Very different indeed—almost a stranger."

Her nose wrinkled with amusement. "But why should you be so surprised, Daniel? His recent project, in fiction, has been to reinvent himself, as you yourself explained to me. So why not in life, too? To live anew, fresh. A bit like Picasso, always renewing himself, we may say. New personality. Why not? He takes his life as seriously as he takes his work. You can see that clearly now, I hope?"

I nibbled on my ham and cheese. "I think I do, Éva. A bit, anyway." I sipped the strong espresso and mused in dumb wonder.

Back in my hotel room, I transferred my musings to my writing pad.

Perhaps it is true that Arthur Ziff has after all surprised most of us with his other life abroad; his other, *new life*. By that I mean that maybe art imitates life here, for real; maybe his fictional personas, who appear before us in one part of a novel in one form, then vanish, and then reappear in a new shape, and who have seemed to some of us like a thin, cerebral invention, maybe they are rather much closer to fictional approximations of the real Ziff, as he exists abroad? The artist who has seen fit to metamorphose himself, in Europe, into a different man, different personality. And if this be the case, then perhaps those elusive protagonists have to be looked at again, reviewed anew for their more rounded, fleshy possibilities?

Perhaps, too, I have underestimated the nature and qualities of genius in Arthur Ziff. The zeal for organization; the ability to create order in nonconventional ways; the remarkable selflessness existing side by side with the narcissistic element; the talent to create a wider and wider pool of unusual characters and usable materials; the personal charisma employed for uses of unexpectedly rich paths; all of this is uniquely Ziffish, we may acknowledge, something akin to the recent fiction. The man has shown an art for living as distinct as the artist's talented style and literary voice.

Can we imagine other great American writers living this other life in a new territory? Hawthorne? Melville? Faulkner? Bellow? Well, perhaps Melville only of them all. (Indeed, were these tantalizing episodes of Ziff in Rome similar to the mysterious and never explained fourteen weeks that Melville spent in Hawaii in 1842?) Which suggests, at the least, the very audacious imagination of Arthur Ziff? . . .

I looked up, massaged my neck in a few slow turns, and lay down on the bed, still gripped by the trance of my imagination. . . . And I had a sudden glimpse into the breakup of the friendship between Melville and Hawthorne, the younger, more intense Melville creating a kind of symbolic, judgmental father in the older, formal Hawthorne, writing letters of admiration and yearning to Nate for closeness. And finally seeing the older friend turn his cool gaze and affection away, uncomfortable with the dense emotionalism of the White Whale author. I wondered: Had this pairing been repeated in some fashion by the older, cooler Ziff and the younger, heated Levitan? And was this project of mine my own *symbolical act of revenge?* . . .

That night, after a late dinner with Éva, we went for a long walk, cruising up and down the old Via Veneto, a nostalgic return for me (from a 1960s visit) to the then fabled street and to my many Cambridge evenings at the movies of Antonioni and Fellini. As we wandered along the long, curving avenue, the once-glamorous cafés now relatively empty, Éva pointed out the social history of the avenue, referring to three or four families of power, whose names—such as Boncampani and Ludovisi—now marked the cross streets. At one corner we passed a pair of painted ladies, a stunning brunette in pencil-striped linen suit (face familiar?), and a plump bleached blonde, with bursting bosom, who winked and gestured to us. Éva laughed gaily and shook her head. "These ladies are still here, but not as bold as before! Look, over here, this monster building was designed by one of Mussolini's architects—Piachentini, I think—in the thirties. Typical Fascist architecture." A massive concrete building housing a bank loomed before us. "Arthur loved this walk, you know."

"Do you know as much about Budapest as you do about Rome?"

"Of course, but a stranger knows an adopted home better than her own. Although I have been named an 'honorary Roman' by friends."

"And your English—where'd that come from?"

She laughed. "Bloomington, graduate school. I learn all about

Hoosiers, Bobby Knight, Crispus Attucks High School, idioms. Later, in Budapest, I watch old *Honeymooners* and *M*A*S*H* shows."

"Why Crispus Attucks High?"

She smiled. "Famous for a runaway slave, and great basketball players. You hear of the 'Big O'?"

I nodded, amazed. "Oscar Robertson was special, yes. I happen to be an old hoops fan. Anyway, foreigners always know America better than the natives."

As we strolled Éva said, "So you watched Italian cinema as a young man? "*Bicycle Thief* was our all-time favorite at home."

I nodded and launched into a reverie/discussion about all the old flicks—*Open City, Bitter Rice, La Strada, E Vittelloni, Nights of Cabiria, L'Avventura, Woman of Rome,* and so on. "You saw them all," she noted, impressed.

And by the time I got home and into bed, I was stirred by all the sacred names and familiar faces of those black-and-white celluloid stars, Mastroianni, Magnani, Lollobrigida, DeSica, Giuletta Massina. . . . Just as I was falling off, it came to me—the ravishing double of the Via Veneto whore—it was the dark-haired beauty Claudia Cardinale. I sat upright in bed, bright alert, eager. (And hadn't Arthur himself dallied with the Roman ladies of the night, especially, I knew, in pairs?) I got dressed, called a cab, and in fifteen minutes was cruising the avenue again, this time in a slow-moving taxi.

Half an hour later the three of us, the two professional ladies and myself, were upstairs in a hotel suite five minutes from the Veneto. The brunette, named Gabriella, was indeed a dead ringer for my Claudia C., shoulder-length dark hair, small, upturned nose, compact face with baby-smooth skin, and spectacular smile; in short black skirt and silk blouse, she was the tall knockout beauty from next door. The second whore was a shorter woman with somewhat frizzy dirty blond hair, with large bust, hoop earrings, and fishnet stockings, and a tough look on a round, pretty face. The latter spoke a fractured English, a help since my pocket-size *Collins English-Italian Dictionary* was rather useless for our business. Not so the pocket calculator I had brought along.

Nina, the blonde, named a sizable figure that I couldn't understand; she used my calculator to show it. The figure was 775,000 lire, which translated into $500. What would I get for the tidy sum? "A *mostra* very lovely," she said, opening her deep décolletage and taking her partner's hand to fondle her huge bosom.

Facing the real women beneath the flowery portrait of ladies with parasols in Venice gondolas on the wall, I interpreted the scene as a kind of contextual research; maybe even, as Prince Arthur knew, a tax write-off? Furthermore, had I not gotten my own advance in part for hands-on, basic research?

"Maybe you want same *mostra speciale* as our American *intellectuali* who comes a few times a year?" She took my arm, sat us down, laughed playfully. "Our *avventuriero*," she said with a wink.

Might I have hit pay dirt by instinct, by coincidence? I sat dumbfounded while the younger woman pronounced her name sweetly—"E-leez-i-beth"—and stroked my cheek.

Nina said, *"Millione cinque-cento mille,"* taking my calculator and showing me the figure, 1.5 million lire.

I digested the thousand-dollar proposition, and thought aloud, "That's pretty expensive."

Nina consoled me, *"E caro, ma vale i soldi."*

We negotiated; I got off easy, 1.2 million lire, or $775. Unheard-of in my preadvance days.

And dark-haired Elizabeth leaned over to plant a flicking wet tongue in my mouth—my Cardinale encouraging.

"Speciale, hey!" The call from Nina brought onto the scene a third young woman, a slim-waisted African attired in a beige linen suit, crisp white shirt, and high heels. The tribal indentations on the face, and the mahogany skin coloring, suggested Ethiopian. As she approached, I stared at her jet-black hair, small, beautiful face, broad flat nose, the sensual, soft skin. How old is she? I wondered. She stared back at me with dark, shining eyes, arms folded, a trace of a smile. Her beauty was subtle, youthful, exotic.

Taken aback by the strangeness and stunning ebony elegance, I tried to focus on the blue-and-white ceramic tile floor, the square glass coffee table and large rubber plant, the contemporary wool rug. A jazz group serenaded via a minispeaker system, from walls of turquoise.

At a hand signal from Nina, Elizabeth turned about, and raised her small skirt so that it bunched up halfway; Nina set my hand on her firm, lace-pantied buttocks, and coaxed my hand to massage the delicious fanny, while her dark associate, smelling of musk, licked my ear teasingly.

"*Dolce,* eh? Lire, now, please."

I took out the stack of funny bills I had with me, some 600,000 lire; she counted it and shook her head. Awkwardly, I found my credit card and said that immediately afterward *("subito, subito")* I'd get the rest of the money from a local ATM machine. ("Ah, Banco Roma?" She pointed downstairs.) Explaining the matter to Elizabeth, she wagged her finger at me in mock warning.

"*Vieni, vieni,*" Nina urged, helping me up and along, following the two women, arms linked, into a bedroom, lit softly by indirect lighting. My heart was shaking.

"Ethiopian?" I asked.

Nina looked at me, then shook her head. "Eritrea. *Capisce?*"

The civil war? I watched as the young ladies broke into a little spontaneous dance, half disco, half lyrical, heads bobbing, hips swaying, pelvises suggesting. I sat enthralled, figuring that $775 was cheap for this private theater, and could have watched the one-on-one sexy dancing all night.

"*La sua famiglia mange per tre mesa del lavoro d'una notte.*"

"What?" Slowly I puzzled out something about the family eating for one night's work.

Beaming, she touched my hand, urging me to watch.

Presently, in a kind of slow motion—my blood pumping—the women kissed, fondled, undressed each other. Every now and then one of them winked at me, flicking a tongue out. One in camisole, the other in black bikini underwear, they sat and stroked their lithe, ravishing bodies, two porpoises intertwining in pleasing play. Nina sat by me in a two-seater divan and caressed me, starting at my neck and chest, then my member through the trousers. Growing aroused, she set my hand deep into her full chest, squeezed down, then took one breast out of her bra for me to nibble on. A sweet-sounding trumpet (Chet Baker?) was blowing, the air in the stylish bedroom was indolent and musky, and I felt my senses swimming.

At some point one of the girls called over for me, and I rose up, unsteadily. What did they want with me? I mused nervously. "Asmara," Elizabeth introduced her friend (giggling at the nickname) and the young woman smiled shyly and took my face to hers. Mesmerizing, aromatic, different. She gazed at me for a full minute, as though judging me, before kissing me softly, holding my tongue in her thick lips. The sensual kiss and ebony beauty lulled my consciousness.

Now, what ensued was something out of deep-sea diving, an aqua blue terrain wherein the familiar was transformed, slowed down, and a dream world emerged. Frankly, I found myself in over my head, so to say, mingling with the young, lithe women (and guided by the mature one), and escorted through the medium of uninhibited acts. For an instant I tried to remind myself that all this bodily confusion was for bookish research. But I was quickly pulled out of such folly by the sly, professional pleasuring. Objects liquefied, aromas swirled, jazz piped, time vanished, and I was transported down, down, into a soft sea bottom of secret games, a man nibbled at, teased, played with, cajoled, by smart, slippery, sensuous creatures.

Soon, after a timeless, slow daze, they were cleaning me (and them) up in a grand bathroom. A large whirlpool bathtub, with gleaming golden faucets and jets, large off-white tiles and heated towel bar with monogrammed bath towels, a thick Mondrian design bath rug and discreet mirrors, soft lighting, the sweet musical hum of piped-in jazz. A postop coital scene performed in a modern art bathroom. An epilogue as good as the play itself, with Asmara and Elizabeth scrubbing me forcefully, two solicitous trainers in white bathrobes rubbing me down as though I were a comic actor after the matinee performance. Their hands were firm and knowledgeable; it was ravishing to be in their hands.

Finally, director Nina called a halt to the proceedings and

suggested that it was time to move on and get dressed; move on from this theater, I figured, back to noticeable reality.

Afterward, down on the street at the Bianca di Roma, I slipped my magical plastic into the ATM slot, hit the English button, and ordered my money. Handing over 700,000 lire bills to the women was like handing over oversized Monopoly money from the bank, no more. Nina hailed me a taxi and, touchingly, the two young ladies hugged me, with Elizabeth nipping my ear and whispering *"buono notte,"* while Asmara kissed my cheek shyly. Saying good-bye to my young teachers, I felt like a schoolboy who has completed his exams and earned his summer vacation.

Leaning out from the taxi, I said, "The American, Arturo. What did he look like? Tall, short? Handsome? *Competente?"*

Nina looked at Elizabeth and said something, causing them to giggle and laugh robustly. Claudia and Asmara linked arms, waved. Nina said, "No worry! *You very much fun!* Come back, ah? *Ciao!"*

Well, what did it mean? Had I guessed right? Or was my over-heated imagination working overtime, trying to fit pieces together neatly, too neatly? In my safe haven of a hotel room I concluded just that, and sought sleep, and dreams of my beauties; but when I couldn't sleep, I stayed awake and took copious notes.

Sitting in the CISA library room the next morning, I realized how much I adored library reading rooms. Book-lined shelves, a few quiet readers, a large wooden desk, angles of sunlight from the high windows, the odors of dust and old books, all this added up to a blessed chamber. Reading rooms ranked right up there with classrooms, playing fields, and erotic zones as favorite turf. And now augmenting this room was an ongoing manuscript, the surprising buoy of my adult life. Pilot rollerpoint pen in hand, I wrote in my soft notebook:

Let me begin this section on Arthur Ziff as a kind of unique American artist with a quote from Ziff, from his *Essays on*

Reading, Living, Lying: 'Middle-class conventions, rules, and mores must not dominate the writer's life, as Melville, Flaubert, Céline, and James knew, but especially in modern days. One of the modern writer's tasks—a painful one, to be sure—is to turn upside down the rules and truths of his upbringing, and then make sure to trod and trample them underfoot. At the same time he must remember what he has lost, and miss it always. Only then will he have begun to serve his true life, as an artist, in a serious and honest way.' Most writers who make such a statement, and there have not been many in contemporary America, will employ those principled words as just so much rhetoric, and, if anything, pay lip service to them in life. Not so Arthur Ziff, as it turns out. He is a man true to his words and therefore true to the idea of the artistic self as the dominant one in the life of the whole man.

Pay attention to the phrase 'a painful one, to be sure,' since it may very well provide a clue to the periodic, apparently immoral or unseemly actions of Ziff the man. Somewhat stiff or awkward in company, proper and conventional in society, devoted to a rigorous work routine, he has tried his best to discover ways of hiding out while carving out original routes to an outlaw territory of society and self. In the media-crazed celebrity atmosphere of American society, where Arthur Ziff is a major, visible figure, he has done brilliantly in recognizing the subtle and vulgar traps of that culture, and sought ways to escape them. An engineer of bridges to foreign territory, a secret scout of new frontiers, Ziff has grown more and more ingenious in constructing ways of inventing and playing out a new life, and subsequently, in his fiction, creating new masks and screens of self.

Consider his life in Europe, both East and West. In Hungary, for example, he has created riches in cultural life and surprises in personal ways that have been nothing short of unique. It is not simply that he has helped launch the new generation of writers and critics through the cultural quarterlies ('2000' and 'Holmi') he privately funded and whose editorial boards he served on; he was also tireless in finding publishers in the West for those writers, and rooms of freedom in Budapest. Just as important, he visited these writers regularly, being there in their time of urgent need, practically, politically. While other writers flew in and out for USIS readings, Ziff was on the ground, as it were, a literary doctor in the grim Communist trenches. Then, for six years, he brought their work to the attention of a Western audience, along with others from the East, in the annual series that he coedited back home. No wonder that when Arthur Ziff appeared in Budapest—or in Warsaw, Prague, or Bucharest—he was treated like a literary god, and referred to, only half humorously, as 'Lord Arthur.' For those serious acts alone, Arthur Ziff deserves, I believe, serious consideration for some special post-Communist award.

Yet for the artist, as Arthur knew well, that sort of behavior means little. In fact, such gestures of virtue can be a hindrance to the necessary life of impertinence, and a sure ticket to deadly fiction. Hence his Other Life, hidden away ingeniously, tucked out of sight, away from the virtuous soul and away from the flocks of admirers, fans, and media paparazzi who hound and injure the modern celebrity artist. There had to be a secret life, one that flew in the face of bourgeois conventions or middle-class notions of morality, a life of furtive, self-imposed exile. And this is where Ziff as General Rommel, master planner, returned to enter the fray, expanding his theater of operations via his real-life campaign.

It was in Rome that I unearthed a fitting piece of that secret life. In that holy city I unearthed some, though not all, of the unholy sites and unknown acts. For there, in the shadow of the Vatican, Arthur Ziff lived like a true underworld prince, creating a unique, viable empire of students, pilgrims, whores, lovers, librarians, and servants, which served as the real-life country for his rich outlaw fictions. For it was there, on foreign soil, that he might walk about anonymously (and safely) at all times of the day or night, and give his splendid imagination—with the help of his full financial resources—all the freedom that it craved to nurture creative impulses. And what he founded there, in its combination of utopian impulse, social experiment, and controlled decadence, all for the sake of art, his art, is nothing short of remarkable.

We can see some of this activity, of course, in characters such as Hayden Aarons—

My shoulder was tapped, and when I looked up, it was Éva, her hair held back charmingly by a turquoise headband. Flashing a smile, she said, "Come along—it's time to take a small journey to one of Arthur's favorite meditative places."

In my writing trance still, I slowly packed up, scribbling a note on where to start in the next day.

On the way out we bumped into Suzanne, the young Swedish student who was writing on Steinbeck. I said hello, offering a lunch later in the week. She said Friday, and we made a date.

Éva and I drove out in a southerly direction from Rome, fighting the traffic. She was a speedy, even daring driver, I noticed.

"Where are we heading?" I asked.

"You've read *Henderson the Rain King*, yes?" I nodded, and she went on. "Bellow has written about Monte Cassino there, though briefly. It is a monastery that was bombed—during World War II, mistakenly, perhaps—by the Americans who believed there were Nazis headquartered there. Later, however, the Americans rebuilt the place, stone by stone almost. You shall see. Quite special, we believe."

Which "we" did she mean? We drove out past small industrial areas to a farming region of rolling hills and green fields. Éva explained how rich this region was in supplying vegetables and produce for the entire region, including Rome, of course. "And if we were to continue straight down on this road, we'd eventually reach Sicily."

"Land of my favorite director, Petro Germi," I said, "and also my favorite Italian writers, Pirandello and Sciascia."

She eyed me. "Arthur always praised your knowledge and literary taste."

Uncomfortable, I shifted to something about the Dutch and Israeli agricultural capacities, and she shot me a quizzical look.

After a bit, she said, "It was at Cassino actually that Arthur got the idea for his large and new, remarkable project."

"Oh?"

"Yes." She nodded. "When listening to the monks chanting." She looked over at me, to see how that registered.

"Which project is this?"

"It's something no one knows about yet. You will be the first. In the West, at least."

"I see. I'm very . . . honored, then."

A long pause while she lit a cigarette.

"It is not for the pages of your book. Unless, of course, Arthur publishes something first."

We zipped past two cars. "I understand," I said. "But then why are you informing me?"

"Because I think you will appreciate him all the more."

Always the same theme. "What is the project, by the way?"

"Wallenberg."

I looked over at her, stopped by the name, her solemn tone, stunned by the subject. "You mean the Swedish diplomat Raoul Wallenberg?"

"Exactly. Rescued Hungarian Jews, maybe as many as a hundred thousand, directly and indirectly."

"That many, really?"

She nodded. "Yes, very many. A great man. An aristocrat. And then he was missing, for many years."

"Didn't they discover recently that he had been killed, or died, in a Soviet prison in the late forties or so?"

"That is the official line, yes. Arthur believes otherwise, however, and is trying to locate the full truth."

"Oh? Where?"

She shook her head and laughed at me. "In fiction, of course. But also in Budapest, Moscow, Stockholm. Even Siberia."

This news was stunning to me, and I tried to take it in. Was it, could it, be altogether true? I said aloud, "You mean he's conducting a search at the same time that he's writing?"

She eyed me shrewdly. "I told you he was a genius, and now you are discovering it for yourself."

She was right on, wasn't she? A genius. "By what means is he searching? Interpol? The U.N.? The recent release of KGB documents?"

"Here. Look up. You see it?"

There it was, perched on a steep hilltop, a low, long, white building. "Like Walpi in Arizona," I admired.

"Huh?"

"An old Indian town—Hopi, I think—that the conquistadors could never conquer, because of the vertical drops of its cliffs."

She shook her head. "Oh, I would like to see it. Will you take me sometime?"

I smiled and said sure.

"Look, it even gets better. The climb is very beautiful, so please do not miss the views."

We wound round and round, up and up, the low monastery looming larger. "How is he conducting that search, by the way?"

"He is carefully organized. There are several helpers; well, perhaps teams of helpers in each country." She smiled, thinking of it. "He has even been granted an audience with King Gustaf in Stockholm. On the condition of privacy—by Arthur, of course."

"Of course," I said, and admired the views, the hills, the strategist. "Doesn't all that take a lot of time? And time away from writing?"

"When you are single as a mature adult," she advised me, "and you have your purpose or mission in life"—she clicked with her mouth and sliced the air with her hand—"you can work very, very efficiently. Arthur explained that to me years ago."

I took that in, and viewed the white houses growing smaller and smaller below. Soon we were in the long driveway of the monastery, where three chartered buses were already parked. She nodded to an attendant, who showed us an upper parking lot.

Presently we were walking up the many steps and into the

gracious monastery, a squarish arrangement of white buildings folded around a large central courtyard, with pillars, levels, and superior views. In the sunshine we took a brief stroll, amid clumps of students and tourists. Then Éva took my arm and led me up another flight of steps, to a quiet corner of stone wall, where a robed monk nodded and opened a huge wooden door.

Inside, another world: darkness except for candlelight, dark woods and bright mosaic floor, vaulted ceiling, long aisle, and about two dozen pews. Up ahead on the dais, four Franciscan monks were singing some Gregorian Chant. We took seats in the back and listened quietly to the riveting music, which rolled upward to the ceiling and around off the walls with deep sonorousness. Gradually the music enfolded us within its circling harmonies.

"It was here that he retreated. Sometimes I went inside with him, sometimes he asked me to wait outside. You can see why. It is a place for, and of, spiritual solitude. And it was here"—she took my hand—"that he took the inspiration for the present important project."

My senses of disbelief and wry skepticism were gradually washed over by the waves of chants and the aura of silence. Whether it was true or not, the great hall was having its spiritual effect on me, as in her tale of Arthur.

I whispered, "The Americans rebuilt this whole floor?"

"Yes. Exquisite, isn't it? And the whole monastery. It took them fifteen years, I believe."

"Then we're not such monsters after all."

She squeezed my hand and looked over at me, her nostrils giving a little sexy flair.

We listened to the deep chanting, listened steadily, and I contemplated the story. This aspect, at least. Was it half true? Even at 50 percent, it was a great tale, a plot imagined by Emily or Charlotte Brontë, maybe. And if it were more than fifty, why, then, Arthur Ziff was something to behold: part general, part saint, part monk (Franciscan? Rasputin?).

Later, outside, we stopped by a hillside cemetery for a picnic of cheese, fruit, bread, and wine.

"Are you saying," I began delicately, "that Arthur is using Wallenberg as a fictional protagonist?"

She peeled an apple with her knife, in circular style. "You know that Arthur would be more subtle than that."

"Yes, of course."

She gave me slices of apple to go along with my brie. "I would say that he is *searching for Wallenberg* in the novel—perhaps in the same way that he searches for the truth about him and his death in life. Isn't that the beauty of his recent work?"

"Yes, I think you have a point."

She chewed slowly and said, "The Jewish element never leaves his work, you see. In one form or another."

"Yes, true enough."

"It gives the work an underpinning in the soil, you can say?"

"Not quite. But I understand you." I took my bite. "Along with the element of sensuality, perhaps?"

She smiled—wanly, I thought. "Yes. The *famous sensuality*. I wish . . . I wish that the . . . never mind."

Puzzled, I poured her a cup of wine and handed it to her. "What is it that you wish?"

She sipped the wine and said, "I wish that things had been different." Then a brave smile. "Forgive the cliché, but don't we all, always?"

"Not quite always," I replied. An allusion to Ziff? "But is there something specific you're thinking of?"

I thought I saw her repress tears in answer.

In the spring aromatic air I felt awkward, and also, curiously, pressed to act in some way. I moved closer to her and took her around, and she nestled in my arms. Nearby, I could see the white and gray tombstones, dirtied by age; beyond, yellow forsythia bloomed. Were the dead looking on, allowed to view mutely the living?

When I looked down at this living one, however, I was quite surprised. She was looking up at me, brown eyes imploring, face smallish and lovely. I couldn't help myself, and kissed her; she kissed me back, once, twice. Perceptibly, her mascara began to run and her lipstick smudge, the rouge loosened; she was turning paler, older. Not a thirtyish, stylish ingenue, but a survivor of fifty.

Yet something curious happened then, inwardly. I was very moved by her transformation, the sudden falling away of one self, and the revelation of another, more vulnerable one beneath. This paler face, of vulnerability and aging, mirroring the deep wish for something else in her life, elicited a new and curious passion in me, much like a new, synthetic element in chemistry, mine made up of elegy and compassion. In any case, I tried to act on it, against my reason—since I had wanted to keep my research clean of relationships and passions—and we were soon stretched on the blanket, extending our mutual field of interests to the level of ardor. Except that my ardor of caring and tenderness did not translate into erect passion, and I wound up only holding her closely, an act in itself appealing. I started to apologize for my performance, but she put her finger to my lips. Then, getting rearranged and smoking, Éva mused aloud, "I wished that . . . we had stayed lovers. When it ended, I was crushed. And have never gotten over it, deep inside. . . . Some passion affairs stay with you like bullet wounds, d'you know?" I nodded, knowing nothing, but hearing the Ziff tag phrase repeated by her. "Yes, it's true, unfortunately." She leaned over and kissed me on the cheek, warmly.

Later, in the car, driving back, she spoke. "We worshiped Wallenberg, you see. All of us, the writers, the artists, the freedom fighters, Gerta, Janusz, Laszlo, Yvette. He was an inspiration to all who had fought the Nazi-collaborators and later the Communists, from one generation of Resistance fighters to the next. So you see, when Arthur took a devoted interest in Raoul's disappearance and death, up at Monte Cassino, and chose his life for a subject in fiction, well, it all fitted together, strangely but perfectly. The great man and the great writer, two outsiders from two different lands and eras who had taken Hungary as their kind of adopted country or child."

I tried to take it all in. "But surely very few people know of Ziff's aesthetic interest in Wallenberg."

She patted my hand. "Very few, yes. And now one more, probably the first American, too."

She had put on her blues/jazz tape, and Julie London was singing "Cry Me a River" from a world ago.

"Where is your son now?" I said, trying to take the pressure away from my persistent subject. "Budapest?"

She zipped past a blue Mercedes sedan. "He's dead. Killed in a car crash with his father four years ago."

"Oh. I'm very sorry."

Turning my head, I experienced her driving in a new perspective. The more I discovered about this woman, the more I learned that surprised me. I was coming to believe more and more in her credibility, at the same time that I grew more bewildered by her ways of feeling, sounding, maybe seeing.

"Arthur told me you play tennis. I hope you still do, because I've arranged a doubles for tomorrow afternoon. All right?"

nine

Back in the now familiar confines of the palazzo library, I sat at the huge table and returned to my own text, scribbling:

'We shall be judged finally by the delicacy of our feeling of where to stop short,' wrote Robert Frost in a letter, an admonition that is worth taking to heart for any biographer. So if it appears at times that I stop short here, in my interpretation of the life of Arthur Ziff, the reader will understand, I hope, the influence of my curtailment. For Frost—himself the subject of the crude excesses of biographers—understood well how private and elusive a life could be, and how bumptious and arrogant those university intruders could be, who tried to enter posthumously into a life armed with apparent facts, half-truths, and tendentious prejudices.

What can I say, therefore, about the nature of Ziff's bizarre, elusive life over in Europe? What was he up to? Was he really a private saint and literary Lord Jim of Communist Eastern

Europe? Was he the real modern artist, organizing all of his considerable resources, including financial, in the service of his mission as a novelist? Is he the true heir of Henry James, our last great transatlantic ambassador of American literature? Is he the aesthetic Rommel of our time, one who understands full well that since a Nobel Prize would never come his way, because of the Nobel's politics and piety and his own controversial content, he would create his own unique strategies for attack and outdo every recent recipient of the award, by working tirelessly and seriously for the state of literature in the modern world?

As the reader can sense, this writer—his biographer, his admirer, his friend—is at times at a loss for words in trying to present a confident interpretation of that peculiar life.

And yet, yet . . . what are we to make of his doings with those unique 'pilgrims' whose life stories he has solicited and paid for? With those students, and servants, at the American libraries in various European cities, for whom he acts as the princely benefactor? With the Rome—and Budapest, Manhattan?—ladies of the streets, with whom he risks exotic dalliances? With the secret crusade on behalf of Raoul Wallenberg, both for his fiction and for history? Is there another contemporary writer so enshrouded in mystery and so enlarged with legend in his life?

I sat back in my chair, stared up at the decaying filigreed ceiling, thought of the original Italian prince here a few hundred years ago, and realized how rich it would be to have a peek at the current manuscript of Arthur's. To see where and how the figure of Wallenberg was set, like the Jamesian figure in the carpet. Maybe I could put some of the pieces of the puzzle together then, and weigh in with some assessments. I wrote next:

> Perhaps the one clear thing that can be said when looking at this life is its glittering ingenuity and resplendent powers, like some brilliantly cut diamond; if Henry Troyat was able to call his subject, Leo Tolstoy, 'a colossal human fact,' what can we say, with reasonable fairness, about Arthur Ziff? Perhaps this: His is a

uniquely designed life, an aesthetically driven life, and it may be fair to call Arthur Ziff 'a formidable modern fact.' Would that be so far off target?

Now, how well does that myriad life translate into the novels and tales? Or, better, does the unusual experience of that life translate with equal resonance and power into the fiction?

Someone was hovering above me, I sensed, so I scribbled a note on my smaller pad to check out "Arturo" with Claudia and Nina on the Via Veneto, before I left in three days. And to reread a few Ziff novels, *Rosenthal's Revenge* and *To Each According to His Needs*. Plus the masterpiece *Goldfeld at Eighty*.

"Hi. We have our lunch today, okay?"

"Oh, sure. Yes."

So, over a cheese and ham sandwich at a local shop, I chatted with the young Swedish student, here in Rome for a few years, to learn the language fluently and obtain her B.A. degree. Freckle-faced pretty, reddish-haired, Suzanne, though she hailed from a small village in the north, was clearly, from her English, an excellent linguist. We talked for a while about Steinbeck, and her thesis on landscape and character—"suggested to me by Mr. Ziff, after my original idea went nowhere." Her looseleaf binder was thick with notes and colored dividers, like a high schooler.

I didn't know how to bring up what I wanted to bring up, said something about the fine Roman coffee, and wondered, "So you did occasional research for him?"

"Yes."

"Like what?"

"This is for your book on Mr. Ziff, I understand?"

I nodded, and explained that I was interviewing several of the students to get an idea of how Arthur organized his research.

She nodded. "Once I did research on Henry James, but the last few times I worked on Mr. Wallenberg."

"Oh, I see. Where?"

"In Stockholm."

"And you were . . . paid, obviously?"

She smiled broadly. "Free trips to my country and to my home. And money. Yes, paid excellently."

"He was always very generous." I sipped my coffee and, figuring the Swedes could handle it, slipped in casually, "By the way, did you happen to have a romance with him?"

Nonchalant, she drank her caffè latte and shook her head slowly. "I have an Italian boyfriend."

Was that a clever answer? "Oh, I see."

After a pause, she added, "He is like my professor, that is all. Only far more helpful. And is he not . . . in his sixties?"

My turn to smile. "Some old men in their sixties still have romances, you know."

Her laugh was small but appreciable.

"And he will help you get into an American university?"

"For graduate school, I hope."

"What did you find out about Mr. Wallenberg?"

She shook her head. "Not very much. Small details of where he lived, family history, his schools, a few old friends."

"Did Mr. Ziff act on the information, then?"

"Oh, yes. He visited the house in old Stockholm and the country house, and even met one of Wallenberg's old friends from university."

"He was rather thorough?"

"Very."

"By the way, how did he speak with the friend in English?"

"Mr. Svenholm's English was not good. I translated for him."

I pondered that. "Oh. So he traveled there *with you?*"

"That one time, yes."

I felt more and more like Sherlock Holmes circling a suspect, or was it rather more like a divorce detective? The many sides of biography were beginning to open up to me. Now, with this Swedish Suzanne: Was a casual sleepover once or twice different from a regular romance? But even if so, what difference did it make?

"Did you have to write up anything on your research?"

"Yes, I wrote a full report on Mr. Wallenberg."

"Oh, I see. Would you have a copy?"

She shook her head. "I gave it to Mr. Ziff."

I nodded, and eyed her fat looseleaf.

"May I ask you something, Mr. Levitan?"

"Of course."

"Are you sympathetic to Mr. Ziff—in your biography, I mean?"

I smiled. "I think so. I hope so."

"I hope so, too," she said. "It would be a pity if you were not, and yet asking his friends these questions."

I said I understood what she meant. "Do you think you might order us another coffee? Your Italian is better than mine. Here." I gave her a ten-thousand-lire note.

"Sure." She got up and went to the cash register to pay, before taking her receipt over to the coffee counter.

Casually, I turned her looseleaf book around and flipped through it, searching for anything of interest. Organized neatly, in literary categories, by color separator sheets. Just as I was about to turn it back, however, I noticed a small photograph autographed for "his friend," and pasted on the orange divider. The black-and-white photo was of Arthur, and the category read ARTHUR ZIFF. As I opened the page, I noticed Suzanne returning with our coffees, so I turned the book back around to her place and waited.

"You certainly do keep a lot of notes. I'm impressed."

She shrugged modestly and set the coffees down. "Many are class notes. I put one sugar in, all right?"

"Thanks," I said, taking my coffee. "So, are there any future projects in mind for you? For Mr. Ziff, I mean."

She sipped. "Perhaps Etty Hillesum."

The name sounded somewhat familiar. I nodded.

"The Dutch Jewish woman who died in Auschwitz and who wrote a very memorable diary."

"Oh, yes, sure. What will you do on her?"

"I do not know yet. But I believe I will be asked to join the Hillesum project team."

I almost burned my tongue on the word *team*. "Really. Tell me a bit about that. It sounds . . . most interesting."

"Well, I am not sure I am allowed to. Please, let me find out from Éva, or Mr. Ziff, if you don't mind."

"Of course," I said, calming her, and me, too, and making a mental note to look at that diary. "I take it you read the diary in English?"

She nodded. "Swedish, actually."

"She was an unusual woman," I recalled.

"For me, one of the remarkable things about working for Mr. Ziff has been the introduction to remarkable people, writers. That is why I respect him so much. His feelings for these mostly dead, European souls, of forgotten honor, are what make the work . . . important and unusual."

I half joked, "Maybe he should win a the Peace Prize?"

"Most definitely, Professor Levitan, and I hope your book will help this happen. That is why I speak to you so frankly about my work here for Mr. Ziff."

I looked at her blue-eyed freckled face, eyeing me directly, while listening to her sincere entreaty. I felt imbued with an added mission for my own project, one that surprised me with its new possibilities. *(Prizes of all sorts, on his behalf?)* At the same time, I wondered about the veracity, or diplomacy, of her earlier words about her relationship to Arthur. Did her own idealistic thoughts for Arthur Ziff interfere with a full, frank disclosure? (What was that little photograph of Arthur—a fan's souvenir, or a personal memento?) But did that matter after all, a small truth next to a much higher hope?

That night, late, I found myself back in a taxi on the Via Veneto, cruising up and down, looking for the familiar pair of ladies. Up and back two or three times, with the Italian driver nearly laughing aloud. No luck. Several other prospects were in evidence, standing on corners or in doorways, but not my pals. I kept a book jacket photo with me, however—promising myself to replace it from the States—ready to try the next night, my last before leaving on Saturday noon. It was a crazy chance, but one worth taking; witnesses for the prosecution, you might say. Would I give them full credit in a footnote? (*Nina, Asmara, and Claudia, pro-fessional ladies from the Via Veneto, have positively identified Mr. Ziff as a playmate in Rome. . . .)

For our last dinner together, Éva took me to the Jewish ghetto, to a place called Giggeto's, a formal restaurant a few blocks down from the synagogue. Over the specialties of the house—fried arti-chokes and zucchini blossoms—we chatted about a future meeting, about my stay, about the book.

"I heard you had a productive meeting with Suzanne yes-terday," Éva said, nibbling. "How did she strike you?"

Tasting the oddly delicious artichokes, I said carefully, "Very honest, very helpful. Excellent student."

"Yes. I think so. I hope so."

"Why 'hope so'?"

"Because she was my choice, I chose her for Arthur."

Central Casting, like for a movie? "I think you chose well." Then I probed, "Is he fond of her?"

"Fond?" She lifted an artichoke, "I think so. But you know, it takes a period of time before Arthur allows trust."

"Yes, that's right."

"Here, have some more wine," as she poured me another gob-letful. "Now that you have a little sense of his life here, perhaps you will want to visit Budapest next?"

"Why not?"

"The routine is a bit different there, as you can imagine, and yet not so much. Nowadays he does not stay as long as before, with the Communists gone, and the political pressures gone, too—his attrac-tion, perhaps?" She smiled. "Altogether, now Eastern Europe is much duller than Rome . . . and yet we have our special interests."

The white-jacketed waiter came for our main course choice.

I shook my head. "No, this is too good to want to add to."

She laughed, and explained to him how we'd have a penne pasta with broccoli.

"Has the *material* here been helpful for you? Of surprise?"

"Both, I'd say."

"You have a more . . . hopeful image of Arthur now?"

"That's a nice way of putting it. A more balanced one, say."

She thought about that and smiled. "Good." She took a few more bites, then said, "You Americans are obsessed with 'balance,' aren't you? That's the good thing about Arthur's work—*it's not*."

I patted her hand. "Touché. You're a smart woman."

We ate and drank. The traffic of new diners was heavy, and the other tables were busy with chatter and goblets tinkling.

"You will think of me a little bit now and then?" she said, raising her glass.

"A little bit," I teased.

"Good. . . . I think you . . . hold yourself back a little from me. But maybe that's because of the . . . situation. Your work on Arthur, your friendship with him."

It called for an answer, but I didn't quite know what to say. "You've become a friend. And we will stay that way, I hope. And naturally we will talk, by letter, by phone."

"And by more modern communication."

I smiled. "Of course, by e-mail, too."

Outside, we strolled in the warm air around the winding cobblestone streets of the old ghetto. "Have you read *History* by Else Morante?"

I nodded, and she continued. "The best novel about Rome during World War II, I believe."

"But I think that maybe Arthur's new novel will be the best about the Holocaust, because he was not a part of it, not injured by it, and because he came to it very late, almost by accident. And only after resisting writing about it for so long. Do you know what I mean?"

"Well, maybe. . . . "

She saw my doubt. "Because he is a master, he will feel the experience from the inside out, and judge the right details, and psychology. Like Stephen Crane, he will write a unique text without having been there, a *Red Badge of Courage* for the Holocaust."

"Well, that's quite an expectation. Actually, the idea still surprises me."

Leaning into me, she said, "He is full of surprises, unpredictability. That is the great lesson of his art, too, isn't it?"

I took that in, her arm through mine. "Oh, I imagine that most art is truly surprising. Otherwise, what's the point? Not surprising in an easy or sensational fashion, but showing a new side to a familiar experience, or maybe an old truth in an unfamiliar one. No matter whether the situation is domestic or wild."

"Yes," she nodded, "I see what you are saying."

"But perhaps his life *is more truly surprising* than that of other artists," I said, trying to accommodate her point in some way. "For my project, of course, it is of great interest."

She turned me toward a sculpture in a small square, showing a nude boy and a tortoise shell. "Piazza della Tartarughe," she named it. "And that is what your book will be, Daniel, a truly interesting work, outside of fashion or sensation. A work of art in itself. That is why I invited you here to Europe, to make sure about this. And"—she reached upward to kiss me—"about you."

I returned it, awkwardly. "These odd sculptures pop up everywhere, don't they? Hard to believe." Seeing the anomalous sculpture emerge in the tiny dark square, I added, almost to myself, "Yes. Maybe as hard to believe as Arthur Ziff writing a Holocaust novel, since he and I have often had fun mocking the 'Holocaust industry' that's sprung up in the past few decades. In novels, unfortunately, as well as television and films."

"Why is this, do you think?"

"Commerce operates everywhere. In literature, too. Even, at times, in writers who should know better. Six-figure contracts sometimes distort values, cloud thinking. Let's walk on."

"You don't think Arthur does it for commercial reasons?"

"No, I don't," I answered truthfully, though tactfully I kept to myself other possible motives.

We roamed through the close, human streets, every now and then passing free-and-easy citizens, nodding a night hello.

Éva said, "Charming now, but not in the late thirties and forties, when the Jews were rounded up and evicted. Some killed. Though it was not nearly as bad as Paris or Amsterdam. Mussolini and the Italians were not Jew-haters."

"How very un-European," I said.

"Yes. Mussolini even had a Jewish mistress, I believe. At least here you will find Jewish names on the doorbells still. Not in Budapest or Berlin. Come, I'll show you."

So we stopped along the street and found di Veroli, Piperno Ajo, DiSegni, Bonfiglioli, Jews all, she declared.

Much later in the night, on my own, I returned to the search for my two witnesses. Up and down, down and up the elegant curving Via Veneto we drove, slowly, for my last look. Beyond humiliation and into mocking self-humor, I was about to give it up when I spotted the pair at a dark entranceway. By the time I alighted from the taxi, they had engulfed me.

"*Che bello riverderti!*" Nina looped my arm, nudged me with her full bosom.

Claudia, in the same white pencil-stripe linen suit and dazzling smile, kissed my cheeks warmly and whispered, "*Ciao, Daniele!*"

They edged me back into the taxi, swiftly fondling me, before I held them off with my hand. "*Un momento!*"

I took out the book jacket with the photo of Ziff, and said (having rehearsed), "*Lo riconosci? Lo conosci?*"

They laughed like crazy, gestured wildly, spoke back and forth to each other. Nina asked me, "*Polizia?*"

To my shaking of the head no, she said, "*Allora, perche?*"

How was I to explain the situation, and in Italian? The taxi driver wanted to know our destination.

"*L'hai incontrato? Intellectuale? 'Arturo'?*" I asked, growing slightly frantic with frustration.

For answer, Nina took the book jacket, laughed mockingly, said, "*Si, certo riportamelo é un bravo rugazzo, quello, e generoso!*" and stuffed it deep into her vast cleavage and stroked my neck, while Elizabeth, my dark, baby-smooth Cardinale double, took hold of me deftly, naming a hotel to the driver.

It took all of my energy and resolve to shake them off, stop the driver, pay him, retrieve the photo, and even tip the ladies a fifty-thousand-lire note for their trouble. When Nina looked at it—and me—offended, I added another fifty thousand, leaving me off the hook softly. They waved at me, and Nina scolded me with her finger, winking at me lewdly.

Back in my hotel room, I realized I had learned nothing. But maybe that was best, after all. Maybe nothing as cheap and easy as the spotting of a john, *especially when he might have been a friend* out on the town. So what if that friend was the subject of a book of yours, the object of a literary puzzle, or the alter-ego invention of a cunning writer? Didn't I already possess a bag of surprise booty, a trove of European dragon treasure, you might say, to take back with me to home ground, for interpretation, for analysis? And for pleasure, too, perhaps?

I said good-bye to Éva the next morning before leaving and told her how weird it all seemed, at times even surreal. "The adventures of Ziff in Rome," she said. "Yes, I know what you mean. The French say, *'Le vrai n'est toujours vraisememblable.'* " But when I asked her the full meaning of that, she laughed and said to look it up when I returned home. "It will remind you of me, eh?"

For that I hugged her warmly, and, as she reciprocated, I felt moisture on her cheeks.

"Oh, yes, one other thing: how do you translate," and I gave her a semblance of the Italian whore's lines, and repeated it.

She laughed. "Go ahead, bring him back to my place. He's a great guy and very generous!"

Before leaving, however, I had coffee with one Chip Matson, an American ex-pat freelance writer who had been recommended as an insider who had known Ziff well, once upon a time. We sat at a small table in the Compo de Fiori, in the northwestern corner of the square. Matson had once gotten a writing fellowship at the American Academy and then stayed on, one of those aging veterans who hung around hot European cities and exploited their expatriate status as their identity.

"Oh, yeah, Ziff *has* led a charmed life here, though I don't see him much anymore." A curly-haired graying fellow who wore a tennis sweater and Yankee baseball cap. "If you have money in Rome, you can do fine, very fine."

"Oh? How do you mean?"

He smiled wryly. "For the record, or the off-limits truth?"

I adjusted my brim against the hot sun. "Off the record."

He nodded and drank his morning beer. "So you want to know what fine, very fine means? Oriental pussy, and young. That's the definition, as far as Arthur was concerned. The choicest stuff just in from Thailand, Burma, China. I mean 'pulchritude,' pal. Fourteen-, fifteen-, and sixteen-year-old beauties, some still immaculate. Smuggled in and out for two-week stopovers, on their way to Amsterdam, London, New York, L.A., wherever the money is, for the family pimps. I envy him, I don't mind telling you, Danny. I envy the son of a bitch." He raised his bottle.

I watched the old vendor hawking French postcards from his stand, amidst the stream of shoppers for fruit and vegetables. What was this sly ex-pat saying, and why?

"African, too?" I put.

"Why not? *If* she was young and a knockout."

He smiled widely. "I'll litigate if you ever use my name in support of any such wild claims, of course. And I doubt if you'll ever be able to prove it. But you wanted some truth, right?"

"What about the Italian whores?"

"Are you kidding? Wouldn't touch them, too old!" The ambiguous smile. "Look, man, he's not just a writer, he's a literary emperor with fame and money. Wouldn't you do the same, or me?" He drank up. "The age of Hemingway is over. And Mailer or Capote. We're living in the era of Ziff." He laughed at his aphorism.

What about all the good things he was doing here? I wanted to ask, but knew better with this old tanned warhorse.

"Yeah, him and me had some good times together in the old days. And I miss them, to tell you the truth. He was a gas—funny and conservative on the outside, but once you earned his trust, you saw the size of his *coglioni,* his freedom to do whatever the fuck he wanted. Then, once he got the big bread, there was no stopping him. A fucking emperor with an erotic imagination and the right city to play in. 'M plus EI=Z' was my formula," Matson said with a grin. "Money plus erotic imagination equals Ziff."

A mahogany-skinned woman stopped at our table, hawking an Eritrean newspaper, and Chip bought one, skimming the headlines. I waited a moment, but there seemed no news about my dalliance.

"For the latest cause," he said.

I nodded, and saw how little I knew about the true identity of Ziff, how romantic I had been, and how tough it was going to be to sort things out, verify, and sum up. In that hot Roman sun, it seemed to me an infinity of figuring, one that was way beyond my mathematical—biographical?—skills. Ziff's Rome suddenly seemed as ambiguous as James's.

Flying back over Europe, I had about two hours of freshness in me, I figured, and got out my spiral writing pad and pen. Rough paragraphs now that would later need polishing, revising, but that didn't matter. What mattered was getting black on white, à la Frank O'Connor's advice.

"Excuse me!" interrupted my seatmate, hitting my arm as she adjusted her armrest, to exchange reading for listening.

Glancing over at her book, I was surprised to see, instead of best-seller fluff, a recent Ziff, *The Devils*.

"How do you like it?" I couldn't help asking.

"Him? Oh." The pretty gray-haired lady lowered her bifocals and smiled in exasperation. "He never fails to amaze me, that's the best way to put it. I read every third or fourth book of his, and he—" she shook her head—"the man's imagination is, well, lurid and weird, but he's brilliant, isn't he? Do you read him?"

I nodded, almost sorrowfully. "Well, enjoy it."

A little laugh. "Oh, that's not so easy, you know."

I smiled, observing her small, eager face and the yellow bow in her hair. "What do you do, if I may ask?"

"Oh, I'm just a small-town librarian, in Minnesota."

"Why the *just*? You're more important than that, an endangered species."

"Thank you!" She beamed and added, "Can you imagine

what *his life* must be like? Oh, my, I couldn't even begin to imagine *that!"*

Right on cue, at thirty-eight-thousand-feet altitude, I thought, not terribly surprised anymore. Arthur Ziff was a national figure, like a U.S. senator or movie star. A ubiquitous presence, even though, to his credit, he avoided the regular celebrity lures. "Well, good listening!" I said, returning to my pad, my notes, my scribbling.

Let me state, rather baldly, that the life of Arthur Ziff in many ways parallels the wild antics of his characters and protagonists. His adventures, or misadventures, are daring and inventive. And yet, Ziff transcends fictional personas such as Harry Freedman, Philip Samuelson, or Irving Schuster in terms of virtue. And therein lies the surprise revelation: *The bad boy of American letters turns out to be the good guy of European literary lives.* Perhaps no other writer in our history has created a life of generous aid to literary counterparts in Europe; a one-man Marshall Plan/Fulbright Award combined. And not merely to writers, but also to academics, graduate students, librarians, libraries. The story of Citizen Ziff is nothing short of revelatory. Moreover, those acts of literary generosity have been performed furtively and nearly anonymously. Who would have thought this of the 'Monster of Jewish Narcissism'?

So what if there have been secret dalliances, or scenes of outlaw whoring? Are these not allowable, even desirable for Writer Ziff? In the scenes of dissoluteness and decadent pleasures I have uncovered, I see no more, nor less, than the rightful counterbalance to the life of extraordinary virtue led by Citizen Ziff. And if the two should mingle at times, magnanimity with dissoluteness, benefaction with manipulation, let us consider that commingling as necessary, part and parcel of the opulent staging of that unique theater called Ziffland.

Indeed, it is precisely in Ziffland that elements of European history and players mingle with American themes and melodies. *[Are there African/Asian elements as well, instruments and/or players? Check out Manhattan or . . . Cape Town? Or maybe Latin American music, to be explored in Buenos Aries or Rio?*] What I am suggesting is, the countries inhabited—or the ones created—by Arthur Ziff are much more varied and international, much more powerfully striated and textured, than what I had imagined when I first began my project. Ziff's is no ordinary life, by any means or standards but rather, an ever-expanding series of lives, a widening universe of selves and acts, motives, too. I've come to think of Arthur Ziff as a kind of Melvillean voyager, one willing to travel to unlikely sites and bring back remade tales of the new regions. . . .

I picture Arthur Ziff this way since—

At this point the 767 veered sharply downward in a jolt of turbulence, and I lost my pad and my breath. My librarian grabbed my arm and held on tight. And for the next fifteen minutes we were belted with hard turbulence, making writing impossible. I stopped composing; and by the time things were settled again, I had lost the fine thread of my thinking, and my inspiration. For a moment or two I felt like Coleridge, interrupted by the traveler at the door while composing his "Kubla Khan." Literary allusion—or delusion—aside, I was grateful for the break; I had much to mull over, new food to digest . . . and interpretation couldn't be built in a day. But *Ziff: A Life* was clearly becoming, *Ziff: A Life?* so mysterious and elusive—and alarming?!—appeared the facts of my subject, the grounds of my interpreting.

ten

The law offices of Bergman, Tendler, Sorenson, and Wong were on the twenty-third floor of a 57th Street skyscraper near Lexington. The offices were grand and took up the whole floor, a far cry from his old downtown place. Larry Tendler was an old buddy of mine, a lawyer introduced to me by Arthur himself. Bergman was dead, his original partner; Sorenson was a schmuck whom Larry hadn't talked to in years; Wong was a relative newcomer, a quiet, unobtrusive specialist in tax law. So Larry more or less ran the large and prestigious practice, which included about a dozen offices; long, carpeted corridors; plush furniture; and a fine research library.

A warmhearted fellow from the East New York side of Brooklyn, a specialist in First Amendment and Civil Rights Law, and recently entertainment law, Larry bearhugged me warmly, and we chatted for fifteen minutes, catching up on the past year or two. Witty and civilized, tall and lean, sporting an Italian wool suit and silk tie—a new chic life in his 70's—Larry had escaped poverty, tough Boys High, and tougher family life to make it up the rungs of *Columbia Law Review* to a high legal station. His boyish face and buoyant laugh were in part misleading. You didn't want to mess with him in litigation, or in briefs; he knew the law, he was fearless, and he loved nothing better than taking on a tough adversary—be it the government, Sony, or a hardnosed Republican law firm. He also had an affection for controversial plaintiffs and political cases, from Castro's Cuba to Dr. Spock, the Chicago Eight to Mario Savio and the Free Speech movement.

He had heard about my biography of Arthur, and listened sympathetically as I talked. (Yes, he had spoken to Arthur briefly on the phone in a friendly conversation, and they had agreed to meet later, if necessary.) "First of all," he asked me, "shouldn't your legal advice come from your publishing house? Who's doing it again, Emerson House? They'll be the lawyers of record."

I shook my head. "I hope not. I'll need you."

"Well, this may be a bit complicated, not just because of them, you realize. Arthur is an old friend. Like you. I can't take sides."

"I understand."

"Okay, go ahead, ask your questions."

"Well, mainly, what should I look out for or guard against?"

He sat on his desk, his sensual lips breaking into a small smile. "You're not writing a novel, so you won't have the license of fiction. You can't simply make things up or invent incidents, especially those that may do your subject harm. If you describe this or that situation, and it impugns the character of your subject, you're going to have to back up that situation with credible evidence. In other words, if you give what you call facts, be ready to produce evidence to support those facts."

Staring at his bookshelves filled with political literature and memoirs, I missed my own fiction. Would Larry go with me to the Via Veneto so we might subpoena Nina and Claudia to the court-room, for example? Or the "pilgrims" of Rome as witnesses?

"Don't look so glum. Arthur Ziff is a public figure, so you are allowed to make personal judgments, and offer your true assess-ments of his work, which are perfectly legitimate. The *New York Times* versus Sullivan established that in the 1950s. You just have to be careful that there is no intent to injure that can be proven, no 'actual malice' that can be shown. That's where libel enters."

"But how can you give a true assessment without hurting someone? Come on. Anyway," I declared eagerly, "I have no 'intent to injure' whatsoever. No 'actual malice.' "

A wry smile on his long face. "It may not be as simple as that. A smart lawyer may find ways to suggest and even document malice, either in your book or in your life. Or both."

In my life? I noticed, on his shelves of American novels, four by Ziff. And searched in vain for one by myself.

"Hey, what happened to my novels? Don't you have them here?"

"Are they missing?" He walked over and pulled a few books away from the front of the shelf to reveal two of mine, set in behind. "Here, one of them is already autographed. You should sign the other for me while you're here."

"Sure," I said, "but why not leave them out front?" I half teased. "No need to injure a would-be client any further."

He laughed. "Of course. These always get shuffled and reshuf-fled according to what comes in."

"So in other words, I should be factual and truthful and—"

"And be ready to back up what you say, if it comes to that."

"Okay. Fine. Though 'truthful' is sometimes not so easy."

"Be prudent then," he advised, sitting with me on the couch. "Look, it's tricky, very tricky, because you'll probably have Emerson's lawyers to deal with as much as, or more than, Ziff himself. Absolutely they'll be more *frightened* than Arthur, and will do their utmost to keep you and the book clean of any controversy."

I laughed sardonically. "Just like our last case together, nearly thirty years ago, when the publisher's lawyers were more terrified of Postman than protective of me? And wound up doing *his bidding?*

"You've got it, precisely."

"So I have to watch out for censorship at both ends—but mostly from my own publisher's lawyers?"

He nodded, and put his arm around my shoulders, like a veteran boxing manager trying to calm and prepare his young fighter for a very tough match. "Look, I doubt whether Arthur would play that sort of game, regardless."

Trying also to comfort me with an illusion? "Oh. What sort, then, might he play?"

He leaned back. "It depends on the book, of course, and what's said in there. If he wants to play hardball, he could probably threaten an injunction on the book before it's published—in galleys, say—which would press Emerson's lawyers into a panic. They'd probably come after you then, to clean up your act. By the way, have you checked your indemnification clause yet? I'll bet it's a partnership. Why not have Gerard send over the contract and we'll find out."

"Okay," I said, feeling more and more like a piece of Jell-O.

Larry shifted tone. "Are you into the writing yet? How's it going? It is quite a subject," he admired, "especially as interpreted by you." He laughed. "Bold writng on boldness, I'd say."

"Oh, it's going," I said, still weak. "If there is an injunction, and I don't agree to the changes that *my lawyers* want, what then?"

"You could find a new publisher."

I tried to fathom that. "You mean while the book languishes, and the legal threat hangs over it?"

"Something like that."

"For how long?"

He shook his head. "There's no telling."

"Sounds a little like Jarndyce and Jarndyce in *Bleak House*. A legal suit that languishes for years and years."

"Oh, you're looking too narrowly at a bleak scenario here. It doesn't have to be that . . . bad. Not at all."

I stood, took six steps to the floor-to-ceiling bookcase, and scanned a South African shelf. "He's first-class," I said, holding up a novel by J. F. Coetzee. Moving on, I held up another. "Hey, this looks interesting." A memoir called *The True Confessions of an Albino Terrorist*, by Breytenbach. "Have you read it?"

"Oh, yeah, a long while ago. When I defended him. Take it, it's a knockout. About his five years in a Cape Town jail."

"Prepare me for my fate?" I said, taking it. "Do you think Mandela will let me in, for my exile? Or does Ziff know him?"

He puckered his lips. "Israel may insist upon 'reverse' extradition, but maybe to give you an award for the book."

"That's true. . . . So it could be worse than that, you're saying, or implying?"

He stood up and mused, "Look, we're big boys. You're writing a book, kind of a daring book, and there could be consequences. Yet the worst ones may not be legal. You're not exactly planning an armed robbery or blackmail and kidnapping."

"So you think I'm better off planning a kidnapping? . . . Anyway, will you read it for me when the manuscript is ready?"

"Sure. But I can't be involved. And we can go from there, all right?"

"All right. Thanks a lot. I understand, and I feel a bit easier."

"Don't feel too easy, or you'll have forgotten what I told you. It's not a novel, remember."

"Even if it reads like a wonderful one, right?"

He smiled the soft smile. "Yeah, even if it *writes* like a wonderful novel. Ask Janet Malcolm."

Before turning to leave I said, "So, where are you off to next? I'm always returning to New Hampshire, you're always leaving for Kenya or Sarajevo."

"Actually, I'm supposed to return to Tanzania to help redesign their legal system. But after the last time, I don't know if I have the stomach for it. Too depressing. I think I told you about it. Took me a long while to recover. We'll see. Otherwise, maybe Prague and Havel again."

I smiled sheepishly. "And I'm off to the woods again, the trees, the grosbeaks, the boys. One of them has a bar mitzvah coming up. Can you come?"

"If I'm in town, maybe I will. Send me an invitation."

"You already received one, I imagine. I'll send you another. Good. And thanks."

I saw the old photo of him and beautiful Jean, his dead wife. We hugged, and I departed.

Flying north on the bumpy fourteen-seater prop plane, I tried to forget Ziff by concentrating on this South African albino terrorist and his gutsy reflections about his long ordeal.

Which was harder, I mused, five years in a South African jail, or five months having to prepare mentally for a son's bar mitzvah, knowing that in-laws and family were coming? There was one great comfort, at least, and that was the absence of a rabbi to pontificate at the occasion. Wife Becka, to her great credit, had managed to find a senior at Ledyard to train Jonathan in Torah and Haftorah, and then to preside over the occasion himself. Since the Hillel rabbi at the college was a fortyish Borscht Belt vulgarian who used popular television shows for his scholarly references on the High Holidays, it was an enormous relief to skip him—and his hippie, touchy-feely wife, who tutored kids for whatever the market would bear. And to avoid his weekly realm, the universalist college chapel, for an antiquated and quaint synagogue down the road in seedy Claremont.

The event was in early May, and though the weather was hard rain, the event soared. Jonathan was mature, poised, knowledgeable; and Josh Rosenberg, the boy's tutor for nine months, handled the ceremony with fluid competence and no sermons. No need, since Jon was articulate in his three English speeches, reflecting on the portion he would read and the interpretation he gave; he was also graceful in his Hebrew chanting, and very handsome in a light blue Italian silk tie and navy blazer. His high forehead, blue eyes, and winning smile were the good looks of a young man primed by a boy's buoyancy. And as the event went on, you could see Jon enjoying himself more and more—a rare happening at such rituals—and it showed in his eyes, his gestures, his laughter. Not Yahweh or the Torah, not the ritual or the packed crowd, could faze him; gradually he rose to the occasion, conducting himself as a thirteen-year-old boy-man of serious purpose and pitched feeling. Gradually I, too, a deep skeptic of the ritual, was won over and moved by his beauty, his performance.

But then I shouldn't have been surprised, since Jon had always proved himself in the clutch, no matter what the field.

Afterward, as I hugged him off to the side, however, I was taken aback, amazed—for who should be standing there, waiting in the wings to congratulate my elder son, but Arthur Ziff.

Though never answering the invitation, he had come up for the occasion. Was the man a chess genius or what? Brilliant move!

He shook Jon's hand, said he had done a fine job, and then released the boy to a circling crowd of admirers.

To me he said, "The kid did well. You, too. You could actually sit through the thing. Rebecca deserves a medal from the UJA." He leaned closer. "Did you hear the one about the doctor in Manhattan who wants to do something very unusual for his son's bar mitzvah? So he calls up this ritzy bar mitzvah agency on the Upper West Side, and the agent says, 'How about a ten-day Caribbean cruise ship reserved just for your guests? That's always popular.' 'Nah, nah.' "Look, Doc, we can book Madison Square Garden, like Richard Todd did for Liz Taylor and—' 'No, no, too fancy-schmancy.' 'Hmmm, so you're fussy. What about a private safari trip in Kenya to see the animals?' The doctor lights up. 'That's it, perfect!' So they book the trip, and they fly over, and are met at the airport by the guides who whisk them away by Land Rovers to the jungle and set them up in an elephant caravan, and they're off. Everything's great, the elephants are a bit bumpy, but the kid and his friends are loving it and the father is delighted. The camps and food are great. They travel for a day or two, and they're seeing rhinos and hippos and hyenas"—and here Ziff produces some marvelous African calls and howls!—"when suddenly they slow down and hardly move, for hours. So the doctor calls out, from his position way back in the caravan, 'What the hell's going on? Why have we stopped moving?!' The guide passes the word up ahead, and pretty soon the answer is relayed back to the doctor, "The bar mitzvah two caravans ahead is having some trouble and is stuck!"

I laughed aloud, the timing so right.

At the reception back at the house, Arthur quickly became the center of attention for a good part of the crowd. Constantly surrounded, inquired of, praised, he was not only the literary celebrity but also the good Jewish friend who had come to his friend's son's bar mitzvah. The famed harsh critic of middle-class Jews and Judaism attending a middle-class Jewish event was a bit of noteworthy news, it seemed to all present. To his credit, Arthur was at his charming best, courteous to ordinary strangers, open and engaged with intellectuals, serious in serious conversation. As a brother-in-law put it to me, "I never dreamed that Arthur Ziff could be this down-to-earth and friendly!" And as a friend said, "I don't think I've ever met a funnier or better conversationalist!"

With me he was cordial, friendly, warm. Not a word was said about that other little matter of interest, my/his biography. Smart, classy. With Becka he was warm and funny: "Hey, you look like you're ready for the next forty-five-year-old stud, not this *alta cacker*." Hugging her, he added, "How'd you stay this good looking?"

And with Jonathan, he was special. Shrewdly, Arthur waited till the end of the day, when most guests had left, took the boy aside, and chatted with him quietly for half an hour. Later, when I asked my son about the conversation, he said they talked about books, Jon describing some of his favorite novels—such as Graham Greene's *This Gun for Hire* and *Brighton Rock*, Maugham's *Of Human Bondage*, and two that Arthur had never read, *Paths of Glory* and *Treasure of the Sierra Madre*.

Afterward Arthur came over to me and said, "The kid has no future in America. *He reads*. And he *understands* the stuff. What the hell is he going to do when he grows up in this country? How's he going to get through high school when they find out *that* about him?"

Two family members approached, and interrupted Ziff's report.

Later, when he was leaving, and I thanked him for coming, he said, "I wouldn't have missed it. The boy's a genius—he can actually conduct a conversation! Next time I'm invited to a dinner party, he's my date. And he told me about the stories he's writing. You should quit, and let him take over. What is it, six years for the next boy? My nurse will bring me up, in my walker!"

It warmed me to see him, and it was no matter or surprise that he had given Jonathan nothing for the occasion. His presence was the gift, I knew.

Wrong. Ten days later something in fact did arrive from Arthur Ziff, for Jon. It came via UPS one late May afternoon, and the familiar mustached driver, Jeff, carried from his truck a good-sized cardboard box to the door.

As I thanked him he asked shyly, "Would you mind giving me a hand? There're at least half a dozen more of these."

Befuddled, I said sure, and helped out. All the address labels read, "Master Jonathan Levitan." The return address was Random House, Inc., 400 Hahn Road, Westminster, MD 21157. Eight boxes in all, so I left them in the living room, for Jon when he returned from school.

And at three-twenty, when I fetched him from the school bus a few miles down the road, I told him he had another present waiting.

He brightened and said, "Oh, yeah? What is it?"

"I didn't open it. But it's different, I'll tell you that."

"From who?"

"Arthur Ziff, I think."

"Oh, yeah," he said casually, "he mentioned he might be sending something to me."

In the living room, Jon set down his heavy backpack and stared, his jaw dropping. Grinning broadly, he said, "ALL from Mr. Ziff? Wow!"

Using my pocket knife, we opened a few of the boxes, and

he began pulling out shining new book after new book, all hard-covers. *"Crime and Punishment,* by Dost-o-evsky," he pronounced, beaming. *"The Brothers Karamazov. The Possessed.* Look at this nice title, *The Idiot.* Hmmm, maybe I'll start him with this, *The Best Short Stories.* Have you read 'White Nights,' Dad? Or 'The Honest Thief'?" I told him I had, too many years ago. His mother protested not to open yet another box, but he resisted her, as well he should have. "Hey, *The Hunchback of Notre Dame.* Didn't I once start this when I was nine or ten?" Smiling widely, he continued, taking out four Thomas Hardy novels and then announcing, "Look, Dad, *Sheba* and *King Solomon's Mines,* which I just reread!"

I turned a book to its spine and showed him the famous logo of the runner with the torch. "This little fellow stands for the Modern Library."

Flushed with excitement, a boy in rapture, he marveled, "Is this the *whole* library? How many books altogether, do you think? A hundred or so?"

I shrugged. "Try two or three hundred."

"W-O-W!" Jon exclaimed, opening yet another box, like Dobbs finding gold in *Treasure of the Sierra Madre,* a character he had written an essay on (for me), comparing the book to the movie, and, of course, preferring the book, as he always did.

"Jon, that's enough, really!" chided Rebecca.

But he had already opened the next box, and held up a fresh one, saying, "Look, a book by Arthur Ziff, *Dorchester Boy.* With his photo, too. He's really famous, huh?"

I nodded, proud of Ziff's fame just then. "Really. Open it."

He did that, and said, upon opening the flyleaf, "Hey, there's something written—to me!"

He read slowly, "To Jonathan, who one day will add his own novel or collection of stories to this library. Your friend, Arthur Ziff." The boy's cheeks, already pink, turned red with pleasure. "What a treasure chest, huh! This is awesome! I don't think I'll have to go to the library for a long time."

As I stroked his tender, exalted face, I couldn't help thinking how Arthur had done it once more, outwitted each and every one of us, friends, family, parents, with his perfect gift for this boy.

"This must have cost a pretty penny, huh, Dad?"

I nodded.

"No words will be able to describe to him my feelings!" he summed up, regarding the note he'd write.

"Yes, they will," I said. "Don't underestimate yourself."

Half an hour later, sitting among piles of spanking new Modern Library books transported up to his room, Jon said, "You know, Dad, this was a GREAT PRESENT. Is Mr. Ziff that rich, to be able to afford an entire library? Did it come from writing novels?"

"Yeah, I think so."

"Then I'm definitely going to be a writer, no question!"

Before bed, I considered once again the ingenuity of the present, in every way, and my son's query regarding the price tag. I also considered the generosity of the gesture, which was Arthur, too. Were the two so commingled, the clever and the generous, that you couldn't actually separate them? Or? . . .

The next morning, in the car on the way to school, Jon said, "You know, Dad, I'm going to figure out what the cost of those books was. It'll be almost a real math problem actually."

"Not really. And the money's not the important part, you know that."

"Yeah, I know," he replied with sincerity, but that thought couldn't restrain his other thought, reflected in his gleaming blue eyes, "but still, it'd be worth it to know. Really."

eleven

Putting aside my complicated feelings for Arthur at the bar mitzvah, I wrote my chapter on Ziff in Europe, calling it "The Travels of Marco Ziff," and mailed it to Pat, along with two other chapters, for his editorial eye. After his reading, he called and we made a date for lunch at Joy Wah.

We met on a misty June day at 1:00 P.M., and after ordering, we went through some niceties before discussing the editorial part. Pat laughed and said, "It was amazing to see Ziff show up at the bar mitzvah, don't you think? God, he is clever! Someone at the event, was it Tom or Mike, said that for sure it would turn up in one of his novels soon, and it would be very very interesting to see just how the event will be depicted. Especially since everyone agreed that it was not only lovely but actually interesting! Do you think he'll write about it?"

I smiled. "Who knows? Maybe it will depend on what I do."

He laughed. "Absolutely. Without question."

"Okay, so how are the chapters?"

The waiter set down our lunch, and beers.

"The two literary chapters go on for too long," began Pat, "we'll have to cut it down later. Also watch out for excessive praise; you're too easy on him. And remember, literary opinions or talk are not going to sell this book. As for the biographical section about Rome"—and here he guffawed raucously—"it's wonderful—except that it's unbelievable. *Totally.* You're writing fiction here, right? Invented the whole crazy scene! Be straight with me."

I shook my head. "No, I didn't invent anything actually. Or tried not to."

He smiled, bemused. "Then maybe you've been set up somehow."

"Set up? By whom—Éva, the Hungarian prof?"

He shook his head. "Maybe. Or maybe by the master himself, through her?"

I looked at him. "Maybe, but I doubt it."

"Well, I don't. 'Cause what you've written belongs in Ripley's *Believe It or Not.* And I'm afraid I don't. Can't. Unless . . . "

"Unless what?"

He shrugged. "Unless he's got a whole other agenda in mind and," he laughed, "it's otherworldly!"

I nodded. "I still . . . don't buy it."

"Do you have any proof of what you've claimed? Visited with

those 'pilgrim souls' of his? Checked out this Budapest lady? For example, how much is she willing to do on behalf of Arthur?"

I wiped my mouth with the linen napkin. "Well . . . a lot."

He wrinkled his brows. "Even including an affair with the biographer of her mentor?"

Guilty, I nodded. "Even including. Well, an almost affair."

He shook his head and laughed hard. "Oh, Danny boy, you are a babe in the woods after all! My God!"

I rebounded quickly. "I'm not sure you're right, Pat. Not at all. In fact, I'd bet against you."

"Oh? How much? What?"

He had a point: Bet what? "That chapter. My belief in it, my interpretation."

"Oh, you should be in Vegas." He laughed hard. "You might nurse twenty bucks all night!" He nodded. "Just teasing. Okay, you're on. Shoot for some verification."

"Like Moritz Schlick, huh?"

"Huh?" He shot me a look.

"A Viennese philosopher who wrote a first-class piece, 'On Verification.' Philosophy 1.1, at Brooklyn College. I loved his name."

"Oh, I see, perfect! Bring him into it if you want, if he'll help you out!" And he shook his head, laughing.

"I'll get something for you, don't worry."

"Otherwise it's out, completely. Right?"

"No St. Ziff, I understand."

This babe in the woods twirled dutifully his double-sided noodles, thinking over the new conundrum and possible solutions. *Had I been had, after all?* By acts of the body as well as words of the mind and spirit? And if so, by whom: the literary grand master or his handmaiden?

We parted at Pat's old Ford Ranger truck in the parking lot. "Keep it going," he advised, and then, blond eyebrows raising, "And who knows? Maybe life is stranger than fiction."

"Maybe especially one man's life?"

When I got home, I found a letter of interest. The writer was the principal at a well-known Jewish high school in Massachusetts:

> *Dear Mr. Levitan,*
>
> *I heard about your book on that* meeskite *Ziff, and I hope you give it to him good! He has done more harm to the Jews than a hundred Himmlers or Goebbels. He is the Trojan horse for our people, a traitor to his tribe, far worse than Milken or Boesky or that bunch of crooks. For centuries on end Ziff's books will be used to stigmatize and demean the Jewish people. Irving Howe said it all, as I'm sure you know. So give it to him good in your biography, expose him once and for all. Let him bleed just as he's bled us, for thirty years now, that SOB.*
>
> *Yours very truly,*
> *Isadore "Izzy" Mintz, Principal*
> *Solomon Schechter School*

I decided to answer the principal immediately:

> *Dear Principal Mintz,*
>
> *I'm not quite sure where or how you learned of my possible project, but I can assure you that truth and honesty will be at the center of my writing. At the same time I believe that both qualities have been at the forefront of Mr. Ziff's ambitions as well, in his novels. The fact that they may have caused injured feelings or bruised egos of particular Jewish groups is not of relevance for the artist. Seeing reality for what it is, especially among one's own, is what counts.*
>
> *As for your historical references, Izzy, I believe that they are beneath you. At least I sincerely hope so, for your students' sake.*
>
> *Yours,*
> *D. L.*

Surprisingly, later in the week came another letter, from Arthur:

> *Just a note to let you know that the boy can write, too. I just received a thank-you letter from Jonathan, for the books I sent, and it was most charming. I'll write him back separately, of course, and I'm going to ask him to give me the honest lowdown on my own novel. (On the other hand, maybe he'll see through* D.B.*??)*
>
> *Again, the BM was a fine affair, free of rabbinical cant and filled with pretty cunt. How'd you get so many hot shiksas to attend? I particularly liked that blond Katherine S., with the long legs and hidden tits. If you can distract the husband for a weekend, I'll come up again. By the way, one item really struck me: When they parted that velvet curtain for the Torah, and stared at it in awe while singing some blessing, and then gave it to Jon to carry it around so that* everyone was encouraged to eye it up close, touch it, kiss it, *I began to wonder if the real model for the Torah in ancient days was the Pussy? I mean, way back, in pre-Babylonian, pre-Brooklyn times, when they were first figuring out how to locate and how to touch the thing—the Torah I mean—and convert it into something really holy and secret. What do you think? Worth a scholarly monograph?*
>
> *Yours in Torah studies,*
> *A.*

Humorous fellow, with a sharp eye and a hard bite. No piety too pious for him. (And yet, had I uncovered a secret life buried beneath that hard-edged, iconoclastic one?)

Should I send Ziff's letter down to the principal for his scholarly reply?

Anyway, I pondered, where do I go from there? How, indeed, was I to verify my Ziff-in-Europe revelations? Return to Rome, then travel to Budapest? And what if I had been taken in? What would be my take then?

Meanwhile, I was teaching once a week for the summer quarter at Ledyard. I taught a course in writing and reading the short story to older students who were coming back for a graduate degree. I preferred these types, who had real lives outside of college, and I preferred, too, the freedom to teach the greats from across the board of world literature. That week I was doing Babel, the Russian genius of economy, who wrote four-to-eight-page stories that revealed whole worlds. I had assigned "In the Basement," "My First Goose," "Italian Sunshine," and "First Love."

Once inside the magical room of literary study, I felt alive, energized, and otherworldly; literary talk lifted and spiritualized me. Twelve students, like a jury, sitting around a large, oval table, the judge standing at the head, the lovely and lucid talk about beauty, truth, perversity, style, voice, character, narrative dissolving the street noise of cars and drills, or the other noise of CDs and movie talk, book chat.

We had gotten some three or four pages into "First Love," and I was asking about the uniquely packed page in which the boy's grandfather, Shoyl, is murdered in the pogrom, his father humiliated by a Cossack on horseback in front of the boy's eyes, and his beloved pigeons squashed. "Why all the chaos? How does the boy take it? And his beloved Galina?" A hand went up, and literary Freida of Fort Worth said, "He can't talk, and goes into a hiccuping binge. Who is Babel? I mean, he's something else, and I never heard of him before!"

I nodded at my smart black high school teacher. "You're right, I should have said a few words about him, though we don't know that much." I proceeded to give a bit of his skimpy biography, beginning with his Odessa childhood, then his soldiering life in the Red Army, and finally his mysterious ending in Siberia, disappearing in a labor camp. "Basically he disappeared, though his death was confirmed some years later; in fact, there's a new book, by the second wife, who claims it took her some ten years to find out the truth about what happened. How come? Life in Soviet Russia, with Stalin and the KGB. . . . "

As the class pondered that, and Marion, the lacrosse coach,

put a question to me about "detailing," I spoke of Babel's stunning use of imagery, but within felt something stirring on my back burner. And presently, while a discussion ensued among the students, I drifted off into my own reverie about those ten long years of *not knowing*. Why just Russia? Couldn't truth hereabouts, the full labyrinthian truth about Arthur Ziff, take years and years to know? And maybe even, in the end, *not really know,* but just guess, speculate? What if one plumbed the depths of Upper Manhattan, both sides (Buda and Pest) of the Danube, his hangouts near the Compo de Fiori, and still came up with the unbelievable, the unknowable, the mysterious? What then? Would Pat, and the biography, the reading audience, all demand something more tidy, more final, more credible?

Why, then I'd have to send them all back to the fiction! To the tricky Ziffland of ingenious personas and disguised narrators—via the return route of perverse turns and tricky curves, ending up, of course, with his full, ironic triumph.

"Are you saying that a great writer can disappear off the map just like that? Without a trace for a dozen years?"

"Well, maybe with some clues. But why not? Ambrose Bierce was a native story writer who went to Mexico one day and was never heard from again, or ever found."

Though in my case, I thought ruefully, perhaps it was to be the biographer who might end up vanishing.

PART TWO

twelve

III. IN RAPHAEL'S QUERULOUS QUARTET, ARTHUR ZIFF HAS given the world his version of Captain Ahab and Hester Prynne combined, in a novel of audacious vigor and unvarnished anger. His Lenny Aaron Raphael is a wronged creature of monstrous proportion, a man so pricked by vile circumstance and so devoted to mischief-making that his malevolence appears quasi-innocent, quasi-metaphysical. As in most of his recent novels, Ziff's prose here is glittering, the energy flowing, and the literary conceit very clever. *RQQ* is a triumph of Ziff voltage, you might say, a hard jolt of 220 amps poured into a circuitry—the late-twentieth-century American novel—that is used to handling 110 amps. The result is a literary power outage, wherein standard cultural lighting and sense go out, and the world is bathed anew in the dark, negative energy of *Raphaelisme*.

Huge in size, deformed by childhood polio, crippled further by his beloved sister's mugging death on the streets of New York, Lenny Aaron R. is a one-man wrecking crew, perverse in life and perverse in his music. A brilliant cellist/composer, Lenny moves from high to low realm with his mobile, brilliant quartet crew, playing on Friday/Saturday nights in the homes of the wealthy and sophisticated, savaging the musical culture of the parents (and Manhattan), and later ravaging their daughters and sons. ('The Julliard Orgy' is surely the funniest, naughtiest chapter in modern literature.) It is a tribute to Arthur Ziff's skillful execution and vast research—his own, or that of the New York Research Agency that serves and numerous other writers?—that he has been able to bring this feat off without missing a beat, as it were, earning high marks from at least one real music critic. ('The post-Schoenberg atonal scale created in *RQQ* is brilliant,' Tim Payson, *Newsweek*.)

If the serious echelons of the Upper East Side come to be savaged by Lenny and his wild boys, the lower half of the city, in the seedy clubs and raucous halls of rock 'n' roll, are also their hits as Lenny moves his satire and versatile quartet down to the lower depths and transforms them into a rock 'n' roll group banging out heavy metal and punk rock demimusic. Cross-dressing and cross-gender fertilizing, the rock band, 'Lenny's Fuckers,' travels on the wildest spree in literary fiction since Alex and friends went on a tour of London in *A Clockwork Orange*. Lenny's Manhattan spree is both funny and vicious, the invention is manic/brilliant, and the language employed by Ziff is the linguistic equal of Anthony Burgess—here, a triumph of the hard-rock mimetic voice. (No surprise perhaps that the Rolling Stones and Michael Lindsay Hogg have bought the screen rights.) And would the lyrics composed by Ziff not do well—as Jon Pareles hinted at in a *New York Times* rock review—if sung by Mick Jagger or Prince?:

> We're gonna come on Monday night, Mrs. Morgan,
> We're gonna make yah feel real good,
> And when we're all done *doin' you*,
> We're gonna make yer Emily feel real good, too.
> And when hubby James comes home from AA town,
> And asks sweetly how your night's been,
> Why, you can tell him all 'bout Murphy Brown
> And he won't say nothin' 'bout his own carnal sin.

It doesn't hurt that the husky-voiced rocker here, Ms. Diana Truth, is a witty send-up of Marianne Faithful, and that her cynical sexual shenanigans are a potent match for Lenny's.

RQQ is the toughest critique of our contemporary culture that we have in modern fiction. Ziff spares no person, no institution, in wielding his potent scalpel, knife, hacksaw, crowbar. You name the good institution, and Lenny Aaron has targeted it—NPR and MacNeil/Lehrer, the *New York Times* and its *Book Review*, Alcoholics Anonymous and the Sierra Club, *Fresh Air* and *Nightline,* the MLA and PC English Departments, Public Television stations and New York publishing houses. And by the time he's through with his all-out laser attacks, there's not much left to hold on to. In all this, Arthur Ziff displays a dazzling intelligence and cultural attentiveness, demolishing the shallow, false, and gutless gutting of our culture, by liberals especially, that has occurred in the past decade or two, on various stages. Lenny Aaron works as the convincing rhetorical vehicle through which our PBS version of culture is held up and observed clearly, without fears, without inhibitions. It is a gutsy, reckless, no-holds-barred performance.

More problematic perhaps is the characterization of Lenny Aaron Raphael himself, and what the author seems to want for him from the reader. For it is not merely disturbance and disgust, along with respect, that is asked of the reader; but also, at bottom, a curious sympathy. That is, Lenny privately holds on to sacred feelings for his beloved lost sister, while publicly brandishing his highbrow idealistic values for music, literature, art, so that his warped and perverse sides are in part understandable, and therefore perhaps forgivable. In other words, Ziff wants his wicked Lenny to be intrinsically liked, sympathized with, even admired, while at the same time making him out to be a wretched scoundrel, a colossal modern antihero, á la Céline.

Can Ziff have it both ways? Has Lenny earned this sympathy? And what of this ambivalent sentient self? Has it been convincingly sketched in and offered up fairly to the reader? Or has it been surreptitiously, perhaps sentimentally, created by the author as an extra incentive for secretly admiring the protagonist and thereby even buying into his other side?

Does this make a difference? If so, how? On what grounds? Yes, emphatically yes, this writer answers. . . .

Too much literary talk for a biography? Not for literature lovers, no—

My unlisted number rang, and I picked it up.

"Danny,*this is Jeanne. I have arrived in Manhattan for a few weeks for a show. Can you please come in? I want you to be my witness to a scene where Arthur used to take me, for his 'fun and games,' when he wished to have his little adventures with me. Can you come this Thursday and stay the weekend? It will be well worth it, for your understanding. Are Rebecca and the boys well? My love to her, please. So can I count on you this Thursday, my dear?"

Taken from my writing trance by this odd plea and promise, I nodded my head, confused.

"Yes, Daniel? I can't hear you."

"My mind was elsewhere. Sure, I'll come in."

A loft in SoHo, large, indirectly lit, sparsely furnished, with a straight-backed chair and a leather horse set in the middle of the floor. A mousy woman escorts us to a comfortable love seat, at the outer, darkened edge of the central area, partitioned off by a wooden railing like a jury box. She puts out her hand to Jeanne, who turns to me, "You have some money?" Bewildered, I say, "Sure. How much?" "Five hundred," the woman replies. Shocked, I explain I didn't bring along that kind of cash. Casually she advises, "There's an ATM downstairs on the corner of Houston. We'll wait. Would you like some coffee, madame?"

Thus, yet again, I find myself down on the streets, using one of the wily black screens to get the cash for more of my basic research. Rome, Manhattan, Budapest, all slots lead to the invisible wizard of automatic financial powers; perhaps one day the technology will be advanced, by '04, to inquire discreetly, "Excuse me, sir, but what is the money for?"

Upstairs, I hand the frowsy ticket-taker the ten new Grants (with oversize faces); she nods a perfunctory thank you and walks off. I take a seat alongside Jeanne, who is sipping coffee from a porcelain cup and saucer. "Ah, there you are at last. I was beginning to think you had lost your nerve."

Lost my nerve? For what?

"I hope it's worth the price of the ticket," I observe, "Chekhov and Shakespeare cost much less."

Cupping my hand, she says, "You will tell me."

Sitar music enters from high corner speakers, a handsome middle-age woman walks out and sits down in the wooden armchair with a cane seat. Of medium size with light brown hair, she is wearing a simple black crepe dress, as though going out to dinner later, and a mauve silk scarf is twirled around her neck. Her hair is studiously wild, straight, stringy, falling upon her forehead, the skin is almost alabaster, and she looks about, to check out what audience there may be. A Japanese gentleman arrives, casually attired in black jeans and a white karate jacket. Olive-skinned, narrow-shouldered, and sturdy, with dark hair in a pony-tail and a black goatee; he is carrying a large maroon duffel monogrammed with a large yellow letter.

As the professor guest takes her upright seat in the chair, our mousy escort leans over and whispers, "Adele is one of our regulars, a professor of drama at a prestigious Boston university."

The man takes out a blindfold and puts it over her eyes, then takes out a bunch of ropes from his bag, carefully arranged in a series, it seems. He proceeds to use the first one to tie her up. The brightly colored orange-and-white rope looks something like a decorated snake, and he employs it with easy dexterity and familiarity. He ties under her arms and loops it to the chair, then wraps it around her waist, pulling it tight, and finally around and under her thighs. He works mostly from behind her, and speaks to her—and to us?—as he labors, using words and phrases such as "the need for authority" and "the sensuality of restraint," and suggests to her, "Adele, *feel all your emotions; don't resist or censor any of them as they flow in.*"

The trumpet concerto pipes in beautifully, as complement. His voice is smooth and he speaks cordially, like addressing a schoolgirl, or a whole class. Now he reaches over in front of her and slowly peels down the front of her dress, to reveal her fullish white breasts, unfettered by brassiere. Using a new rope, shiny white like a jump rope, he winds this up and down and across her breasts, once, twice, making a kind of bandolier, and squeezing the bosom harder as he ties tighter; at this Adele begins to moan softly.

"Pain or pleasure?" I ask low.

Jeanne smiles, somewhat oddly. "Both." Then, leaning toward me, she whispers, "About now, Arthur would have me put my hand on him, and hold him." To dramatize, her hand comes to rest on my thigh. "Like an adolescent boy."

Is she inviting me to do the same, and become that boy? . . . Or is she inventing? . . . Lying? (Arthur's caution!) . . . I say nothing, but nod and look on, nervously adjusting my legs (and releasing her hand). The dim lighting, theatrical lady alongside me, bizarre act before us, some fifty or sixty feet away, give an air of filmy unreality to the room. *Was I inventing the scene?*

Leaning into me, she murmurs, "Arthur studied this master carefully, trying to adapt his methods to us at home. His 'research on the extreme,' you know. The pig."

She sets her hand on mine and holds it firmly. I take this as a spontaneous response to her fear and maybe excitement, no more.

The gentleman proceeds now around to the front of the seated woman, takes out a canary yellow twine, and, removing the scarf, draws the rope precisely along the bared flesh of her neck and breasts, with apparent exquisite torture, for Adele begins to moan aloud and plaintively swoon, "Please, please, let me!" For response he places a small pink rubber ball into her mouth, muffling her. Her forehead, I can see, is beaded heavily with perspiration.

Next to me, Jeanne is sitting at the edge of her seat and leaning forward and nodding, nodding, like a schoolgirl raptly watching a magic show, gripping my hand tightly.

"Are you all right?" I whisper.

She nods, far away. . . . Then: "Watching a true master at work is compelling. On this Arthur and I agree, always."

Our view is partially blocked by the fellow, but I can make out the woman's free hands now permitted access to him, and also presently, her mouth is given its freedom, also to work on him.

Two large tears, I see, are rolling down Jeanne's cheeks.

In an uncharted territory myself, I say nothing. Ravi Shankar (?) has given way to a sixties rock song, "Devil Woman." My head spins with a host of semilit surfaces and thoughts.

In a few moments Jeanne says, "Cruel but beautiful, don't you think?" Cathartically, she is wiping her eyes and nose with a Kleenex, glued yet to the situation. "Like the essence of a great scene, without the extraneous dialogue."

I replay that remark and wonder how much truth, how much rationalization is in it.

"Arthur thought Strindberg," she murmurs. "Something Strindberg was getting at in his wildest scenes."

Oh? Should I check that out?

Soon—or long?—afterward, the woman is untied, she sinks to the floor and holds her master around his hips, and he in turn cradles her tenderly. Her head is shaking in sobs of satisfaction.

"Come, let us leave." Jeanne stands, pulls me up, and escorts me through the dim hallway. (Mousy guide informs us, "Next week Mistress Magda will be performing, if you want to reserve now?")

Exiting, I ask, "Tell me, did he *really* take you here?"

"Daniel, don't be a child! Was this so terrible, so . . . *mauvais?* You must really tour Manhattan, then. You have much to learn!"

Outside, in the 6:00 P.M. twilight, the air cool, the cars whisking by, pedestrians walking past, a panhandler approaching, all are surfaces of another realm indeed, one of familiar rules, shapes, and proceedings. For me it all adds up to a sum of surprising comfort, a rush of common relief.

"Now, where shall we dine?" Jeanne asks cheerfully, linking my arm. "Have you been to the new French restaurant in Chelsea? No? This will be my treat, Daniel. Can you find us a taxi?"

I look up the street and also search her face. "But don't you have a rehearsal, or performance?"

"Oh, it's a commercial I have come in for," she notes breezily, "and we shoot mornings. Look, there's one. Shall I whistle?"

"Sure, go ahead." And as I watch her put two fingers inside

her cheeks and suddenly blow loudly—a suede blouson-attired veteran of city streets having fun!—I think how shrewd and elegant the French can be, in decadence or in deception.

At home again, my mind still adrift with the bizarre SoHo scene, I returned to the mundaneness of the writing game. Back at my stand-up desk, I fiddled with notes, pages, old photos. Locking in on one, I studied it closely, and felt ready to try some local hometown biography. (Had I postponed it out of a kind of anxiety about trekking in the new vein?) Taking the eight-by-eleven black-and-white photo over to my regular desk, I sat down, opened my laptop, and began writing:

> In the 1952 class portrait of the graduating class from the Boston Latin School in Boston, Massachusetts, we see the seventeen-and-a-half-year-old Arthur Z. in the first row. Sandwiched between two smiling peers, Arthur is distinguished by his stern countenance, his dark-eyed stare of determination and intelligence, the high forehead and fiery shock of dark, curly hair (with pompadour), the firm prow of the indomitable chin. Even in that innocuous black-and-white photograph, if you examine the boy with the dark blazer and wide Windsor knot closely, you can see a face inscribed with a future, an ambitiousness not to be denied. Do photos lie? Yes, of course; but not in this case.
>
> School records, yearbook scribblings, comments from old chums, teachers, and principal draw a picture of the same relentless march to success for the young man. Medium built at five-eight, young Arthur made up for that dimension with his powerful drive, early accomplishment, exalted peer stature. Here's the yearbook take on the young star: 'Stay out of his way, and salute as he goes past,' and 'Watch out, Hannibal!' Favorite song: 'Buckle Down, Winsocki'; Favorite books: *In Dubious Battle* by Steinbeck, *USA* by Dos Possos, *Studs Lonigan* by J. Farrell. Imagine, a three-way literary deadlock in the early fifties without citing Hemingway or Fitzgerald! Individual taste, even then. Favorite movies: *Duck Soup* or *A Day at the Races*, *The Thin*

Man, and *The Best Years of Our Lives*. Outrageous humor, dry wit, and high fifties seriousness. The whole package of firm, discriminating taste is already evident. With this kicker: Favorite actor: 'I prefer writers.'

'He was a young man who could cut you down in class if you appeared stupid or lazy,' noted Henry Powers, his old principal, 'and it didn't matter whether you were faculty or student. But if life had seriously assaulted you with a crippling blow such as polio or a parent lost to war or illness, he could lift you up. The worst sin was lack of loyalty to Boston Latin; if you didn't take the school seriously enough, you'd feel it from young Art. Did you know that with his fourth book, *The Carnal Confessions of Rabbi Shmuel Siegel*, his first major commercial success, he sent us an unsolicited check for twenty thousand dollars earmarked precisely for the library? We used it to buy books, update the desks and shelves, and invited him to come and see it. And one day, impromptu, he just dropped in, and was spotted in the stacks. That had been his favorite hangout, you know.'

Mr. Powers' comments were augmented by an English teacher, Andrew Nelson, or 'Nellie' to the kids. A lucid bachelor in his seventies, he explained the unique features of his favorite student. 'He had his own ideas of excellence at a very early age, and if you thought otherwise, you'd have to argue it out with him. He was a fierce debater, both informally and formally, you know. I remember an essay he wrote for a school contest, "On the Nature of Friendship," where his prose was flowery and ornate. But I knew that he had been reading Henry James and was now trying the style out. I was one of the judges, and the two others felt he was showing off, and that his florid style should not be rewarded. I thought it was a brilliant imitation. Anyway, I lost out, and he lost as well. You know what his response was? He smiled defiantly and comforted us both with Joyce's adage for the artist: "Silence, Cunning, and Exile." After he graduated he wrote me once a year, brief, witty notes or postcards catching me up on things in the big world. And much later, when my second cataract wasn't working out and I was having problems reading, he personally came and got me from my farmhouse in Montague and drove me into the city to see the specialist he had found. In two weeks, I was reading again. That's Arthur Ziff, if you please.'

Another memory comes from Jules Goldfarb, a classmate but not a close friend. 'Oh, I remember I couldn't stand the bastard, he was arrogant as hell, a prime know-it-all who wouldn't show me the time of day. Part of it was, I know, he despised my Orthodox upbringing and religious faith. I wore a yarmulke, you see. Then one day a few of the tough guys got a hold of me in the schoolyard, took my lunch money, called me a "little kike," and gave me a bruise or two. Art heard about it, saw me after school, and asked the whole story; the next morning he marched straight down to the principal's office, and demanded action! No ifs, ands, or buts. The principal couldn't believe it, 'cause anti-Semitism was rare at BLS. But would you believe it, old Mr. Powers called the thugs in and told them if anything of the kind happened again, they'd be suspended from school! That was Ziff's balls then, and his clout. And you know what? He still never gave me the time of day!' Laughing, Mr. Goldfarb, a Boston lawyer now, added, 'When I read the same incident in *Dorchester Boy*, I couldn't believe it. Right there, just as it was in life, hardly a change! Amazing, huh?'

Clearly the dominant force in Arthur's life then (and later) was his romantic, somewhat heroic mother, who died prematurely at age forty-four of pancreatic cancer. [That was the official medical report; but Ziff speculated in *Judith: Dying Days* on whether she had not taken her own life at the suffering end, an ambiguity that he seemed to prefer.] There was never a moment in the boy's life when this woman did not shower the boy with her overwhelming love and moral teaching and, at times, her deep yearning to escape mundane surroundings. A sixth-grade teacher all her life, she was a beautiful woman, blonde with blue eyes whose parents had come over from Vilna. Her influence on the boy lasted all his life. One of his earliest memories was her early reading aloud to and with him, all sorts of books and stories, from

The Jungle Books to *Jude the Obscure*. Her voice was lyrical, he recalls in the powerful *Judith: Dying Days*, her reading style unemotional yet pointedly dramatic. Ziff's admiration and love for her may be seen in the fact that he dedicated not one but two books to her, and that his most poignant book was that extraordinary memoir about her, reconstructing her last painful but alert days, aided by his early memories.

Furthermore, and probably more importantly, his famous cold eye or clinical outlook (and style) on the world was surely a response to his mother's suppressed yearnings to escape, her unrequited romantic side. Never would the son suffer under the same burden of emotional or overemotional weight. Hard analysis, not heartfelt yearning; the scalpel, not the burning lamp, would be his method for survival, and a spur to his art. (See the famous suicide scene in *Goldfeld at Eighty*, which Ziff describes with the cool eye of Mishima, not that of a sentimental American.)

I will not try to vulgarize the relationship here by contrasting Arthur's later relationships with women in the light of the intense one with his mother. That would be an exercise in popular psychology, be it pop Freudian or pop Kleinian. Suffice it to say that the life of Judith Cohen Ziff, and the loss of her at age sixteen, exerted a tremendous influence on Ziff, akin perhaps to Proust's lifelong infatuation, in art and life, with his own mother. (See H. Bloom's ingenious interpretation in his *New York Review* piece on *J:DD*.) Let it be said immediately: The sensitivities of the artistic boy, the reverberating chords in later life, and the subsequent transformations in fiction are not to be explained by popular conventional categories or measured by standard psychoanalytic yardsticks. Nor are future relationships or specific erotic scenes with the women of his adult life to be reduced in explanation to that single early, albeit powerful relationship.

Next to literature (and the mother), young Art Ziff had a passion for baseball and his beloved Boston Braves. (While most of his buddies were Red Sox fans, he embraced the Braves, until they betrayed him by leaving town in '53.) He especially appreciated pitching. 'Spahn and Sain and pray for two days of rain' was inscribed, along with Flaubert's *'Le mot juste,'* on the inside of his loose-leaf book. In fact, he kept a separate composition notebook with lineups of the old Braves, and notes on his favorite players (e.g., Warren Spahn, Alvin Dark, Sid Gordon, Eddie Mathews) and even wrote little essays on the art of pitching. Years later, of course, this boyish passion was translated to the literary page, when he wrote his celebrated short story in the *New American Review*, 'Pussy and Pitching,' that long, hilarious account of his salad days on the mound and on *mons veneris*.

Braves Field and Boston Latin were his two homes away from home, you might say, and both held places of honor in the boy's heart. Consider a few remarks from an early notebook: 'Are R. W. Emerson, Cotton Mather, Henry Adams, or George Santayana more hallowed because they went to BLS and became intellectual forces, than Warren Spahn, Johnny Sain, Crandall, or Mathews? Is a three-story brick building on Avenue Louis Pasteur more sacred than a playing field on Harry Agganis Avenue? I think not. I prefer to honor both, mind and body, thinker and player, Boston intellectual and Boston Brave. . . . '

One of student Ziff's favorite teachers was the Greek and Latin master, Dr. Marnell, who wrote me this about the young man: 'He had three distinct talents, as I recall, and they were rather intertwined. One was his great ability to organize his time for work or for play. He would have done very well at a French *lycée;* the French, you know, honor and train the young in organizational clarity in their essays. A second was his first-rate eye and pen for satire, which began in earnest, I like to think, in my class on classical satire. (He preferred Aristophanes and Juvenal, as you may imagine, to Horace or Petronius.) The third was his utter lack of shame, which revealed itself unabashedly in his writing. I remember vividly his portrait of an elite Boston public school, three-story brick situated on the Fenway, and run by a group of well-meaning but uptight, arrogant, antiquated masters. The portrait, written for the literary magazine, was biting, vitriolic, brilliantly written, embarrassingly on target, and shameless.

As was his scandalous version of *The Merchant of Venice*; two of my colleagues wanted to censor both, and punish Arthur. Thankfully, they were outvoted. But you said a Hail Mary when you heard that young Art Z. had a new piece upcoming in the school magazine. Well, sir, good luck with your project. If I'm still around and kicking when it emerges, and my latest eye surgery holds up, I shall certainly read it.'

One other influencing power in the years of youth was the force and play of young women in the boy's life, especially Michelle F., an Irish lass from Wellesley; Julie L., a Brookline Jewish girl; and Nina Z., a young Italian woman from the North End. At seventeen, Art Ziff was already a ladies' man about town, and a very catholic one in his variety of tastes. Apart from the intrinsic biographical interest, however, it is also useful to see how all three female friends returned to play their roles in Ziff's fiction, and, from what I've been able to discern, have their parts embellished, let me say, with a certain rhetorical gusto (and what part self-serving invention?).

For example, take Michelle F., or, as she's called in *Dorchester Boy*, Colleen M., the 'light brown-haired debating whiz who gave young Jake such superb blow jobs, and in such creative places as yellow school buses or Honors Society meeting rooms, that he named her affectionately his 'Princess of Orality.' Now a high powered financial exec in Boston, twice divorced, Michelle responded to her portrait with—

The fax beeped and I held off, fixed by the slow, creaking noise, and figuring that it was a good place to stop for the day anyway—to paraphrase Hemingway, parking downhill, in case the battery was dead the next morning.

The fax read: FOR NEW UNIV. OF TEXAS PRESS BOOK OF INTERVIEWS WITH ME, EDITED BY PROF. A. PETERSON, THEY NEED PERMISSION FROM YOU TO REPRODUCE OUR TWO INTERVIEWS. A ONE-SENTENCE NOTE WILL DO IT.

SORRY, NO CASH HONORARIUM INVOLVED, JUST GLORY OF ACADEMIC AUDIENCE.

YRS, ARTHUR

I felt relieved, for some reason, scribbled a one-sentence note of permission, and addressed it. I recalled the two interviews, their intellectual seriousness and satisfaction, the written-out questions and answers, the serious exchanges between us, both honest and literary. And as I felt the pleasure of the memory wash over me, I also felt a certain burning sensation in my gut . . . guilt, mingling with the pleasure? Was that to be my long-term internal payment, apart from whatever external one I might receive? A sort of life-time sentence that could only be commuted by . . . by what, whom? Judge Ziff himself?

thirteen

A curious thing was happening, I realized, as I labored over my personal WPA project on the life of A. Z. My juices were running strong again, flowing as they hadn't been for quite a while. A Tropicana intellectual passion perhaps, mingling with a Welch's white grape of ironic playfulness. I was feeling alive again, ego-alert, id-forceful, superego-relaxed, at one with my strengths. In other words, I was getting back to my own green days of life in my thirties, premarriage sublimity, when I was a free and easy fellow, on the loose in the playgrounds of my Cambridge streets, looking out for this Kunderian hitchhiking game or that seesaw Bellovian encounter. At my Centre Street railroad apartment command post, near the old Orson Welles and down the street from Richard Henry Dana's nineteenth-century home, I was riding my own *Two Years Before the Mast,* on the waves of heavenly Cambridge radicalism. Teaching, writing, street-scouting, I was an asphalt sailorboy, ine-briated by the sport of ladies and the theater of sixties politics, having been trained in my youth by the Norwegian Merchant Marine in how to travel to tricky places and dig myself out of dif-ficult traps.

(For example, when I was a seventeen-year-old *dekksgutt* (deckboy) on the SS *Fernwood,* and arrived in Bergen to meet my teenage pen pal Gerta H., I discovered while having a post–white-sturgeon dinner cigar with her father in the sitting room that I had become engaged to the appealing young woman by means of my friendly letters! Well, that was a bit of news, and I had to figure out what to do: spend a few decades at sea, returning home twice a year or so to see Gerta, gulp down North Sea herring and cream sauce and increaseth the family, or else, how to get out with the markings of an honorable Brooklyn boy? I decided on a modest exit, explaining to Gerta the next afternoon on a walk to a Bergen quay that I had first to go up to Standefjord to try my hand at whaling and to "think over matters," since I hadn't realized the full stakes—not to mention charms—of my cordial letterwriting. She cried, but accepted that, and I learned one lesson about foreign culture: Know the customs before committing yourself to paper! And much later on, I learned a curious literary lesson: how my Norwegian experience could become the stuff for another's protagonist; see R. Rosenthal's youthful history in Arthur's *Rosenthal's Revenge*.)

Another way of putting the matter was to say that I had become, since my Cambridge batching days, a rather conventional being—a husband and doting father, trapped by all the 1,001 ropes and ties of marriage and fatherhood that rendered helpless any former or would-be Gulliver. Not helpless but Lilliputian. My passion for the boys had kept me in the marriage, for two reasons: I knew what it was to live in a banged-up home, and I couldn't bear to leave the aromatic presence of my tender, fluttering boys. I savored the moments and scenes with the kids too much: my bedtime made-up tales while lying alongside them, the endless hours of building Lego creations, the theatrical dress-ups and clever made-up dramas in the living room, the pond swims and soccer games in the meadow, the evening bicycle rides on our bumpy dirt road, the serious talks with mature Jonathan and the first evenings of 6-year-old Gabriel reading, Mozart and Bach played on the cello by the little one, and the jazz trumpet blowing by the elder, the meticulous attention given to Frisk the white rat and Glint the Siamese fighting fish—in sum, being there to observe the slow, upward curve of their growing and learning, like the uniqueness of watching a novel unfold and spread in surprising directions. All this daily pleasure, created in my late forties and early fifties, was too rich, too special simply to jettison, and make do with one- or two-evening-a-week visits. Not for now, anyway.

But I had become conventional, let me confess, and that was comical. Imagine Danny Levitan, a playful, polymorphous soul turned into a weatherworn, monogamous man! (Well, practically.) Imagine yours truly, a devoted antifamily man, attending an in-law function—a bat mitzvah here, a comic anniversary cruise on Norwegian Cruise Lines there—and not storming out, raging. (Well, some raging.) Consider the rowdy boy of forty-five putting up with shopping, loading dishes in the dishwasher, attending—or worse, giving—polite dinner parties with all the deadly trappings, while all the time behaving well, playing the good boy. (But you liked it as well, no?) Can you picture dear Captain Ahab laying the fire, setting out the tableware and linen napkins, greeting guests and chatting about property tax rates and campus politics? Ah, talk about twenty-five years of hard labor—in gentility! And more. Imagine D. L. teaching, in the new world of the Orwellian Politically Correct University (OPCU), but having to forgo a full educational affair with a smart young coed for fear of risking all—being plastered on the women's Most Wanted bulletins, roasted by ideological judges and scarecrow administrators, and forced to flee! No, you had to be virtuous and acquiescent and chaste nowadays in the academy—well, you get it, a professional bore, a professor of repression. Forced conventionality—a true killer. Death to brain cells, poison to blood pumping.

And a gradual killer of the imaginative life, too. There was the rub that especially hurt. The last few books had shown the demoralizing burden of that overload of conventionalism—too much virtue, politeness, supine gentility. Good for Local Author stuff. The prose style softened, the mischief muted, the anger gone. Hence, novels that were "orderly," "decent," "crafted"—the true obscenities of literary praise. *(Yet, was all this true, Danny boy? Or convenient rationalization just now?)*

Now, the Ziff project seemed to be routing me back to that earlier outlaw energy, back to youthful romp, to scenes of frenetic disorder. I had gotten off my bad-boy track, and I needed to get back on it for the sake of my sanity and health. Trying to find the real Arthur Ziff was spurring me on to find the real Danny L., I began to see, and so, full steam ahead, no matter what A. Z. would do! (Or how furtively virtuous he might turn out to be!) The point was, *I needed my own life back again, pal!*

Already there were signs of renewal signaling to me: a new novel forming, a hard-boiled rewrite of a favorite medieval Romance with Levitan realism filling in the cracks of the romance, to reveal a new angle of viewing. I had written fifty pages, and it was flowing hot and strong. And I had allowed beacons of green light from distant females to beep on my (e-mail) radar screen: a signal from an old flame living in Austin, Texas, a blip from an ex-graduate student, in Lunenberg, Massachusetts. Not to mention the cue from Budapest, via Rome, of my literary ombudswoman. I was up and receiving again, ready and open for all comers. (At nearly sixty, Danny boy, were you really ready?) As yet, just flickerings.

The next day Pat called, checking in. "Any 'verification' yet of the European stuff? Is he a secular saint, or is it all a grand hoax? And by the way, shouldn't you have a chat with his old buddy, that ex-editor friend in New York, what's-his-name?"

I nodded. "Teddy Feuerstone, of course. Sure." I jotted down the name. "Before Budapest, the lower depths again. Fair enough. Thanks for the tip." Before hanging up I said, "I like that secular saint label. Do you remember the last literary one?"

"No, who?"

"Albert Camus."

Digesting that, he laughed raucously. "Wouldn't that be something, if Ziff turned out to be our Camus?"

"Anything is possible," I replied calmly, while inwardly excited by the incidental discovery and association of the unlikely pair. Not Rommel, but Camus? I had my work cut out for me, didn't I?

The idea of Camus being the man behind the mask of Rommel

was not that far-fetched after all, not in the Ziffland of Scarlet Pimpernel disguises. Wouldn't it be the greatest irony indeed if the fellow standing behind the bad boy of American Lit. was also actually the moral man of European letters? Then the most brilliant disguise of all would have been effected. Life imitating art, say; as with his fictional protagonists, Ziff would have transformed himself, incognito, on the old Continent, outwitting the nitwit native critics and the pious Jews. I walked around my farmhouse, contemplating the refracting brilliance of the artist. Moral scrupulousness, Camus/Wallenberg scrutiny, hiding behind the facade of the campaign strategist and Manhattan narcissist; ah, there was trickery for you, reader, of a Ziffian sort. (Come to think of it, did the rumor of the teenage Jeanne L. being the lover of Camus, before the Spanish actress, play a role in Ziff's choice of girlfriend?) And if I were exaggerating, and it wasn't entirely—or even more than half—true, would not 50 percent or so be good enough for literary news? For major revelation? For a revolutionary view of Arthur Ziff? And maybe, too, for a reevaluation of the contemporary model of an American man of letters, here the naughty rogue, but over there, in Europe, born anew, as noble hero? . . . How was that for reinventing the self while shifting the old literary paradigm as well?

In *Mendelsohn's Meditations*, Harold 'Heshy' Mendelsohn, the artist-protagonist, is masturbating in his ex-wife's Cambridge apartment, in one of the key scenes in that startling novel. The scene is characteristic for its relentlessness and emerging scope, and for its being a classic example of the powerful theme of narcissistic pleasure/degradation that Arthur Ziff has made his own and brought into modern Western literature. I quote:

'Sitting in his favorite chair, the frayed leather stressless recliner, where Heshy could lean back almost imperceptibly the hotter he got, as he had done hundreds, or was it thousands of times, he started out with a few lewd pictures of two recent women. He held up the first shot, a three-by-five of the twenty-seven-year-old NYU grad student who had mailed him this photo (and others) of herself with her skirt hiked up high and bare snatch showing, and her inviting note on the back: "Does a post-feminist vagina look so different, Mr. Mendelsohn?" and he began stroking his prick tenderly. He proceeded to recall their playful times together, and the way Dina loved to fondle or suck him on the sly in darkened movie theaters or beneath dinner tables. A long minute of staring at the alluring hairy triangle, while recalling the Gerbers' Upper West Side dinner party, with the political argument raging and her hand unzipping him. Smiling above, she fondled and teased below, (Heshy afraid, but oh, so taken with the sweetness and the risk.) Now he pulled slowly upward and played with the head, mimicking the way that Mary S., his Catholic social worker, liked to hold him, and he lifted up her small black-and-white snap. Blond, sharp-nosed Mary, who bore those great weighty tits that she hid in loose sweaters and that he loved to uncover and hold, squeeze, suck upon until she cried out; now he proceeded from a tender stroke to a more vigorous stroking, especially from way below (almost reaching the anus), which she would perform lovingly, and he imagined an angelic smile spreading on her Meryl Streep face as she licked his balls and below. The Instamatic of Mary that he held before him showed her baggy sweater lifted, her bra pushed down, and the firm, weighty breasts emerging upward; oh, that got him going good, real good (maybe a trifle too fast?). In the thick of fleshy things and memories now he alternated long, purposeful strokes with tender fingertip teasings, an exquisite alternating rhythm that never failed to recall Michelle from his teenage days, the delicious debater who, down through all the years, remained in his mind as his finest masturbator, maybe even better than himself? (Or was that due to memories of youth?) He was coming close now, maybe too close just yet, so he restrained his strokes carefully and squeezed his cock hard periodically (darling Dina), wishing he had an old photo of Michelle in her daring bikini bathing suit from Plum Beach days, but he didn't, so he simply focused and recalled the demure face turning coldly powerful—a turning that excited him—with the passion of her control over her beloved prize (his member), as she contained him to a perfect tee; and finally Heshy had to stand up now, prick out and held by imagined Marie, and go to the bathroom, where he would shoot his load while recalling Mish's Radcliffe dorm on Linnean Street with her roommate studying soc sci ten feet away, and Mish, beloved Irish Mish, unable to resist offering her beautiful cunt for him to lick in the dark bathroom, offering it right up defiantly, breaking free from good girlness and whispering for him to "do it, do it!" Oh, he was there now, daydreaming of licking and nibbling at her beautiful wet mound and inner folds, Mish draped awkwardly over the bathtub and he would make it slow, yes, very slow, and come long and hard, Hesh and Mish, again back there, with the towel spread for his knees! And he'd stretch it out, good and long and steady, but spiraling it out and upward and allowing wildness to take over, yes, yes, darling Mish, ohherlovelytightcuntalwaysdrovehimdelirious! . . . [*MM*, p.128]'

A typical (if long!) passage from *MM*, evincing Ziff's flexible and versatile prose and his great pervasive theme, which has been laid out in many of the books but never at such gutsy, all-out-driven length as in the *bad and wicked MM*. (See his private note to yours truly after writing the last page of the novel.) What Melville did for blubber and the whaling industry of nineteenth-century mercantile capitalistic America in his *Moby Dick* sea epic, so Ziff has attempted, in his *Mendelsohn's Meditation* ego epic, to do for the masturbatory industry of twentieth-century narcissistic America. A far-fetched parallel? Highly exaggerated? Perhaps. But perhaps not. For in his semidemonic quest for degrading pleasures, Arthur Ziff, via his self-pleasuring protagonists, has pointed to the frayed ends of society as we have known it, and the expanding boundaries of the life of Self in fantasy, in memory, and even in social reality. Captain Ahab's drive for retribution is matched by Mendelsohn's innate sense of spite or Rosenthal's mad drive for revenge; and contrary to the fairy tales of most modern writers, there is no sign of redemption here, no surreptitious play for healing. (Is it any wonder that competitor Updike, no slouch himself in the narcissism/sex department, would go after these books hard in his retrospective review of *MM*?, damning Ziff and his protagonist with phrases such as 'a surprisingly soft, specious nihilist,' and 'a black humorist gone solemn and humorless.')

Unlike Molly Bloom's poignant and elegiacal act of masturbation, Heshy Mendelsohn's acts of jerking off are the final sum of fury and survival in a world without faith, social coherence, or philosophical underpinning. As Pascal said about the self without faith a long time ago . . .

No, not Pascal just here, and I deleted that; first, more Ziff.

Let's consider the paragraphs just after Mendelsohn has completed his private act. I quote:

'Heshy washed himself off carefully, and tenderly tucked away his working member, grateful for its steadfastness. Well, once a day still—and that for how much longer?—now that the early-morning erections were but a memory. Feeling easy, he proceeded to the living room, and to his upholstered reading chair by the mullioned window. To read for an hour or so, no phone calls, and observe the changing light. His meditative time. He sat down, his fragile back propped by the firm chair, picked up the *New York Review*, and saw that the late-afternoon coppery color had already been effaced by the softer colors of evening and slow-moving dark clouds. He had marked a piece by Theodore Draper to read, and the correspondence; then, perhaps half an hour with his copy of collected essays by Shapiro on Romanesque sculpture. Mostly ignorant of the subject, he admired their elegance nonetheless. He sipped from his goblet of wine; just the one before shower and dinner. Body relieved, he tuned the mind now; if there were a woman around and they had just fucked, forget reading, thinking. Too much time spent in the bed, and then in the polite chat following. Save it for weekends when Gina came up; two days a week was plenty. Only useful way to live. Thank God he had gone back to masturbating in his late forties, and canned all that popular rot about the regressiveness of the act. The usual cultural brainwashing. Anything to shove you back into its great trap of people and marriage, and away from solitude and yourself. Well, sure, for most of the well-trained sheep, that was fine prop agenda; what the hell would you do with your solitude except piss it away in distraction, boredom, loneliness? Now they had their computers to give them the illusion of thinking, as though working the Internet was like reading Plato. Save all that for NPR and its culture geniuses; he preferred his own rituals, any day. Give me jerking off and Shapiro or Chekhov, rather than the banality of today's noise, in person or on the media. Look, the pink was dissolving and mingling with dark blue, and turning to mauve. Lovely. Aesthetic. Subtle. Who would be insane enough to give up this private viewing for society, sex, chatter? He knew the lesson well, having been that insane once upon a time, of course. Never again, buddy.'

I paused.

Has the world of contemporary solipsism ever been more finely tuned than this? Has the case of the narcissistic self ever been better stated or dramatized than here and elsewhere in *MM*, for better and for worse? Look back a few hundred years and see what the great Pascal said. . . .

As I searched for my quote, the fax beeped, and I held off, realizing I was ahead of the game for tomorrow.

I closed down my file, my machine, and waited for the creaking page to wend its way upward and out. Meanwhile I scribbled a note on comparing the late work of Ziff with that of his contemporary Updike. Both had started out in the fifties and were going strong in the new century, both still interested in the sexual life, in style, in aging and the end of invincibility.

SURE I'LL MEET YOU AND DISCUSS OUR MUTUAL FRIEND. HOW'S BREAK-
FAST AT BARNEY GREENGRASS ON UPPER WEST SIDE ON 25TH AT 9:00 A.M.?
TEDDY FEUERSTONE

At the original Manhattan hangout for early-morning choles-
terol and calories; why not? . . . In Budapest, or Rome, would I get
gossip and rumor, served up along with Nova Scotia lox and
toasted bagel?

Not that rumor and gossip were the only things that I expected
from Teddy F.; after all, he had known Arthur for many years, ever
since they were grad students at Ann Arbor back in the 1950s. And
then he had been his editor on several of the books, and for some
magazine pieces, too. Did he see Arthur anymore? What was the
New York scoop nowadays on Ziff? Was it true that Arthur had isolated himself, a little like his Mendelsohn and Goldfeld protagonists, all old friends more or less dropped? (Or him dropped by
them.) Well, not all of this would be particularly relevant, I knew,
but the journey and/or investigation had to proceed there first,
regardless. For, whatever the elusive truth was about Arthur, the
spin it got in Gotham City was its own interesting news, like a
curious message received in a corked bottle that has floated in
across the oceans from Shanghai or Hokkaido or Ulan Bator. Who
knows? Maybe Ziff had been to those places, too, spreading his
unique kind of goodwill. You know, Lord Arthur in the Far East?
(Or, more likely, one of those outposts where Danny Levitan was
headed for, before this project was finished?) Well, first, Barney
Greengrass's joint, for the news and catch of the day. . . .

fourteen

A scene from the past. The setting: my six-room walk-up railroad
flat in Cambridge, between Harvard and Central Squares, around
the corner from the old Orson Welles movie house. My seedy pad
of fifteen years. It's an overcast day in the seventies. Arthur and I
have returned upstairs, after lunch at the corner Irish Pub, and he

repeats his amused delight at the studentlike digs. ("Reminds me of my youthful days as a grad student at Ann Arbor," he notes, "the best years of my life, only I didn't know it. So I went out and got married, thinking it was the mature thing to do; maturity meant learning to live in hell for five years.")

We sat in the modest living room, he on the door-brick home-made couch and myself in the Morris armchair. I began to talk about the clapboard house up at the corner on Dana Street, home of the writer Richard Henry Dana. Chitchatting, while A. Z. waited for a crucial return phone call from his publisher, about his two new books and his future with Doubleday. The negotiation had started before lunch with his powerful editor, and had continued between us, through lunch at The Plow, some three and a half hours of talk—money and personality talk. I was witnessing yet another side of Arthur's personality, his capacity for selling him-self, his work.

"Oh, yeah, *Two Years Before the Mast,*" he mused. "I never read it."

"I loved it as a boy," I said. "Read it first in *Classic Comics,* and then as a real book in the old Harvard Classics."

"Is it readable now, do you think?"

I shook my head. "Doubt it. A boy's book. Stick with the White Whale, which I don't think ever made the Harvard series. Maybe Charles Eliot thought Melville was a Jew and left it out."

"What do you mean?"

"The editor of the series was a classic anti-Semite, as well as president of Harvard."

"I didn't know that," Arthur retorted, a fan of such items.

I continued, when the phone rang and he jumped for it. Then he pulled back and said, "You answer it."

"Okay." I went into the tiny spare bedroom, off the narrow foyer, and picked up the receiver. The caller asked for Arthur Ziff?

"Sure. Hold on."

I set the receiver down, walked back to the living room, and pointed to Arthur. "You're on, kid. Good luck. Now, don't mess up."

He winked, patted my shoulder, and entered the unlikely

negotiating room, a six-by-ten cubicle holding a single bed and a bookcase. He spoke in a measured voice, I could hear, and sensed that this was not his editor talking, but a new fellow.

For about thirty to forty minutes they went at it, bouncing their demands and pleas from Cambridge to New York, sometimes reasonable, sometimes heated. The numbers were staggering, enough to buy the triple-decker house we were sitting in, open a solid pension account, support a writer for a few years, and still have enough to live on comfortably for three or four more. Who was the new voice at the other end? I wondered. Company lawyer, editor, CEO? I tried in vain to get back to my own novel but gave it up, and sought reading instead. Gogol stories, for teaching the next day.

"Look, Jay, that's the figure, four hundred fifty for *Lustig's Last Game* alone, not for both. But my strong preference is to sell both at once, and that figure is eight hundred. And at that it's cheap, believe me. You know you can lay off both books to the paperback houses the same day you buy them from me and recoup your investment. Before you even start to print them."

A long pause, while Arthur listened. I tried to focus on Gogol's "Nose," and his lightning imagination, but my interest was helplessly elsewhere.

"Now look, Jay, don't give me any of that loyalty crap!" Ziff upped the ante on the voice, "You guys have done all right with me through the years, otherwise you wouldn't be talking to me now. And don't cry to me about sales in the book business; that's your problem, not mine. If you don't want the books at these prices, tell me and I'll go elsewhere, okay? And we'll see how I do on the open market. Think it over. I'm here till five, and after that it's over, off the table, I'm a free agent, like Curt Flood, remember?" The receiver went down, with careful emphasis.

He emerged, in his chinos and soft denim shirt, and shook his head. "Can you imagine, trying to pull that stuff with me about loyalty when it's all about money? The fucking liar."

"Who was that?"

"Jay Donaldson, the president. Trying to chew me down and he's not even a member of the tribe! You know how they work:

Edgar gets finished working me over in the morning, then they turn me over to big Jay D, who plays the wounded aristocrat betrayed by one of his disloyal peasants. Actually, he's trying to soften me up for the next call. Who the hell is that coming from, the janitor? Or maybe the 'genius' head of marketing? Who has informed them that they won't be able to sell *Rosenthal's Revenge*. 'Too negative.' Christ. Do you have some seltzer around?"

"Yeah, I do." I went to the kitchen and poured out two glasses for us. "I loved that bit about Curt Flood."

He smiled pridefully as we returned to the living room. "Yeah, I liked remembering old Curt. Of course, slick Jay probably never heard of him."

"He cut out to Denmark for that year, didn't he, and a great center fielder," I recalled aloud.

"You bet. Changed the game, all by himself. Gutsy." Downing his seltzer, Arthur said, "If this keeps up, I may need some aspirin. Cheesus, what's a guy gotta do for his million bucks?" His eyes glinted with mirth. "I'm giving them two fucking books, not one, and if they can't get their money back, they should hire a new 'marketing genius.' That's what they call him, you realize. Me they call the selfish writer, the ungrateful shyster-thief. Well let them get their next novels from the marketing genius, right?"

"One day they will," I said. "Anyway, they'll come around," I said, knowing little except Arthur's tenacity, shrewdness, leverage.

"Would it have been easier to have let Lauri K. handle it?" referring to his old agent.

"Are you kidding? The first time they yelled at her, or told her what the marketing head said, she would have caved in, come back to me, and explained how we have to be reasonable, give in. For that I would have forked over sixty or eighty grand. This way I make the calls, keep the stakes where they should be, maybe push it right to the edge, and make them sweat it out."

"How 'bout you?"

He smiled warmly. "I'm not sweating, it's not my money."

I laughed. "And Edgar doesn't even want *Lustig's Last Game*!"

"He hates the book, hates all sports." He smiled benignly, took out his small pad, checking his notes. We started to talk about Gogol, when the phone rang.

"You take it this time," I said.

"You know, it's kind of nice for them to understand that there's someone else here, either an adviser or friend, sort of eavesdropping."

"A little extra humiliation, huh?"

He got up and went to it. Suddenly he called to me, "It's for you. One of your writing students. 'Do you have a minute?' "

Embarrassed, I stood up.

"Sure, give him two," Arthur said, adding ironically, "Negotiations can wait."

On the phone I spoke to Gideon Hersh, who was having a problem with "dialogue." I answered his query and told him to work it out.

"He sounds very serious."

"He is, *very*. He admires your work, by the way, but says you're not in a league with Rilke."

"High taste, huh? Tell him I couldn't read the *Notebooks*. Can you?"

I shook my head. "Not too easily," and the phone rang again.

"Your turn," Ziff said. "If it's Gideon, tell him he spends too much time on the phone instead of at the typewriter."

The voice from the morning, for Arthur. His editor?

Back in the living room, I said to Arthur, "Now, don't be nervous, this may be the last act," accepted a light punch, and sat back down. It being three forty-five now, the theater was closing down soon.

Arthur, in the operating room, announced himself and paused to listen. "Yeah, Edgar, I hear you, go on, but just one thing pal, don't put that prick president on again, he's insulting. And I may lose my temper. Go ahead, I'm listening. Hold it, let me get my pencil out here. . . . "

For about half an hour this negotiation went on, in a different tone, about paperback splits, royalties, foreign rights, dates of publication, and so on. "You know, if you weren't around, Edgar,

I'd have been out of here, no deal, no more Ziff at Gotham. Jay Donaldson could have published the books of the marketing genius. Meanwhile, I hope you make advertising use of the extra fifty grand I'm giving back to you guys instead of putting it into CEO lunches and stock shares. And you know what? You watch: *Lustig's Last Game* may surprise you, in reviews and sales. . . . Yeah, you're on, it's a dinner bet. Look, I gotta get going, draw up the contract and send it over to me, I'll be back in town next week and have my lawyer look it over. And we'll have a lunch. Yeah, good, and get yourself a raise for this deal, you kept me aboard." He hung up.

Back with me, he slumped into a chair. "I need another shot."

Grinning, I got the seltzer bottle and poured him a refill.

He took a long drink. "This bottled crap doesn't compare with the old spritzer bottle, does it."

"You have a point." I lifted my glass. "Congratulations. A good day's work. You can be my agent anytime."

"Yeah, I'm not too bad."

"Seven-fifty for the pair. Plus 60–40 paperback rights. Not too bad, I'd say."

"Shah," he put his finger to his lips. "No one hears of this."

I nodded. "They did get you down by fifty. Smart concession."

His eyes twinkled and he said, "Not really. A necessity. I have a friend at Bantam, and knew what they were going to pay, tops, for the pair. So I knew what Gotham could afford."

I shook my head, marveling.

"But what about that million you mentioned?"

"I have to accept my paperback cut, don't I?" A smile. "Tell you what: let's go for a long walk, then pick out a fancy French restaurant, pricey but good, and I'll treat us. Okay? Let me take a pee and we're off."

And while he used the john, I went into that narrow bedroom to use the phone, realizing, once inside, the historical nature of that unlikely room. Cramped, dark, musty, with just enough room for the radiator pipes, bed, and bookcase, it looked more like a phone booth laid horizontally than a center of high financial doing.

But maybe if you were going to do your own literary bidding, and create some sort of American literary history, this was the space.

"Okay, kid, let's go. Hey, should we invite old Grace? Do you ever see her? You know, shabby as it is, I envy you this place."

Ravishing scene, isn't it? All the drama of a wily character in action, a true American agent/artist. But: would I ever get to keep the scene in? How? Would any of the lawyers permit it? Without documentation, witnesses, video corroboration? (And what about the Jeanne L. materials? . . .) Would *I* permit it, my own private superego-censor? Doubtful. Well then, leave the scene to sweet memory, the cunning power and energy of the great Ziff at work selling himself, his work, on a most unlikely stage, a closet of a room. . . . Was there any other artist who could work the practical side of the street with such bravado and success? (Young Mailer or mature Picasso? Maybe. Or old Odysseus, master of tactics?) Further, was that unique promotional power, that forty-gigabyte driver ego, not connected somehow with the power of the ingenious writer and his cunning persuasive narrators? Somehow, sure. So revere the memory, nurture it, let it flourish and bloom somewhere safe, in the hothouse of fiction, say, where one can disguise the scene, dress it up here or there, and slip in some of the hot truth. (Or you might try to slip it in here and now, slide it by the lawyers and self-censor, and take your chances with the consequences later on, with Ziff perhaps, but also with the critics and readers, who want their artists pure and uncontaminated, all Keats and Shelley. Well, why not?)

Still, a ravishing scene, don't you think, *auteur* Daniel?

fifteen

In Budapest, the November weather was gray but not as cold as New Hampshire, and the Erzebet Hotel in downtown Pest was comfortable and convenient. ("You can walk practically everywhere from there," Éva said when arranging it, especially to his favorite reading room at nearby ELTE University library, "and Arthur has stayed there of late when tiring of the Gellert.") After a long day of teaching, Éva came by for me at 6:00 P.M., and hugged and kissed me hello.

"Good, you've made it," she said, dark eyes shining. "I am very pleased. There's a coffee bar a few meters down the road. Let's go there before dinner."

At the Café Karolyi we sat at a small black Formica table, surrounded by a youngish crowd busily chatting at the dozen other tables. The bartender was a slender blonde in a tight jersey, who was chatting with a female friend on a stool, both smoking, while the waiter was a young man with a thick mustache, overlarge jacket, and harried manner; the whole room reminded me of a Czech film of the sixties, a den of amateurish charm. Pencil and pad in hand, the waiter asked for our orders, in Hungarian, and Éva ordered a white wine spritzer while I asked for a brandy and soda. He was a bit bewildered by "brandy." I explained, through Éva, and he nodded with apparent understanding and marched off.

"A popular place," I said, charmed by the cozy informality of the room; a few odd American movie-star posters, understocked shelves of vodka and whiskey, the small, black, round tables.

She smiled. "The young people are always drinking coffee. And these places are very different from the old-style coffeehouses."

"I wouldn't mind visiting one of those, too."

"So you've come to Budapest at last. To see for yourself, perhaps, Arthur's distant outpost, and the peculiar stories I have told you of?"

"Something like that. And to say hello again."

She took my hand. "I think you will find it of interest. I hope so. Forgive me if I don't treat you as a tourist, but more as I treat Arthur, a person with real work to do."

I nodded. "Precisely what I'd hoped for."

"Good. We begin tomorrow, yes?"

"Yes," I agreed, just as the waiter returned with our drinks. He had indeed brought the brandy in a separate glass from the soda water. Éva toasted my stay, and I raised my glass to hers; sipping the brandy, I realized, from its rich smoothness, that the young waiter had probably brought me cognac.

"Everything all right?" she asked.

"Just fine," I answered.

"Just keep an open mind and you will be surprised. Now come, I've made a reservation at a restaurant in the Jewish ghetto, and we can walk there from here. One of the reasons that Arthur stayed downtown was so he could walk to the synagogue, the museum, and the ghetto. And for the food at The Carmel, which he trusts— he's very fussy, you know." She laughed halfheartedly.

The next afternoon, at two o'clock, Éva picked me up in front of the grand old law library, in her small red Opal. We headed over the Elizabeth Bridge, crossing the wide Danube, more brown than blue, and drove up to the hills on the Buda side. Traffic was heavy but moved along smoothly. We passed through the Castle district and wended our way farther into the mountains. In fifteen minutes we parked on a narrow cobblestone street by a rather shabby apartment building of four floors. Walking around to the gated entrance, we entered the pleasant yard, dignified with weighty old beech trees.

"Look, souvenirs of World War Two," she said, indicating the pockmarked exterior. "This place used to be a military officers' building, so the apartments are a bit larger than usual apartments."

As we climbed up three flights, I noted the drab, peeling walls of the hallways and asked when they got around to painting.

"Oh, every thirty or forty years, maybe," she said, nodding hello to a young neighbor heading down. "There is not much money in the city to keep up proper care."

Her fourth-floor apartment was cheerful, however, with one large, spacious room serving as dining room, living room, and study, with high ceilings and oak floors and a window offering a view of the yard and a huge beech. A long, narrow dining table was set in the center, and off in a corner were a wooden desk and computer setup. While she put up tea, I wandered around the room, looking at the large mahogany 1930's bookcase with glass doors, a Chinese plate on the wall, and to the side two family photographs, and another of a group of Hungarians gazing at a toppled statue of a huge Stalin during the 1956 uprising. I sat in one of the two leather chairs with wooden arms, adjusted the seat, and leaned back, looking out at the lovely beech and beyond.

She brought in two mugs of tea and I said, "This is really comfortable, like my old Morris chair, which I stupidly gave up. It had wonderful wide arms, perfect for correcting papers on."

She sat down opposite me. "I don't know the Morris chair, but I had this pair made by a Romanian carpenter friend who comes to Budapest for work and uses my small, spare bedroom. In exchange he made me the chairs, according to my design, actually. For my back, when reading."

I asked her about the oddness of a foreign carpenter and found out about Romanian poverty, and the two countries' history of hostility, dating back to World War I and the Romanian acquisition of Transylvania.

When I nodded dumbly she said, "You Americans think that only Count Dracula lived there, but it's a real place, was always ours, and still has a huge Hungarian population."

Recalling childhood, I said, "Yes, I see what you mean. I think Bela Lugosi frightened me more than anyone else when I was a kid at the movies." I laughed. "Anyway, I like your place. It's informal and bohemian—cluttered with papers and books, which speak to me."

"Oh, is that the way you work?"

"More or less, yes. Chaos—controlled and personal."

She laughed, her dark eyes shimmering. "Just the opposite of Arthur, as you probably know."

"Well, each to his own, right?"

"Come," she said, motioning me, "take your tea and let us get to work. It's not often that you are in Budapest."

"Good point." I stood and followed her across the room, to her work area, where she gave me a chair to sit alongside her. "This is a spacious room. Is it typical of apartments here?"

"No, no, much larger than the average. And you know who I can thank for it?"

I looked at her, at first not getting it.

"I do not have forty-four thousand dollars, you know, to buy such a place. Nor do my colleagues, or most citizens. After a lifetime of savings, and a sale of my studio apartment in Pest, I had about twenty-two. The rest came from our generous friend."

I nodded, letting that sink in. Well, he could be generous, I knew. But was this true? Yet, 22 g's for Ziff was like 220 bucks for me, chicken feed, so why not? (By the way, how much was Arthur worth altogether, 3, 4 million? Or more? Wasn't that relevant now, considering these unusual European activities? I'd have to work on Z's economics. A successful writer was like a CEO these days.)

She had sat down by the computer and was already at work, typing. "Do you play with this? The Internet?"

"Well, not really. I mostly use word processing."

"Ah, you're missing out on all the real fun. You can go anywhere and speak to anyone in this little space. You should know it, and become adept. It's most ingenious."

I nodded. "Is this my Internet lesson now?"

She shook her head, reading the screen and typing in orders.

"That machine looks fast. What sort or speed is it?"

"Oh, a year-old Compaq, a Presario with a Pentium 2 chip. Plenty of power for me and for our work."

An IRS write-off for Arthur? I sat there, surprised, at a loss for what she was doing, but seeing how sitting here nowadays, in this out-of-the-way corner of the world, you could be right smack in the center of consciousness as well. Talking to Paris, New York, a whorehouse in Nevada, or a remote hamlet in New Hampshire. . . . Internet powers, e-mail pleasures . . .

"Now here, please look."

I peered closely and stared at a welcome page: http://www.wallenberg.com. Two paragraphs described an Institute that gave "Grants, fellowships, and/or other financial aid" for those with "unusual or noteworthy tales pertaining to the Holocaust." The director was Professor E. Kertesz. I shook my head, baffled.

"Arthur's Web site for this project. The odd name you see

there, Danush, was the nickname of a lost Holocaust child from Budapest. It is here that Mr. Ziff receives his global messages, from the wounded, the sick in soul, the mute survivors, secret pilgrims, whatever . . . here they have their chance to speak, to confess, to really exist."

I tried to take in and digest what she was saying. "I find this hard to believe. I mean, Arthur couldn't care less about the Web or cyberspace or such—"

She put her finger to her lips, silencing me. "Mr. Ziff may not care to use the system himself, but it is very valuable for his purposes. It was my idea, actually, and he agreed that we try it out. An immediate success. What he reads are my selected printouts."

"What do you mean?"

"I print out the best stories for him to read, save them, and send him a packet once a month. Then when we meet, here or in Rome, we make our judgments, on rewards, fellowships, and who shall receive what." She nodded at her pupil, to make sure I was following. "Look, I show you—I purposely haven't yet opened up this week's mail, so we can check together how many letters and inquiries have come in. Let us see. . . . " She clicked a few times and six names appeared: Jiri Menes from Prague; Prof. Jack Ira Bayliss from Muncie, Indiana; Edith Licht from Jerusalem; Seth Garber from St. Jean de Luz; Adele Sloan from Montréal; and Bruce Knudson from Grand Island, Nebraska. You see?"

I saw, all right, but understood little, believed less. "Okay, let's read one of these things."

" 'Things,' Daniel, they are not. As you will see. Come, sit where I am, the angle for seeing the print is better."

I exchanged seats with her, she clicked on Adele S., and I watched as the print on scrolled in, from Canada.

Dear Sirs, I have heard about your Jewish Healing Program from a sister in Toronto who has worked with the Bronfman Foundation and on the Internet. I hope you might be interested in my tale. Let me begin by saying I am embarrassed to write to you my story, but my sister has always insisted that I tell it. I have tried to write it in a memoir, but it has never gotten very far. That means, please, that the proposal and summary have never been accepted by a publisher. Several have written me saying the story has been told already, people are tired of the topic, and that perhaps I should move on with my life. But I cannot move, since I have just arrived at the truth about my life, and am stuck with it. I am a child of Holocaust parents, my mother having died in Auschwitz, my father having survived it, and I have been embarrassed or ashamed to admit this, throughout my life. Why? I can't tell you, but that has been my secret secret—for it was a secret to me, too, for most of my childhood and adulthood. I lived abroad, in Paris, for eighteen years, most of the time with two men, an Algerian and a Frenchman, and neither man ever knew this about me. I never tried to hide that I was Jewish, only that I had had anything to do with the Holocaust. It was only four years ago when I attended a memorial service for my father, who I had always resented for never talking to me about those years, that a flood of emotion broke through me, and I understood the lie and the shame that had shrouded my existence for many years. It was a terrible revelation, I assure you, and afterward I went back in memory and replayed the many scenes and decisions of my adult life that were shaped by my unknown veils of illusion and delusion.

Why I sought to hide this truth, allowing it to fester inside of me, and how it influenced my relations with the men in my life, and the women, too, both in Montréal and Paris, is what I would like to write about. Also, of course, the relationship with my father, which I now see was poisoned by my resistance to the truth in his and my biography. Also, since my breakthrough, I have conducted my own personal research into our family history, gone back once with my sister to Warsaw, and found out more and many shocking details.

Alan Lelchuk

So, will you help me now with some financial aid in my quest to speak and seek the truth?

I looked over at Éva and opened my hands in helpless query. "What do you think?" I asked.

She shrugged. "So-so, nothing unusual, too many generalities. Let's see another." She leaned over, her musk smell invading me, and clicked us on to the fellow from Indiana, Jack Ira Bayliss:

To Whom It May Concern:

I am a professor of history here at Ball State, a former teachers college and not a very prestigious place. I have been here for thirty years, after taking my doctorate from Wisconsin, where I studied with Dr. George Mosse, who you may know was a great scholar of Nazi Germany. My thesis actually was a study of a single platoon of German soldiers; I tried to discover who was a Nazi and who a soldier, what ideological/personal conflicts might have obtained for individual soldiers, and what happened to the group afterward. (Mr. Goldhagen has been kind enough to cite my work in a footnote in his recent flawed but important book.) Though I came from Holland, I had known German as a boy and later traveled to Germany, where I did hands-on research in a few cities (Ulm, Erlangen, Nuremberg).

The truth is, I did not care to reveal my own personal biography, or that of my sister's, ever before in America; we are children of the Holocaust, but in our own perhaps odd manner. You see, our parents perished to save our lives; they used their resources to buy us passage out from the horror show, but not enough, once they were turned in, to buy their own freedom. (The so-called Dutch Resistance was mostly a postwar myth, by now fully exposed.) So while they perished in Ravensbruck, we came here accompanied by a pair of Jewish strangers, at ages six and eight, and were adopted from an orphanage, curiously enough, by a minister's family in St. Paul, Minnesota, an honorable couple who raised us in the Lutheran Church. They were stern, judicious, hard-working, and raised us as their own, along with their three natural children. Sarah (now Susie) and I questioned little until high school, when we encountered some anti-Semitism, directed not against us, mind you, for we were good little Christian kids, but against a new Jewish girl who had moved in. It was at that point that my private world began turning upside down, as I started having discussions with my adopted father (Pastor Noordsy) and then my sister. It was very hard for her, however, to come to terms with her being Jewish; too much was at stake for her to abandon the Christian community.

Indeed, even for me it was only at the university in Madison that I felt freer to understand matters, and once I took Prof. Mosse's course on the Nazis, I decided to abandon my Lutheran identity once and for all. Did I become immediately or openly Jewish? No, not at all. One change at a time was all my psyche could take. I tried, and succeeded, in avoiding the whole issue. In fact, I more or less agreed with a colleague at the time who said the Holocaust was long over, it was past history, and time now, some forty years later, to move on, and give the Germans a fresh slate, and so on. That was my view, too, which I upheld consciously and assertively; I even went so far as to mock, in a sardonic and cutting way, those who kept clinging stubbornly to the Holocaust like limpets on a rock: survivors, vocal rememberers, conference organizers, Yad Vashem types, et cetera. (When asked by my dean if Eli Wiesel should be invited, I would smile wryly and comment that he was not a very serious scholar. He never came.)

I had lived a life of long concealment and lying, out of shame and misguided understanding. And what brought me out of the closet, if you will, was a colleague in history who gave a talk questioning the Holocaust, and then proposed teaching a course on the subject, emphasizing denial. I found myself, for the first time, growing emotional and chaotic in a department meeting. I volunteered to debate the fellow, and, during the heated affair, in front of maybe five hundred students, I came to acknowledge for the first time that I had been a Jewish boy and was a survivor. I must tell you, this open confession was as much a shock to me as it was to several colleagues, and the shock traumatized me for weeks. So much so that I had to consult a psychiatrist, and take a leave of absence for a term. When I returned, however, I was calmer and more determined. From then on I was a Jew, as an adult man and as a historian. (The revisionist course was not taught, and as the dean of the college later told me, it was my explosive confession onstage as much as my intellectual argument that swayed him.)

I craned my neck, and read the professor describing how his sister broke with him over his conversion, choosing to remain a Lutheran. Wounded, he takes a trip to Amsterdam, researches the town records of his parents (father a prominent doctor), and discovers an elderly couple who had known his parents, and who escort him to their old apartment on the Amsteldijk canal, 109 I. (They explain to the professor that there is probably government compensation due him for that apartment.) There he meets the current occupant, a lovely Dutch widow, and they soon become good friends, and try to reconstruct the tragedy of how it happened, that the assimilated professional parents, with a circle of good Christian friends, were sent to their deaths. A project which is currently going on.

This work has given me new life, new energy. But what I lack is a new voice.

I cannot seem to find a proper, appropriate voice to tell this tale, my story. I keep falling back on my history professor way of narrating events, and the result is dry, heavy on fact, and rather boring, an injustice to the material and my strong feelings. So what I wonder is this: Might you know or employ a ghostwriter who can tell my story with delicacy, with the force of a personal voice? I would be gratified if I

*could be matched up with such a person, a person of sensi-
tivity, knowledge, and writing skill. May I add that I prefer
a European personality, one who has a familiarity with the
recent past, and perhaps, too, a Jewish sensibility—which
I'm afraid I lack, too—rather than one of our mechanical
types. (It would be useful if he/she could come to Muncie, and
even perhaps accompany me to St. Paul to visit my sister; but
if not, I could visit the appointed writer in a European site,
since I visit Amsterdam often now, having become engaged to
that same Dutch widow who occupies my parents'—and
my—old apartment. Our wedding is next summer.)*

*Thank you very much for considering this odd but urgent
request. I first heard about your unique program from the
Holocaust Studies Program at Indiana University, and Professor A. Rosenfeld.*

We looked up, and over at each other, "Looks pretty interesting. What do you think?"

"Yes, I believe so, too," Éva said.

"Do you actually employ a ghostwriter?"

She smiled with seductive ambiguity. "If Arthur estimates the
project of worth, as I estimate it to be, I'm sure we will find
someone suitable. Either here or there."

"Of course, back home we'd get a voice in English, not Hungarian, Czech, or French," I said. And then, half teasing: "Or even,
if Arthur would perform the service himself, we'd get a literary
voice as well?"

She eyed me curiously, her small-featured, lovely face trying to
gauge how to take that remark. "Yes, of course, but what is it
exactly you are suggesting?"

"Well," I said, trying to figure it out myself, "this is good stuff
here. Maybe the Wallenberg novel he's working on could use some
of this material, don't you think? It's a very rich hoard."

Eyeing me again, she stood up. "Do you mind if I smoke? I'll
open the window." As she opened it a few inches, she retorted, "I
think you are very clever, Daniel. Should I open another file?"

"Sure," I said.

She proceeded to click twice, scrolling onto the Nebraska chap:

Dear Yids:

I had heard about your Internet conspiracy, and finally located your weasely Web site with its smarmy camouflaged notice. You kikes are relentless, aren't you? Still looking for blackmail and extortion money wherever and however you can get it. And now smearing the Web with your JEW HOWL for attention! Give us a break, will you?! Christ, for how many years and years are we supposed to foot the bills for what happened in Europe? You got the Swiss banks drumming up money for you, money that never belonged to you but that you're holding them up for, and now you're coming aboard the Web under that sneaky bulletin board victim appeal, which is no more than a hidden agenda on how to get more loot out of us Christians (or is it us "goys")? Just tell me this: For how much longer will you appoint yourselves as the Professional Victims of the Western World? I know, the "Chosen People" was getting a little tiresome after the first few thousand years, so it was time to get a new public relations tag to hit us with. Can you give us a statute of limitations for this Victim act, maybe another century or two? So maybe I can freeze my body and brain and wake up when the nightmare is over? Look, I'm a C.P.A., and I have a great idea for you guys: How about going public with an IPO offering for the NASDAQ exchange and sell shares in the company—Professional Jew Victims, Inc. (PJVI). Sound good? I'll even be your accountant, and we can both hit it rich.

I smiled to Éva. "Charming fellow," I said. "Do you receive this sort of stuff often?"

"Oh, every few weeks we get the hate mail, yes. Mostly from America, too, interestingly enough."

"Maybe they surf more?" I figured, leaning back. She asked if I'd like fresh coffee. I said sure, decaf.

"Here or at a coffeehouse?"

"Here, if it's easy, and meanwhile I'll read one more of these appeals. Just one question for now," I said. "Why is he doing all this here, in Budapest, and not in New York?"

She smiled, the lipstick a bit thick, and shook her head. "Come, you know Arthur. He trusts no one in America, not real trust. And the whole point of this enterprise is privacy, utter privacy, otherwise it is all ruined. If Mr. Ziff did this on the Net at home, through a secretary or computer person, it would be circulating all through New York in forty-eight hours."

"So what? I mean, then what?"

She laughed at my question. "They would be lining up at his door, night and day, for handouts. The 'news' would run, as gossip, of course, in every New York newspaper and popular magazine. The whole serious effort would become comical farce. Arthur used to paraphrase Hegel, that whatever happened in history would reappear in America as farce—pop magazine or Hollywood farce."

Well, that seemed rather true, I figured. Yet, the whole picture? . . . I let her click on the keyboard, and on-screen appeared the message from Edith Licht of Jerusalem:

Dear Sirs:

I was born in Minnesota (a farm in Thief River Falls), and after Christian schooling, I went to the University of Minnesota in the 1960s, where, in my third year, I took a course from a visiting Israeli scholar in literature. We got along very well, both in class and outside, and became good friends. He was tall, energetic, pompous, and played the accordion beautifully. To make a long story short, we gradually fell in love, and after graduation, I joined him in Israel, despite all the protests from my parents and family. There, he had divorced his wife, and he married me. Without his urging—in fact, almost against his will—I began to study

Judaism, and a year later, I converted. Y. didn't mind that so much, but soon afterward, when I began to take seriously the laws of Halacha, and insisted on keeping kosher, he grew very upset. Y. was a secular man, who had grown up in a Labor socialist atheist family, and was much more tolerant of my Christian upbringing than he was of my Jewish religious devotion. This friction continued to escalate, however, and, not being able to tolerate his increasingly mocking sardonic manner, I left him and went to Mea Shearim to live, in the heart of Jerusalem. There I found peace in my beliefs and my soul. I soon made friends with Ruth Blau, the famous French Catholic convert who married the Orthodox rabbi leader of the Neturei Karta movement.

It was Ruth who helped me find my next husband—in fact, a boyhood survivor from the Chelmno death camp in Poland, who was now a widower with two children. We married and had two more children. Life with Moishe was very difficult, however; he was a good man, but wounded, a closed soul, who could never let me inside to see his heart, or what was left of it. Bitter, morose, short-tempered, he wished more to die than to live, I think in great part because of his guilt for surviving while his parents and brother had been gassed. You know how it is with Holocaust souls, I am sure. In any case, we lived simply, in poverty, with Moishe bringing in a few dollars selling Shabbas candles and prayer books, and myself working as a gan metapelet (kindergarten aide) in a religious school outside the district. We grew so poor one year that I had to accept a secret check every few months from my mother or sister, along with religious charity. When Yigal died of lung cancer, mercifully, at 55, from smoking three packs a day, I realized I had to make a change, or myself would go under from depression. So I found a modest apartment across town in Bayit V'Gan, took the two young children with me, and began afresh, getting a job as a part-time teacher of English in the local high school, and eventually becoming full-time. In fact, I became suc-

cessful at the school, even asked by the principal if I'd replace him for a year while he took his leave.

And then a sort of odd mitzvah *occurred, which only G-d can provide. For the first time in twelve years I returned to Minnesota to see my dying father and family, and afterward my old college and country friends threw a reunion party for me in the Minneapolis Marriott. Far from being uninterested in my life, they were amazed by what I had done. (Can you believe that they catered the lunch with* glatt *kosher food? And that they were fascinated, not offended, by my wig and shawl?) What impressed them the most, I know, was my strong religious belief, my sense of firm purpose. A good number of them were divorced and openly restless. So I was not too surprised when half a dozen asked, or implored, to visit me in the Holy Land.*

When I returned home, the zealous interest of my Christian friends stayed with me, and I became newly aware of the fact that I, too, had been a Christian one day long ago. I began reading books on millennialism, and became quite interested in the nineteenth-century woman Clorinda Minor from Philadelphia, who led a small group of Christian Zionists to the Holy Land in 1849, but who died unfulfilled at age forty-six in 1855. And I thought this: Perhaps it is my real mission to complete her work. To lead the next group of Christian Zionists to the Holy Land. To help the true Jews here—not the assimilated ones who wish to be like everyone else, and who care more about the State than they care about G-d, or the laws of Halacha—to help the Jews reclaim their Judaism. There-fore I am writing you now, WALLENBERG *Institute, to ask for your help in carrying forward this important idea, and to resume bringing our Christian friends of Zion over here, to help us prepare the land for the* Moshiach *in the same way that we prepare our house each week for the coming of the Sabbath. Forgive me if I say that I feel uniquely qualified to be a torchbearer of such a potential movement, having been a member of both camps in my lifetime. Thank you for your attention.*

My address is 324A Bayit V'Gan Street, Jerusalem. If you need to reach me by fax, I may receive one downstairs in my local shop: Edith Licht, c/o SHLOMO's Electronics, 972-2-6011727. And I have a telephone: 972-2-6527930. (But please, never on Shabbat, *beginning Friday at sundown.)*

I paused, and shook my head in astonishment, disbelief. "Is this for real?"

She lit her cigarette. "You're as good a judge as I am. But why not?"

I scratched my neck, stared out at the leafless beech tree. "I came here to . . . try to confirm certain things. But these stories . . . they seem farfetched, let's say."

She nodded, inhaled, then stood and opened the window a bit more. "I understand."

"Will you send this one on, for Arthur's reading?"

"I think so," Éva said. "A bit 'farfetched,' as you say, but of interest if it's true."

I stood up and walked about, holding my mug. Stopped at the black-and-white Cold War photograph on the wall from '56, with a group of Hungarian citizens gazing at the toppled statue of Stalin. Better than early Olitski, I mused. "Quite a time that was, huh?"

"Yes, rather unbelievable."

I turned to my curly-headed friend. "Then or now?"

"Both actually," she retorted. "While the uprising occurred, it was incredible, I recall, and later, looking back, it was also hard to believe. Like a movie, maybe."

"Fact stranger than fiction, to forgive the phrase?"

She smiled brightly. "Some of history is like that, I imagine. The more . . . radical events, perhaps?"

"Perhaps," I repeated, pondering other matters. "But how would you verify if those letters or inquiries are truthful? Like that last one, from Jerusalem?"

"Oh, if Arthur took a serious interest, we'd have friends there check her out, I'd imagine."

"I see. . . . Look, why don't we go out for a walk, and maybe see a bit of old Budapest?"

"Sure. Excuse me for a minute first."

She left the room, and I moseyed back to the computer, took out my pocket notebook, and copied the facts of Mrs. Licht's whereabouts. Scrolled back to the Ball State professor Jack Ira Bayliss, jotted down his details, too, and also Adele Sloan's in Canada . . . Why not? I repeated.

In half an hour we were walking along Andrássy Street, a tree-lined wide boulevard in downtown Pest. The day was cool and gray. Rows of low buildings from the grand past lined both sides.

"A little like Paris," I said, "only the trees are thinner and the buildings need some upkeep."

She took my arm. "The old, beautiful trees were killed by the terrible pollution. They had to be cut down. These are all young. Upkeep is out of the question!"

We strolled along the pleasant avenue, busy with pedestrians and small autos, and passed the charming old opera house, where statues of composers were perched high on its front. "It's the same architect who did the one in Vienna," she pointed.

I nodded. "So in other words," I began, "those appeals for aid come in, and Mr. Ziff and you choose whom to help. And for his side of things, those wild letters, true or not, provide him with rich material for his own upcoming novel?"

She squeezed my hand. "You are very clever, even ingenious, Daniel. But I'm not sure it works just that way. Not so simple."

"Of course not," I averred, realizing the density of the equation, especially as it was performed by the alchemist Ziff. "But tell me: Why Budapest, or Hungary? Why pick this town to operate out of? It's so . . . "

"Out of the way? Remote outpost? Exactly. Mr. Ziff never follows the crowd; otherwise he'd have taken up in Prague, everybody's favorite. You know, darling little Prague, home of Kafka, Havel, and Kundera, the Velvet Revolution, and sensitive intellectuals—no no." She shook her head. "Precisely because Budapest is *out of fashion*, you may say, its people rugged but . . . not really that charming or attractive, the language impossible, et cetera, et cetera. He saw what others couldn't or wouldn't see— even what our own people can't appreciate. We are too defeatist, pessimistic, you see."

I considered that. "Perhaps he chose Budapest simply because of you?"

She smiled, but wanly. "He knew my city first, thank you. And if it is not in the interest of his art, no woman will influence him otherwise. Or man."

I paused. "You know, the Ziff fingerprints that I'm seeing here and in Rome are very different from those that are on view back home. For example, just before I came over, I had a breakfast with an old editor pal of Arthur's, and he claimed that Arthur did nothing but eat lightly, sleep regularly, swim, walk, and write daily. That's it. Hardly anything else."

"Hardly a life, you mean," she laughed. "Of course, that is the Ziff that Arthur wishes to project in America, especially in New York." She took my arm. "Shall we stop here for a coffee?"

A beautifully intricate stone building was tucked between two nondescript buildings, and at my initiative we climbed the dozen steps from the street. The inside was dark, with a porter behind a cage, and an elegant, curving, marble stairway that we climbed. Secret niches with saints suggested a onetime church; now it functioned as an art institute for students, with an exhibition currently on. Its three large viewing rooms were well lit and alive with odd pieces of sculpture, photographic slides, charcoal drawings, and video installations. Several pairs of onlookers strolled about, chatting in Swedish, German, French.

"English is pretty foreign here," I noted. "Easy to be anonymous for an American. Another reason for Hungary, huh?"

"You are beginning to see some of our natural qualities for Arthur. Just look at this laser beam and the way the photos are arranged, up along one wall and down across the floor, crazy! I am so glad you diverted us in here, I would never have known of it."

She pecked my cheek. "You two have much in common, curious about everything. Come, shall we take our coffee?"

We stopped at the Müvész Kávéház, an Old World coffeehouse down the street. Lots of tobacco smoke, huge wall mirrors, gilt-edged pictures and an old chandelier, delectable cakes under glass. A variety of clientele in poor jeans, cheap sweaters, ragged suits.

We ordered our coffees, divided a single apple strudel, and continued our chatting. Éva got into telling me about the great Hungarian soccer team of the early fifties, the Aranycsapat club that won the Olympic Gold Medal in 1952, when I noticed a slender, blond-haired man whose likeness I recalled immediately.

"Hey," I pointed, "that one is a dead ringer for the old movie actor Leslie Howard, a favorite of mine. Ever hear of him?"

"You mean *The Scarlet Pimpernel*? Philip in *Of Human Bondage*?" She laughed lightly. "A hero of mine, too. Leslie Stainer was born in London to Hungarian immigrants, April 1893, and died fifty years later. Yes, there is a striking resemblance. Did you not see his photograph on the bookcase? Or the poster in the bedroom?" I shook my head. "Well, he was one of our romantic idols after the war. Did you know that Arthur is very fond of him, too? Loved the idea that one of the most elegant English gentlemen in all of movie history was actually a Hungarian Jew."

I sipped my strong coffee and contemplated all that. Maybe I was being a bit narrow with my Rommel conceit, and needed to include the debonair movie actor along with the general? . . . Éva had gone back to her story of the great soccer club, and I thought of my old Brooklyn Dodgers during those same years. So while she named the unpronounceable likes of Lorant, Lantos-Bozsik, Grosics-Buzanssky, Kocsis, Zakarias-Budai, Hidegkuti, Puskas, and Czibor, I thought of my Reese, Robinson, Cox, Snider, Campanella, Furillo, Hodges, Erskine, Roe, Newcombe, Shuba. And as I made her write down those names on a paper napkin, I wrote down my names for her to keep.

"Memorize my lineup," I advised, "and you're eligible for a green card immediately."

"Tell me: Is there anything *you two are not alike in?*"

I smiled. "Oh, yes. He's famous and successful, and I'm at the other end of things. Come on, let's get back to our walk."

And as we journeyed up the grand avenue, Éva filled me in on the recent history of the place, beginning with World War II and the Hungarians getting hit by both Nazis and Russians, then the relentless Communists for four decades, and next the corrupt, incompetent regimes ruling since. While she talked and I scanned the wide boulevard, I returned to my Budapest task, balancing my levels of wonder and skepticism. In my mind, I was filled with more and more of those incredible tales, computer voices. Were they authentic? Or ingenious fakes? How could I find out, *verify*? That was crucial, before all this whole *bubbemeisser* went too far.

On the way back we stopped off at a well-known bookshop—in this city of bookshops—Irok Boltja (Writer's Bookshop), high-ceilinged, winding spacious rooms of literary books, including an English-language section, with two by Ziff in unfamiliar British editions. Gazing at the photos of Hungarian writers on the walls—Mátai, Krúdy, Nádas, Kosztolányi, Attila—I thought again how I'd have to somehow verify what I was being told. And then hook up the whole complex operation to Ziff. Was I up to such sleuthing? Was this what biography was about? Might it, could it, all be true? Or was it the cleverly devised Internetscape of this crazy lady from Budapest?

And was I no more than a simple pigeon set up in a strategic, bizarre literary trap by a cunning writer and his devoted accomplice?

Back in Éva's Buda Hills apartment, I was shown the small autographed photograph of Leslie Howard on the door of the mahogany bookcase, and I nodded my approval. I then sat down by the computer to absorb more global appeals, stories. I noticed in the corner a long file cabinet for floppy disks, marked WALLENBERG. Would I get permission to view those, too? Presently, while the next group of witnesses and survivors proceeded with their appeals, I construed a plan of attack, to begin right off, maybe tomorrow, without forewarning to Éva. Leave a note, create an emergency, hop a jet; if I wished to return in a day or two, I could, easily enough. That's what the hundred grand was for, Danny boy, to check out cockamamie stories, bogus e-mail players, and find out who was who—who was being serious, who suckered.

So I traveled through the next three grim tales, of Holocaust misery, murder, loss, memories, scars, and the poignant appeals for aid and redemption by the Wallenberg Institute. Even more strongly than before, I felt an urge to get out, escape, verify! And later, all through our cozy dinner at the Kispipa Restaurant, I felt the same urge propelling me.

Back at my hotel, alone, I made a few calls to get a flight out the next day; nothing open, so I knew it would be at least Thursday before I could get out to my first destination. For Wednesday, I was anchored in Budapest.

sixteen

Spared the files for the day, I was instead shown the ELTE University of Elte, where Éva taught, and the Doheny Synagogue, a fifteen-minute stroll from my hotel. The first was a five-story cement building, once a Catholic school, then the home of the Communist Workers' Party; in Éva's shabby office, on a wooden bookcase, was a red metal inventory tag imprinted with "Mszmp" for the Hungarian Communist Party. "A memento from a few decades ago, which I hold on to," she said with a smile. Soon I met a colleague, a poignant Jewish linguist, about forty-five, who was, Éva informed me, trying to take care of her sick, elderly mother and herself on $250 per month. Bespectacled Judith Zirkowitz perked up when I mentioned Ledyard College. "I once visited a friend there, it was so green and spacious, like a fairy tale." She was right; next to Elte, my college was a fairy tale. At the more modern library, across the central yard, we ran into another colleague—"a great friend of Arthur's"—a tall, lanky professor of Central European history who implored us to come by for a drink later. We thanked Professor Sandor.

The Doheny Synagogue was another matter. Far from dreary Stalinist architecture, the grand Doheny was flowing with Oriental splendor via Moroccan arches, mosaic tiles, gorgeous dark woods, stained glass windows, soft desert pastel colors.

"A feast for the eye, not very Western," I noted.

Éva laughed. "Almost complete, some six years of work. It's the restoration of Europe's largest synagogue, with the help of friends here and abroad."

I understood. "Like Arthur Ziff?"

"Oh, no, he wouldn't touch this sort of project. This is for the likes of Tony Curtis and his daughter, and other 'big *machers*,' to use Mr. Ziff's term. For him, it has to be more. Come, I will show you."

"Tony Curtis?"

"Sure, his family too were Hungarian Jews."

She escorted me out of the exotic Doheny and around the corner, down a side street, past the ruins of a temple and grave-yard ("the 'Heroes' synagogue"). She walked us another fifty yards or so, to a black iron gate and modest courtyard. The small sign read: "Raoul Wallenberg Square." She pointed to the sculp-ture in the yard, a huge, weeping willow tree made of steel whose branches seemed to be draping with a silvery spray. "We ran a national contest, and the winner of the commission was a non-Jewish sculptor. Arthur contributed to it, anonymously, of course." Really? Seeing a guard inside, she motioned to him, and he unlocked the gate for us to enter. MEMORIAL OF THE MARTYRS was inscribed in Hebrew on a huge black three-pronged gate posted in front of the tree. The silvery effect was caused by small silver tags, resembling army dog tags, attached to the branches; each tag contained a name, I noticed.

"For every Hungarian child or family murdered," she began, smoking now. "Some are still blank, awaiting names. They are sent in from all over the world, Los Angeles, Toronto, Paris, Israel, Spain, from old family members, friends, Gentile witnesses who hear about it. It is quite a collection, yes? Well, we had six hundred thousand Jews at one time. . . . lost about two-thirds. Come, walk about it."

We strolled about the splash of silver metal branches and around the small courtyard, faced on one side by a vine-covered building, the Bet Midrash. The stunning sculpture seemed incongruous here, bizarre. "Well, it's certainly placed strategically," I said, "set up in this obscure little courtyard."

She nodded and looped my arm. "Yes. Arthur felt it should be seen only by those who really wanted to search it out, find it, and that it not be just another tourist site." She paused and looked up. "The survivors or families who see it are very moved, and honored. All the more so, it seems, that the site is private and the gift anonymous."

I wanted to ask the total cost, for possible use in the book, but I refrained. Vulgar. Again I had to ponder if her statements were true, or perhaps another invention by Assistant Saint Éva? The air was cool, the clouds were low, and the ordinary side street suddenly took on the aura of the sacred. Fittingly, we found ourselves walking through it in silence, and myself in some wonder.

Much later, in the early evening, we stopped at the impressive Wallenberg statue on the Buda side, on the way to Laszlo Sandor's apartment for a drink. ("He would be insulted, I'm afraid, if we didn't. Arthur comes here at least once on every visit.") His place was on another scale from Éva's, huge, elaborately furnished, with a lovely view of the city from the outside balcony.

We were shown into the salon/study, a vast, dark room with old, serviceable furniture (like one's aunt's from the 1940s), oriental rugs, bulging bookcases, a few token paintings, and one wall of black-and-white photographs.

Having served us drinks, Sandor sat in a deep chair across from us while his wife, a short, red haired therapist, sat on the brocade couch, cooing to and petting their Irish setter. A tall, lanky man in his fifties, Sandor was attired in a frayed suit and dark tie. His longish face was marked by extra-thick dark eyebrows, a high forehead, and sunken cheeks. He seemed to have the languid movements of an aristocratic temperament; or was it just fatigue?

He asked what I was doing in Budapest, and I explained that I was doing research for a biography of Arthur Ziff.

"A worthwhile subject, by all means, from what I've seen and read. A cultured man. I like Arthur quite a lot."

"I understand the feeling is mutual." I sipped my dry sherry and asked him a bit about himself, what he taught, his family.

He adjusted his horn-rimmed glasses and began talking, starting with his job as the head of several departments at the university, and his focus on Central European history. And when I asked him about the photos on the wall, he took me up close and identified his grandparents, who taught in Liszt's famous music school in Budapest, and his mother, a pianist, who resembled Laszlo and was a dark beauty.) Soon, back in his chair, he was narrating a tale of family renown and gloomy ends: the eminent doctor father killed in an accident when the boy was two; the passionate mother a suicide at fifty-one; and just a few months ago, a close brother dead by hanging. He spoke in a perfect British English, and his willing frankness was in odd contrast to his aura of resignation.

After a while his wife, a lively lady, brought in a light meal of potato pancakes and vegetables from the large coffee table.

The conversation wound to his connection with the Communist Party in the sixties, and, once again, he spoke with surprising candor. Crossing his long leg in a gesture of emphasis, he proceeded to relay a tale of a mistaken act (the post he assumed for a few months), personal betrayal (by his education minister boss and friend) and severe consequences (first a nervous breakdown and then the distrust of certain friends and colleagues). "I suppose it was the worst time of my life," he said with wonder, to which his wife answered, with a nod of anger, "I can assure you it was." And when I asked him why he had joined the Communist Party in the first place, he responded, in a semiplea for understanding, that he thought it was the best way to help the country. As he continued to explain his actions, while trying at the same time to fathom them, there was the curious tension between the open need to tell and the mysterious contradiction of his actions.

And gradually, in that old-fashioned, poorly lit living room thick with books, rugs, heavy furniture, and dark memories, with the past assuming an almost unnatural grip on the present, a past of gloom and defeat clamping down to make the present a suffocating, endless hour of exhaustion, I began to get a sense of Eastern Europe. I also felt a rising affection for this fellow, who, it turned out, was not in his late fifties but ten years younger. He was a man trapped, at every turn, and he was pleading his case, his dense case, to me, a stranger; was it a confession rather than plea that I was hearing after all? Well, all I knew was that back where I came from, in amnesiac Easyland, they didn't make this sort of intellectual—not anymore, at least.

Before we left, Professor Sandor repeated how much he admired Arthur. "What surprised me was how cultured he was. Not narrow, like many American writers. Even Erdös, when he dropped in one evening and spent a few hours talking with us, remarked on that later. So I'll look forward to your book. And if you wish to have a lunch at the university, please give me a call. Here's my card."

Afterward I felt exhausted, as much by the turns of grim history as by the depths of Sandor's biography.

"I can see why Arthur feels such affection for him," I said, sitting in the car. "By the way, I didn't want to sound stupid in there, but who's Erdös?"

"Our greatest mathematician, who died just last year." She started the engine and began the drive back down. "What Laszlo doesn't know is what followed from that chance encounter. Arthur saw him again, privately, for dinner, and came away understanding the odd nature of the man. " 'Another Jewish genius, like Kafka, only in math!,' he said. And when he learned from me how Erdös lived, very simply with his mother, with no university job or money of his own, just help here and there from friends, Arthur had me open an account for him at the local bank, in dollars, so he'd be free to come and go as he pleased. Erdös had this peculiar habit of dropping in on a conference in Prague or Jerusalem, or a class at Harvard, on whim, without notice, and contribute to the discussion. No one ever knew who officially backed the account, though a few suspected it was Soros. Ha! Erdös, of course, couldn't care less."

The next morning I was up before dawn, left a note for Éva at the front desk of the hotel for when she showed up at noon, and took off in a minivan taxi for the airport. I had claimed an emergency departure, on a personal matter, without saying a word about destination. (No tip-offs.) I added that, with luck, I'd be able to return shortly to continue the interesting visit.

During the nearly four-hour flight, I alternated between dozing off and notetaking on Budapest/Wallenberg, Arthur, and Éva, my Holy Spirit triumvirate of power and mystery. What was going on? The farther I traveled to expose deception, the deeper I plunged into surprise truths. Well, maybe this last leg of my current trip would pull apart the deception once and for all and expose the poor wizard behind the curtain. *Just verify.*

Though it was late afternoon when I arrived at my digs in sun-splashed Jerusalem, I had a sudden second wind after a shower and took a taxi up to Bayit V'Gan, on the far side of town. Crossing through heavy traffic, we wended our way up the curving road, past the Holy Land Hotel, finally reaching the top of the hill. The views were easterly and heavenly, looking down on the small, golden city of modern buildings and old walled town. Even if I didn't find Mrs. Edith Licht, I could verify Shlomo's Electronics, if it existed. The driver let me off on a wide street lined with two-story white Jerusalem stone houses. Suburbia on a ridge. I found number 324A easily and, as though I had expected it, saw the name on the mailbox in English and Hebrew. I climbed the flights of stairs. At 3A I found the "Licht" nameplate, of Armenian blue ceramic, and stood still. Surprisingly, I was sweating, from heat, nerves. What was I doing?

I used the elaborate doorknocker and was greeted by a teenage girl, who, in accented English, called for her mother.

A handsome, fiftyish woman, smooth-skinned, wearing a kerchief on her head and a knitted shawl, asked what I wanted, in English.

"My name is Daniel Danush. I'm connected with the Wallenberg Institute, and I understand you've submitted a project to us."

A beat while the information registered. Then she exclaimed, "Oh, my!" A wide smile creased her well-proportioned face as she opened the door for me to enter the apartment. "Please come in. This is so unexpected that . . . that—"

"Of course, thank you, I understand, this is just a preliminary interview, Mrs. Licht, as I happened to be here temporarily for other business, and the Institute asked me to talk with you informally, before matters progress farther."

"By all means. Please, sit right here, and I'll make you a nice cup of Russian tea, with lemon. With some brandy, perhaps? Chaya, put the kettle up, will you? And you'll have a piece of nutcake, too, yes? Chaya, *nu?*"

So I sat there, in the living room with the vase of red and purple anemones and the bookcase with the blue *Encyclopedia Judaica,* waiting to perform my part in the ongoing charade. I stood to observe a curious object on the wall, in one corner, and when Mrs. Licht reentered, bearing her cake, I asked about it. She squinted and smiled, embarrassed, "Oh, that's my *get.* You know what that is? My official divorce certificate, from the rabbinate. I had it done in calligraphy."

Pampered by the tea and cake, I proceeded to ask some apparently pertinent questions, and sound authoritative, all the while feeling more baffled and confused than ever, and even somewhat guilty. She answered my questions with poise and modesty, speaking in an odd accent that seemed a mix of the American Midwest and the Polish shtetl. A decade or so in Mea Shearim, Jerusalem's most religious neighborhood, had worked its peculiar transformation on her original Minnesota inflection. Anyway, the trick was on me, you might say. I had come a long way, in a hurry, to prove that . . . Edith Licht was real, and the e-mail to www.Wal lenberg.com/ was real, too. But so what, regarding A. Z.? How would I hook him up with all this *meshugas?*

"Come, you'll have some dinner with us, Mr. Danush? I have some stuffed derma, and kasha varnekas, and—"

Closing my small spiral notebook, I smiled, shook my head, and stood up. "This has been very informative, Mrs. Licht. Thank you very much. You'll be hearing from the Institute in the not too distant future, I'm sure. And I wish you the best of luck."

The smooth-skinned, Swedish-faced Orthodox Jewess smiled gracefully, took my outstretched hand, and held it for a moment. "You understand Yiddish, sir? *Zei gezunt!*"

I nodded, released her grip, and got to the door.

"I should call you a taxi?"

"No, I'm okay, I think I'll walk down to the hotel and find one there, thanks."

She gave me a little wave along with a shy, amiable smile.

Outside, the wintry air was springlike in the early evening. The sky was turning mauve and dark blue, with shoots of pink, and touched the mountains and city below like a painting. For me, one closer to El Greco than Chagall.

I stayed one day in Jerusalem, to see a mutual friend of Arthur's and mine, a writer. We met for coffee downtown at the Anna Ticho house. We greeted each other warmly, chatted about families, and eventually turned to the topic of Ziff.

I told him about my book on Arthur and that I was coming across some unusual, unbelievable things in my research.

The round-faced novelist clapped his hands, smiled broadly, and replied, "It doesn't surprise me. Not at all. He is amazing, Daniel. Like a *wizard*. Anything is possible with Arthur Ziff. Anything! You must believe it. I have seen it myself. One day you are a nobody, then his *wand* touches you and suddenly the world knows you, wants you, you're Someone! That's his power. So why should it surprise if you find out things that appear to be unusual, or extraordinary, connected to Ziff? No, no, it's exactly the reverse—it's the appearance of the ordinary that you must be skeptical of with Arthur. Look, we Jews have always had our men who can speak directly to God or lead amazing journeys through the desert—we don't call them wizards or magicians, we simply acknowledge them. But they do wonders." He put his hands on my wrists and gripped hard. "He has a force, a power, that is undeniable, and that is what you must write about and discover!"

Carefully I released his hard grip. "And what if that 'force' is not exactly for moral use always? But comes sometimes with ambiguous motives or consequences?"

His round race had grown red with excitement, and he took off his spectacles and wiped them with a handkerchief. He was smiling wildly. "He is one of us, and beyond us. Not a mere writer. I know it and you know it. He is a force, and 'moral' or 'immoral' are not the right terms by which to judge him or describe him. It's the genius you must look at, turn over and over like a diamond, examine, and with love, Daniel, like a jeweler gazing on a beloved gem."

I nodded, and thought about the loupe I had been using. "But you do have to make sure that the diamond is a diamond and not something else, a brilliant . . . copy. So there has to be some skepticism along with the passion, skepticism and careful judgment too, no?"

His smile was beatific now, as he lifted a salt shaker and turned it this way and that, catching the sunlight. "Look at the genius and expect the unexpected—*if there's illusion or fakery,* that may simply be *a part of the genius,* understand that, and come to terms with it." He lowered his voice and grasped my hand. "You know, Daniel, people here read his books and interviews and think he is an enemy of the Jewish people, when the truth is, he *loves the Jewish people; no one loves them more.* You see what I mean, how genius is exactly misinterpreted?"

He seemed so sure, so transcendent in his belief just then that I didn't see any point in criticizing his generalization or making vital distinctions. No, no, I instead enjoyed his round face lit up that way, beaming—he, who, some fifty years ago, was a young boy wandering alone in dark forests and strange towns, adrift, familyless and countryless, one who would never dream of beaming again in life but who now still held the saltshaker as though it were an icon. He knew all about the unbelievable, all right, the unbelievable and the miraculous.

seventeen

The return to Budapest was the right thing to do. We spent three more days going through the crazy stories and poignant appeals, digging into her collection of files on disk, an inventory of Holocaust scars and pain. ("Oh, there's more, much more for you to see here and in Rome," Éva remarked, "but we'll wait for the next visit, eh?") Clearly Arthur had enough rich material for a Wallenberg trilogy.

Further, I also met with several other writers and intellectuals who had befriended Arthur. I came away convinced he was regarded, if not exactly as a god, at least as a visiting hero, a prince of favors. They revered and cared for him, cherished his every visit; a feeling of mutual reciprocity prevailed, it seemed. All told, I felt I had indeed "verified" certain matters, at least on the European level; now, somehow, I had to confirm all that back on home turf. It would be very useful to interview Arthur, of course, even though I also knew the difficulties of that approach. Meaning, he could simply say "not available"; or else spin his version of things, and that spin itself, though dazzling, would be distracting. . . .

Was all biography such thorny detective work, just to arrive at the topsoil of facts (that necessary loam for seeding interpretation)? Were writers in particular clever double agents about their own lives? Masters of conscious disguise, invented multiple selves, careful smoke screens? Or was all that just a specialty of one Arthur Ziff?

Budapest, Jerusalem (and Rome?), and Arthur's audacious performance and striking virtues there, all seemed so odd and remote back home, and especially back up there, in New Hampshire's north country. My whole view of the man was turning topsy-turvy, opening his real character up and out, into a full-fledged Ziffian protagonist, and maybe beyond that. Such heroic honor, such original rectitude, was indeed a surprising, supreme irony. *If it was all true.* . . . Did it mesh with the Ziff that Jeanne had described in sordid detail, the Ziff that past friends and foes—and even I— knew? Would the world believe this other Ziff? . . . Did I? (*"Look at the genius and expect the unexpected,"* advised the Israeli writer of miracles.)

I had returned home in time to celebrate Becka's birthday, her forty-ninth, and it was a quiet but lyrical affair. The boys brought the cake and candles into a darkened kitchen, and I had hired a local young flutist to play baroque music in the living room. Becka looked (rather) radiant in her Italian shawl and white blouse, and was duly surprised at the sudden live flute playing Scarlatti. Her wide smile and the boys' beaming pleasure at the success of the party told the story. "The music was a great surprise," she acknowledged, "how did you find her and her in?"

I got to work immediately, writing up my notes, tidying up earlier chapters, and sent the whole package (a few hundred pages) down to Patrick.

He called me in forty-eight hours. "Look," said Pat, "a lot of this stuff is rich, very rich, but soon you've got to get some order into this book, it's supposed to read like a biography. Go easy on the lit crit, and think about tying together the three-to-four-page bits and pieces. They're not coherent chapters yet. Start to shape a chronological narrative, all right?"

"I must, huh?" I wasn't amused.

"You must. Beginning, middle, end. You've got reams of material now, so it's about time to write a more cohesive account, okay?"

"Okay."

"And have you started to think about an ending? There should be one, you know."

I paused. "Not really. Can I wait till life catches up?"

He laughed nervously. "Don't get any fancy ideas. Calm and steady will do very well, coming after all the 'revelations.' "

I tried to consider matters, eyeing the late-afternoon light tippling my low mountain. "Can I project a future?"

"Sure, but remember, I repeat, it's a real life, not a novel, right?"

"Right, though it can read like a novel, I repeat?"

"In the plot it already does—which some of the best biographies do anyway. But we have to be prudent here, especially with the kind of discoveries you're making."

"Or alleging, huh?"

"It better be *making,* for both our good!" A laugh. "Keep it up but also go out and have some fun. Don't make this book your life!"

To that innocent proposition I murmured, "Oh?"

On that Thursday morning, having delivered Jonathan to school at 8:00 A.M., I returned home, where Becka was helping the little one get his boots on for his school delivery.

"You know, you're working so hard on this project, traveling here and there," she said, while scrambling to get her own briefcase and tote bag ready for her teaching, "gotten all that money, and yet you're still driving your old jalopy. . . . How old is that Saab, anyway—ten, twelve years? Why don't you go down to Clarement and buy yourself a new one?"

I looked at her as though she had asked me to go to England to perhaps buy a tank. A preposterous notion.

Gaby's little face lit up. "Yeah, Pops, that's a great idea! Get a 9000! Do it, really! You need one."

"He's right. You deserve one. Look, once in your lifetime you're *allowed* to buy a new car, honest. We leased the Honda to see how I'd like it in winter, over this road. But the Saab is a car *you know and like,* so. . . . C'mon, Gaby, let's go, you can lace 'em up faster than that!"

Left alone, I sat with my coffee, the *Globe,* and my four-cereal-and-banana breakfast. Afterward, instead of heading down to the Levitan Ink Mines for the day, I got on my jacket and boots and headed out.

Dean Hill Motors on Charlestown Road was an hour drive, and my favorite place in the Upper Valley. Of course, I had only known the Service Department in back, where they had worked on my old Saabs for the past twenty years, keeping them going. Now, however, I was suddenly dealing with the front part of the dealership, the showroom of sales, offices, and new vehicles. The change in feeling and atmosphere, from blue-collar utility to white-collar salesmanship, was dramatic. Never before had I come here equipped this way, armed with a checkbook that could actually buy a new car, always justifying to myself that no new car was worth the outrageous overpricing. Ha. *To have the money to be a sucker was a native pleasure.* To be sure, never had I felt my blood tingle with this chemical mix of fear, 60 percent, and power, 40 percent. Z = S + ct (Ziff = Saab + college tuition).

Young Jim Landrigan, son of the original owner, showed me three vehicles inside, then escorted me out to the lot to see a few other models. Catching me lingering by a fire-red convertible, he said, "Go ahead, take her for a spin. Here's the key."

"My son thinks I should try a 9000," I apologized.

He laughed. "Smart boy. More powerful, more luxurious, and far more space. Here, try this one."

I walked over to a blue 9000 model, which was emphatically larger and boxier than the odd-looking 900s that I knew so well. It was hard for me to break from my habit of twenty-five years: the two hatchback 900s, before that my chunky 99 sedan, and before that, Becka's stellar 1970 96 model, the low green scarab with the indestructible engine (a modified Ford tractor engine) and amazing traction, a car that had trekked through all obstacles, slashing rain and snowstorms, two blizzards, deep mud season ruts, and sudden potholes. That Saab had been our winter salvation.

Sitting in the bigger 9000 beast I felt disloyal, out of place. Shaking my head at Jim, I got out and walked back over to the compact 900s. Meandering slowly, I found a sleek black 900, a four-door hatchback with turbo. Feeling immediately at home in it, with the same dashboard features as my 900S, but enhanced by the luxury of the soft leather seats, I switched on the engine and eased away. Out on the two-lane road, I headed south toward Charlestown, feeling the car's swift pep and taut handling. Soon I was cruising at fifty-five, came up behind a slowpoke, and stepped down, hitting the turbo; whoosh! I flew past. The burst of speed surprised me, the sheer power of 185 horses exhilarated. I cruised at sixty to sixty-five and felt quietly seduced by the ride, the handling ease, the control around curves, the deep comfort. I mused, was a book going to buy all this? But why not? Hadn't a few other books bought my house and land?

If the ride was smooth and lucid, the negotiation in the showroom was painful and complicated. But not outwardly. The sticker price was $32,465; they would give me a generous $2,000 for my 1992, a special dealer's reduction, and sell me the car for $29,500. Sitting in the chair across from the young man, I felt suddenly weary, my chest and legs weak; I had the money but not the will. The thought of spending that kind of money on a car hit me like a fist, and it showed. (I repeated the mantra for aid.)

"Are you okay, Mr. Levitan? Would you like some water?"

I nodded slowly and tried to straighten up. I had an urge to call Becka and ask her for reassurance. But I sat there, helpless, trapped.

"Here you are, Mr. Levitan." The young man handed me the cup of water.

Sitting, he talked about the Saab warranty, the Dean Hill services, taxes and license fees, et cetera. But I wasn't listening, I was too ill, unhappy, semiparalyzed. I couldn't wait to get out of there.

When Jim asked what sort of financing I'd like, I told him I'd write a check, and he gave me a look that read, "Really? Well, I had no idea, sir!"

Soon, I realized it was time to do it, and, like facing surgery, I took my checkbook out from the inside pocket of my winter parka and forced myself to take up the pen. I repeated a mantra: *This is good for you to do, you can afford it, and one day soon you will even enjoy your new Saab.* Near tears, my chest pressured, I forced myself to write out the absurd figure of 29,500 and signed the check. Accepting it, he thanked me and told me how happy I was going to be. I couldn't wait.

I drove home as though I were returning from the hospital, slowly and carefully, not wanting to shake the stitches too much. No use of turbo, no spurt of ego. Just drove. A necessary deed I had performed, a surgery of spending money on myself, and only sometime later would I be allowed—by myself—to appreciate it. Weary and wounded, I drove into my driveway with the new car. With relief I left it and went into the house, walked straight to the study, and got to my routine—turning on the radio, starting the fire, opening my laptop. Spent the day working and trying to forget my morning operation. The steady, dull quiet of the day was a blessing.

But when the boys got home from school at three-twenty, all that changed as bedlam broke loose. Jonathan, grinning broadly, said, "Dad, it's REALLY sharp! I mean, the black color and the hatchback are awesome. We have to go for a ride immediately, and test the turbo! Especially before Gaby does some damage."

Sure enough, there was little Gaby, auto connoisseur par excellence, at the wheel of the car, in full pretend.

Becka said, "It's handsome. You did well. *Mazel tov!*" And she pecked me on the lips.

Outside, Gaby was all smiles, anticipating high pleasures. "Pops, it's great! Only one thing: Why didn't you get the 9000? Remember, we talked about it."

I leaned down and kissed his soft cheek. "The truth is, I couldn't get used to the different feel of it. It was too . . . big, boxy. I tried it, but didn't like it nearly as much."

"Besides, Gaby," Jon explained, "Dad is loyal to his 900s."

"That's okay," the seven-year-old mogul relented. Then sought to console me, and him. "It's got turbo, and REAL leather, right?"

"Right," I said, sliding in, while Jon called out to his mother to hurry and join us for a quick ride.

Presently, we were heading out on Route 118, a road without much traffic, north toward the White Mountains. I cruised easily at fifty-five, urged on by the enthusiastic boys.

"Very comfortable ride," admired Becka.

"Hey, Pops, there's a truck up ahead. Can we try the turbo?"

Driving up a long, curving hill, I came up a few hundred feet behind the pickup, waited until I had a clear view and broken yellow line, and said, "Okay, hold on!" I pumped down, jolting the turbo into action and propelling us by the surprised GMC.

"W-O-W, Pops!" exclaimed Gaby.

"That was REALLY COOL, Dad," said Jon, with a grin, in the back. "I thought we were going to take off!"

Becka was nodding. "You better be careful with this thing. It could be very tempting."

For the rest of our maiden voyage I cruised easily, while the kids luxuriated in the leather or cried out for more speed, and Becka admired the spanking newness and comfort. ("The ride is extra-smooth, isn't it?") For me, it was a kind of relief from the day, and I actually had fun. Driving back, feeling the quietness of the engine and the sure control, the precise handling, I felt as though a period of healing and recovery was already beginning.

Indeed later, observing the sleek Saab sitting prettily in the driveway with the boys and Becka, I was relaxed enough to enjoy its sensuous shape, and Jon's words, "It's like our own black Hornet, huh?"

Recovery welled up for the next few days, as I started to get used to the idea of the car, and the possibility that I was not the most stupid and immoral man in the world. Also, I was back to wordsmithing, leaving the notetaking behind and beginning to write. On Friday, feeling calm again, and working, I got a call from Pat, who, after greetings, asked, with care, "Have you read it yet?"

Huh? "Read what?"

"*The New Yorker*. Obviously you haven't. You might want to, very soon."

I paused. "How bad is it?"

"Well, you should see it first. It's on the stands now."

"Concerns my book, right?"

"Well, not in a direct way."

I paused. "Concerns me?"

"Yes, I think you could say that."

Could? "All right, I'll get it."

"Sit down when you read it, okay?"

"It's that bad, huh?"

"Well, let's say it might catch you off-balance."

After the call, for ten minutes I deliberated about continuing work before driving to Hanover. At the bookstore I bought the magazine and walked to the basement of Baker Library to read it. There, beneath the gaze of Orozco's wild Antichrist staring out from the huge mural of the Mexican Revolution, I read a short story by Arthur Ziff, "Survival of the Fittest." It concerned an over-the-hill writer who, once upon a time, had been of some interest, writing with real vigor and anger, à la Céline. But now, in deep middle age, he was losing out—losing his career, losing his confidence, losing his material. Furthermore, he knew all this, and though he tried to hide it from friends and college colleagues, he couldn't hide it from himself or his wife. The story was poignant and comic at the same time, and the protagonist, Steve Lussiter, certainly won a certain amount of sympathy from the reader, at the same time that his condition of humiliating pathos is laid out fully. It ends on a melancholic, rather drastic note, with Lussiter on the verge of a nervous breakdown, crying on a pile of rocks at his New Hampshire country home.

The tale had sympathetic touches of sad Tommy Wilhelm in *Seize the Day,* and the nihilistic protagonist in Hemingway's "A Clean, Well-Lighted Room." But it also had aspects of the character that were less impressive, more open to ridicule—his hypocrisy, his hucksterism, his pettiness, his dishonesty. Not to mention details close to my own life:

> Lussiter's errors of life judgment and overzealous pursuit of career, at the expense of friendships, honesty, and self-criticism, were reflected in the recent books, where flaccid prose and juvenile themes had come to dominate the work. What hurt the most perhaps was that Lussiter knew this, down deep, but was powerless to shift ground, to change directions, and so he continued to go after the cheap and easy ways out. Put another way, it may be said that the more Lussiter tried out "virtuousness" for his characters, to appease the critics who had been displeased by his past nastiness, the more meretricious did they seem, and the more false did the novels become. So he was losing out, both to the shallow critics and to his

deepest self. If Lear's famous cry had been "A kingdom for my horse!" Lussiter's cry might be "A kingdom for one of my old novels!

I read all this with a pounding in the chest, and weakening in other parts. Standing and walking about after a first reading, I felt weak in the legs, and perhaps feverish, too; I seemed to understand, for the first time, the violent and aggressive figures in the stylized mural hovering above me. It wasn't about capitalism and the Revolution, it was more personal—the ripping out of one's heart and the defaming of one's integrity. (I recalled how, in the 1930s, the Ledyard College president and trustees, reacting to the sharp pressure from some powerful townspeople, had tried their best to get the mural whitewashed and Orozco thrown out of the place, because the great painter was a Communist. The tiny art department had threatened to quit, saving the day. Now, of course, it was a great plum for the college, its chief tourist attraction.)

Having made my way from one end of the basement to the other and back again while the innocent undergrads studied and chatted at the long tables, I sat back down, and reread the story:

> Even the solitary walks that Lussiter took now were full of self-recrimination and increasing doubts; what had once been two-mile hikes of country pleasure and nature watching were now reduced to one-mile treks of looking narrowly, seeing a stray beer can here or an old tree gouged by a snow plow, and swearing at the state of things. No longer was it a routine walk of refreshing idleness, so necessary for the writer's calm, but instead a forced march by the superego, as brutal as any the Army could require. New Hampshire country life was becoming a punishing internment camp in Steve's middle age.

I looked up, perspiring, wondering . . . how many were reading it *and projecting me?* Let's say 1 percent of the six hundred thousand circulation? Or just a half, three thousand readers? Substituting Levitan for Lussiter was not too difficult. . . .

I returned to the text for one last look:

> The family, too, had sensed the fragile edges and loosening threads of Lussiter's life. His son and daughter—

Ah, how *thoughtful,* he had substituted a daughter for one of my sons.

> —looked at him at certain moments and knew something was frayed, not right. 'Hey, Dad, why don't you answer me? I asked twice if you could take me down to Jesse's so we could study for the test together. Is something wrong?' And wife, Judith, grew rather alarmed the way he forgot about some obvious items like taking out the garbage or calling the plumber: 'I really think you need to talk to someone, Steve. Things are going from bad to worse, and I'm worried that you might, well . . . do harm to yourself or blow up at me and the kids.'

Even the literary agent entered the story:

> It was clear enough from Jean-Marc's response to the recent collection of three novellas that he was not eager to try and sell them. 'Maybe put them away for three months and then look at them again?' the shrewd gentleman had recommended. All of this carping or nibbling came in bits and pieces over a period of a year, so that it was a little like Lussiter standing on a tiny island, and watching it gradually erode right in front of his eyes. And when friends stopped calling, for one reason or another, it was clear enough to Lussiter that he was in the struggle of his life, for his career and his writing, for his family, for his literal survival.

I looked up, breathed deeply, eyed the wild characters above me.

Why did he write it? I wondered. Simple, I answered. It was a warning shot across the unsteady bow of my ship of state. A quick shot, not to sink the boat, but rather to slam it, change its course, alert the captain. That was all, sonny boy.

I had had enough punishment for just then, and departed the basement and the Revolution. In my car, bruised, incensed, I drove home, making sure not to hit the pedal too hard in turbo-fury, trying to come up with a plan to alleviate my burning injury. Well, no one said it would be easy, right? And this was just a warning, I reminded myself. When I released the wheel, my hands hurt.

I put a call in to Arthur when I returned home, and much later, he called back.

"So how goes it? Did you hear the one about—"

"I liked your friend Éva very much," I interrupted. "She, and Budapest, are special."

"Well, well, you do get around. Oh, Éva, she's a saint. I call her my Éva Marie Saint, remember her? What the hell were you doing in Budapest?"

"Researching you. You lead a rather unusual life over there, on the other side of the old Curtain."

"Oh? Tell me about it."

Smart. I paused. "Well, you're not such a bad fellow, it turns out, not nearly as bad as Gloria and Midge think you are. In fact, *maybe you're the saint.*"

A deep-throated laugh. "I'm sure you can get the New York crowd to believe that, all right. Yeah. Try that pitch out and they'll send you to the loony bin."

Not now, on the phone, did I want to "verify" those matters.

I shifted tone. "Why'd you do it? Why go after me again?"

A pause. "What do you mean?"

" 'Survival of the Fittest.' "

"Oh, come on," laugh number two, sardonic-over-lightly. "Don't be so sensitive. Do you really think that people will imagine *you* in that story? Please, Daniel."

"*I imagine me,* Art."

"You? Are you that down and out? Come now. Get real, as they say—Steve Lussiter is a composite figure, not based on a single model. You of all people should know that. I can name two or three writers I had in mind. But if you insist on seeing yourself as him, well, what can I say?"

"Well, I took it as a shot across my bow. A shot of deterrence, from writing the biography. And it's got cheap shots in the piece, all the way through."

Ziff made a sound with his lips, and I could feel that he was thinking about whether to continue the discussion. "You know, Danny, you're a smart boy, a good writer, and an old friend who's been down on his luck. That's why I'm continuing to listen to you now, and to stay in touch with you—*despite yourself.* You're not the easiest fellow to take, you know. The truth is, I'm a little worried about your connection to reality these days. Believe me, I've been through that sort of thing, and it's no fun. Are you talking to anyone?"

He had moved me around the board with his customary agility. Moved this way, edged that way, I was forced to back up. "Well, what was that joke you wanted to tell me?"

A pause.

"There's this old Jewish couple," his voice warm and inviting again, "Morris and Ethel, and Morris is dying, you see, on his last legs, at home. Now, while Ethel is tending to him, Morris is praising her and what she's meant to him. 'Ethel, my dearest love, before I go I want you to know you've been the best wife a man could ever hope for! The way you've taken care of me, looked after my every need, Ethel, it's been wonderful. And taking care of the kids, this house, the family, the cooking. What can I say, except Thank you, my dear.' 'Ah, Morris, sshh, don't talk too much.' 'No, no. You know, I can even now smell the cooking, the aroma of the strudel coming from the kitchen, *oy.* You know what? I can't resist asking right now for a taste of that strudel? May I, dear?' Ethel shakes her head. 'Of course not. It's for *after the funeral.*' "

Despite myself, I laughed like crazy, and he did, too, for a long minute.

"Look," I finally said, "I do want to talk with you at some

point about your European . . . work, or activities. If what I've discovered is true—"

"Hey, you write what you want to write. It's your book, not
mine, remember. I'm not cooperating. You do what you have to do."

A classic Ziff line. I nodded, and realized that the subject of
the call, his short story, had long ago vanished, and there was in
its place a different tone and focus. And no way I could bring it
back. I had not done a very good job of challenging or attacking,
had I?

"An unauthorized short story for an unauthorized biography,
huh?" I tried to joke.

"All right," he called an end to my shenanigans, "you take care
and don't take any more hits now, imaginary or real, right?"

Later, I wrote down a small list of literary friends to check with,
about the story. How many of them, I wondered, had read the
piece, and maintained a tactful silence with me about it? What
were their thoughts? . . . Should I read it again, and maybe use it
in my own book? Just how? . . . Yes, I would have to see him about
his Europe, and put certain questions to him; he already admitted
he knew Éva, for starters. Even if he claimed total ignorance or
took the Fifth and remained silent, I'd have offered him the opportunity to talk. Necessary.

In the next few days I went about the business of compiling
notes, checking certain facts in the *Contemporary Who's Who of
Writers,* adding a writer, an old grad student, a society girlfriend,
and two other names to my list of persons to check out while I
chauffeured the boys to basketball games, trumpet and cello
lessons.

By the end of the week I received a note from a friend at
Amherst who had read the *New Yorker* piece. "It's a blood sport,
literature, isn't it?" he wrote sympathetically. "First you have the
critics, then you have the writer-friends. Tough stuff. As they say
in the hoop game, was A. Z. making a Statement??? Well, what was
it? And how'd you take it? Cheers, Dick."

Smart aleck Dick. I dropped him a note saying what I thought the Statement was, and adding that I was recovering well enough. I was actually coming up for air when I was suddenly hit by a different sort of blow. From below again—the prostate.

It was on Sunday night that I started bleeding while peeing. I had had an episode of this sort some six months earlier, and my doctor had run tests, of the blood and urine. X rays, MRIs of the bladder and the kidneys. Negative. Then he had sent me to the chief of urology, a rather shy, handsome Irishman from Dublin. After reviewing the pictures and my history, he had performed a painful office procedure with a scope called a flexible systoscopy, and concluded that it was not cancer but calcium stones and my enlarged prostate that were causing the trouble, and we should keep an eye on it. He explained concisely what was happening, prescribed a drug for relaxing the bladder, and told me to monitor it and get anther PSA exam in six months.

Well, here it was six months later, and I was bleeding again. Badly. My heart began to pound when I saw the red blood mix with the urine, and I hoped against hope that it would be a one-time episode. When I went to dinner that night across town at a friend's house, and he asked me how I was, I acknowledged that I was somewhat nervous, since my prostate was acting up. And all through the tasty dinner, while the talk flowed about his stay at Spelman College, I kept thinking about my problem and decided to hold off on using the bathroom there. Later, at home, I peed in the snowbank in the driveway, and was startled again by the flow of blood. I kicked snow to cover my shame.

What followed was a misery of two more days of the same fear and dizzying humiliation, as I continued to piss blood. No pain, just thick blood. I said nothing to Becka, but cursed my luck, and did my best to wipe the rim and outside of the toilets. At last, on Tuesday morning, I was forced to call my GP and head in, a woman's pad on my penis, for an emergency visit, shlepping Gaby, at home with a cold, with me. After checking the toilet bowl and the dark blood and blood clots down there, the doctor called the urologist, who urged me to get up there swiftly, as he was headed out of town at 4:00 P.M. ("This could be anything, bladder cancer, something internal breaking, stones, so get there pronto, okay?") With that cheerful sense of urgency, I gathered up the mature little boy for the ten-minute ride up the highway to the new Hitchcock Medical Center.

At the Urology Department on the fourth floor, I went through with the bureaucratic paperwork, the questions about insurance coverage from a fumbling receptionist at the desk, and then waited, hoping I wouldn't have to pee again before getting inside. Meanwhile, Becka, who had been teaching when I called the college, arrived, and offered Gaby a "chicken nugget" lunch over in West Lebanon. "I'll come back afterward, and maybe you'll be out by then," she said.

"Maybe," I said, and to Gaby, who had been such a grown-up little buddy, I put my hand on his tender face. "Hey, I didn't realize that KFC is your new favorite place."

"Oh, yes," he said, beaming, after staying grave for my situation, "Mom gets me fries and a milk shake, too!"

Kissing him, I told him what a great pal he had been.

The procedure inside the office was on a par with any Marine boot camp, stripping you of any illusion about holding onto your dignity. First I undressed completely, and got on a green johnny; then I had to urinate into a plastic container, in a tiny bathroom. I bled into the cup and into the toilet, the thick, maroon blood smearing the toilet and my fresh johnny. The prologue to horror. Next, in the adjoining eight-by-ten room, I obeyed the older sour-puss nurse, making sure to be extra polite, and lay on the high, narrow, adjustable bed.

Dr. McCabe was a trim, handsome man, brown hair graying, features small and words spare. He greeted me cordially with Irish accent, had the nurse put an extra pad under me, and said, "I'm glad you made it right over, so we could have a look at what's going on before I leave town in a few hours. Just lie back." I did. Uncovering the johnny, he wiped clean the messy penis, held it firmly to plunge a Novocain shot into the orifice, stinging! "When did it start?" he asked and as I explained the sequence, he teased, "Shoveling snow out in Mascoma, eh?" and got his scope and hi-tech equipment ready while waiting for the shot to anesthetize me.

The lights were dimmed, a viewing screen was raised (opposite the doctor), and the nurse stood by, ready to aid.

After setting up, Dr. McCabe inserted the flexible tube down into my penis, sliding it down farther and farther, stinging me at the depths. Then, craning his neck, he began to scope his position out, like a Cousteau searching the underseas habitat. He turned his tube this way and that, slowly. "Now let's make a little turn here," he'd say, sending a sliver of pain down through me, then looking up to view his screen. "It's hard to see, so much bleeding," he bemoaned. "Can you urinate? Go ahead, see if you can." Though I had little power to operate anything down there, he soon said, "Ah, yes, that's better." In some fashion I could feel the puddle of piss and blood that I was spilling all about my lower half, but I didn't care much. At some point he called in an assistant doctor, a young female urologist, introduced her, and began to share with her the pictures on the screen of my messed-up bladder and prostate, which looked to me, when I glanced up, a little like Mars scarred with reddish veins. His assistant induced in me feelings of humiliation for three or four seconds before I returned to my scraping abysmal discomfort. "I don't see any growths," Dr. McCabe turned his scope slowly, like a submarine captain using a periscope to search for danger. "See that mound of stones over here? The bleeding is coming from there somewhere," he spoke slowly, searching for the source. "Ah, there, I think that's it," and his assistant assented. "Now let's just try to get a few photos, can you move the camera just a bit, yes? That's it, good, good." By now I was gritting my teeth, squeezing the bed and the nurse's hand, each minute going by like a month.

"All right, we're just about done, Dan, just hold on one minute more so we can check out this one other area and make sure we see nothing else . . . that's all right, bloody, but no growths, no tumors . . . good."

As he raised his head and began to bring the tube out, I was left in involuntary tears, from relief as much as from pain.

"You get cleaned up, and we'll chat." He wiped me with some antiseptic, asking, "Are you all right?"

I nodded slowly, drained.

Slowly I gathered myself, while the now forgiving nurse was wiping up my lower lake of urine and blood. My johnny was a mess, I saw, removing it in the bathroom. I did a poor job of washing my blood-stained pubic area, knowing I'd have to wait for a shower at home. I dripped blood into the toilet and set my pad into my shorts. *So this is life, too, understanding now why people may want it to end. Which was worse, betrayal of the spirit or betrayal by the body?*

I sat in his small office, waiting. The nurse gave me a cup of water, which I drank, though with some hesitation (not wanting to pee again).

Dr. McCabe entered with my file, touched my arm, said, "The good news is that it's not cancer. You have a great deal of blockage of the bladder, the prostate is very enlarged, and the bleeding is probably from all the pressure—a combination of the stones and squeezed veins, and maybe an infection there as well. So first we have to stop the bleeding, and then I think we should do a TURP, or a transurethra resectioning of the prostate. Here's what we do." He pointed to a graphic chart of the organs on the wall and began to explain what a resectioning means. While he spoke, in his clipped Irish accent, I was still stunned from the procedure, but I thought how I wouldn't mind if he operated just then, so I could avoid the bleeding and another "procedure."

"Now, as for the present situation, you're going to have to lay low for the next couple of days, drink lots and lots of water, a glass every half hour if you can do it, get off your feet and don't do anything strenuous. And I'm going to write a prescription for an antibiotic to take twice a day for the next ten days. We've got to stop that nasty bleeding by Monday or we'll have to do something. Okay?"

I nodded, and asked when he could perform the TURP.

"Well, I'm off to Houston until Sunday . . . then next week . . . let me write the prescription, and let's see my operating schedule." He departed.

I sat there in a daze, wondering what next, when I noticed a copy of the current *New Yorker* lying on a table. *Next*, huh, Danny?

Wouldn't Arthur already be taking notes on the situation?

The next four to five days were the hardest of my adult life. I peed blood, thick, wine-dark blood, often with bits of clots, every hour or so; I'd stand by the toilet, waiting for blood drips to conclude, then wipe clean my member and the toilet; next, tuck a sanitary pad into my underwear and leave. And look forward to drinking yet another glass of water so I could pee blood again. Nights were the worst. I'd get up two or three times, and in a sleepy stupor, trudge to the bathroom to perform the same bloody operation, bending over to clean up the toilet rim while trying to avoid dripping blood on the floor. It didn't help when, one night, I missed a few drops on the rim of the toilet, and Becka asked if I could be a bit more careful, so Gaby didn't have to see blood when he used the toilet the next morning! . . . All told, I didn't know which was worse, the hourly humiliation and constant fear, or the actual physical injury of infection, stone buildup, and endless blood? By the end of the week the two had melded into a kind of psychic volcano of overflowing blood-lava terror, and I had the sneaking thought that if things kept up that way, I might very well break down mentally, too.

Did Ziff call it right, then, when he had projected such a fate for his protagonist Steve Lussiter? Should I call and ask?

I didn't have to, for on Friday, during the siege, Arthur called and invited me to meet with him after all, to discuss what I had "discovered in Europe."

I expressed my interest in the visit but told him it might be a while now, because of my situation, which I described briefly.

"So you're finally learning about middle age, pal? Well, I can tell you all about it. What's the bleeding like? And what's that procedure called? I don't know it. And when's the surgery?"

I thought how it was a pity that Lussiter wasn't created by Ziff just a few months later, for then he, too, might have some prostate trouble thrown into his troubled pot.

Work was out of the question in my feeble condition. I sat in the lounger, legs up, trying to take periodic notes on a legal pad, but every hour or so, having to get up awkwardly to hit the bathroom again. It was a unique hell, at home, with my own body providing the real drama of one's life as an ongoing wound, one's life as a virtual prison, not some existential metaphor for a no-exit play.

Could Ziff have dreamed up a more ingenious or potent punishment for one of his fictional protagonists? Well, Danny boy, why not lend him your life just a bit more and let's see how he uses it. Was he right? Was I falling apart in every way?

With "Survival of the Fittest" seeking to expose and torment me, and the flow of blood continuing to ooze from me, the prospect of surgery was almost like a relief. At least a light at the end of the tunnel from the present bleak situation.

eighteen

After Lussiter, I understood clearly that Ziff could and would use me, my life, freely in his fiction, and I should feel no qualms about using him, too, when the situation presented itself. It was not surprising that we had an ongoing rivalry, as writers and men, since we were so similar in many key elements—erotic appetite, artistic freedom, adventurous imagination—and no matter how often this rivalry went underground, it continued to run, like a deep aquifer. And since any life was worth examining, and any rich life particularly worth transmuting, we were both fit and natural material for mining, no matter what our Yaddo "prenuptial" writing agreement had been. (So the rivalrous flow could pump both parties as well.) Now, had Arthur been fully aware, fully conscious, when he had first written of me in his fiction, or only dimly aware, semiconscious? Probably the former, but maybe the latter. But insofar as my current Ziff project, one thing was crystal clear: I needed to be as free and daring as possible in discovering material, following leads, pursuing the authentic Ziff. My own self-pact.

The surgery went well, an hour of high-tech performance with a microcamera and vacuum/scraper manned by my skilled Irish surgeon, with my legs hoisted up and set into stirrups. My enlarged prostate was trimmed of calcium deposits, and, like a New-Age shave, reduced to normal size. When I woke up, I felt a little like Gulliver, roped to a catheter and an IV, the one transporting blood and urine from my bladder to a plastic bag, the other trickling water into my bladder to keep it irrigated. My legs hurt, I felt sore below, but I greeted Becka with a stab at humor and felt relieved to be through it.

In the next few days I looked for any inch of comfort on the bed, and continually checked out the color mix in my bag, watching the dark red fade perceptibly into a kind of pink champagne. The right stuff! The visits from the boys were heady, especially the little one's detailed questions about the fluids. I was also pleased to see half a dozen friends come by, envying them their bodies of easy movement and health. At odd moments, I mused humorously: Had Ziff somehow managed to put me in here, a body shot to go along with the literary one? (A touch of madness mingled with lucidity.)

Meanwhile, my wiry Irish surgeon had come by, checking on his work, and shocked me by jerking out the catheter (to exchange it) without any warning, causing me to scream out and be reproached by him sternly in front of four residents. Only a minute later, realizing his error, he whispered an apology to me. And the next morning, on a six-thirty visit, he cradled my head and whispered yet another apology. Two small gestures of gentlemanly honor that turned him from a doctor to a man, a fellow whom Dr. Chekhov would have nodded to.

I started to feel guilty about the doctor's remorse.

An hour later, as they were serving breakfast, the second surprise arrived, on the telephone.

"So, can you still get it up?" asked my other perfectionist, Arthur. "Have you tried masturbating yet? Or is it all over for you?"

I smiled. "All over. And good riddance, too. What was it that Sophocles said when he reached eighty, 'How happy at last to be rid of my bondage to sex.' "

"Hey, you beat him by more than twenty years. *Mazel tov!*"

"Good point."

"You know, you are now allowed to ask the nurse to help you jerk off, did ya know? At least in the New York hospitals. It's all provided for in the new HMO contracts."

"Thanks. I'll check on it."

"So how are you, kid? And how was it?"

"Not too bad," I said, and narrated a bit about the surgery and recovery. Then, noting that he knew about prostate cancer but not this stuff, he started putting specific questions about the procedure and my problem. "Hey," I said, "I still have my ninety days' option to write my own stuff down, right? To get it into a new novel, say?"

"Oh, was it ninety days? I thought sixty. But sure, go ahead, take the full ninety. Why not? I'm a generous guy. In any case, how long are you in the hospital for? It turns out I have to run up to Burlington, Vermont, tomorrow to see about something, and if you're still there, I'll stop in and take a peek at your nurses. Are female ones permitted there anymore, or just gays?"

"Yeah, there are a few left. But I'm scheduled to get out tomorrow morning. If you feel like driving down to the house, you're invited. It's about two hours."

"I'll see about the timing. I have a six-fifteen return flight."

"What are you doing up in Burlington?"

"Oh, just some research. Hey, did you hear the one about. . . ."

While he told the joke, I wondered—research? The only thing it could be was to see Raoul Hilberg, and I realized (of course) that it was Wallenberg time. Recalled a word from Éva about that smart, sardonic Holocaust historian. The punch line was funny, as usual, and I laughed. "Now, don't forget to check on that special HMO privilege with your nurse, and take advantage of it before you leave. I'll call you tomorrow if I can make it." Click.

Tough and funny Arthur. Hard as nails. Warm, too. Oh, well. I had my breakfast—they had only omitted the bagel and the banana—and I made do with the Corn Flakes and milk, and institutional coffee. A call from Rebecca, and I explained how I'd have to wait for the doctor to arrive, at about eleven, to see if I was fit to leave, "maybe without attachments."

I took a slow walk out into the corridor and circled the floor, feeling rusty but okay. The attached plastic bag at my hip felt like a peculiar extra limb, and I realized how a lot of men live—in cumbersome daily humiliation. If I could get home without that catheter, I'd be a happy patient. But at that moment, bladder hooked up and trickling, I didn't see how it was possible to pee on my own again.

In bed I drank a glass of water, lay back, and fell into a reverie about a long, early stay at Yaddo, when Katherine Ames was still the queen bee of the hive, that elegant lady from Minnesota who treated her favorite workers-in-residence like her adopted children, all in need of special care. A handsome, white-haired woman in midseventies who dressed formally and aired a lively wit, she had been running the artists' retreat since the 1930s—helped by a sweet-tempered Swedish groundskeeper and an eccentric Boston spinster—with a mix of midwestern charm and rectitude. We, the neurotic worker bees, sat at the long dinner table and conducted polite chatter during the good dinners (and elaborate desserts). Many found the formal dinners and forced chat unbearable; Arthur and I looked upon the boring event (and Katherine) with deep fondness. They were part of the whole meticulous ritual, a clockwork of routine and dullness that made the working hours of nine to four so cozily insulated, so conducive to invention.

An evening arose now in memory, when the well-known playwright and humorist Hal Schechter was with us. He had just received a note from Katherine, in which, in her tiny handwriting, she cautioned him to eat his food more slowly—he chewed much too fast, and she was a bit worried. Hal was taken aback by this memo, wondering what to make of it, but Arthur and I calmed him, saying it was a memo of care, not admonishment. Really? Oh, yes, we counseled, privately amused. And then, watching him, I observed his hesitating bites, his eye glancing this way and that, checking on who might be observing his rapid jaw movement. The dinner chat rambled on about the latest political fiasco by Nixon, and a new ghastly mugging in Manhattan.

Afterward we adjourned to the music room, where we gathered

as usual for another half hour or so to drink our coffee and talk, listen to music, read magazines. The point was to enjoy each other's company after the day's solitariness and the evening's separate ways.

This night, Hal was offering us a first reading of his new play, and we were cordially recruited to be his captive audience. "Now you know what it's like in Attica," Arthur whispered as we sat. "Could be worse," I advised, "could be poetry." Hal, a short-mustached fellow with an amiable sense of humor, explained the context of the play—why, if he was going to read the opening?—and proceeded to set up a small tape recorder so he could later "re-hear" it for himself. Then he began to read the first act, about two friends meeting at a restaurant just after their thirtieth high school reunion. While the wives were in the rest room the buddies bantered, kidded, replayed their past in a bath of nostalgia; soon the wives returned, the Jewish one rather vulgar, the other more English-majory sophisticated, she being the former girlfriend of the first one's husband. I looked around at the four other guests—two painters, a composer, an older writer—and they seemed fully engaged and entertained. Arthur sat straight, drumming his fingers lightly; I focused on myself playing in a sandlot baseball game. Hal's play was high-schoolish in material, sparked by one-liners of easy humor and collegiate "wisdom"; all told, it was about forty minutes of private embarrassment, and I felt a growing sympathy for him. Yet when it was over, the small audience burst into clapping and high praise. Katherine added a modest accolade. Arthur and I chipped in with polite words, and, with Hal circled by admirers, we sneaked off.

"Do you think he chewed his food too slowly?" I wondered.

"Oh, yes, for the reading," Arthur answered. "That's why the tape recorder was there, to speed things up later on."

Over in West House, where we lived and worked, we played a game of Ping-Pong on the rickety table in the downstairs lounge. Soon we were joined by Jenny O., the fiery New Zealand novelist we were both fond of. Frizzy-haired, ruddy-faced, and highly wired, she loved slamming the little white ball, not caring if it flew upward, into a wall, or onto the table, laughing with girlish glee. To her the game was licensed teenage fun, a chance to let out years of repressed energy. In youth she had been locked away for a breakdown in a mental asylum, kept there for a decade by the Byzantine system. Arthur and I were happy to indulge her, screaming too; for half an hour we three were naughty children on the loose. After a few games, we said good-night.

Upstairs in the Pink Room, Arthur's abode, we had a drink.

"Subtle theater by Hal, huh?" Arthur began.

"Reminds me of Chekhov."

"Yeah, just about. I hadn't thought of that. It'll be a hit on Broadway, you watch. Or Hollywood. Cognac?"

"Sure."

He poured our drinks and brought them over to the living room area of the immense, ornate room—usually given to a composer/pianist, because of the grand piano in it—a few old-fashioned love seats and overstuffed chairs.

"Speaking of Chekhov," I said, "you should read these novellas I've been reading. Two of them are knockouts: *An Anonymous Story* and *A Dreary Story*."

"I've never heard of them. I know *Ward Number 6*, of course, which is not too bad."

"Not too bad and far better known, but these two may be superior, or more unique. About fifty pages each, but they read and stay with you like novels, they're so densely felt and imagined."

He sipped his drink and asked what was so special about them.

"The compression, the material, the maturity. Very little wasted motion. The strategies, and immediacy, of the narrators. It all looks so easy, so simple, and yet you know their seamlessness is the hardest thing in the world—that's why you can't imitate him." I took a sip. "Want to hear a page?"

"Sure."

I went next door to my modest room, got the Oxford paperback, and returned to the couch. Showing Arthur the photograph on the jacket cover, I said, "Have you ever seen Chekhov look like this? More like an actor than a writer, huh?"

Taking the book, he observed, "Looks like a patient to me. One who knows his own end."

Yes, I could see that. *A Dreary Story, from an Old Man's Memoirs,* I began, started from the beginning and continued on into the second page of the Hingley translation.

At one point Arthur stopped me and asked me to reread a passage:

> But I write badly. The bit of my brain which controls the writing faculty has ceased to function. My memory is going, my ideas lack consistency, and when I put them down on paper I always feel I've lost all feel for their organic links. My construction is monotonous, my language is poverty-stricken, and feeble. I often write things I don't mean, and by the time I reach the end of what I'm writing, I've forgotten the beginning. I often forget ordinary words, and I always have to waste a lot of energy avoiding unnecessary sentences and superfluous parentheses in my writing. These things are clear evidence of declining intellectual activity.

"That's pretty good. I wonder—"

A knock at the door interrupted our talk. He stood up, went to the door, and opened it. Sam Appel, a painter, asked Arthur if he wished to join the group for a drink downtown. Back early. Arthur declined politely and returned to his couch.

"Go ahead, let's hear some more."

I smiled inwardly. Literature always came first with Arthur.

> As to my present mode of life, I must first mention the sleeplessness from which I've been suffering lately. If anyone should ask me what constitutes the essential core of my life at the moment, I should answer insomnia. From force of habit I still undress and go to bed at midnight exactly. I fall asleep quickly, but wake up between one and two o'clock feeling as if I hadn't slept at all. I have to

get up and light the lamp. I walk up and down the room for an hour or two, and look at long-familiar pictures and photographs. When I tire of walking I sit at my table—sit motionless, thinking no thoughts, experiencing no desires. If there's a book in front of me I pull it toward me mechanically and read listlessly. . . .

I read to the bottom of the paragraph, which went on through page three. I closed the book and looked up. "I think I have a new interpretation of the jacket photo now."

He smiled. "That's terrific stuff. I'll read it when you're through. You have taste, *boitchek*. How 'bout a small fill-up?"

"Sure," I said, feeling smooth from the cognac, the Chekhov, the comradeship.

We drank and talked for another hour and a half about Chekhov's narrators, characters, themes, and the making of novellas. A night infused with the aromas and fragrances of literary talk, so characteristic of nights at Yaddo with Arthur. . . .

Here, in the hospital, I was now being prodded by a nurse who wanted to take my temperature, pulse, vital signs.

The warm feelings of my memory stayed with me throughout the day, like a piece of theater the night before that remains in your head and heart despite the ordinary distractions.

The next morning the catheter was removed, I attempted with trepidation to pee. To my surprise and glee, I succeeded, with only minor burning, and a few drops of blood. My urine flow was stronger than it had been in years, decades. (I could challenge the boys now!) Young Dr. Curtis congratulated me and said I was free to leave later that morning, once I had "voided" a few more times and everything checked out well. No need to bring home the bag or catheter. I was a liberated man.

I felt better than I had in weeks from the news, and couldn't wait to get home and get to work—on my body, my spirit, my project.

Later, at home, when Arthur called and said he wouldn't make it after all, Mascoma was too far, I didn't mind. I had a stack of mail, a new boyish flow, renewed energy, and a warming memory. Plus one of Becka's fine dinners to look forward to, either "a risotto with leeks and salad, or chicken marengo, whichever you prefer."

And later, after the superb chicken, I went through the mail from the past week, searching for something of interest. I found several letters, from unlikely sources. The first came from the Fidelity lady, Michelle Kathleen Farrell:

> *Dear Mr. Levitan,*
>
> *I've had a chance to think about our conversation of a few months ago, in my apartment, and feel that more needs to be said about the subject. (I must admit that my daughter's input here has helped prod me into writing this note.) So, if you wish to come down to Boston again, we can have a dinner this time, and hold a fuller discussion of your subject and my old connection to him.*
>
> *I suppose it is fair to say that I feel better prepared to speak more candidly on the whole matter, or affair.*
>
> > *Cordially,*
> > *M. K. F.*
>
> *P.S. My daughter Sabrina has asked to send you her best regards. Obviously you made an impression upon her.*

Three cheers for daughters, I thought, prodding their moms to speak up, confess, reveal their promiscuous youths!

I wrote her a note, saying how happy I was to hear from her, and as soon as I was up and around again, I'd contact her. Hello back to her lovely daughter.

Another note came from an old grad student dropout, a favorite of mine, Dorothy Grudjen. From a small town in central Massachusetts, she scribbled on her four lined, crumpled pages, asking why I hadn't answered her letters, and talked about her life today in Ashburnham. She was living in an old farmhouse, cooking dinners for the ninety-one-year-old owner in exchange for free room and board. With her was Buck, her huge, untrained Siberian husky who had already ransacked other places, and she had picked up a local boyfriend, "poet, (unpublished but *very* good!) playwright, bass player, possibly a genius of sorts. . . ." She was writing her poetry steadily ("I've got 214 poems now") and getting acceptances, too, in places like *Potpourri, Hayden's Ferry Review, Old Red Kimaro, Melting Trees Review, Soundings East,* "maybe *Peregrine.*" The other side of this self-destructing blond Dorothy—she was a true literary kid, someone who read Russian writers on her own and understood them wonderfully. Also a fledgling writer of talent. As for everyday life, she was way out of her element, the details overwhelming. But might she be of help as a literary assistant? Run around and do some literary footwork, and maybe an interview or two? A full literary sensibility, she was always out of work, impoverished, and could use the dough. But could I use the chaos? I'd think it over before asking.

A third letter came from a professor of Jewish studies up at New Paltz, asking if I might come over and give a talk on Arthur Ziff. "As the biographer and friend of Mr. Ziff, you'd give a truly valuable lecture on the most important Jewish writer of the nineties. Naomi Krasno is right, it is simply amazing what he has done recently, isn't it?" After naming some dates and a payment, he added, "I want you to know how much I've admired your own fiction through the years. As a 'Brooklyn boy' myself, I especially appreciated your own take on the old turf." Well, that was a nice extra pat, wasn't it? If you couldn't come up with the big bucks, you better come up with the right strokes.

But why not try out a few of my notions and discoveries in the hinterlands? Like trying out the play in New Haven before taking it to Broadway for the big judgment. How would Arthur as Lord Ziff of Eastern Europe play, for example? The bad literary boy a mask for the virtuous man? Would they buy that turn of identity? Could I sell it? If so, maybe try it out on The *New Yorker*? *Atlantic*?

The next ten days I was slow-moving but clear-eyed. Recovering from surgery meant seeing things anew, fresh. The big maples in the front yard, ready for sap harvesting, the slender white birch stand across the road, ready for spring ogling. The birds would return soon, the yellow grosbeaks, swallows, hawks, all but my cherished purple martins; their old house was too battered, and I hadn't a chance to get it repaired. Fussy and unforgiving, the iridescent, purple-winged beauties might never come back. The light in the sky was lengthening wonderfully now, in late March; the pink shoots and mauve shadows stayed patiently at twilight before being swept over by the slow flood of midnight blue.

Relations with Rebecca were smoother, too, in convalescence. The fighting sprees, my eruptions of anger, her stubbornness, had ceased. A kind of temporary truce had been called, out of fairness; one of the combatants, after all, was *hors de combat*. Now, this battling, you understand, was not without its charm, its attraction. The scenes displayed two actors in full passion, my fury and contrariness, Becka's counterfury and willfulness. We could have sold tickets to these frays. And why not? Did rural folk have better shows to watch? Doubtful. In the provinces the shows, too, were provincial, and our fights were main events, fit for large arenas.

In this forced interlude of quiet, I decided to reread Ziff's "Survival of the Fittest," feeling I could get a better handle on it now, a more objective, perhaps more equable view. But as I read, in my study, the sentences turned in me like screws tightening:

> The once-vigorous prose of Lussiter now contracted and folded under the weight of piety and sentimentality; the early muscular ideas had become soft commonplaces, clichés; the protagonists, once steaming with sexuality and protest, now sagged with tepid appetite and low libido. What was left, it may be said, were the skeletal bones of a once lively, fleshy writer. The writer knew this, somewhere, but couldn't accept it. What injured the most was not being able to acknowledge the failure aloud to himself while feeling it viscerally, subconsciously, since the wound only festered, and produced the puss of self-contempt.
>
> He stayed away from all incendiary materials, book reviews, literary magazines, cultural sections in the

Sunday newspaper, anything that might stir in him the embers of his buried past, when his name existed and he *counted* in those journals. . . .

My chest congested, my breaths were coming faster.

And now I came upon a paragraph that I seemed to have missed in my first reading:

The situation with Sarah grew slowly more problematic, sad. Both knew it, but could do little about it without outside help. (She had asked him several times to talk to someone, a good local therapist, and he had nodded, but wondered what a counselor could do—write a literary review of one of his books that would open eyes and reclaim his reputation?) Shaky and doubtful about himself, Lussiter began to have doubts about his wife. Why was she spending so much time up at the Shumachers, especially with John, the congenial, handsome Orientalist? Was it simply for the piano accompaniment he played with Josh? Or was there *more?* And wasn't it particularly ironic if there was a real affair going on, since Lussiter himself had often fantasized an affair, but never had had the guts to try, with the willowy blond country wife who could be so kittenish and sexy when she turned it on about half the time?

I smiled ruefully, recalling the letter that Ziff had written after the bar mitzvah, when he referred specifically to her, and suggested he'd visit again if she were invited. How ingenious to bring her into the story, too. So, Becka cuckolding him with his good friend would be a formal memory now, maybe a more permanent fact via the fiction than if it were merely a fact of life?

For now when he went out to his studio, he sat at his desk by the window, the computer open, the morning light flowing in, the music on, everything ready except the creative juices. Dutifully he sat, occasionally getting up to pace the room or take a walk outside, circling the cabin, poking at leaves with a branch and hoping for the right idea or character to emerge, only to return inside, write a listless paragraph or page, and check his watch for the approaching lunch hour. Indeed, it was that last hour of waiting and hoping, while feeling fatigued and empty, that proved to be the most arduous. And when he finally came back to the house and he saw his son—

I stopped. Had to. Stood up, walked. My heart was beating too fast. The warning shot was slamming my kidney. Take it easy, I cautioned, take it as Chekhov would, calmly, with deep understanding of the petty foibles of man, and forgiveness of his follies.

BUT I WASN'T THE WISE DOCTOR! I WAS JUST PLAIN OLD DANNY LEVITAN BETRAYED AND CUCKOLDED BY THE ZIFF FICTION!

This was America, the big Barnum and Bailey three-ring circus. All attention was focused here on the main ring; no more St. Petersburg, Paris, London, no more calm and objectivity. And now in that ring a tired old elephant named Levitan, a red ribbon and silver bell tied about his leathery neck, was being put through a comical/sad routine by his shrewd trainer.

I walked outside and trudged the logging road loop, spotting a small pile of deer droppings and, while taking care to keep my footing on the uneven terrain, wondered if I should try to follow him and join up with his family. Better to stay put out here in the wild woods, where life was far safer than back home.

nineteen

A few days later I took my first laptop laps again, first answering the e-mail and next trying out a few Ziff pages. To Michelle I wrote that I was happy to hear from her again, and looked forward to seeing her and having a "franker" discussion sometime within the next month. To the university professor I said I'd be happy to come and give a talk; call and we'd fix a date.

Then, seeking to rev up my book engine after the break, I returned to my elusive subject. Stay fair, judicious, I cautioned.

I drafted several pages on the major writers of the era, trying to place Ziff among them, especially the three Jewish ones. My rough assessment claimed he was the boldest, most risk-taking, and most energetic, in theme, style, and imagination, despite the flaws. To trek in Ziffland you needed to be an adventurous, gutsy reader, ready to face surprises and dangers. (A little like the biographer?)

Let's have a brief look at the major Jewish writers of the past several decades and see where and how Arthur Ziff fits in. Obviously the major figures have been Bellow, Malamud, Roth, and Ziff, or as Bellow once dubbed them, the 'four Marx brothers' of the literary trade. My own metaphor for the entire group is that of a flock of notable birds, a literary Parliament of Fowls. For example, I. B. Singer seemed to me a charming and vivid hummingbird, with a haunting song, whose appeal was his exotic East European plumage. In Norman Mailer and Joseph Heller, E. L. Doctorow, and Grace Paley, we have witnessed *tour de force* flights by a quartet of hawks who have rightfully captured our immediate attention. And a good variety of birds has flown over with notable markings and voices, whose calls have proved to be of resonant interest to the astute observer, birds like Ozick and Helprin, Elkin and Wallant, Henry Roth, Leviant, and the Golds, among others. In sum, an impressive run of different-generation flocks flying above us in post–World War II America.

Of the four major birds, however, I shall focus on Arthur Ziff and suggest that in this balding eagle we may be witnessing the most singular figure of them all. Notable in his conceit markings, striking in the voice, Ziff has provided us with the most spectacular flights in recent aviary history. Flouting all variety of hazards and risks, he has made an increasing number of daring journeys into exotic and offbeat destinations, often flying low fearlessly, dangerously. A far-reaching, risk-taking creature, his booty has proven to be more audacious, if not always more aesthetic, than the other three eagles. To put it another way, he has upped the ante on what he's gone after, abandoning caution to seek relentlessly the most unlikely sources of nutrition and sanctuary.

Discarding the metaphor, let us consider what the apparent causes are for such daring genes. Where do the guts and vision come from? One answer is, in part, excellent *groundwork*. Arthur Ziff is his own private scout who, having flown the home coop of Jewish pieties and genteel middle-class mores, goes out alone to explore uncharted territory; later, no matter how unique or extreme the finding, he will report back on it in the fiction. That is why the books are written with a confidence bordering on arrogance, a cockiness that offends many. Cocky to the nth degree is this Dorchester pathfinder about the nature of his journeys. And no hired gun for the *New York Times* or Virtuous Middlebrow reviewer is going to deter him from chronicling those treks to unusual destinations, or from reporting his hard-earned truths, extreme as they may be.

Have there been unwanted trade-offs here? Let me ask whether in Ziff's deployment of ingenious techniques and clever literary conceits, real substance has too often been sacrificed. If it may be observed that A. Ziff's work lacks serious emotional depth, it also may be said that this absence is painfully apparent in most contemporary writers, save for the great Bellow. Is it not a sign, a symbol, of the way life is lived in our time, where the connections between the individual and society, or the individual and self, are tenuous at best? Perhaps. Where the need for Something New, Something Hot, is always pressing? Sure. And is the absence of emotional and moral depth—the heart and soul of Proust, Kafka, James, Joyce, too—a strong piece of evidence against the ultimate gravity of our best novelists, including Ziff? Be that as it may, Ziff's work provides the reader with an alternative content, let us say, via the extreme experience or radical conceit, and this may be its ultimate (dark) reward to the serious reader. . . .

I backed off and considered my assessment. My extended metaphor (of an aviary) needed fine-tuning and cutting. I was clearly abbreviating the depth versus ingenious techniques argument; it required much more careful scrutiny, precise examples. And what did I mean by moral depth? Certainly Proustian morality was something much richer, more complicated than the journalists or moralists (e.g., J. Gardner) could ever imagine.

At my stand-up desk, I also wondered whether I had already bought into—subconsciously, anyway—the perceived life of Ziff in Rome, Budapest, SoHo. And the intimate life with Jeanne? With Éva? . . . *Come now, pal, where's your skepticism? Your critical guard against slippery ways, changeable masks, subtle deceits? Self-alert: Innocence is no virtue in this project, but a suicidal quality. So think clearly, critically, act with sophistication, and do all this soon, before you wind up torpedoing your own SS Ziff, just as you've launched it!*

The door buzzer rang, taking me away from my cautionary self-counsel.

A stocky middle-aged man was at the door, with a huge station wagon filled with children and wife, sitting in the driveway. Dressed in a dark, sloppy suit and wearing a wide-brimmed black hat, he gave the appearance of an Amish fellow.

"Mister, I'm on my way to Bethlehem, up this road is good, eh?" he said through the screen door. His teeth were yellowish, and he gave off an odor.

Somewhat startled, I saw he wasn't Amish but Hasidic. "Yes, you can go straight on this dirt road and hit 118, then go north to Route 25 to Plymouth, where you hook up with 93 north."

He nodded and, smiling feebly, said, "You're the writer, yeah?" He pushed the screen door ajar. "The Jewish writer?"

I nodded dumbly, a bit afraid, and astonished.

"The same one who's *shreibing* a book on Arthur Ziff, yeah?"

In a fog of bewilderment I nodded slowly. "But how did you—"

Permitting himself in with a gesture of helplessness, he stepped inside and stood, removing his hat and wiping his brow, in the tile entranceway.

Shaking my head dumbly, not believing this, I started to speak, but he beat me to it.

"Please, you'll do something for the Jews, yeah? You'll tell the world about this Jew-hater, yeah? Tell how much damage he does to the Jewish people with each new book, more than any of the anti-Semites. Why, why does he do it? For money? For fame? *Nu,* so what else is new?" He took hold of my arm. "But I'll tell you the *real* reason why. *To please the* goyim, that's why. *To show them how brave a Jew he is. How independent,*" he mocked, *"how liberated."* He was tightening his hold as he worked himself up, and I had to pry his grip loose. "Sorry, mister." He tilted his head sideways. "It's a *shanda* for all Jews, never mind Conservative, Orthodox. That's why he's permitted to say these slanders, because *they* support him, *they* want him to shame us."

"Who? Who supports him?"

He shook his head at my innocence. "The *goyim,* who then? He's their tool, you see? No more, after the Holocaust, can they say these things aloud about the Jewish people, the State of Israel, but through him, they can. *Farshtey? Redst Yiddish?*"

I nodded, half lying, but feeling more and more oppressed. "Look, I better get back to work, so if you'll excuse me."

"Why not?" He adjusted his huge hat back on his square head.

"But how'd you find me, out here? Or know I was writing—"

"Doesn't matter, my friend." Gripped my arm again, with strength. "What matters is what you do. If you write true things, expose him and his *fahshtunkenah* thoughts about us, you can do a *mitzvah.* You understand?"

I had gotten him outside now, and tried to count the children— four, five?—loading up the boat of a wagon.

"Tell me," I couldn't resist asking, even though I was trying to get rid of him, "what happens if I find out surprising things, like that Mr. Ziff secretly does many good things for Jews? Is it a *mitzvah* if I speak the truth about that, too?"

He looked at me for a minute, puzzled. His dark, stubbly face broke into a grin. "So you're full of *chochmas*, eh? *Arthur Ziff secretly doing good things for Jews?* Go tell the goyim, they'll believe it, sure. One day they'll anoint him king of the Jews, you'll see. But in the meanwhile, mister, tell the truth." He gave me a feeble handshake and lowered himself into his gray Caprice, loaded to the gills with kids and goods. Almost immediately he leaned out, asking, "My Esther can use the bathroom maybe?"

Huh? "Why not?" I said, and escorted a little pig-tailed girl of about eight through the house. Afterward, gurgling a glass of water, she murmured, "I wish we were staying here for our seder. I hate where Papa schleps us." Big dark shining eyes, intense face. "Tasty water."

I delivered her back to the car. "I like your Esther."

He made a face and responded, "Between you and me, she's a *farcrimptar*." His fedora set on his head, he started the car.

Backing out the driveway, he nearly plunged over the railroad tie and onto the lawn. I took note of his New Jersey license plate and realized, as I waved, that I hadn't asked his name.

What a character! Between his mad demonization of Arthur and Éva's crazy intimation of sainthood, where did the truth lie, the accurate assessment? Did the common Jew really hate him that much? How about the uncommon one?

Was he really admired so much by his Gentile readers, for exposing his brethren so scathingly?

If the man remained a controversial mystery, did any of that have to do with literary quality?

Well, one thing was becoming manifestly clear: Arthur Z. was not just a writer but a phenomenon, an American phenomenon. (A subtitle?)

In the next few weeks I took it easy, walking to get my stamina back, taking notes, watching the buds of green emerge on bushes and trees, and poke up along the gravelly banks of the road. Healing inside, I had time to meditate on my difficult literary task. Was I expecting to find some hidden secret in the Ziff life that would open up new vistas, paths of understanding? Discover something new about the nature of the modern artist that would stun me? Scratch the surface of an old friend and uncover a genius? (Or a postmodern version?) Unearth a link between living biography and ongoing work that was somehow new? I walked (with dog), poked with a crude walking stick, and pondered.

If there remained any question about Arthur's resistance to my penning his biography—and the full motive of that was still mysterious!—the warning shot had settled it. He had fired, and it had landed, and my *kishkas* were still smarting. Now what would happen if I proceeded out again—what would he do next? Sink the vessel? (And the captain?) He had infinitely more power than a mere mortal writer or ordinary citizen could imagine. (*Really? Come now, Dan, curb the paranoia, for godsakes!*) Literary power, legal power. Shadow-of-influence political power. Yet if I knew this, why chance my ruin for a scary enterprise that, in the end, might not work out or fulfill itself? Was it worth it? *Was I being stupidly self-destructive in the guise of noble explorer?*

In those weeks of recovery the family took it easy on me, it should be said. The boys actually listened to me, especially the little one—the spark plug of chaos. Gaby listened when I asked him to cease running his noisiest trucks alongside me when I was reading in the kitchen; and Jon, when I asked him to fill my woodbox with maple and birch logs, actually stopped his computer or reading and did it immediately, instead of the usual "in a little while," which lasted all day. The ease startled me. And Becka was consistently cordial and concerned; dinners were actually raised an elegant notch, I was relieved of cleaning up, and she ran small errands for me in town without fuss. Arguments were few, and quickly stopped. In sum, those few weeks were like a vacation from family life. (Should I do surgery quarterly?)

In Boston two weeks later, at Hammersly Bistro, a swanky

South End restaurant, I sat with Michelle Kathleen Farrell over dinner. Attired smartly in a gray plaid suit and maroon silk scarf, she sipped her Beefeater martini. "You look good for postsurgery, what was it?" she asked, Wellesley accent intact. After hearing, she noted, "It's a regular epidemic. You're the third guy I know in the past few months to go under the knife for prostate. Except the other two had cancer tossed in and their erections tossed out. Don't you ever drink?"

I held up my goblet. "Is wine not drink?"

A face. "I suppose so. To some."

The waiter came and took our orders, French double lamb chops for her, and veal marsala for me. House salads, and a Bordeaux.

Across from me, in the dim light, she was pretty and robust in her deep middle age. The auburn hair permed; the oval, smooth-skinned face (crow's feet wrinkles covered well, true); the small, upturned nose; maybe a County Cork Kathleen overlaid with prep school and suburban varnish.

"So you said you'd like to speak more candidly with me," I opened. "Please do."

She drank, and declared, "The rules are simple: Some things are off the record, and if I say 'off,' you'll kindly abide by that. Agreed?"

"Sure," I said, wanting to hear everything and negotiate later.

"And my lawyer and I get to read everything written about me beforehand, agreed?"

I laughed. "Not agreed. What I write you can read later on, like everyone else. But I'm not stupid enough to slander you, and I'm not out to harm you."

Her strong chin protruded slightly. "Will Arthur have an opportunity to read things beforehand? And change or refute what he wishes?"

"Of course not. Mine is not an 'authorized' biography, you know. I'm the sole and final authority." Was I? Easier said than done, perhaps?

She nodded, mulled things over. "You sound honest. And

prudent. Well . . . the thing is, we did have a hot little affair back then, and I probably explained it away too quickly, too casually in my apartment. As Sabrina hinted that day and"—she smiled ruefully—"elaborated upon later to me."

I nodded and sipped, and made room for our salads.

"Saby was a bit jealous that I was seeing you tonight," she said with a smile. "As I said, you made an impression."

"Or Arthur Ziff did. As he probably did on you, in those early days."

"You could say that. On me and on others, yes. He had a . . . powerful personality."

I nodded and tasted. Could I entice a fresh memory to go with the fresh Bibb lettuce?

"So it wasn't just a brief romance—a passion of youth, say?"

She looked at me, amused by my awkward description. "Well, no, it went on, as I think I mentioned, at the 'Cliff and maybe a few periods after that. By the way, I don't see any notetaking or tape recorder?"

"I have the notepad in my pocket," I acknowledged, tapping my jacket. "You were saying, 'periods.' How many?"

"Several. After I graduated from college, for example, and well, later on, after my marriage broke up, too." She paused and nibbled and drank, finishing her second martini. "You could say I, we, were hung up on each other, even after we went our separate ways. You might call it an affair of stamina." She smiled wryly. "It endured high school, 'youth,' college days, a couple of marriages. . . ."

"Did Arthur not have girlfriends through all those years?"

"Of course, many, plus a wife."

"So you were his 'steady,' it might be said?"

She laughed, for the first time with pleasure. Flashed a splendid row of teeth. "He had many steadies, and live-ins, too. But I was his first, his 'original *shiksa,*' as he put it, the model for all the rest. He would always tease me with that, which at first made me furious. But actually, I grew rather pleased, as I grew more familiar with his peculiar notion."

The waiter returned now, took away our salad plates, and laid down our entrées.

"Looks good," I observed.

Her face was relaxed, though she might still flash a wary look, and altogether she seemed at ease, unlike that hour on guard in her apartment. I tasted my veal and fresh asparagus. "It's good, and the portion is even sizable. So it's not just a yuppie joint. . . ."

She laughed, observed, "You have a certain street charm, don't you." She was about to speak again when a well-dressed woman came by, leaned down to her, and said, "You really timed the sell perfectly on Ascend Communications, dear." A smile, a pat on the shoulder, and she was off.

"This is a hangout for some of the Fidelity gang. They think it's an extension of the office." She drank from her second glass of red wine. "Money, when you have plenty of it, and it keeps coming, is shit. You give yourself the illusion that making it is fun, but *fun is what I had with Arthur.* Fun as in *pleasure.* Boy, that was fun." Her nostrils flared slightly. "The truth is, he was probably the love of my life. I know I never needed this stuff"—gesturing to the glass in her hand—"when I was around him."

I nodded, and paid attention to the color filling her face.

"It wasn't just the sex, which was a rush, a great rush," she conceded, "he's very inventive." Took a breath. "It was the talk, the jokes, the satiric hits, the curiosity level about everything. Do you know he once visited me at my office for a morning and actually watched the way I worked? Took notes on everything and asked a thousand questions. God, is he ever curious!"

At that I took out my small spiral pad and jotted down a few sentences—the increasing passion in her face, the thrust of the prow chin. [See Colleen in *DB*—check out Fidelity office scene.]

"So you found something of interest at last! About time!" She roared low and waved for "Manuel" to bring us another bottle. "Spanish and Indian waiters are my favorite, dark, somber, ravishing in their service." Eyes glistening, she drank. "You know, I love his books, once I started reading them again. Funny, sexy, earthy. As for the portrait of 'Colleen,' who gives a shit after a while?

You know, life goes on, and besides, others look at the portrait very differently. Like Saby, she thinks it's really cool that I was the original. And," she whispered, "to tell you the truth, I did used to be rather . . . sassy in the sack. Sure, I'll 'fess up. Hot with Arthur, anyway. But we seemed to get each other going pretty well."

I paused while she took some breaths and wiped her lips.

"So I seem to be shooting my mouth off, huh? Not very proper. Or ladylike. Well, fuck ladylike. Those days are all gone, dear, after fifty or so, if you've got half a brain."

Manuel brought us a second bottle, uncorked it, and poured. When he departed, I asked, "So he gave you great pleasure. How about anger? When and how did he get you angry?"

Turning her goblet and peering in it, she considered, drank wine said, "Oh, he pissed me off, sure. Small items. As for big anger, well, maybe once or twice, I suppose. Stood me up once, when we had made an important engagement. Another time, years later, when I had waited a month to see him. Then there was the absolutely worst moment, when he asked me to say that I had 'been with him' "—she scraped her lower lip with teeth—"to cover his ass for a celebrity he was jamming. She was not only famous, she also happened to be married at the time. Tell me, how do you separate anger from jealousy, huh? With me it's impossible."

She poured herself a glass of wine and topped mine off.

"Which woman?" I put delicately, watching her eyes.

"The big one, Miss *Shiksa* USA." She laughed derisively. "You know, he's so fucked up in his mind about Jews and Gentiles that he himself *doesn't really know when he has genuine affection for a woman and when he's simply jamming a* shiksa *to fuck the* goys. Do you know what I mean, Daniel? *He loved me,* I know, and he admitted it several times, but he jammed her 'cause she was *the goy goddess* of our whole fantasy-driven WASP country. Can you imagine me in my Prudential apartment getting called from the *Globe* and the *Herald to check out his alibi?* The bastard!"

She quaffed more wine, her face twisted with memory. I offered, "Yes, I see what you mean, that's a difficult situation. . . . Which goddess?"

She put her glass down, wiped her wet lips with her napkin, and gathered her wits. Squinting at me, she said. "So you don't know, huh? No clue. Am I the only one, then, who really knew? Hard to believe. This whole little bit is *off the record,* my friend, you understand?"

I nodded.

The waiter came by with the dessert tray.

"We'll split the dark chocolate cognac cake, fair? My big weakness," she said

"Sure."

The waiter nodded, laid out two dessert plates and the single slice of cake, and departed. I cut it nearly in half and gave Kathleen the larger piece. I took a bite and said, "I see what you mean."

"Divine, isn't it?" She smiled.

I nodded. "No, no clue."

She took a second bite and brought it slowly to her mouth, licking the fork of the last bit of chocolate. Deliberately she cut the next bite and said low, "Off the record, Daniel, our mutual friend was jamming a Princess from Main Line, Philadelphia. Isn't that sweet? And I had to fucking alibi for him. The bastard." She shook her head slowly, still entranced. Flung her head back slightly and said, "Isn't it always true, and rather inconvenient, that the best stories are those you can't repeat or even tell? Happens again and again. You can't use it, and I never said it. And should you attempt to turn this dirty little rumor into a fact, you'll have your balls cut off and placed in your hands by the bevy of lawyers and suits that will come your way. Honest. Irresistible cake, isn't it?"

I tried to catch up and also taste the cake. "It is good, and even a touch tart. . . ." A new path of possible understanding had opened up possibly, *if the tale were true* and not a gilded fantasy of this inebriated lady. Indeed, it would help explain the great wall of Ziff resistance to my working on a book about his life.

Figuring I had one more shot at this window of news before it was shut tight, I said, "You couldn't *prove* what you said, however, could you? I mean, if you had to."

Her nose wrinkled and mouth moved for a telling moment. "Yeah, I could probably 'prove' it, if I needed to. But I don't need to, and won't, my friend." She murmured a hiss. "The bitch! Beneath it all, beneath the glamour, just another low Irish bitch."

She called the waiter and ordered us two cognacs.

Seeking to defuse her emotion, I said, "How long has Sabrina known Arthur? Do you think she has anything to contribute?"

"Oh, I think you can count her out of this," and she nodded at the coffees set before us. She raised her wine glass, and saluted, "To your biography. May it win awards and prizes!" She drank. "Hey, you haven't asked me about the young budding genius called Art Ziff whom I knew from the BLS. He was quite a fellow even then. I remember the time when my mother and father took us out to the North End and Dad went into his 'hate Adlai Stevenson' spiel and Art took him on pretty strong, saying how. . . ."

As she drank and recalled the politics of the fifties via the battle between her dad and "Art," I was scrambling to find solid ground for what I had heard. Was it the jealous babble of a jilted girlfriend? A hot rumor she had heard, and embraced with perverse eagerness? Or the real thing, a journalistic 'scoop'? But what could I do with it? Give it over to Rupert Murdoch? To Evelyn Waugh? (How about Arthur Ziff?)

All the way back to her apartment in the taxi I listened with one ear to the teenage goings-on of smart, arrogant Art and smart, hellish Kathleen, while the other ear was still listening to another part of the story. All the time my hands were rather full in guiding the robust but shaky lady in negotiating doors and finding keys. At the end of the evening she apologized for "getting heavy" that way, but the memories weren't easy for her, she explained, and next time she would do better, stay clearheaded.

I told her she had been nothing but charming and helpful, and I'd be in touch. She offered an embrace and I returned it.

Driving on Storrow over to Belmont to stay with friends for the night, I took nostalgic pleasure in the little yellow lights blinking from the Cambridge side of the Charles River, especially the MIT buildings, and the curving Saarinen dorm. My old playground of

Cambridge rushed upon me, my seedy railroad flat near the Central Square where I had written three, four novels, my teaching days over in Waltham, and my roaming days on the energetic politicized streets, the friendships with Borsky the Russian bear and great critic Rahv, with Flora the wonderful painter and Elsa the eccentric photographer, and with Arthur the famous writer who had served as my literary big brother. As I replayed the remarks from the evening to jot them down later, I realized there was not much I could do with what I had learned—well, not much that I wanted to do. Meaning, Arthur's private life was Arthur's private life, after all, and why the hell would I be the one to reveal or expose that life for the ordinary world and for literary gossip or chitchat? (Besides, had Arthur done anything with it yet?) No, my preference was to create my own interesting wild life of him, there in the biography; and yet ironically what I had learned would probably be *quite unbelievable there,* of course. (So you see, Danny boy, you've wound your way right into the middle of a Ziff novel!) I wouldn't mind hearing about the matter from Arthur, and going through all the high details and rich Ziff commentary. But he'd never do it, unless, of course, I said—and I couldn't help grinning to myself here—I was giving up the project, abandoning the biography, in exchange for hearing the best biographical bits about the most famous romance in recent American social and literary history? (Indeed, a romance that would change our view of our own history, to some extent.)

Now, that would be an agreement, a contract of philosophical and fictional irony that would be worth its weight in literary gold. Why, that contract alone would be publishable in the *New Yorker,* don't you think, Daniel?

Naturally, the first thing to do was to get on e-mail and try my luck around the globe, in trying to figure things out. In many ways this form of impersonal communication was best, I was learning, for strange inquiries and intimate questions. To my friend Éva in Budapest I e-mailed a message: [I was gambling here that she'd keep this between us.]

I have just heard an outrageous tale, or rumor, to the effect that A. Z. once had an affair with a very famous American lady back in the Sixties. Do you know *anything of this wild story? Can it possibly be true, or partially true? (Brief encounter, say?) If you don't know, what do you think? Is there any hint/evidence of such a fantasy affair? This is off the record, not for publication.*

On the back of Jonathan's door there was a poster of the human brain, and, walking past, I stopped and studied it. Was it the "most complex organ in the universe," as some called it? I saw a convoluted surface turning in on itself with deep folds and odd contours, squished into inches of flesh and bone. I took note of the two cerebral hemispheres, connected by something called the corpus callosum (and other axonal bridges), and tried to imagine how thought and perception, taking place as nerve impulses, raced through and across the cortex. Might the brain of Ziff really be slightly different, perhaps, those nerve impulses racing in more daring tours of the regions, zigzagging with more speed? Was I studying only the obvious, manifest side, the least interesting? Was it better to study that brain at a site like the Max Planck Institute for Brain Research in Frankfurt? Would scientists there be better able to account for the marvelous variations of reality, the screens of illusion, the surprising leaps of imagination and play, that I was confronting in the life? Seeing the structural variety of neurons (shown as tracings from "Golgi stains"), I admired the treelike Pyramidal cell, the bushy Purkinje cell, the spidery Large Cell of Reticular Formation, the birdlike Ovoid Cell. And I mused . . . was it rather an electrical question, one of neurons and cells linked in ancient networks, not a literary one of books and affairs, linked in the life of a complex living writer, that was most fascinating? In other words, did I need to add, for my project, a research team of neurologists, phrenologists, and brain scientists to get the full story, to separate the lies from the truths, the imagined from the actual?

"Hey, Dad, what's up?" Jon put, standing by my side. "Game of Ping-Pong?"

"Sure," I said. "Let's go."

Presently, downstairs on the screened-in porch recently opened after winter closure, we were warming up, hitting the little ball back and forth.

"That's a good poster, huh?" he noted, rallying with me. "Didn't know you were that interested in the brain."

I nodded. "Let's see if you remember how to get fifteen points off me," I teased.

"Oh, yeah?"

"If you get fifteen, you get the new bicycle seat you wanted."

His face lit up with the challenge. Not an enthusiastic athlete, he had taken to Ping-Pong and tennis, making use of his southpaw side delivery, in the serve. And when he won four of his first five serves with a hard, quick, crosstable shot to my backhand, I was proud of him. He smiled and said, "How about twenty or twenty-one points?"

In his second teenage year Jon was a handsome lad with a full shock of thick brown hair, blue eyes, and smooth, tawny skin. Indeed, I wondered how the hell he had gotten to be that handsome. He didn't look like Becka or me, but rather as though he had had a grandfather in England somewhere, not Russia.

I played hard, using my entire repertoire of unorthodox serves, but he responded well, making some fantastic returns, and we were even at fifteen. Wearing his best grin of barely restrained glee, he said, "Should we up the wager, old chap, and include a cyclometer for a win?"

"Cocky, huh?" I smiled. "Sure, whatever that gadget is. But what happens if you lose?"

"I'll owe you a full afternoon of work."

"That's too good to pass up. By the way, where'd you get the 'old chap' designation?"

"Philip's colleagues call him that, especially when Mildred gets him down."

"Philip who?"

He shook his head in dismay. "*Of Human Bondage*. Ready?"

The next five minutes were a flurry of wonderful points, with

Jon returning two of my slams for winners of his own. Just like that we were knotted at twenty apiece.

"You know you've played so well, you don't deserve to lose," I said. "Let's just give you the seat."

He beamed and said, "Nope, we made a wager, and I'll live up to my side of it."

Each point now was tense, and after three ties at twenty-one, twenty-two, twenty-three, I was delighted when he hit a shot that just nicked the table edge and flew away, to seal the victory. I walked to his side and took hold of the beaming boy's hand in congratulations.

"You did it, pal, you did it."

"You played all out, 100 percent? No holding back?"

I nodded, took his cheek, and kissed it. "You beat me fair and square. Your returns were awesome. Where can I find that fancy speedometer?"

I found the pleasure of my son beating me for the first time to be surprisingly keen, partly because it meant a step up for him in ability (and pride), and partly, I felt, because it was a sharp contrast to my own father and his arrogant victories over me in chess.

In the next few days I marshaled my interview notes about youthful Art Ziff, and sat down at my laptop. I had garnered several interviews in person from his college days at Brandeis, and a few by letter and e-mail from his graduate days on the West Coast (where I had yet to make a necessary journey). I reviewed some pages.

'To me, the seeds of his genius were already on display here, though maybe we planted one or two ourselves,' opined Stanley Rosenthal, a retired Brandeis prof. 'You had to realize we had some very, very bright boys here, especially in that golden era of the 1950s, but young Art Ziff was quite special. A strong Jew on the inside, but antiethnic on the outside. Impeccable sense of himself and his natural superiority. His own best critic often, but also a listener, a top student. Fully clad with a protective armor and shield, and an impressive array of weapons. Accepted no babble from any of his profs, and actually had some fiery confrontations with fellows like Abe Maslow in Sociology and old Max Lerner in American Civ. Always in the attack mode, but with a sense of fair play. What else? Canny, cunning, crafty, the prose style and the young man. What else can I tell you? Oh, yes, cross him and he never forgot it. I did, just once, and even though it was inadvertent in my case, he was not very forgiving.'

When I asked him what ensued, what was the consequence, he explained, 'Oh, I became the subject of a virulent satiric essay in the college magazine. The English teacher as prissy pedant, a feeble imitation of Sam Johnson. Believe me, it was no fun.'

I skipped down several paragraphs.

'He could have done most anything, really. What I mean is, he had the *mind* to be a first-rate historian, literary critic, social scientist. In the History of Ideas program, for example, Frank Manuel, a giant in the field and one of the great teachers, admired the hell out of him, as did Harry Lubasz, another bright colleague. But he never got on easily with Howe or J. V. Cunningham, though Marie Syrkin swore by him too. English got him, in part because of Rahv really; Philip became his early mentor, and, if you recall, published his fiction in *Partisan Review* when Arthur was still an undergrad! Can you believe that? Right there, in the company of Sartre, Mary McCarthy, Lowell, Ignazio Silone, Bellow. I mean, you're talking heavy hitters. And you know what? His story grabbed real attention. Of course, it became part of *Dorchester Boy* a few years later.'

I made notes to meet with a few of his colleagues from those days, for corroboration or correction. And skipped to a Stanford letter I had received.

The truth was, he was never at home here, or at home in Wallace Stegner's Writing Program. The writing classes and the Fellows bored him. They were interested in success as measured by more traditional standards, you might say, and he was interested in success measured by literary greatness. Also, he and Wally never hit it off that well, though they were cordial with each other. And the place just wasn't intellectual or cultural enough for him; he used to call it 'Leland Stanford's cow farm for Western playboys,' and he was partly right then. So when he left as soon as the year ended and headed an hour north to Berkeley, it was understandable.

UC Berkeley in those days was probably the best university in America, all told, and Arthur flourished there. Mark Schorer and Josephine Miles immediately took him under their wings, and he was comfortable—although with Ziff you could never really go that far. But the atmosphere was intellectual and dynamic, and the women were plentiful and diverse. He was a TA for a couple of years, which suited him, and although he was an elusive man, he had several buddies, including one fellow from Chicago, a jazz enthusiast, who occasionally took Ziff to the San Francisco clubs. (If Markman is still living, you might speak to him.) But, you see, he was a rising national star by then, appearing in the New Yorker, the Atlantic, and Partisan Review, *and Berkeley was a big enough pond for him to swim in for a while, and be noticed. Just for a while, though; only two and a half years before he called it quits and left. I always thought his little corrosive satire about academic life,* Tavel's Long Tenure, *set out here, was one of his best, an underrated little gem. . . .*

I realized I had done little as yet with those California years, and needed to. I jotted down "Markman" and a few other names to contact out there, if they were still around. How was he as a teaching assistant? Might I be able to locate any of his old students? And jazz clubs back then? (See *RQQ*.) "Elusive, man," even as a grad student TA. I still had much work to do, obviously.

Later that evening I returned to my computer and, on e-mail, I found a response from Budapest:

In confidence, Daniel, frankly I say to you that in Rome once I did hear rumors about a romance between an American Jewish writer and a famous American lady. I remember asking A. Z. about the rumor, and he laughed it off, and that was that. But who the Lady was? I never discovered. (Though I assumed it to be the once First Lady of Camelot.)

Do I think that is a possible scenario? I believe there have been many, many rumors concerning Mr. Ziff through the years, and do not take them very seriously. You shouldn't either, in my opinion, without much solid evidence.

When will I see you again? And where? Somewhere soon, I hope, Daniel.

Your friend, Éva

Prudent counsel. But a rumor in Rome may have been a fact in New York or the Berkshires. How to find out, conclusively?

Start with Arthur . . . and get nowhere?

Besides, if you do find out, what could you do with it? Mark the file "Inadmissible Evidence" and lock it away for fifty years. Is that how the best secrets of biography are kept?

twenty

In the next few months I worked hard, both at the desk and on the road. I hit California, New York, Boston/Cambridge, and made arrangements to see Éva (and Jeanne) in the fall, maybe in Europe. In the writing, despite Pat's counsel, I was not trying to compose chronologically—book or life, it turned out—but rather at assorted points in the life depending on my mood, my newly gathered information. (On the big secret rumor, the apocryphal story, I still had found no hard evidence, learned nothing really new, only met with more rumors and metarumors on the subject.

I had not yet contacted or confronted Arthur on the subject. Fear? Prudence?) Magazines called and wrote but I declined all invitations, interviews. Slowly but surely I was rereading Ziff's large *oeuvre* of novels and stories, essays, memoirs. Nearly twenty books made it a rather daunting task. (My calls for any Ziff correspondence had produced paltry results.)

On the sun-filled day of the summer solstice I was writing away when I heard on public radio a promo pushing the Freddie Flynn *Bright Morning* show, and her guest for that day, on the eve of the reissue of his *Collected Stories*, Arthur Ziff. With some excitement and trepidation I got my tape recorder ready for the 4:00 P.M. interview. Not that I expected anything of real usefulness for me, but it would be amusing to hear Arthur handle Freddie, a panther swatting a fly. Amusing, and what else? . . .

After the opening introductory remarks ("Arthur Ziff is by now one of the two most recognizable writers in America," and here I projected coy Freddie adding, "and the only one who may have been 'jamming' the princess"), the host noted how much she had enjoyed rereading these stories since they first appeared. She then named a few of the tales and asked, "If you could change any of these stories and/or attitudes, how would you change them?"

Arthur responded coolly, "I'm a bit confused as to what you mean by 'could.' Of course I *could* have changed things in these stories if I'd chosen to, but if you'll allow me, I think they stand up pretty well. Perhaps technically I can improve on them, yes; but I feel that would be somewhat unfair to the youthful writer."

A slight giggle. "Well, have your attitudes toward these Jewish protagonists and characters changed? Or toward the Jewish people and traditional customs? After all, you do have a reputation among Jews that is, let's say, controversial."

"My, Freddie, but you've put so many questions into that question that I don't know which one to try to respond to."

"Well, you know what I mean—do you still view Jews in the same way as you did more than forty years ago?"

"But how did you see me as viewing them then—with a critical eye?"

"Yeah," she roared in her high lilt, "you can say that!"

"But it's my job as a writer to view things and people and beliefs with a critical eye," he retorted, having secured her in the trap. "Jews, too. Yet because I viewed them critically, that did not mean that I didn't value Jews highly, or love them." A pause. "But perhaps you'd be better off asking me specific questions about particular stories or characters."

A little laugh. "Well, at least you're living up to your rep as *one difficult interviewee*. Anyway, in "Horns of a Dilemma," your character Joshua Mulshin has this problem of deciding how to do his son's bar mitzvah, given his disdain for the rabbi. Here's what he thinks, quote, 'Can you imagine having to deal with these pontifical characters with their religious piety covering their crass asses just because they've been ordained? Who said the Jews weren't as stupid and vulgar as the next religion when it comes to hiring little bureaucrats to be His middlemen?' Now, my question is, Is that what you think, too?"

"Oh Freddie, come on," chastised Arthur in his best pedagogical voice, "you know well enough that what a protagonist thinks is not necessarily what an author thinks. The two are not exactly the same."

A hard cackle. "Now, don't go disingenuous on me. Are you not putting down Jews, rabbis, religion here? And do you not stand by that?"

"Joshua Mulshin is caught, as the title suggests, on the horns of a dilemma—on the one hand he wants his son to go through the ritual, and on the other he doesn't like the way the ritual is handled institutionally, especially by this rabbi. It's not a very complicated dilemma, you know. So he speaks his mind rather frankly, in an outpouring of frustration. Now, to equate my protagonist's thoughts during his emotional dilemma with my own thoughts on the issue is, as they say, a bit of a stretch."

Laugh of exasperation. "All right, all right. So you really have nothing against bar mitzvahs, just the rabbis, right?"

A moment of silence. "I'm sure you have other stories and specific questions, Ms. Flynn."

I listened to Freddie trying her best to articulate literary questions, and Arthur correcting her questions, her terminology, and then, once the question had been framed properly, answering adroitly, in fact giving a little education to anyone who cared to have one about how to read a story. This went on for two more stories, maybe seven or eight minutes more of a Ziff introductory class in the short story.

"In this late piece," Freddie pursued, " 'A Lesser Assimilation'—very clever title, by the way—David Lesser, a Jewish professor, is involved with Geena Swain, a WASPy financial consultant, and you write this: 'For David Lesser this was his way of committing himself, sleeping with the Other and therefore constantly reminded of his own tribal affiliation. It was a bizarre assimilation, to be sure, a reverse run, you might say, but it worked. And, for extra reward, he had learned more and more about the field of the Gentile, which, after all, was the only major playing field in town." Is that how *you* view Gentile women, Mr. Ziff, as well as the value of assimilation?"

A pause. "Freddie, is Flynn your real name?"

"*What?!*"

"Is Flynn your family's original name, or an adopted Americanized name?"

The pause was tense. "Well, that's rather irrelevant."

"Yes, I agree, it's the sort of personal question that is intrusive and uncalled for, similar to your question to me, I believe. Now, should you frame the question within the context of the story itself, and ask about David Lesser's views on these matters, that would be much more on target, more relevant."

Sighing perceptibly, Freddie called for a small break, repeated the name of her guest, and returned to the interview.

"Now, Mr. Ziff, while you have this new edition of *Collected Stories* out now, I'd like to ask you about two other projects, one by you and another *about you*. [*Uh oh. I trembled.*] Let's look at the former first. Is it true that you're working on a new book about the Jews, a kind of Holocaust blockbuster that will in fact blow away lots of past ideas and impressions about how you view them?"

I could feel the resigned smile. "Yes, I am working on a new novel, and yes, it does concern a Jewish theme, but that's about all I'm at liberty to say about it."

"Well, is it fiction or nonfiction, may I ask?"

"Let's say it's a little bit of both."

"How intriguing! Can't you give us a little something more, a kind of coming attraction? And will we have it by the end of next year, say?"

"Oh, I have no idea when I might have it ready for the publisher. As for a coming attraction, let's say that it is drawing upon all of my resources, and then some. It's a big, challenging project, yes."

But how did gossipy Freddie find out? A careful leak? With Ziff there were no *careless* leaks.

"Well, okay, since we can't get anything out of you on that subject," she commenced, "can you comment on the project *about you*, being done by an old friend of yours, Danny Levitan, himself a writer?"

Suddenly named, I felt like a co-conspirator, and held onto my armrests before pressing the eject button and parachuting out.

"All I can really tell you is that I know little about it," Arthur retorted. "I am not cooperating on that project, you know."

"What do you think of Danny Levitan? Didn't you use him as a figure in a book or two, in a rather derisive fashion?"

"Oh, Freddie, I know that *being provocative* can be a useful interviewing technique, but really. Mr. Levitan is a fine writer—an underrated one, I might add—and I hope he writes a fine book."

Ah, *clever,* that pat on my back!

"Look, Mr. Ziff, some people are saying that this book will be the real thing, a work that will reveal sides and truths about you that will be new and startling to your fans. And lead to a serious reevaluation of your life, and perhaps of your work. Another view is that this could be a work of writer's revenge, a kind of payback for some of the hits you've delivered to Mr. Levitan. Either way, it's obvious that he has known things about you that could be considered off the record, say, and remarkably . . .

embarrassing? How do you feel about it? Which path do you think he'll take?"

"Freddie," he said in exasperation, "I really think you should ask Mr. Levitan those questions, since I haven't the foggiest answer and, quite frankly, I don't much care. It's his book, not mine."

"Okay, that's an idea, maybe I will ask him those questions."

My heart fluttered crazily.

"But in the meanwhile, I'm asking you, Mr. Ziff: Is it not true that the biographer in question was once upon a time a great friend of yours, and therefore, as it is with all of us who have had good close friends, they might be privy to some uncomfortable stories, well-guarded facts? And that you, of all writers, have made such facts and tales about yourself a deep guessing game, an intentional puzzle, a multilayered mystery, which would make this book all the more . . . eagerly awaited, perhaps?"

Light laugh. "You mean to see if I really am, deep down, some sort of child molester or pedophile recidivist?" A cordial voice now, playful and easy. "Or maybe a secret synagogue-goer? A big contributor to Gush Emunim? Maybe a part-time Mossad agent? Or maybe even"—and he paused for effect—"an ex-lover of Madonna?"

Freddie laughed raucously. "In line, huh? Hey, that would be a hoot, wouldn't it?!"

"No, not really. You know, in fact, I lead a rather ordinary and dull life, early to bed and early to rise, writing my several hours daily. That would be the only real secret to be revealed."

"Oh, sure, I bet!" Giggle of disbelief. "Now let me turn to something else. It's been said by one or two literary critic friends of mine that the two best writers in America today are probably John Updike and yourself, but that neither of you is likely ever to win the big prize, the Nobel, because of the content of your books, especially the explicit sexual content. Do you feel that there is some truth in this observation? And if there is, do you think that's fair?"

"First of all, Freddie, the best writer in America today already has a Nobel Prize; his name is Saul Bellow. Second, though I'm flattered by your friends' assessment, I don't think it's appropriate for me to respond at all, since writing for prizes or thinking about prizes is beyond my scope."

Of course.

"Oh, come on, you can *say something* on the subject!"

"Something? Well, sure, I'll say this: No subject should automatically prohibit or deny an achievement, any more than a particular content by itself should affirm any achievement. Rather, it should be *the way a subject is treated, the care and devotion, the skill and the talent that are brought to bear upon particular material that count for literary accomplishment.* Do you see what I mean? Neither sexual extremity, nor political outrageousness, nor moral offensiveness should count if we are measuring a writer and a book, but rather literary sensibility and literary talent. Now, does the Nobel always look just in that literary area, so to say, look there and only there? No, I don't suppose so. But the judges are human beings, as fallible as we writers, so I won't presume to judge."

"Even though they may be severe in judging you!" she laughed at her own prescient remark. "Anyway, I want to thank you for your time, I know you don't give interviews often, and I want you to know that I enjoyed immensely your *Collected Stories.*"

"Why, thank you, that's very nice of you to say."

"I hope you'll come back and join me when your new novel comes out, or even when Mr. Levitan's biography appears."

"Well, let's take one step at a time."

"You've been listening to Arthur Ziff, whose new edition of *Collected Stories* is being reissued by Modern Library. And please stay with us. Coming up in the second half is a talk with Natasha K., the outspoken rock star from Moscow who is tearing up Europe with her latest CD, about to hit the charts here, *Western Perversities.*"

I turned off the radio and recorder and tried to digest it all, including Moscow rock. Hopeless, completely. Should I call Freddie and offer her the full scoop—unnoticed virtue, unreported dalliance? Or fax Ziff, call it quits?

In the next weeks I sat at the desk, planning, writing. To my surprise, my plugging away had now turned out some 225 pages of rough draft and many isolated paragraphs. The semblance of a life was unfolding.

A smart, willful boy devoted to ambitious learning and schooling, and rooted deeply in his Mattapan/Dorchester neighborhood and family. A literary star at Boston Latin in his teens, and then a Brandeis boy brimming with confidence and carving his own path. From high school youth onward he had a rather precise idea of his future as a serious writer. Meticulously organized, supremely driven, cuttingly witty and ironic, the dark, sturdy young man was powerful on the page and dangerous as a student. [Give that example of the sadistic trick he played on his sadistic, anglophile English prof who had belittled Arthur's work in class.]

Though he was a devoted son, and always contributed money to the household from youthful jobs—grocery clerk, delivery boy, movie usher, busboy—he also was an independent soul early on. On his own at fifteen he traveled down to New York, regularly taking the train from South Station to review various plays (*Iceman Cometh* with Jason Robards, an unknown *Six Characters in Search of an Author,* Bert Lahr/Alvin Epstein in *Waiting for Godot*). At sixteen he journeyed to Paris and London for two weeks. ('The French drink coffee with style, the English speak English with style.') At Fenway he made it a point to meet Dom DiMaggio, the Red Sox center fielder and Joe's little brother, interviewing the quiet 'Little Professor' for the student newspaper and comparing his fielding to Williams' hitting. In all things he was an independent soul, cultivating his own taste.

What he possessed early on was the desire, and the power, to record experience, and in the recording, to interpret its deeper meanings and seek out its full potential. Like young Wordsworth, whom he quoted at length in a *Paris Review* interview, young Ziff believed in the power of art to re-create experience and to discover there its redemptive truth and beauty. 'I want to bring order to chaos,' he wrote solemnly when he was a seventeen-year-old senior at BLS, 'and writing appears to be my surest path to do this. Only in art can the disorder of life find a pattern.' (Though later he would spin a different message: 'Writing for forty-odd years has taught me that art, far from bringing order, stirs up the full chaos and disorder of human lives and their experience.') In short, already as a teenager, he had a very precocious sense of a special mission.

Alongside this serious side ran a flourishing playfulness, a wild imagination, a mischievous personality. This young Arthur (unlike young Werther, say) was a keen ladies' man, an artful conversationalist, a lethal prankster (see above). Walking a fine line between moral rectitude and polymorphous play, he displayed very early a paradoxically firm but flexible self, it may be said. Gradually a Picasso of masks evolved, in which the same tension/equilibrium was solidified; later, in fiction, this Pimpernel of ego disguises served the writer well. Morality merged into aesthetics and vice versa; certitude and attitude mingled with contingency and modernist relativity; the result was a much more complicated and ambiguous sense of the moral self than the conventional one, in the protagonists and in the life.

I backed off, stood up, circled my study, and gazed out at the gray-blue skies lowering upon Mount Tug and Smarts Mountain. Where was I getting to? Was there a result I was heading for as yet unknown to me? A changing *raison d'être* for Ziff as well in all this?

My mind returned to Freddie Flynn's words (echoing Ziff's), asking if Danny Levitan was engaged in a Writer's Book of Revenge?

I needed to get this clear in my own mind, I felt, so in the next few days I decided to see a shrink and see what he—and I—came up with.

In Dr. Harry Friedman's wood-paneled office in Norwich, Vermont, I sat in a leather armchair and proceeded to lay out the groundwork of the odd situation. ("A first for me, too, I must tell you," the seventyish man said with a smile, "and I'm not sure you've come to the right office. Maybe it's a literary doctor you want?" he said kindly.) But in any case, the smooth-shaven man with gold-rimmed glasses and white hair listened intently, asking questions about my past, both family past and Ziff past. ("Does he resemble your father in any way, would you say?" "Not that I can think of." "Does Mr. Ziff have a volatile temper, too, perhaps?" "Well, no, his fuse is a slow one, you might say, though when it ignites it stays hot for a very long time." "Did you two share women friends at any point?" "Hmm . . . once I did have a girlfriend he had spent a night or two with, but he was never a boyfriend of hers." "Do you think he might have repressed his own deeper feelings about her and resented your attachment?" "Possible, but I don't think so. He was pleased, maybe amused, by my seeing her, and even encouraged me to write about it." "Did you?" "Yes, I did, but in the final draft of the novel, I removed the section." "Due to something Ziff had said?" "No, not at all. It was my call entirely.")

For the first week's two sessions we went through these sorts of circling preliminaries. In the second week he opened with, "Tell me: What are your feelings toward Mr. Ziff nowadays? Can you describe or articulate them?"

I paused. "Well, I guess my frankest response would be a kind of ambivalence. I admire and like very much many sides of him, and maybe less other parts. Sorry, not very original."

"Ambivalence, that's fair. Let's go to the writing. Has he injured you personally there, do you feel, and with intention?"

The late-afternoon sun reflected off his glasses. "I suppose the intentionality part is very difficult to assess. . . . Maybe one part has been intentional but another part . . . not."

"How do you mean, 'not'?"

"Well, as part of his overall satiric purpose in a particular novel, I was one of several, or many, portraits, say."

"And do you feel now the urge to get back at him in your book?"

Eyeing his credentials wall, I wondered if we writers needed our own wall, for self-certification. "I don't think so. I hope not." I questioned myself, "But maybe so?"

He nodded. "How is the work turning out, then? Can you tell from that?"

"You mean, is the biography an attack on him? I don't think so. In fact, if anything thus far, it's an *endorsement* of him. And what

I've uncovered, for the most part, is laudatory—*if certain things can be documented.*" I held out my hands.

"How about his work? Do you come down hard on that?"

The wooden-cased Swiss clock ticked away on a shelf. "No, not really. I criticize some books, some elements, and praise others. So . . . so far I *think* it's rather balanced. But who knows? Maybe I'm kidding myself, and you."

"Maybe, Danny. What would a general reader—like myself, say, who has read a few of Mr. Ziff's works—feel on reading your book? Anger or ridicule or mocking derisiveness at Mr. Ziff?"

"I don't believe so, not any of those feelings."

"Are you disclosing any facts or information that you know may be untruthful or intentionally harmful?"

I shook my head slowly. "I think I'm trying to contain—or mitigate, if anything—unpleasant news or nasty rumors that are or may be unverifiable or apocryphal."

He leaned back, crossed his arms. "Mr. Levitan, either you're a very capable liar, to me and to yourself, which is possible, or you know yourself very little, which is also possible. Or it may be that you are trying your best to write a fair biography, with all the pitfalls of subjectivity. I wish you luck."

"You mean? . . . "

"I mean"—he stood up, sighing—"you have my full approval to go forward without a guilty conscience. As far as I can see, you seem reasonably aware of your motives and the dangers, and if what you are writing approximates what you've been saying, then your resentment has been kept to a minimum, and you have a clean bill of health from me. As for the legal or literary bill," he laughed—with mirth or mischief?—"that's a whole other matter."

Did the doctor know something? I wondered, taking his hand. "One other thing, sir."

"What? 'sir,' " he teased me.

"Do you get the sense that I'm . . . *strong enough* to get through this? To write the book and then, later, handle the consequences?"

He eyed me directly. "Oh, I think you strike me, Daniel, as having reasonable ego strength, yes. Otherwise you wouldn't have come to me the way you have. And which consequences do you have in mind?"

"Oh, the loss of the friendship, for sure. And, as Arthur has warned, the probable nasty reviews from the literary community."

"Well, I think you're already distanced in the friendship, you might say. So a little more distance will not destroy you." He patted my shoulder. "As for the reviews, you can't predict those. And you're a pro, you've been through those before. So maybe that warning has some self-interest in it, to begin with? Reviews don't kill, do they?" He smiled benevolently.

I faced squarely the light blue eyes and sincere gaze and saw that he had little idea of the down and dirty literary wars. I silently repeated his query in my mind. *Do they kill?* Well, sometimes. And maybe the good doctor had little idea altogether of my "ego strength," or weakness.

"Good luck, Danny, and will you autograph my copy?"

"Sure." And I thanked him.

"By the way, do you have this much anxiety when you're just making things up, like when writing a novel?"

"I guess not."

"Good. Then just pretend you're writing a novel. Why not?"

"Yeah, why not?" I asked, too, though I think I knew the answer well enough.

I went home feeling cleared, as though I had come through a trial and been acquitted. I had a drink, watched the news—more Middle East troubles—and, after dinner, tracked to my study to check mail. Drowsy from the wine, I opted instead for a quick nap to energize myself. I lay down on my rug, my head on a small pillow, dozed. . . .

"Daniel, will you listen to something I once wrote?" came the sober voice of a faintly familiar bearded gentleman, who, I saw when I looked up, had seated himself in my armchair.

Alarmed, I sat up, holding my knees in my arms.

This figure read from my old Dell paperback *Six Great Modern Short Novels*.

"Now, envy and antipathy, passions irreconcilable in reason, nevertheless in fact may spring conjoined like Chang and Eng in one birth. Is envy, then, such a monster? Well, though many an arraigned mortal has in hopes of mitigated penalty pleaded guilty to horrible actions, did ever anybody seriously confess to envy? Something there is in it universally felt to be more shameful than even felonious crime."

Did he pause or did I, to gather the full import of those startling words from the startling apparition?

"And not only does everybody disown it but the better sort are inclined to incredulity when it is in earnest imputed to an intelligent man. But since its lodgment is in the heart, not the brain, no degree of intellect supplies a guarantee against it."

Here Melville stopped, looked up from the page, and nodded, just as little Gaby burst into the room, aflame with emotion: "I'm in big trouble Dad, with Mom!" Yet as he narrated his mischief, I replayed the words of the ghost of the somber writer, who had appeared—been summoned?—to deliver those dark sentences from *Billy Budd,* which struck me as harder wisdom than the lenient judgment of the day. "More shameful than even felonious crime" lodged within me.

In the evening, on e-mail, I found a new message from my friend in Budapest:

Dear Danny,
Although I have nothing new to add to your question about Mr. Z.'s possible affair with a celebrated lady, I do remember that Arthur once told me that he had written a novella for the "posthumous life," one he could say nothing about but that he had a special feeling for. And since I was to be his literary

executor, he wanted me to read it, after his death, and judge then its ultimate worth. If I thought it would hurt his reputation in any way, then I should simply destroy it. Do you think that this could have anything to do with your subject? Naturally, I thought this most unusual, but said nothing to him, then or afterward. That is all I know about the manuscript, and I'd prefer if you did not bring it up again.

Yours faithfully, Éva

A secret unpublished novella, reserved for posthumous judgment? That was very unlike Arthur Ziff, a writer for the here and now. How might I ever pursue it, *verify it?* Was it possible?

I sat down at the computer to try out a paragraph or two on the invisible affair and mysterious subject, paragraphs that also would remain invisible to the large world, off the printed page. I composed:

If the purported affair with Ms. G. K. did in fact happen, and it was not written about or at least not published by Arthur Ziff, then we have witnessed a first in his life. For in the past, no real event was too sacred for entry into Ziffian fiction; in fact, the opposite has been true. Why the secrecy now? What does it mean? And does this not alter our view of Ziff? (Further, does it not alter the American social and literary landscape as well? For if the Miller/Monroe marriage was the hottest crossover ticket in modern highbrow/lowbrow cultural theater, what, then, about the Kelly-Ziff relationship? What are we to make of that mysterious and astonishing coupling, the true WASP princess (albeit Irish Catholic) of elegant benevolence and beauty and the metaphorical Jewish prince of literary wickedness?

Again, we may ask: Did it happen? And will it reappear in a piece of literature, in the form of this secret manuscript? What did Arthur Ziff make of the romance? How did he interpret it? Through what imagined protagonist view it? If it was true that the chief Jewish writer of the post-WWII American era, who was most concerned with Jewish-Gentile relations, was intimately involved with the chief handmaiden of White Anglo-Saxon Protestant America, its reality and its dreams, then a literary fable about that involvement would be of supreme interest and fascination. [If, of course, the novella concerned that situation. But would it be secret otherwise, postmarked for a posthumous delivery?]

I reread my words and realized that they were a bit overwrought, somewhat melodramatic. Yet it was difficult not to be, with such loaded material. Would Arthur's new manuscript give a clue at all? Doubtful. Would Arthur himself allow a hint in person, perhaps inadvertently, by body language? Possible, but doubtful. But an interview had to be tried. Remember, as the Holocaust writer had warned, he was a man of miracles! And whenever you thought you had him figured, locked into a fixed identity, whoosh! There he went, escaped! Only to transform himself again, a postmodern Houdini.

When I informed ruddy-faced Pat of my unproven discoveries, my editor roared with amusement and skepticism. "Where are you getting this stuff, in Oz-land, the *X-Files*? It's wild, just wild!"

"I know." I nodded in sympathy, scooping Chinese noodles.

"Can it be documented, either of these things? A secret manuscript? That's charming enough, *if* it's earmarked for posterity. But how the hell are you going to tell?"

"Break into his studio and see if it's hidden there?"

His mouth opened, eyebrows raised for a full five seconds or so. "My God, you *are* kidding, aren't you?"

Was I? "Yes, I am," I confirmed.

"That would be something though, wouldn't it?"

"Yes, that would. Maybe a first ever literary burglary?"

He looked at me quizzically. "And as for news of the affair with the lady, well—" he shook his head—"*if you could document that, that would make the book very, very hot.*"

I leaned across and tapped the back of his hand. "But I'm afraid I'd never be able to write it down for print, *even if* I were able to document it—which is highly unlikely."

"Why?" he said, referring to my reluctance.

"Oh, for many reasons, including the legal. Chiefly I think because that would become an overriding focus of discussion in the reviews of the book. And the rest of the biography would be almost beside the point, marginalia." I smiled. "That's not why I'm writing my three or four hundred pages."

He nodded. "I see your point. On the other hand, you still have an obligation to find out the whole truth, if you can."

"True, and I will, if I can."

His blue eyes fixed me. "This has turned into a real adventure, hasn't it?"

I ate. "And it's not over yet."

He gave a little laugh. "You say that with a worried tone."

Sipping beer, I said, "Wouldn't you, if you knew that it wasn't over yet?"

twenty-one

During the next weeks of the summer drought I was doing several things at once: writing my three to four pages daily while considering underlying interpretative lines; still searching for hard evidence for the hearsay romance and that apocryphal novella; and keeping up with my other sources of biographical reference. Then there was the little matter of keeping up with my own life, such as putting in time with the boys, chores and pleasures. Also, deciding it was time to get some feedback—or hitback—I handed in 250 pages of manuscript to Pat for his perusal and comments.

A great writer needed a mission, I had written, and Arthur Ziff's mission of recent years, I thought, was to be a mature European writer here on his native American soil. This was no small ambition nowadays, where the turf was swarming with innocents and sensationalists, minimalists and mandarins, gross imitators, gothic romancers, ignoble savages. No, Ziff was not interested in making the *New York Times* bookchat culture page;

rather he wanted to create a body of work that was going to remain on record for a while—these days, a few decades, say?— and be remembered for its singular portrait of the (Jewish) writer/protagonist in America, as well as its critical look at the society in the last years of the twentieth century. And remembered, too, for its firm prose style: the increasing polish and hard fluency, the assertive determination to beef up the sagging paragraph and the texture of literary narrative, in an era of eroding interest in the force of realism. In other words, Arthur was not going to give in one iota to the fads, fashions, and meretricious notions of the day in literary circles. He was after the biggest prize of all, not the Swedish one, but a place in the gallery of American literary greats, alongside Melville and Hawthorne, James, Wharton and Dreiser, Faulkner, and Bellow. Would he make it? That remained for posterity—future readers, critics—to decide, but that was the ambition. (*If there were to be* future readers, not just video game players. . . .) Therefore his work needed to be framed and read within that large aim.

I wondered: Would the apocryphal novella add to the oeuvre or subtract from it? Where and how might it surprise? How would the famous characters be portrayed, camouflaged, altered? Would its chief interest be as a roman à clef, or something much deeper, richer? Indeed, would that enticing work, *if it existed,* open up yet another piece of new territory for this ever-original novelist? . . . And would it change seriously one's view of the life, of the man himself? These were intriguing questions, which remained to be investigated. (*Maybe a break-in was not so loony, for the sake of real answers?*)

As I said, I kept up with the rituals of my daily life with a seaman's rectitude. The same mix of cereals and sliced banana for a breakfast of texture; yogurt, nuts, and fruit combo for my monkey's lunch; the dinners wide open, as long as they included red wine and green salad. My two or three weekly tennis matches (despite tennis elbow), two-and-a-half-mile walks, bicycle rides accompanying Gaby (and Jon) back and forth on the bumpy dirt road (or swimming in the pond while Gaby screeched and splashed). And the puttering around outside, in the garden helping Becka, or mowing, or maintaining the clay court. At the center, the five solitary hours in the depths of the writing mines, laboring, tapping away, scratching for pay dirt. Days of boredom, hours of beauty—my rituals of necessity. A dull life at fifty-nine—and a failed life, too, right?—especially alongside the brilliant, ingenious, and evolving life I was writing about. (Or imagining?)

Just after Labor Day two things occurred: Jeanne L. was publishing her memoir of life with A. Z., and she was coming to New York to promote the English-language edition. And Éva was coming over, too, to see Arthur and to attend a literary conference in New Mexico. (ISCLT, the International Society for Contemporary Literature and Theater, met yearly, usually in Europe. How poignant, a loyal band of a hundred literary pilgrims trekking around the world to talk books!) Would I be able to see them? (Perhaps, as Éva asked about a day with Arthur *and* me.)

The reviews of Jeanne's memoir were 99 percent gossip, 1 percent critical prattle. Endless magazine babble about the "explosive collision of two cultural superstars, two cultures." Before reading her book, I had wanted to finish a relevant section in my own manuscript. When I did read it, I breathed easier. No danger to me in "My Ten Seasons in Hell"—no probing inquiry about two lives, no hard facts of the intimate life. Rather the familiar litany of complaints about Ziff's arrogant, bullying ways, Mme.'s victimization, his lack of respect for her work, et cetera. Little new, little insightful. As I expected, the diary had been much too personal, too hot, for Jeanne to assimilate and translate into public view. Hence no talk of compulsive masturbation, voyeurism, cunnilingus, bondage games. I understood, even sympathized. A great actress was not a serious writer. Besides, all of her really valuable material needed to be borne aloft, by the wings of fiction (or biography?); the house of autobiography was much too proper, self-protecting.

To her note asking me what I thought, I replied that it was "a most interesting tale." What else could I say?

Yet the memoir was useful for me in a couple of ways; it cleared the path for me to say what I wished in my own book, without having to contradict Jeanne, and it gave me an easy and immediate reason to contact Arthur now. Jointly we could mock the ridiculous hoopla and publicity concerning the book.

Meanwhile, I had turned up someone interesting in Somerville, Massachusetts, a fellow named Ernie "Bo" Strevens. A desk clerk at the Sheraton Commander Hotel in Cambridge back in the 1970s, he had kept a detailed journal of the comings and goings of guests, I had discovered. Why? For blackmail? Anyway, I had arranged a meeting.

Pat called to report to me about the manuscript and said, "I think we can discuss it in full when you come down to Boston; the lawyers for Emerson want to have a little powwow with us. Okay?"

Stunned. "Huh? What's going on?"

"A 'precautionary meeting,' they claim, so I wouldn't worry."

"Should I bring up my own lawyer from New York, that pal of Larry Tendler's, as a 'precautionary measure'?"

A little laugh. Pat said, "I wouldn't. No need to make it adversarial unless it's necessary. Let's just hear them out."

"Well, at least you'll be there, acting as my second."

"Just don't come out swinging, remember."

At the offices of Emerson House in downtown Boston, Pat and I sat down at a long conference table opposite the pair of corporate lawyers, James Sweeney Jr. and Charles Everitt. The atmosphere was cordial, beginning with the opening polite chatter. "Do let's use first names," Everitt said, shaking my hand firmly, "we're all on the same team here."

I smiled inwardly at the platitude, the falsehood, and pictured him with a team cap—Harvard Law (HL), or Emerson House (EH)?

Sweeney was a cherub-faced blonde of about forty-five. "Well, we look forward very much to your heralded book. The whole firm is quite excited about it. In fact"—he lowered his voice—"there's even a buzz going around about it winning a Pulitzer!"

I took the stroking in stride. "I wouldn't bet the house on it. Or my advance."

Small laughs. "You never can tell, can you?" opined Charlie Everitt, tall, lean, graying, tanned; Maine sailing, I figured. "And Ziff is a really great character to write about. I've read a few of his books, they're quite . . . audacious!"—he smiled at his word— "and certainly they make you curious, and even wonder an awful lot about the man himself."

"Well, in any case," put in Sweeney pleasantly, "we just want to run through a few basics with you now, beforehand, so there's no chance of a misunderstanding later, when you hand in the completed manuscript."

I asked. "Is this usual procedure for your authors?"

" 'Jim,' please," beckoned Charlie amiably. "Usual procedure? Oh, I don't think there is such an animal when it comes to books, Dan. But, to speak candidly, perhaps this is a bit unusual—though it's not surprising given the highly charged subject you've chosen. And we have had a preliminary letter of inquiry from Ziff's attorney."

Aha, so it's started! I took a few deep breaths.

Now the pair began talking about public and private life in America, the differences between British libel laws and ours, what constituted invasion of privacy, etc., and Sweeney brought up that curious term again. I interrupted him softly. "Highly charged? Arthur Ziff is not exactly a double agent who worked both sides of the fence, and I've produced startling new evidence of the agents he's done in. He's a literary man, that's all."

"That may be the case," interceded Charlie Everitt, "but still there are legal matters involved when you're dealing with a real life, even if he is a public figure, a celebrity."

He smiled benignly, and I wondered again if it was indeed a "real life" I was dealing with. Or was it more tricky than that?

"After all," said Everitt, "your research may turn up, how shall I say, shocking allegations that may not be supported by actual facts."

Sweeney added, "And which Emerson House may be responsible for."

"Well," I acknowledged, "I think I understand that. The difference between allegation and fact, I mean."

"Good, good, that's all we're reminding you of," Charlie cheered. "To have all supporting evidence for your claims."

"Yet I'd be amiss here," Sweeney persisted, "If I didn't also remind you of the indemnification clause in your contract. In other words, *you are responsible* if there's litigation involving points of libelous information in the book." He fixed me squarely. "I'm only saying this, again, as a prudent precaution."

Taken aback by this, I mumbled, "Sure."

"Here, let me read you this, it bears your signature, I believe?" He held out to me, or waved, the book contract, and I, somewhat dazed, nodded, as though this legal sheet of paper with my signature on it were a confession of guilt.

Then he took back the pages and began reading, in a neutral but firm voice: " 'Section 2. Author's Warranty: The Author warrants that he is the owner of all the rights granted to the Publisher hereunder; that the Work is original and is not in the public domain; that to the best of his knowledge it does not violate the right of privacy of any person; that it is not to the best of his knowledge libelous or obscene; and that it does not infringe upon the statutory or common-law right of anyone.' " He looked up at me—to check if I were still sitting, breathing?—and continued: " 'In the event of any claim, action, or proceeding against the Publisher by anyone else, based upon any violation of the foregoing warranties in connection with the publication or sale of the Work, (a) the Publisher shall have the right to defend the same through counsel of its own choosing; however, the Author may join in such defense with counsel of his own choosing at his own expense, and (b)' "—he coughed, and I knew I should have brought Larry's pal up from New York to be with me—" '(b) the Author shall hold harmless the Publisher and any other seller of the Work against any damages finally sustained in any such action or proceeding or by way of settlement, provided, however, that no settlement shall be effected without the prior consent of the Author.' "

He paused momentarily, fixed me, then went on, and I was already replaying some of the sentences in the warranty, about the right of privacy, etc., wondering if I should confess verbally right there and then. " 'If any claim, action, or proceeding is instituted, the Publisher shall promptly notify the Author and may withhold payments due him under this agreement between the Publisher and Author to be held in an interest-bearing account. In the event no legal action or proceeding is instituted or imminent within twelve months from the receipt of a claim, the Publisher shall release all withheld sums.' "

Of course, in my case it would mean returning all the money. And return the Saab, too?

" 'These warranties and indemnities shall survive the termination of this agreement.' "

In other words, I was forever indemnifying them?

He laid the paper aside, and, like a thoughtful judge in button-down striped shirt and tie, awaited my reaction.

For a long minute there was silence, broken only by the sounds of the cars. I half expected to be sentenced. Though I had signed at least half a dozen book contracts over the years, all of which probably contained such clauses, I had never heard one read aloud to me directly; the result was a quivering of my legs and a congestion in my chest. I tried to conjure up a few of the scenes to be declared off-limits, of my book, but immediately stopped; it was too perilous. I sat there, limp, looking at the clock on the wall, the fine wood paneling.

After what seemed like ten minutes instead of one, Pat said, "Well, it's standard stuff, no more no less. Right, gentlemen?"

"Oh, yes, standard stuff," retorted Charlie. "We just wanted to make sure your client—I mean *our author*—understood clearly what the lines were, and what to avoid." He smiled affably.

"Oh, I think he does, he's been through this before many times," asserted Pat casually. "Right, Danny?"

I nodded, and eked out the word "Right." My head and the room were swimming now.

"Good!" chimed in Sweeney. "I'm glad we're all on the same playing field on this. We don't want someone going out of bounds on us and then claiming, later, that he didn't know the rules."

"I'm sure we'll have no problems whatsoever," said Everitt, standing. "By the way, any date yet for a finished manuscript?"

I sat there, exhausted, and couldn't dream of completing anything.

"Maybe another six months?" Pat ventured for me. "Or a year?"

"Terrible question to put to an author, I know!" teased Charlie. "But as I said, we all look forward to it exceedingly! It'll be on top of my list!"

They shook my hands, patted my shoulder, helped usher me out as though the ordeal, the (first) trial, was over, and there was nothing more to worry about. I felt weakened, exposed.

Pat and I strolled out together. The sun peeked forth from beneath heavy clouds. A sign?

I asked, "What the hell does a 'preliminary letter' mean? A warning, eh? And do you think they were squeezed by someone on the phone as well? Christ."

"Don't get paranoid now. I'll check on the letter."

I nodded sadly, remembering Delmore Schwartz. "Even paranoids have their enemies. Right?"

Huge cranes and one-ton trucks and yellow hard hats were moving and digging everywhere, carving up the streets of Boston. I observed them with unusual interest.

"You behaved well, restrained yourself. Good."

I smiled. "Did I? Just fear, and paralysis. What words, obscenities! It's not enough we have to write the fucking books, but then we have to be blackmailed and insulted by corporate jerks. Whew, what an occupation. Well, maybe restraint, or fear, *in there,* will mean more freedom, more gutsiness, inside the book. If so, fine. Do you think they'll actually read it?"

He shrugged. "Depends on how long it is."

"For prurient reasons, if at all. Well, maybe I can get some pornographic scenes in it, featuring a few respectable lawyers out for some fun? That should wake them up."

"Hey, watch it!" Pat pulled me as a car veered by. "Just don't get any fanciful ideas."

The federal judge who was coming to town for a conference and for dinner with me had been, some thirty years ago, an ex-student, dropped from Mount Holyoke for smoking marijuana. I had met her in 1969 in a Cambridge laundromat reading Jane Austen, and

I talked with her out of curiosity. Tall, wild-frizzy-haired, sloppily clad in jeans and sweater, she was reading *Emma* for pleasure, not a paper, and professed a passion for reading. When we discussed the novel, I was taken by her observations and asked if she wanted to write an essay on the book, as I was a literary prof and maybe could help her. After her amazement she said sure, and a week later I received at my office eight well-written, intelligent pages. She showed a real sensibility. On the telephone I asked her to do a paper on George Eliot, and lo and behold in two weeks I received ten handwritten pages on *Middlemarch*. Once again, first class. This kid belonged back in college, without a doubt, and so, in the next few months, after several more essays and two more discussions (she came from a Boston suburb and a crazy Italian contractor father family), I wrote several letters recommending her. Sure enough, by midterm she had been accepted back into school, not prissy Holyoke, but the University of Vermont. "Why are you doing this for me?" she asked, bewildered. "Austen and Eliot need their readers," I answered glibly, not really knowing the answer myself, especially since I had stayed clear of romancing her.

Anyway, she had worked her way up through college, Emory Law ("Litigation, Criminal"), lawyer, and then, of all things, judge. Through the years she had stayed in touch by card or handwritten letter, even paying a visit some fifteen years before to New Hampshire. About five years ago she had been appointed to the federal bench in Atlanta, and here she was, visiting town for a three-day conference. Was I free for dinner? At Sweet Tomatoes trattoria in Lebanon, we chatted and I tried to *see* the bedraggled student in the current judge. The hair was shorn and bleached dirty blond, the facial skin was pulled taut, the nose was sharper, more Roman, the trim figure was clothed in a dark velvet suit and white blouse, her shoes were low-heeled patent leather. The disheveled college kid had become a respectable middle-aged adult, very respectable.

As we talked, I realized that one of my more obscure reasons for wanting to see Diana Cappelli was her high legal status; for some reason I felt I'd benefit from the proximity, Ziffwise, now or later. Over chicken cacciatore (me), linguine, bluefish (her), I asked what sitting on the bench was like. "Well, most of the time I miss not being able to write letters while I'm up there, it would be very convenient." I laughed, and pushed her to tell me about some of her trials. Drinking a glass of wine, she narrated a long, intricate murder tale concerning a gay doctor (Jewish), a drug-dealing carpet owner (also gay), and the brutal beating to death of a black man at an Atlanta party. What made the case so Byzantine, for starters, was the fact that the carpet boss filed for a mistrial based on the fact that his lawyers had been in on the drug dealings and therefore couldn't have represented him honestly. They, on the other hand, claimed that client-lawyer privilege would make that charge inadmissible in court. Now as she went on explaining the Byzantine tangle, I saw the same quick, animated intelligence of the young woman who had discussed *Emma* three decades ago: "To tell you the truth I didn't quite know how to handle the whole thing, so I went down to the fourteenth floor and asked my mentor, Melvin Cohen, what to do. He's the brightest legal mind I know, and he helped sort things out. So it worked out, and I was very proud of the decision I wrote. Would you like to read it sometime?" "Sure," I said, eager to see how the prose style analyzing Austen performed on a murder case.

I asked her how she had become a judge in the first place, and she explained, without pretense or apology, the political clout of her ex-husband, a crazy, shrewd Hispanic who had migrated north from Miami. And when she was nominated for federal judge, it was none other than Jesse Helms who had put a "hold" on her because of the FBI report that pointed out her tainted drug days of the 1960s. "I made it with five minutes to go in the year," she proudly exclaimed. "Sixty-six others of the Clinton era didn't."

In the car, slightly high and enchanted by the combination of the original twenty-year-old student and the forty-eight-year-old woman, I started the engine and took her in my arms. My kiss was meant to say, "I'm delighted to see you, and to see how well you've done." To my surprise, she returned the kiss with full-tongue ardor, and I found myself drawn into a whole other scene.

In the four-poster bed at the old-fashioned inn, she was passionate and uninhibited. "It's so good to be with you like this," she whispered, running her fingernails along my flanks. "If only you knew how long I've waited for you to be back in my life again." Were these commonplace words true? Was this where I was, I thought, back in her life because of this impulsive action? Holding me fiercely and moving with abandon, she was soon crying out so loudly that I had to cup her mouth and caution her to go easy, easy. Her trim figure fit mine well, she was calling my name intermittently as we fucked, and I felt the tender care of thirty years before emerge surreptitiously, as though it were not merely this older woman I was with, but that hungry, pristine kid, too. Erotic scents wafted upward, mingling memories, and I conjured up a balloon of swirling time raising up our younger bodies for a weightless half hour and then parachuting our older selves down slowly. She kissed me repeatedly ("You saved my life, you know, as I've told you so often!"), and I held her close, feeling a protective warmth.

Somewhere in my drifting thoughts, I also sensed my old pal as a possible ally in any future war with the lawyers (A. Z. or publisher). *Was it her turn to save my life now?* As the land mine planted slyly in my unconscious exploded comically, I kissed her cheek, aware of my paranoid follies, fantasies. (Should I e-mail her later on for names of her judge friends in Boston/New York?) "We won't lose touch again, will we?" she implored, and I nodded my head in firm agreement, though I hoped I would never need her.

What would account for the schizoid tendencies in Mr. Ziff? I refer to the honorable schoolboy, playing by the old-fashioned rules—meritocracy over ethnicity, achievement over self-promotion—and the Jewish guerrilla boy, attacking from behind every bush. On the one hand the urbane, witty, intelligent writer who is the most civilized of fellows at the dinner table, and the no-holds-barred bounty hunter of personal lives, the professor of the extreme life? (He didn't have a subject, he had a target.) Why the profound transfer, and might we locate the psychological transfer station?

Let me speculate here and use D. H. Lawrence's dictum, namely that within every writer there is a male and a female side. [I was not going to employ here the hearsay remarks about occasional cross-dressing; hearsay from Arthur to me, of course, but still, hearsay. As Pat would ask, where's the evidence, Danny?] Biographically speaking, Arthur was his mother's boy, as I've intimated earlier, and one resulting consequence of that devoted attachment was, surprisingly perhaps, a lifelong cherishing of the female. On the other hand, there would emerge a rather disdainful, even savage, reaction against the weaker male figure (the father). Inevitably the repressed dam in the man would give way, and release a steady river of critical sentiments in the novels. [Cite here Kurt Eissler's study of Goethe and the sister attachment. And show, too, in the fiction how this sentiment is translated.]

Now, in our current era of ideology, the question may be put, Is there a homoerotic element operating in all this? My own response to this is the following: The question itself is framed inappropriately. For what is of real matter and pertinence are the uses made out of various impulses and tendencies by the artist in the work, rather than a critical judgment of the artist by an abstract formula of gender rightness. Let me be specific here. In the scene where M. Goldfeld dresses up like a woman—a three-page scene of meticulous detailing—and then goes for a night walk in downtown Boston, stopping by Shreve's and entertaining, for a few minutes, an attempted pickup by a well-dressed male, we have a portrait of pain, humor, and poignancy. The psychological adventure and the memorable near-rape that occur are the products of a startling imagination; what is crucial is the element of credibility in those remarkable scenes. In other words, the judgment of the scene should have less to do with ideological correctness and more to do with artistic excellence. And there is little doubt that the turning of Goldfeld's inward disturbance into a situation of near-ridicule-disaster is managed with tonal delicacy and professional aplomb.

Just as we may say, with some certainty, that these fantastic pages could not have been written by a male artist who did not possess within him much of the female in understanding, impulse, and drive. [Add now the actual cross-dressing? But how? And how to verify it???]

The slipping into the soul and body of the female has been managed before at an external, formal distance by other writers, to be sure; but nowhere else has this 'slipping into' transformation been done with such intimate skill and authenticity as in the portrait of Manny Goldfeld breaking down and traipsing about in padded bra, panty hose, eyeliner, and rouge, on the streets of his youth. It is one of the superbly artistic scenes sculpted by Ziff, his homage to Mann's Aschenbach, 'Goldfeld in Boston.'

twenty-two

At Ziff's house, by his invitation, we were eating pasta and Swedish meatballs courtesy of Bigan, his physical therapist and recent weekend buddy (though he had known her longer).

"I had no idea this was so elaborate," I said. "A version of *cholent*. Must take hours to make."

"What else do you think they do in Malmö?" observed Arthur, "except cook, fuck, and wait for the mail to come?"

"You are very amusing," Bigan retorted casually, a big-boned, light-blond woman of midthirties. "Arthur has an agent in Malmö, you know? I am glad you like the dish. He will never eat it."

I nodded, savoring the rich mix of veal, pork, beef meatballs.

"Do I taste beer in here also?" Arthur nibbled at his broiled fish.

"And did you know they saved Jews there, too?" Arthur added. "No kidding. Explain it, dear."

"Oh, it is not such a big deal, relatively speaking. At our local convent they took in Jewish women from Poland I know, and kept them there until the end of the war. Pretended they were Catholics."

"Really. How many?" I asked.

"Several hundred, maybe near a thousand altogether. And a few thousand in other parts perhaps. Before my time, you know." Her wide smile revealed prominent cheekbones. Altogether her face was filled with wide, ample spaces, in the cheeks, forehead, chin.

"How did you know about it?"

She shrugged. "Oh, we knew in childhood, but also Mother told us all about it when she spoke of the war."

"And what happened to them?"

"Many went to Palestine, during the illegal emigration, before '48. Some, not too many, stayed and married Swedes." She gave me a second helping.

"Don't be modest now, tell the whole story," Arthur said. "It took nearly a year before I learned that her grandmother has a tree planted in her honor in Jerusalem as a Righteous Gentile. Sometimes the Jews get it right, but not often!"

"Oh, Arthur, please." Bigan brushed his poor humor aside again and poured wine for all of us.

"Please, Daniel, some cabbage?"

"Well, I'm not really too wild about cabbage."

"Oh? Have you tried it with flax oil? You should, I believe."

"Listen to her, honest," Arthur nodded. "She'll make you a new man. Look at me, resurrected before I hit seventy!"

"Excellent for the skin. Here," and she served me. "Tell me how you like it."

When I looked at Arthur for aid, he held up a forefinger, cautioning me.

I followed orders and tasted it. I had had worse. "Not too bad," I offered generously. "Better than the old cod-liver oil."

Arthur shook his head. "Jewish wiseguy, that's all."

"Well, next time I'll give you it with tamari oil, heh?"

"Oh, sure," I said, and vanquished the taste with the wine.

"We don't get the essential fatty acids, you see. Anyway, I have much work to do," she said, standing. "I'll leave you two and see you a bit later, hey?" She gave me a little bow and pecked Arthur on the cheek.

"What kind of work?" I asked before she departed.

"Working on her repression and neurosis. What else do Swedes work on?"

Bigan shook her head. "*You* are the wise guy. I study nutrition now, at night of course. A bit late in life, but . . . it's quite fascinating. See you later for a dessert, maybe?" And she exited.

"Nutrition, on top of . . . all that?" I put. "Didn't I see her in one of the old Bergman movies?"

He gave a little laugh. "She's something, isn't she? First she repairs my pinched nerve and atrophied muscle, which the doctors failed to do for ten years, and then she takes on my life. From soup to nuts, including complexion. Bigan Lisolette Anderssen from Malmö."

"If I go over, can I find a sister?"

"Sorry, but the sisters are taken. How about a brother? There's one of them left, I think. And you know what?" He winked mischievously. "He's even better-looking."

I paused and tried out, "And I thought Éva from Budapest was rather terrific."

"Oh, that's right, you met her. Yes, she is rather terrific actually. But fifteen years past prime. And a tortured soul."

I nodded. "Yes, I heard the story. Quite moving. Like her devotion to you."

Eyebrows raised momentarily, then an enigmatic smile. "Decaf espresso? Why not?" He began setting beans in a small, elegant European machine.

"Actually, I found out many surprising things when I was over there. As I think I told you on the phone, astonishing things."

"Oh, really?"

"Yes, really. Do you want to hear a few?"

He gave off a little laugh. "Oh, you're free to speak here, you know. Though I am wired, you should know that." He pointed at the ceiling light fixture. "Go ahead, tell me what you want."

"Well, for one, I found out about your Wallenberg Institute on the Internet," I began and went on to give a brief rundown of the letters I had seen (I left out my quick trek to Jerusalem). Soon the steam machine was hissing and emitting little explosions, like a miniature battle. "What do you think?" I asked, concluding.

"It's ready," and he proceeded to pour our espressos into two demitasse cups. "It's not Budapest or Prague, but it will have to do." He brought them to the round oak table and served us.

"Is it true, then, you behave very differently over there?"

He sipped, swallowed, sat back. "You are persistent, aren't you? But don't you get it? I'm not cooperating. This is your bag, your book. I'm out of it. Absent, away."

I sipped, too, and crossed my legs. "Fair enough. You're my subject on paper only, but not here. It's a nice little wrinkle isn't it? You're *only real there.*"

He eyed me and sipped some more. "Whatever you say."

"I'll add only one other thing: The way my book is going, it's making you much bigger, grander, than you appear to be, or were thought of previously. Not grander perhaps than you thought of yourself, but grander than others might have thought. Or even wished."

A slow, wry smile. "I think you're trying to flatter me somehow. There's no need, really. None at all. Do what you have to do, say what you have to say, and see what happens. I've offered you my cautions before. Now, what else shall we talk about? Madame Lemaire's refined memoir and her impeccable memory?"

On impulse I asked, "Tell me: Did you really take Jeanne to that bondage parlor in Manhattan, where she dragged me?"

His eyes narrowed for a moment, his smile was ambiguous, he sipped. "You know, I'm going to allow that one, to show you my tolerant spirit. Jeanne's second marriage, as you know, was to a famous English actor, a bad drunk and near psychotic who used to beat her—for 'erotic purposes,' of course—and who persuaded her into anything way out. From drugs to taking her to that East Side 'Japanese-style' rope joint. Well, she hauled me there one night, complaining I was so staid and conventional, I was a bore, a hypocrite. So I accompanied her." He nodded. "She got off on it, too."

"And you: How did you like it?"

Stern, then relaxed, he said, "How was it? Not without its

interest. I liked the music, Ellington's 'Mood Indigo,' as I recall. The instructor had taste. Look, I'll tell you once again, anything you ever hear or read from that woman, on the subject of her and me, take the opposite as the truth. The complete opposite. I told you a long time ago, she's not merely furious at me, but a raving neurotic, pathological liar, and an actress. She will make something up, and a half hour later, she'll believe it's a fact. Do you understand? Until you see and feel the mechanism operating, you can't believe it. Look, I'm starting to shake, get hot, even now, a few years later! More coffee?"

Then, as he proceeded to parody the book and mock the tattle about it, I tried to consider my options. But I quickly felt that I had few, other than to push forward, push through, and let the chips fall where they might. Besides, I felt, laughing at a bit of humor, his "No" meant I was writing a freer, more unauthorized biography than otherwise, a great advantage. I was admiring the view from the kitchen through the long living room and out into the fields and meadow when Bigan reappeared and announced that she had made "ris alamalta" for our desserts. Were we ready for them?

"Sure," Arthur said, taking her onto his lap, "and later, if I'm very good, will you help me get into my Dr. Dentons before tucking me in?"

She slapped him playfully and got off.

Later, about nine-thirty, with Arthur and Bigan retiring early, I was sitting in the thick, cushioned armchair reading the *Times* and drifting off with Safire running the Sharon cheering squad for the six-hundredth time. Suddenly I was seized by a wild idea, or better, a hot impulse, jolting me awake, head spinning. Dare I? . . .

I knew if I waited too long and considered the proposed act, I wouldn't do it. Too irrational, dangerous, foolish.

Quietly I walked out of the room, found my pocket flashlight in my overnight bag, and slipped out the back door. The air was cool, the cicadas were chorusing, and I waited to adjust to the near pitch darkness. After a minute, listening, I proceeded, on the grass where possible, and glancing upward at the large farmhouse for lamp light. Good boy—in bed for his early *schluffin*. Within 150 feet I was standing at the entrance to the writing studio. I didn't think the front door would be left unlocked, and it was not. Carefully shielding my small beam, I walked around the wood-shingled one-floor bungalow, checking the windows. The three I came across in front and side were shut securely. At one point my foot suddenly sank in a small hole, twisting my ankle!

I cursed and moved through the shrubs around to the back of the house. The first window was closed, too, but the second, in the far corner, was actually ajar several inches. Seeing its height, I looked about, found a good-size rock and a few old boards. Laboring, I pulled over the boards and set them on the flat rock for an extra inch or two. Raised on my lift, I was able to reach the window. Opened four inches, propped by an old-fashioned accordion-type bug screen, the window was easy enough to push open, way upward, while maneuvering the screen out. Exerting myself, I boosted myself up, getting one knee onto the sill, then the other. Balancing the flashlight, I realized I was landing in the bathroom—maybe the reason for the window left open in the first place. Dropping down inside, I banged my head on the window and felt somewhat exhausted, bruised. No blood, however. Now my heart began to beat wildly as I realized with a shock where I was and what I had done.

Slowly, carefully, I made my way into the large main study, where I knew Arthur did much of his writing for six or seven months of the year. Not much had changed, though to be here now was very strange. Rows of bookshelves, the main desk and the files, the stand-up desk, the handsome pine walls, and the old photographs. Though I knew the place from the old days, it now felt like coming into old Matadi in Central Africa. Was I still an ordinary citizen, with rights and protections, or a biographer out of control, an out-and-out criminal? My thumping heartbeat gave me the answer!

Meticulously I began my search for that apocryphal novella, starting with the desk, the second desk, the open vertical wood file. I kept my light beam as low as possible, just in case, and hoped that the batteries were as good as on the bunny commercial. Next, onto the standard filing cabinets, three in the corner, which would be a monster to go through. Taking a throw pillow for my knees, I knelt there and began to investigate. Just then, a creaking floor noise, then a scuffling sound, and my body froze. I waited, and heard a quick scattering in the attic. Mice at play, Danny in panic.

Back into the files. In a horizontal cabinet, alongside an old copier, legal-size folders, a financial section (banks, muni bonds, mutual funds), a large correspondence section, IRS and CPA files, property taxes (town), Legal. . . . Another section, foreign rights, 1990s fan letters (four files worth on various books), Awards and Honors, Honorary Degrees, Friends' Crits, Journalism (pieces), Interviews (three sections), Contracts (four files' worth). . . . In the second cabinet I found manuscripts; I shut my light, listened . . . all well, I began my search there. Speeches, articles, short stories, the long list of the novels. . . . In another row, I found the Discarded section and grew encouraged. I opened each file, hoping against hope. . . . Fortunately I knew what I was looking for, in length at least; a novella-size manuscript anywhere from 50 pp to 175 pages. But no luck—nothing I found was on target, either in length or in subject. I kept searching. . . . My watch read 11:10 and I was thirsty, sleepy, fatigued.

I stood, my knees creaking, gazed about inquiringly, and discovered an adjoining kitchenette, added on since I had been there. At the faucet I craned my neck and gulped a long drink of water, avoiding a glass carefully. Splashed my forehead, my face, cooling off. At some point, I told myself, I must call off the mad search. But not yet. A wash cloth dabbing, careful refolding, then back to the mines of manuscripts.

Ten more minutes of futility. Near my end. In the bottom row of files in the last cabinet I saw a curious file labeled "Dead Letter File." A borrowing from old friend Bartleby (the Scrivener), one of our favorite subjects of discussion. In a daze of exhaustion I opened the surprisingly thick file and found inside a manila envelope containing, within that, a typed manuscript titled, "A

Fateful Affair." I sat down legs crossed on the floor and skimmed the first lines with my krypton beam. "In the obscure ways that fate hooks us up with a destiny unforeseen—a fate so very contrary to that declared centuries ago by Heraclitus—I first met her. In this case, fate was a matter of contact lenses, and a mutual optometrist in Cambridge, Mass. . . ." At this point I paused, my breath coming fast, to wipe clean my eyeglasses with Kleenex. Knowing I could not read the whole work with a flashlight, I stood up, looked about in the shadowy darkness, and tried to figure out the best, safest spot to read it. For I knew clearly this was it, now or never. . . .

In that same barnboard bathroom in the back of the studio, on the folded-down toilet seat, beneath a sixty-watt bulb, I proceeded to read "A Fateful Affair" reading it in an alert trance.

In that unlikely site, with the small cone of light, I read intently, swiftly, checking my watch periodically. The book was a small novel, maybe 150 pages, and I knew I didn't have the time to go through it thoroughly. The tale mesmerized me, not simply because of Ziff's usual attention to the perfect detail, the strong sentence, but also because the content was so surprising and original even for Arthur Ziff. What I mean is that the full Ziffian irony was set up against the writer himself—not the usual halfway measures—and the tale was a love story, so you had irony working alongside real passion. Ziff, the great ironist at others' expense, was here criticizing himself, implicitly and explicitly, as he narrated this grand affair, this passion of his adult life. It is a tale so secret that he acknowledges, early on, that he will forgo publishing this story:

> I will write it because it compels me, but it shall remain with me in ms., until and perhaps after my death, a manuscript, not a book. For reasons that perhaps will become obvious. And thus the sharpest irony: the truthful passion of my life will remain a private affair, and not be subject to my greedy artistic alter ego, who, like some hungry shark, waits for me to live my life so it

can immediately devour the experience. No, no feeding
this time. . . .

But the biggest shock was that it had nothing to do with the
alleged celebrity romance. Had that been a Ziff smokescreen, an
elaborate disguise, for the real thing? The story—or memoir—still
in draft stage, concerned a famous writer named Arthur Ziff, who,
in middle age, meets by chance at an optometrist's shop in Cambridge, Mass., a young lovely dark-haired lady while both of them
are being fitted for contact lenses. The young lady turns out to be
a Brandeis senior, witty, bright, dressed in jeans and suede jacket.
They exchange pleasantries and a few barbed wits, she enters to
see the optometrist and emerges some twenty minutes later and
explains how contacts won't work for her after all, her astigmatism
is too severe. And she departs. Next Arthur sees Dr. Woolf, who
tests him, and in response to Ziff's query, discovers that the young
woman is the daughter of a rather famous rabbi in New York, a
well-known figure both in and out of rabbinical circles.

Arthur pursues her, first at Brandeis, and later in Cambridge.
(It took me a few lines to get used to Arthur writing about
"Arthur," and his shifting point of view, first to third person; I
knew I would have to photocopy some of this stuff.) He contacts
her that evening and they have a quick coffee in Brattle Square,
Charna leaving early because of schoolwork. This charms Ziff:

> Imagine, knowing who I was yet leaving me for Soc Rel 2,
> or some other luminous course, and thinking nothing of
> it other than "it's been nice." Was there a greater insou-
> ciance or freedom from celebrityhood than that? Yes,
> there was one; when I invited her to my public reading
> the next day, she checked her schedule and declined,
> saying, "I have an important paper to write, sorry.
> Another time."

> On the taxi drive back to Boston, Arthur played
> and replayed the accidental meeting, the brief evening
> tea stop, the handshake good-bye; and the young lady's

dark good looks and quick smile. Curiously enough, he had been invited several times to meet the famous Rabbi, but had declined, not needing another rabbi in his life, though this one was known for his political liberalism and unself-righteous ways. Was that really possible? Ziff wondered.

Though the young lady ("Charna, please, not Jenny!") doesn't attend the talk, she invites him to her Cambridge home for Friday night dinner, if he is staying in town. He is scheduled to depart for New York, but stays on, surprising himself, for the curious twenty-one-year-old with the long black hair and vibrant personality. He arrives, bearing a bottle of dry wine and, to his further surprise, she has set a white linen table, complete with candles, and offers him a yarmulke. Taken aback, charmed again, he accepts it politely. She proceeds to light the candles and recite the Hebrew prayers, covering her eyes with her hands.

"What's that mean?" "What? Welcoming in the Shabbat?" She shook her head. "Do you know at least how to bless the bread maybe?" A wry smile, and, out of his past, Arthur offers the prayer. ("Baruch ata adonoi elohenu. . . .")

"Well, you know something, and even have a decent accent!"

Appreciating her praise, he sits and appraises her as she serves the dinner, a young Jewish girl in white blouse and black skirt, and a black velvet vest. He can't get over the fact that he's sitting here and doing this on a Friday night, as though he were a thirteen-year-old boy in Roxbury.

"Don't by shy, please!" she admonishes him, only half joking. "Try the chopped liver, it's really not bad. What do you think?"

He tastes the chopped liver—and finds it firm and not too dry, and he nods. "Pretty good." He pours the white wine, she claims only a half glass—"Can you drink the stuff really?"—and he sips it slowly, an Australian chardonnay.

"So what do you think of this horrible right-wing Israeli government, allowing the settlers to dictate political policy? Feh, disgusting, isn't it?"

He smiles and will play the devil's advocate: "Well, they have a right to live where they want to, don't they?"

"What, are you crazy! Sure they have the right, but then they have to live under an Arab flag. Of course, this they won't do. Here, you have to try everything, yeah?" She passes him a plate of roast chicken, carrots, and small potatoes.

Gradually, as the evening progresses, Arthur finds himself in a different world, one wafting back from his childhood, a Jewish world circumscribed by ritual and atmosphere. One that he had sharply revolted against and mocked in his adult fiction. But here he doesn't mind it, actually, because this Charna is so much at home here; nothing is done for effect, it is all natural and fluid. He wonders, too, about later, afterward: Is he supposed to make, or does he want to make, a move on her? And have the same repetitive experience as always? Or should he simply leave it, her, alone, as this pure Jewish angel he has run into at the optometrist's, a sign to him of something new? Sure, let her be with her young boys and do whatever she wishes, stay virginal, give blow jobs, accept awkward fumblings, whatever. . . .

Only Charna has her own agenda for such matters, and later, after a two-hour dinner and all-purpose discussion, in which he is impressed with her sense of social justice and knowledge of Jewish history, she brings up the matter in a curious way:

"So, where are you staying tonight, at some *goyishe* hotel? Do you want to stay here? You can, you know."

What is he hearing? What is she saying?

"You mean you have another bedroom or? . . ." he asks.

"Come now, we're not children, you know!"

But she is a child, of course, a complete child to him; she's twenty-one, and he's mid-fifties, so she could easily be his daughter. Yet, is this what attracts him as well? He ponders, this childless man who has missed out on having his own daughter.

Well, he'll play it as it lays, so to speak.

"Sure, I'd be pleased to stay, but perhaps it would be best if I slept . . . on the couch, over there."

"Oy!" and she makes a face. "I can't believe this, *bist du mishuggah,* I offer him my bed, he's a famous writer who writes about sex, and he turns me away! No one will believe this. Sure, stay on the couch if you will. Go ahead!"

"Yes, it may sound funny, that's true, but after all, you are very young, I don't know you well, and—"

"*Genug, genug.* I have enough lectures in my life. I'll make up the couch."

"Look, your father—"

"My father! Why bring him up now, here? Are you crazy? Don't bother me with him now, for Godsakes!"

So now he understood, seeing the redness in her face and the fury in her tone. The father is a problem for her, good man that he is supposed to be. Saints shouldn't have to be fathers, too, he figures. Go easy on this.

Presently, she makes up the couch with sheets and blanket, and, making a face, says, "So does this look comfortable?"

"Yes," he says, lying down briefly, "it's not too bad."

She shakes her head in exasperation, waves her hand at him, and walks out.

I lie there, in the dim light, amused; at myself, at the situation. The air is a bit stuffy, but that's the least of it. A pair of black-and-white photographs in the corner draws me up, and there I view what are probably a Hasidic rabbi and wife and several children—an ancestral family?—and a younger couple at a wedding, perhaps Charna's parents. I am touched, and return to the couch. I flick off the light and try to sleep. In a few minutes there is a sound, and Charna eases into the room, wearing a white robe and nightgown, and crosses through to the kitchen, opens the fridge, removes something, and quietly retraces her steps. I observe her moving back through, barefoot, long dark hair unfurled and sweeping down her back, a sexy biblical Jewess. But I stay put, and silent.

In the morning, she has put out lox and cream cheese along with the challah, and says, "So, you slept well? You want coffee or tea? I still can't believe it, you slept out here when I invited you. . . . I can't believe it, and neither would anyone else! *Oy gott!* Here, give me your cup."

She had such beautiful mobility in her face, her gestures were abrupt and almost comic, she seemed always to be in a hurry or impatient. I had my breakfast and we chatted amiably—she was smart, witty, and irreverent. I passed to the door, coat in hand. I thanked her for her hospitality, the wonderful dinner and lodging. "Really, I enjoyed it very much."

"Yeah, so much that you took the couch over me! Go on, go home."

"Look at it this way: Suppose I told you that I want to see you again, but, had I slept with you last night, maybe I wouldn't have; maybe would have viewed it more like . . . a repetitive or familiar situation for me. What then?"

She shot me a weird look, like I was a true madman. "Yeah, well, call sometime. Meanwhile, good Shabbos."

I returned her greeting with the same and kissed her cheek, but she gave me her lips instead. She leaned her body into mine. I grew quietly aroused.

And I was off. I took a cab to South Station, and from there the Amtrak to New York. Her animated face, her unsentimental piety, her Yiddish ways and sarcastic wit, stayed with me.

And so began my intoxication with the young woman, my feelings of endearment balanced by my feelings of eroticism, my sense of her Jewishness infecting me, my feel for her youthfulness enhanced by my own sense of middle aging. In other words, I was assaulted by a rich mix of feelings, contradictions, anxieties. All rather exhilarating. I went on with my New York and Berkshire life, occasionally receiving e-mails and notes from Charna, all of which I answered faithfully. I even had the occasion to be invited to a synagogue to hear the father, Rabbi Wallerstein, give a sermon, and this time I went; I was most impressed with his words of poetic religiosity and civil rights passion. Afterward I was introduced to the man, small, slender, goateed, with penetrating dark eyes, and he shook my hand powerfully and complimented my work. "The pleasure is mine, Arthur, I read your books with great interest, even when they provoke me in an unsettling way." I thanked the rabbi, declined his invitation to join a small group for a late-night bite, and saw Charna's face emerging from the rabbi's.

When next she e-mailed, I wrote her back, spoke of our brief meeting and his fine sermon. She answered immediately, "Yeah, everyone puts him up on a pedestal. I would, too, if I weren't his daughter."

It takes another nine months before Arthur begins sleeping with the young lady, who is active and eager in bed, a willing student, too, and the affair goes on for more than half a dozen years. Arthur is affected as much by her style of Jewishness as he is by the young woman herself; she is charmingly Yiddish in her love and inflections, and scholarly in her knowledge. Indeed, he begins a journey of discovery of Judaism through the romance.

I came to understand, through Charna and her serious knowledge, her Yiddish humor, tenets, and ideas of Judaism, that I had had little idea of, so watered down had it become through suburban synagogue ways and

American institutions. I felt free, for the first time, to pursue real ideas in Judaism, and to witness authentic ways, in being close to Charna. I learned for the first time the true meaning of Hasidism, its history of authentic rebellion by means of emotionalism and spontaneity against the armies of mainstream Judaism, rather than the corny weddings and costumes of the current ilk, or its materialistic modern appearance. And while I didn't convert in any outward or notable way, I came to discern and appreciate what Jewishness was about, in its better, pristine forms, not the current suburban bastardizations and euphemisms. So Charna came to mean more to me than merely herself; she was important as symbol as well (which I kept private, of course). In a word, I was taking a serious journey through her, riding on a river of Old World Jewishness with the up-to-date young woman, which enhanced the attraction.

I pulled back from the pages, craned my neck, adjusted myself. The material was striking, for who would have dreamed this stuff of Ziff, the master womanizer, the arch-Jewish satirist, the modernist artist? (No doubt, a secret manuscript about a WASP princess was more likely.) And perhaps he knew this, too, in his way, and was not willing to sacrifice his image of bad-boy tough Jew for this new revelation of deeply feeling Jew. (Ashamed of publicizing this feeling?) Also, was he keeping quiet to protect the real Charna—and maybe her family, too?—who would easily be recognized in the real world? Far from bad boy, maybe he was a good boy after all? Ah, the irony! All this care and sacrifice—no public book, but private manuscript—on behalf of the young Jewess?

Was this revelation of personality and revolution of character significant reason why Arthur would choose to keep the novella private? Or at least contributing factors? After all, the fact that Ziff, the *enfant terrible* of American letters, was also a reflecting Jew and solicitous man—well, this could impinge on his literary persona, a persona carefully cultivated. And yet it could also be said that this was in keeping with Ziffian reality, in which stunning surprise was the key ingredient. Once again he was performing a unique somersault of self, a flip of personality, this brilliant circus acrobat. What a discovery, and yet I could do nothing about it!

Later in the novella the eminent rabbi, hearing a rumor of the union, writes the eminent novelist a letter:

"Dear Arthur,

It has come to my attention, through a trusted voice, that you have been having a romance with my daughter. If this is the case, my dear friend, I ask that you think of putting a halt to this immediately. You see, Charna, despite her surface, is a fragile psychological soul, and a long, casual affair, passionate as it may be, can only cause profound and long-lasting damage to her psyche and balance. I know that you will not want to contribute to that sort of situation. I will only add that you being some thirty-plus years older than she does not suggest a suitable union for the long run. Therefore, sir, please think of what I am saying here, imploring you, for the sake of Charna, our beloved one. Naturally, this note is one of utter confidentiality."

Interesting, that phrase "our beloved one." Does the rabbi mean the mutually beloved of Arthur and himself? Or the beloved of him and his wife? In any case, Arthur does not answer the rabbi, but it is not long thereafter that he writes a note to Charna canceling a weekend rendezvous and suggesting that they ease off for a while. The note is brief and solicitous, ending with, "Don't worry kid, I am not abandoning my feelings for you, or you; just saying let us try a cooling period. That way you can concentrate on your final exams and papers, and I on my new book." *Enfant terrible* behaving once again like an English gentleman!

Time passes, some years, and Arthur writes more books, gets even more famous, becomes a true international star. Every year, on

Rosh Hashanah, they exchange phone calls and/or cards for the New Year. Charna goes to graduate school in Michigan, goes through a few more boyfriends, and Arthur reflects,

> I observed her from afar in her growing career, even furtively attending a talk she gave on Jewish mysticism at a conference, and was impressed by her knowledge in the area, and her deft skills at analyzing the variety of mystical testimonies, in figures like rabbis Joseph Karo, Abraham of Granada, the Gaon of Vilna, Ba'al Shem Tov. In her high calf boots and mesh stockings, her black hair flowing and bright eyes shining, she was as much Hedy Lamarr as she was serious scholar. Oh, I was taken all over with her; a budding movie actress embedded in the star Jewish pupil. For a moment I pondered whether she was also dressed nattily underneath, with her style of vivid lingerie. Luckily, no Hollywood agents attended these conferences, only dry academic types for whom sex was a medieval concept. I couldn't resist dropping her a note saying how much I enjoyed her performance, and she e-mailed me immediately, "What! You were there and didn't see me afterward! You coward! Glad you liked it. Come to Ann Arbor! For a shabbat and weekend!"

That border, between piety and sensual wanting, between tenderness and irony, is preserved throughout; and the sparse but elegant prose style, the signature of the late Ziff, adds a bravura style to the whole tour de force. No antimemoir this little book; no peekaboo postmodernism here; no typical sensational opening conceit to capture the reader; rather, a kind of Tolstoyan simplicity in narrating the tale, affording the reader a glimpse into a writer composing in full leisure and confidence in his art, while at the same time shaking loose all the presumptions of past artistic journeys.

It was getting late. I looked about edgily, I skipped pages . . . she gets married in her late thirties, Arthur still looks in on her, like a long-term project, and we have this:

I longed to see her all the more as she was removed from me; to see the mature changes in her youthful face and body; to hear the infectious laughter and cascading Yiddishisms; to be the recipient of her acerbic wit and brainy rejoinders; to see the mobile expression in her face when we argued and she made or heard a new point, or to hear her special unrestrained moan at the height of her lust; but I stayed away, believing my years with her had left their indelible mark, not all for the good, and if what I was left with, in place of Charna herself, was memory and beauty, memory and sadness, memory and this elegy, so be it. In the end I would serve her best in this manner—the manner I knew best—and perhaps she would serve me best also, in her unbeknownst way, for after all, we were both joining together at last, joining in serving a mutual master, she and I as humble servants to the master of art.

Had Arthur Ziff ever written or felt more poignantly? Or shown more boldness than in declining to publish this passionate, artful novella?

Moving back into the study, I spotted the copier, a Canon like mine, and staying still to listen for any possible noise outside, proceeded to copy a small batch of pages from here and there. . . .

What Ziff had done was take his unknown autobiographical affair and write a small novel of immense readability and exquisite prose. The great cynic and anti-Romantic had written a riveting passion tale of two unlikely creatures filled with unusual depths of emotion (for Ziff) and surprising turns of character. No tricky postmodern gimmicks here, no avalanches of wit or rage, just hard, precise sentences on personality, culture, and the anatomy of emotion. From a chance meeting at that optometrist's office to secret trysts in Cambridge, Maine, Vermont, Antigua, the affair unfolds, with no resolution in sight at the end, à la Chekhov's "Lady with a Pet Dog." (Indeed, the epigraph came from that memorable story.) As the writer-protagonist narrates his tale, the reader is confronted with layer after layer of revealed shallowness and biases of the character, which soon infiltrates his own self-conscious meditation. For the first time, Arthur Ziff exposes his narrator to full irony and criticism by the author, no self-protective devices or artifices set up.

Moving back into the study, I thought what a stunning performance it was, in every way, a cross of F. S. Fitzgerald prose with Tolstoyan lucidity. "A Fateful Affair" struck me as Ziff's finest work, the crowning work of a lifetime oeuvre. And the fact that he was now hiding it away, out of sight of a celebrity-hungry culture, preserving it for posterity alone (if then), was just as remarkable. For a long minute I pondered. . . . but it was too risky, I was too tired, and the thought of having breakfast and then trying to sneak out with the manuscript in the morning would be akin to trying to get out of old Moscow with a Samizdat manuscript. My watch read 2:20 A.M. as I got back down on my knees to return the sacred text back to its manila folder, back into its harmless-looking Dead Letter File, and finally back into the bottom row of cabinet number four. How would I ever be able to verify this, write about it? Answer: never.

Wiping my wet brow, I found by chance a slim file alongside marked "Switzerland," and saw in there a packet of letters. Debating whether to chance it, I heard a noise that seemed to come from the front door . . . this resolved my ambivalence and I closed the cabinet softly, swiftly.

And suddenly, I imagined a scene, imagined it so so strongly that it felt as real as what was happening.

A shaft of light flashed down upon me, in my floor position, and when I looked up, there was Arthur Ziff, a sturdy figure in white terry bathrobe, standing inside the front door, holding a long black flashlight and staring down at me on all fours. . . .

The next morning, when I came down at eight, I heard a surprising sound of disco music coming from one of the rooms. Not finding anyone about, I made my way down the corridor toward the steady, rhythmic beat. At the large room that used to be a study for one of the ex-girlfriends, I saw, through the ajar door, a sight I wasn't prepared for. Bigan, in royal blue spandex shorts and yellow tank top and white sneakers, was working out aerobically to the tune of a disco CD. Up and back she was marching, then stopping to twist this way and that, throwing out a flank here, arching a hip there, stretching arms wide, bending in tune and craning her neck, stopping in place to run, legs pumping high, the music blaring.

"Cute, huh? Every morning." Arthur was at my side, arms folded, admiring. "I set my clock by it, 7:30 A.M. promptly."

I nodded in awe.

"Sexier than miniskirts or underwear, right? Come on, I bought some bagels and lox for us, to show you I was thinking of your health, too."

I paused. "Oh, I thought I'd do some aerobic training first."

"Come on, smart aleck." Presently, in the kitchen, he put up the coffee, toasted the bagels, and gave me a section of the *Times*. "How about the Style page? Or do you want the Style-News?"

As I read the sports and the coffee brewed and we chatted news and baseball, I recalled my journey of the night before, how delicious it was, the literary sleuthing and the late reading. To have hunted down and unearthed that treasure was worth it all, I figured, the scary madness . . . the dark fantasy ending to the night, with the discovery by the lord of the manor. Curious, how I couldn't even win *out there,* in fantasyland.

"So, what'd you do last night after we went off to sleep?" Arthur asked, giving me my cup of coffee. "Make use of my special magazines? Or stick to the high road and read literature?"

I smiled casually. "High road, I'm afraid. Some Arthur Ziff, actually."

He shot me a look—was that anxiety or fury, I wondered—before relaxing and quipping, "Yeah, I'll bet."

Later we sat in the living room and talked. After a bit of New York gossip and a description of how isolated he had become down there ("I see no one, absolutely no one, save for Bigan") I asked him if it were true that he was writing a novel concerning Wallenberg and the Holocaust.

His eyebrows arched. "Why would you think that?"

"I've bugged your computer, that's all."

"Oh, I see." A slow, sardonic smile.

"No kidding—have the Jews really gotten to you after all these years? And you've finally decided to take on the Jewish question, set it into full account?"

He eyed me. "That's odd, since I thought I had been taking that account on for twenty books or so."

I nodded. "Well, not quite this directly perhaps."

The sardonic smile faded, giving way to a cordial look. "It's not a bad subject, heh?"

"Actually it's quite intriguing, especially in your hands."

He laughed. "Conning aside, Wallenberg was a rather interesting Swede, don't you think? One whose motives were not all that pure or clear, as it turns out."

"I know, I've read up on him a bit. Good subject for Bergman, maybe? . . . Or Arthur Ziff?"

He gave me a look. "Why would you read up on Wallenberg?"

"Why not? He wasn't exactly obscure, and with the recent stories shedding doubt on his and his family's wartime virtue . . . well, what do you think of him, or what have you *made* of him?"

He drained his decaf espresso. "An unlikely hero, don't you think? An aristocrat who took unnecessary risks. Saved a lot of Jews. Unfazed by the threats, rumors, myths."

"Sounds a little like someone I know."

"Oh?"

I locked his gaze. "You."

A little smirk; then, as he saw I was serious, a guffaw. When it subsided, he cocked his head at an odd angle to study me. "You were never without imagination, Danny. Sometimes in excess."

"Well, isn't it possible that you may be an improbable hero, maybe even a savior of sorts to certain Jews? What do you think?"

"Me?" He crossed his legs, attired in corduroys. "Possible? Sure. But probable? I'd say no." A skeptical half smile. "Be that as it may, if you're thinking of putting forward that sort of spin into your book, who would believe it? Come now, try that interpretation and it will be the subject of Comedy Central festivals from the Adirondacks to Elaine's. Ziff—a friend of the Jews, an unlikely hero, wow!" But he was not smiling, just facing me soberly.

"So in other words, if it were the truth, then it would be impossible to try to put in the book. Or too foolish."

"You got it, pal. Too foolish."

I eyed this sturdy-in-the-flesh Jewish sphinx who had the answer but wouldn't supply it.

"Why? Do you yourself believe it?" he queried.

"Good question. I don't really know."

He emitted a little laugh. "Well then, you might imagine how others might take such news, those a bit less friendly, say. Forget it, Danny, forget the whole attempt at 'getting the truth' for this book." He shook his head. "You see, even if you got it, you, or any good and honest writer, wouldn't quite know how to handle it, and in the end, for your own good, for the book's reception, would be forced to suppress it."

He folded his arms and stroked his severe beard. I felt his *presence,* a presence of honed steel and cunning, while I felt *less there.* Oh, yes, he would play Wallenberg well, impersonate and reinvent him in print with mimetic voice and aristocratic conviction. A performance to watch and listen to—like Olivier playing Iago, or Raoul.

I nodded and drank my water. "Anyway, how's your book coming?"

"Besides imagination, persistence, too. You were never short on that, either." He paused. "My new novel? Oh it's fine, just fine."

Where am I to go now? I mused, facing his titanium stare. Sneak through the back door to the truth after all—another entry into the study to copy, verify my booty? Was it possible, was it worth it?

"Hey, you guys, get with it," called out Bigan, in blue and yellow Adidas sweats. "Ready for a walk? You'll never eat my goose for lunch if you don't get some exercise!"

Later, at lunch, I ate the goose with a new sense of foreboding: book doubt.

"Well, you haven't said anything yet. How is it?" Bigan put, smiling.

"It's delicious," I mustered, feeling that both this saucy goose and my own innocent one were cooked just perfectly. "Couldn't be tastier."

twenty-three

Suddenly I was in Budapest again, propelled by a recent Éva e-mail hinting at a new lead—"a curious friend of Arthur's is now in town"—and taken by that loyal scout to a home on a residential street in Buda, an ivy-covered three-story stucco house, once a private abode, now six apartments. After a near-silent taxi ride, Éva deposited me at the front gate with the caution, "I know nothing of this visit, or address, please remember." Excited, I rang the bell, and by return buzzer entered a small, rundown courtyard where Judith Fodor awaited me at the massive front door and directed me around back on a narrow path. In the 5:00 P.M. twilight I made my way, greeted suddenly by a smiling, slender bearded man wearing a yarmulke and cardigan sweater. Speaking a reasonable English, he showed me into a long two-room basement study, the larger holding a desk and computer, a second with a few worn upholstered chairs and low, round table. Bookshelves lined the rooms, and books and papers were piled everywhere. I was seated and offered a drink, which Dr. Fodor proceeded to make. *(From him I was to hear about Arthur's grand passion?!)*

"Are you a rabbi?" I asked the strange fellow.

"No, no." he smiled affably. "I am a scientist, actually. But I also try to be a good Jew." He brought over two whiskey glasses and a bottle of Palinka brandy.

He welcomed me with a *l'chaim!* We drank, and I asked him if it were true that he was a friend of Arthur Ziff, who visited him regularly.

"I suppose you could say we are friends. I'm fond of Arthur."

"What do you mean, 'I suppose'?"

"Well, we study together. That is how we met."

"Study together? Study what?"

Restraining a smile for my gross ignorance, he explained, "The texts. We look at Bible and Talmud together."

I took another sip, skeptical of the words I was hearing.

"Bible passages?" I asked.

Of course. "For what reason? Or how did this come to happen?"

Gently he chided me, "You have asked Mr. Ziff himself?"

"No, I haven't. But I doubt whether he would tell me. I am writing a book on him, you know. A sort of biography."

"That would be a difficult labor, I imagine." He laughed lightly. "But still, you should ask him."

"Look," I rejoined, growing strangely impatient, "are you implying, sir, that Ziff is turning to religion through you?"

"Please, call me Ferencs or Feri, not 'sir.' " He shook his head and smiled. "No, I did not mean to imply that."

"Then what?" Perplexed, slightly annoyed.

"He simply studies passages with me. For example, with the Bible, I read the Hebrew, and we work from that to the English translation."

"Which translation, the King James?"

"Oh, among others. For gentiles, laymen, it still serves. But for scholars, its inaccuracies are too many. Several recent translations have been less . . . fanciful, truer to the Hebrew, stronger. Like the recent translation, or retranslation of the Rosensweig version, in your country a few years ago, by Fox, published by Schocken. You are familiar?" He lit a cigarette.

I was on a different track. "But why? Why?"

"Mr. Ziff is a serious man, and interested in the texts. Why? You'll have to ask him for that."

I took the last of my peach brandy. Heady stuff, the Palinka, the news. "Do you also read . . . commentators on the passages?"

He nodded his head back and forth. "Of course. That's where Talmud comes in."

"So you do a kind of Midrash study with him, then?"

He shrugged vaguely. "You could say that, but please, our

study is most informal." He had a low, gravelly voice, belying his rather graceful manner.

He offered me another drink, and I accepted a half shot.

"Tell me, Ferencs, are you a professional at this? I mean, have you trained for this sort of study?"

He smiled radiantly. "I could ask if you are trained for your sort of study." He tapped my arm playfully. "I am only joking you, Daniel. Yes, I have had some training in this. In Jerusalem I studied with my old chemistry teacher, Yeshiau Leibowitz; in New York I spent a few years with the great Lieberman, who also taught me about the stock market!; and I spent a winter in Boston working with Soloveitchek. Three different kinds of scholars, and Jews, but very shrewd, deep readers of the texts."

"I see," I muttered, realizing his pedigree was far superior to mine. "Could you give me an example, sir?—I mean Feri."

" 'An example'?" his eyes glinted. "How do you mean?"

"Well, a passage you and Mr. Ziff actually would read, and then discuss, analyze."

His smile revealed nicotine stain. He unbuttoned a button on his plaid cardigan, leaned back. Sighing, he rubbed his scraggly beard. "Maybe we leave this for a later date and time, yes, Daniel?"

Stymied at a good moment but not wanting to push him too much, I replied, "Would you know, Feri, if Arthur has studied elsewhere—with others like yourself I mean, in different cities?"

He put his hands out wide, palms up. "Could be. I am not the only one interested in such matters."

"Like New York. Or even Rome?"

"Why not? There are scholars and *chochems* of repute in both places. But you should put these questions directly to Mr. Ziff!" he said happily. "Don't you think he would answer you, Daniel?"

Would he? "Not if he wanted it kept secret," I remarked as casually as possible, knowing I'd get nothing from A. Z.

He nodded, smoked the stub of his cigarette, observed me.

An intercom buzzer rang. He got up and spoke, then announced to me that he was being called upstairs for his family dinner. "I'll call you a taxi."

"Yes, that would be nice."

As he dialed City Taxi, I looked about, hoping for something, a sign, some evidence. . . . On a shelf, I spotted an edition of Ziff.

"Oh, may I have a look?" and I took down what looked like the Hungarian edition of *Mendelsohn's Meditations,* leafing inside. Indeed there was Ziff's signature, written large, under a line, "To Ferencs Fodor, a good man and friend."

"You know the book?" he put. "It has many interesting ideas, and Jewish propositions. Come, I'll walk you out."

He led the way on the darkened path. At the front gate he asked, "Maybe next time, you come for a *Shabbat* dinner?"

"That would be lovely," I said.

"Good. I return in two weeks. You will call Judith?"

I explained that I'd be gone by then, but perhaps he could supply me with a name or two in New York that might be a good source for inquiry.

Shrugging, he took out a scrunched envelope and wrote down a few names while the taxi pulled up, and waited.

"A pity you won't be here. When do you return? All right, you'll come for *shabbat* then? A date." He extended his hand, and when I shook it, he took mine in both hands. "There are many kinds of Jews, Mr. Levitan, and a wise one embraces all."

The mercury lamp above revealed a radiant look on his face, and for some reason I was reminded of the last scene in Malamud's *Magic Barrel,* where the matchmaker's daughter is revealed in sin as a prostitute. Only here it was Arthur Ziff, revealed in virtue!

In the taxi ride back across the Margarit Bridge to Pest and my hotel, I pondered the meeting, its long-range meaning. Was this the most charming, or the most alarming of my discoveries? It had been worth the journey, but could it be corroborated?

Arthur Ziff reading the Jewish Texts secretly was something special. Far more bewildering than anything lewd or literary—a little like Ahab shifting course, away from his mad pursuit and toward a calmer place where he might have more time to read and study. . . .

* * *

In New York I met up with Shmuel Cantorwicz, in a Riverside Drive apartment near Columbia, where he taught. A bulky, bushy-browed man, seventyish, he greeted me amiably in frayed white shirt, wide, loud tie, and gabardine cap.

Taking my arm, he escorted me into the comfortable, high-ceilinged living room where we sat on worn leather chairs and were served tea, sponge cake, and brandy by Esther, a small woman dressed in a skirt and blouse.

The high windows afforded a view of Riverside Park and the Hudson River.

A few minutes of polite chatter, and I proceeded to my queries.

"Yes, Mr. Ziff has come by for discussions in recent years." An accent, but I couldn't place it. "He is very curious intellectually, you know."

"Is he actually studying with you?"

He sipped his brandy. "Well, it depends on what you mean by 'studying.' We discuss, he asks questions, tough questions"—he gave a robust laugh—"and I try to answer." He shrugged. "Sometimes I manage. You don't drink, Daniel? A little schnapps is very good for you! Try the cake, too. And please, take one, straight from Havana." A long cigar, still wrapped.

"How did he get started on this," I put, diplomatically holding the cigar, taking a bit of cake, sipping, "and when?"

Puffing his cigar now, Shmuel recalled, "Well, Saul wrote him a note, that's how it started."

"Saul, which Saul?"

"Which Saul?" He stared at me, a naive fool. "Lieberman, of course, the Talmudic scholar. Who else? After Scholem had put down Ziff's work publicly—in *Commentary*—Lieberman, who was my mentor at JTS, you see, wrote Ziff a note of support, telling him how much he enjoyed his books and how he was very much in the Jewish tradition. Just like Saul, a freethinker. So they struck up a friendship, which was more or less passed on to me." He looked concerned. "You're not trying it, come on!"

I puffed, coughed. "I see," I said, bewildered by all this.

"Esther, maybe a little water for our guest, yeah?"

It amazed me to find that Esther had been sitting there, hidden in a corner. Who was she?

"But what did Ziff want? Or still want?"

"To talk, to see texts, to understand materials."

"For a new novel?"

"*Ver veis?*" He shrugged, finished his brandy, inhaled, and blew out smoke slowly. Esther brought me a glass of water in a crystal glass on a silver tray. He nodded, and I drank a bit. "Arthur's his own man, goes his own way. You know that, I'm sure."

I did, didn't I? And was continuing to learn it.

"What texts?"

"Everything, from Torah to Talmud—and various tractates of interest." He leaned forward, his chin emerging as a force, and a huge ash dangling from his cigar. "I tell you in candor, Mr. Daniel, Arthur has made some comments about the *Tosafot,* for example, that I actually found very . . . insightful. And original. The boy's got a *Yiddishe kup!*" Without glancing down, he caught the ash at the last second, for deposit. "Saul was right—Ziff could have made a big, big scholar if he had wanted to enter the field. But he's doing all right in his own field, eh? Tell me, do you think he has a chance for a Nobel, or is his work too earthy, too *schmutzidikah*—for the reserved Swedes?"

I said I didn't know, trying to handle my cake, tea, brandy, and cigar, and when I tried to push him about when Arthur visited last, or would visit again, Shmuel dismissed my questions and advised me to speak to Arthur, also suggesting I visit again, next time I was in Manhattan. "Where do you live again, in *Yenemsvelte?*" he laughed. "Why not? Jews have always made good farmers! Do you farm up there?"

As I was leaving, escorted by Shmuel, who took my arm again, I asked him who Esther was, and he said, "My sister-in-law, who survived. Our Hannah didn't."

"Oh," I mumbled, perplexed.

"When you come next, remind me to tell you a wonderful story about some New York Jews who went to Petaluma in the forties to chicken-farm communally. Fellow travelers and fellow *meshuganahs,* you know? Safer in California with their chickens than back in Minsk or Kiev with their borsht and beliefs. Goodbye, *sei gezunt.*" He squeezed my arm and gave me a little wave.

Flying and driving home, I felt I had now gathered the final pieces of the puzzle. Arthur was developing his spiritual side *furtively* all the while, right along with his secular doings. Europe was not merely for mischief, adventure, philanthropic idealism (and recovering Esther Licht tales), it also was for private learning, higher education. Once again Ziff was ahead of the field, by a full length or two, the Secretariat of American letters. For him, the words, the texts, were the mission and the passion of his life. So why should I, or the rest of us, be surprised by this turn of events?

While scribbling away on his novels for the world to see and be occupied with, he was up to something deeper underneath, his personal *midrash.* The public surface was emphatically secular, cool, and carnal, the interior thickly meditative and subtly Judaical; it made for an incongruous, exquisite whole. (No wonder, such rich and layered content to his late novels.) The solo pathfinder was delving into the great Jewish books, the deep textual mysteries—the Talmud, Kabbalah (probably), commentaries, Apocrypha—with the help of private guides and select tutors plucked from around the globe. How princely, how Ziffian.

Given Arthur's accomplishments thus far, it made good, logical sense. Now he was competing or joining forces, in his own artistic way, against the great older heavy hitters of the tradition— Maimonides, Rashi, Rabbi Ben Ezra, and others. Inevitably, down the line somewhere—in *Wallenberg,* or after—a grand novel would emerge—another of those major paradoxes, another exploration into uncharted territory.

(Or was I getting it wrong again, extrapolating from a few bits of evidence an overglamorized and melodramatic whole? Was he simply loading up the train for another ride on the Ziff Express to fictionland? Nothing spiritual, just practical digging, necessary spadework?)

PART THREE

twenty-four

TIME—FOR ME—ENTERS A STRANGE REALM WHEN I'M WRITING. No longer run by clocks or bound by calendars, it is measured by the accumulation of pages, the development of story, the fermenting of elements. Measured in this fashion, it moves differently from the ordinary, and produces a flow like an alert somnolence, a self-induced creative trance. And unlike erotic passion, a briefer intruder on clock time, this trance is a long one, winding and burrowing its way down and deeply for months and years, resembling in this sealed chamber nothing so much as a long, grave illness.

I worked on my Ziff for nearly another year, making it my real life, while my other, more illusory one spun about me in a kind of secondary rotation. There was little unusual about this; when you're taken down or sealed away by a serious book, it immerses you so completely that the daily routines—domesticity, friends, teaching, public events—pale in comparison. Put another way: The heat and the intensity reside inward, in the leased residence of art, while on the outside, ordinary life parades by, unaware. ("I write, therefore I exist," was my revised motto.) So while the Bush right-wing regime ruled and journalists stayed quiet, the Mideast raged and African famines grew, the Internet wired up China, cyberspace made hostages of our natives, and the new hackers frightened Wall Street and gave new importance to obscure geography, while all the world's events tumbled on, I spun my surprising roller-coaster tale. Over my desk I hung Kierkegaard's words, "Purity is to will one thing."

Accommodating Pat, I gave *Ziff* a cohesiveness, chiseling the material and shaping the narrative, deleting odd bits and pieces, weaving in my interpretations of the man, the life. Yes, I had praised much of the work too highly and had to reassess soberly. Certain books emerged anew (DB, J:DD), others sank (MT, TEATHN). On the whole I was impressed by the inventive forms, the ambitious sweep, the reach for originality. I was less impressed by over-ingenious conceits, rhetoric doing the work of emotional power, and noticed the falling off of latter halves of books. Depictions of class, of place, Jewish-Gentile relations, were exacting and humorous. Indeed, the humor, both high and low, was always effective.

Maybe the most difficult task was to try to describe that complex mechanism by which the civilized, humorous, urbane, refined gentleman reflecting on his subject was suddenly transformed into a dead calm shooter, amoral assassin, hunting down his target. What was the transformer? How did it work? What lit the fuse? The two sides of the man, the honorable schoolboy and the ambushing guerrilla, seemed to act themselves out in the novels, the calm composer of those lovely, lucid paragraphs and the vengeful looter breaking and entering into all sorts of characters and scenes with a gleeful hatchet and wild spray paint. I attributed it to the suave WASP element of the man and his mischievous alter ego, the rebel Jewboy. (I gave credit to the audacious conceits at the beginning of his works, those brilliant laser shots at the readers in the first fifty pages.)

As for the life, I recalled a few more old scenes, found several new ones as well as characters (especially a boyhood buddy), but little to dislodge the intriguing mysteries, ambiguities, intangibles, which I left intact. My decision was not to tie the ribbon neatly and provide a final resolution, a perfect order or clear meaning, but rather to let things fall as they might, loose-ended and playfully amoral, intentionally gray and ambiguous, as grainy reality mingled with saintly glimmerings. (Éva sent me videotapes of six poignant interviews with Roman pilgrims.) At times I fancied the mission of my book as a kind of space probe launched toward a remote planet (Z-10) whose topography and chemistry were totally strange and whose nature was shrouded in layers of deceitful gases and shifting moons. Naturally, I had to ground that metaphor with hard facts and judgments.

Among the latter, I was pleased by a few of the more speculative paragraphs:

> Mr. Ziff is perhaps the best representative of the Spirit of Inauthenticity in modern letters. With vigor he has debunked the myth of the self, derided the whole notion of what it means to be authentic. In his books and life he has forged another kind of identity, an anti-identity that has mocked the Trilling/Howe era of personal authenticity and moral value, the ruling philosophy from Hemingway to Bellow. In its place Z. has created a system of multiple selves, subversive moralities, metamorphosing values—nothing less than a sly weapons system firing torpedoes at the 'authenticity' of human lives, personality, self. . . .
>
> As a Jew, Arthur is perhaps best seen as contemporary and new, but not the sort introduced to the world some fifty years ago in Israel, the tough sabra or sunny kibbutznik. (Nor is the model the old Luftmenshen scholar or rabbinical *cheder* boy.) Rather he offers a rude independent man, a post-Enlightenment, post-Holocaust persona, free of the old ways (guilt), the old beliefs (religion), the old restrictions (taboos), the old pieties (tribal history). He cares about himself first and foremost—'himself' being American/Jewish simultaneously. Cares about the Jews when there is an event or crisis of anti-Semitism, but otherwise, not particularly. Cares about the Jewish past, but is not imprisoned or haunted by it. It may be phrased that he is a Jew on personal demand, when conditions of life or writing call for it. The narcissistic Jew, yes, but perhaps beyond that, through the famous fiction and self, an *embodiment of the Jewish people through history*—a condition created by the Christian world and by the Jewish Bible—in short, the narcissistic Jewish people. Hence the arduous paradox and exacting play of Ziff's deceptive life.

(Of course, I could not comment on Arthur's devotions, as exemplified in the hidden "A Fateful Affair.")

Spirituality pervades the later novels, with a subtlety and beauty that is rare in modern fiction. Give credit to the Jewish sources for this intense flame in Ziff's late works, to those same texts that have been attracting scholars' attention for centuries. At the same time, let me say that Ziff's transmutation of that material is an act of skill and unmatched ingenuity; not Singer, not Bellow, has turned the trick so forcefully. Only perhaps in Kafka do you see that act of subtle transformation and balance taking place, whereby the spiritual is felt simmering just beneath the surface of secular plot and subject, where theme is experienced as prayer, where words accumulate slowly into a mesmerizing chant. Let us salute the mastery of Ziff in these last books, and give credit to the deep sources that have nourished him privately, away from the world's eye, for a considerable time.

Curiously enough, however, as I proceeded toward the end of the book, I was filled less with satisfaction or growing elation and more with anxiety, pressure. Yes, I was afraid, even scared of finishing, handing it in, and then facing the inevitable angry music, first waiting around while the news broke out about the book, subliterary "news" and lurid rumors, and then the "literary" reviews that would follow. I even found myself checking in on the mirror once or twice a week, as though to check on my physical reality; I was discovering a thinner, balder D. L., with more lines in the face, a look of doubt in the small hazel eyes. If it were possible to get writer's insurance for a hot project, I would gladly have taken it out, a kind of Peerless Umbrella Policy for a Dangerous Literary Folly. I felt the fear and pressure from all sides—my publisher, Arthur, his attorneys, the journalistic and literary worlds, the magazines and the media, and from myself. Had I done the right thing? Had I written a just book, a good book, or . . . a self-deluding exploitation? . . . a long, misguided rocket folly? . . . Would it make it off the launching pad, and fly? If so, for what ultimate purpose, toward what destination?

So the finishing line became, instead of my victory line, the line of fear and trembling. I approached it with my two or three daily pages of slow progress, like a slow train on schedule, though I worried about the true end. At times I projected that to be a vast (toxic) landfill, where the book would be dumped, along with all other live garbage, to be buried or burned, in a giant heap of mangled steel and awful stench. That image distracted me as I wrote on and on. So finishing was not fun, but trepidation; to change the image, I was running those final laps with uncertainty, vulnerability, not ease or confidence. What a last irony, I pondered, racing toward my career end, my final crashdown?

Another, deeper irony, of course, was what I had *left out* of my *Ziff*: the tale of Arthur and his long-term girlfriend, the material of—the very fact of—"A Fateful Affair." No way could I negotiate that rich stuff in without hard evidence, and I felt a great shame, even dishonor, in its omission. For it was less the fact of the affair itself than the resplendent short novel that it had inspired, a work of exquisite, deceptive simplicity in the vein of some of the great short novels [*Daisy Miller* (James), *Ward Number Six* (Chekhov), *Summer* (Wharton), *The Great Gatsby* (Fitzgerald)]—a fact I couldn't even note down, or discuss, and that, as far as the world was concerned, didn't exist. Do you see how the news of this book, and Arthur's refusal to acknowledge its existence, let alone publish it, would have changed the perception of the man? Not to mention the cerebral writer who, now for the first time, was dramatizing the world of powerful emotion, opening up for the first time to depths of emotion never before available. Now it was buried forever. . . .

Feeling that omission added to my despair and triggered my sense of literary insufficiency and a curious disingenuity.

Friends helped, consoled, especially Pat. The boys were boys, playing and mischiefing, and they provided surges of high cheer. Whether Gabriel was playing Bach on his new 3/4 size cello or learning to catch a football, face downward, body tense like a frightened doe, or Jon was blowing his horn accompanying a Chet Baker solo or running straight up a steep mountain trail for his high school cross-country team, they buoyed me. Their boyish battling, their buzzing motion and noise, their intrusion on my time, all that used to disturb me now upped and transported me away from my endless days in Ziffland. And Becka, too, was helpful, kindly, in running our routine. . . . Literature helped, like the novellas of Stendahl, Chekhov, and Melville, which I read and reread. Nature, too, which brimmed with moments of beauty, the brisk hikes in the scented woods of autumn, the ice-cold lake swims in late May/June, cross-country skiing in the silent woods of winter, the sighting of a blue heron slowly circling the meadow pond. These distractions lifted briefly the large mass of despair gathering over my head and within; only to pass, and leave the sense of futility. . . .

Inevitably during this extended period, I found myself dropping out of society, losing interest in people. Large parties were out of the question, and dinner parties were painful exercises in tact, strained wit, staying alert. For a while I turned into a kind of indoor ornithologist, studying this one's voice, that one's plumage, this one's taste in books, pictures. Their judgments, opinions, struck me as nothing more than easily received wisdom, wearied, predictable. I ceased going out, at last. Old friends, academicians, aroused little interest, save as memories of the—deluded?—past. It dawned on me now how few of them were conversationalists with something real to say, or with a way of narrating a story that had clear purpose, an edge of wit or point of revelation. They chitchatted, gossiped, laughed, spoke of kids or career, emitted the right political opinion (liberal), offended no one. So I retreated, backed off, held out. A newfound recluse. Just when I could have used an intelligent person to talk with seriously, argue against, maybe even read a bit of manuscript to, I found no one. Too bad I was writing about Arthur; he would have made the perfect companion.

Of course, the rumors and gossip swirled, and hit me one way or another. *Publishers Weekly* and the *New York Times* would hint occasionally at fantastic revelations, scenes with real names (if not persons), and for a week or two legal alarms would go off, shattering my rural peace and silence. Immediately phone calls signaled and faxes beeped in, asking for interviews, clarifications, putting questions. Again I held off, returning silence. A movie deal was signed and sealed in the culture column of the *Times*;

unfortunately, I had heard nothing about it. Through it all I remained steadfast with dull routine, driving the kids to school, coming back to a bagel or cereal and a long coffee with the morning newspaper, and in my study, turning on the computer and radio. Ready then for the day's solitary work: focusing, writing, revising, writing anew. Accumulating the pages, shaping the narrative, trying to be balanced, scrupulous, smart.

While I wound down—inwardly, too—during those long months, the family moved upward. Little Gaby had progressed on the cello to rich Marcello and elegant Bach, his vibrato becoming a passion. (And his mischiefmaking had been augmented by articulateness, and making things up, especially against little enemies.) Jonathan had begun in earnest his teenage rebellion, employing ingenuity and moodiness—driving Becka crazy—while mingling the Simpsons and Seinfeld with *The Way of All Flesh* and *An American Tragedy*. His jazz trumpet had taken a step upward, too, hitting new high notes, thanks to a new teacher. All the while Becka was proceeding with her female side of Proustian recording, completing her eleventh volume of a long-term memoir of Lives of My Sons, begun when Jon was born. Handscribbled in lined hard-backed six-by-nine books and kept continuously for more than 16 years, they recorded phrases, sentences, acts, gestures, motives, reactions, a detailed Declaration of Maternal Observation. And since she could write well, they formed a new kind of subliterary genre, a mother's diary.

Éva e-mailed:

Dear Danny,

I am very glad for your last visit, brief as it was, I felt it closed the circle, yes? Budapest misses you! I hear occasional note from Mr. Z., who says he knows nothing of your book. His Wallenberg is nearly done, I understand. Judging from the two chapters Arthur sent me, to verify Hungarian rural towns and Budapest street names, it will be one of his very best books. The material is haunting, and Arthur has gotten into the minds of the victims, especially two young boys, like

no one else. Mr. Wallenberg lives through A. Z.'s fiction! I
hope you will be able to see it before you finish yours. . . .
Any further news on the missing woman or apocryphal
novella? How far are you along? Any other late discoveries,
reinterpretations? I long to see what you will come up with,
altogether. So does the literary world, if I'm not mistaken. As
I mentioned to you before, I am hoping to be in your South-
west for a conference this summer. Will we be able to meet?

I answered Éva warmly, saying I'd love to see the chapters if
she still had them and cared to send them on, as it might be difficult for me to get ahold of the manuscript. Yes, if the timing and
the writing permitted, we would try to meet.

Next, via airmail I heard from Jeanne, in Paris, who wrote:

Mon charmant *Daniel,*
Why the long silence, my friend? Is it busy times, or
something else? And did you ever respond to my memoir? I
forget now. (The publisher sent you a copy?) I realize I am
not a true writer, but I tried my hardest to give a sincere
account of our life. Of course, I could not confess everything;
my upbringing, natural timidity in writing, and close
friends, made that impossible. That is why I am hoping you
have been able to use my journal notes in a productive
manner. Have you? Naturally, if so, I do want, no, I must
insist, on viewing the manuscript before publication. You
will agree, of course.
Are you coming over to the Old World anytime soon, my
friend? How is the charming family? And Rebecca?
Warmest greetings to her, please. And to you!

I wrote Madame a cordial letter, explaining carefully the long
and arduous work it took to compose a biography, and the many
hurdles, internal and external, I had had to jump over. And in a
single sentence of tender diplomacy I reminded her of the document
she had signed, giving me permission to use the diary notes as I

saw fit, as long as there was no intent of injury or malice. I offered nothing in the way of showing her the manuscript beforehand. In fact, I had used her diary entries with as much circumspection and care as was possible; I certainly tried to reveal her point of view, though, at the same time, I countered her material with Arthur's vehement denials and his miniportrait of her character. It was a balancing act of some delicacy, to be sure.

The young woman of Ziff's youth, Michelle F., checked in (on Fidelity stationery) with a four-page letter with more details, chronicling more of their careening on-again, off-again romance, giving me a clearer picture of the indelible mark that Arthur had left on her.

The Encyclopedia Judaica invited me to contribute the article on Arthur Ziff for their planned revised edition due out in 2002: "Jews from all over the world, from Australia to England, Canada to the Americas, will read this landmark work. We already have sold twenty-five thousand subscription editions, and we believe you are uniquely qualified to write the updated article on Mr. Ziff."

With gratitude I declined, and suggested instead they try the noted Ziff scholar Professor Éva Kertész in Budapest.

Two weeks after I had handed in the whole manuscript and was having a small celebration at home, I received a call from the publisher's office, asking if I might come in and have a final little meeting with the legal staff. In shock I called Pat, and he said yes, he had heard about it and it was necessary; we arranged to meet.

Once again the same two fellows, the same conference table, and the same deceptive cordiality. "Look, we want to be absolutely fair about this, so if you'd like your own lawyer present, that's fine and we can wait," said Jim Sweeney, "although this shouldn't take long or be too painful."

I shook my head, having checked with Pat beforehand. ("Do I need to shlep a lawyer up here for this?" "Oh, I don't think so.")

"We're simply going to put several questions to you, a simple deposition," advised Charles Everitt, "and that should be it. Remember"—he smiled affably—"we're all on the same team together here, all right?"

Ah, that mythical team again! Where was my logo cap and vacuum cleaner and morning cheerleader song for Hoover?

"Let me run down a series of brief questions, and then go back and ask each one individually, okay?" Jim Sweeney Jr. said, turning to his yellow legal pad. "Now, everything you claim here as fact you know to be true? I mean, you have credible witnesses, or you were there yourself?"

Charlie Everitt asked, "Were any of the . . . more extreme or unusual scenes invented by you, for example? Or embellished by you in any way, let's say—

"Maybe even unconsciously embellished, perhaps?"

And as the questions continued, I realized immediately the obvious thing, the obscene irony: I was going to be forced to fib a bit to these lawyers—well, let's call it lie—otherwise my book was headed for indefinite delay, euphemized change, and gutless pieties. It was not that I had "intentionally lied" in the book, it was that memory itself was deceiving, and writing down accounts was a process of getting a piece of the truth, not the whole. And besides, what the hell was truth, let alone fact? What these legal jerks determined? Are you kidding? . . . Read my *Ziff,* I wanted to say.

So I nodded or shook my head accordingly, said yes or no appropriately, gazed at the mahogany walls and pleasant wall landscape and figured I gave it my best shot in the book, I was not going to be held up here in a conference office by Harvard Law School twits covering their firm's tail. Sure I had to make up some things, create my own furniture, as it were, sketch in my own background, to give certain scenes credibility. Was it "lying" if I re-created a facial tone, a skin coloring, a living room in the Vermont countryside? Sure, in the basics I was as straight as I could be, as honest, but even there, maybe I was inventing, right?

"Now, would you please sign this sheet right here, which simply says that what you've told us in this deposition is the truth?"

The sheet sent shivers up my spine, and I felt the room, with its hot air and heavy atmosphere, closing in on me. Needing air, I scribbled my name, shook hands, and departed with Patrick.

"Here we go, huh, into the wild blue yonder?"

He laughed raucously. "They get paid to worry, don't worry."

"Oh?"

"Think of the other side, how he might be worrying!"

But before my prepublication incubation period had gone by, it was my turn, yet again, to sweat.

Out of the blue, on a lovely September afternoon, I received a copy of the *New Yorker* in the mail, with a paper clip on page 42, marking a new short story by Arthur Ziff. "The Pursuit of Happiness" was the tale of a young writer, Jay Mendele Katz, who, while working on his first novel at MacDowell Colony, meets Josephine Fields McEvoy, a smart young journalist from New York society, also working on a first book (on Vietnam). The affair between "Mendy" and "Josey" was the focus of a hilarious account of a poor Jewish boy and a high Episcopalian girl, switching in locale between Josey's swanky Manhattan and Mendy's seedy Cambridge. The tale was rich in class detailing and comic in class contrasts, moving from Mendy's Brownsville tenement origins to Josey's Upper East Side brownstone, and angling in on clothing, accent, food, and manners. Following closely my own romance with Joey Parnell back in the late Sixties, "Pursuit . . ." was driven by a sharp, mocking tone and acerbic play toward the protagonist. At best "young Mendy" comes off as a foolish naif, and at worst, a humiliated social climber. (In fact, Ziff had originally urged me on in the romance, claiming it would be a great and useful education! My initial reluctance had in fact been based precisely on Joey's exalted background, which, if anything, I was prejudiced against, and, did indeed, learn about. Well, Arthur had been right, in life.) The scenes between Mendy Katz and Mrs. Chandler Trowbridge, Josey's mother and a well-known New York society lady, were worthy of high Waugh. As I read, I alternately laughed and winced, nodded and felt knifed. If the protagonist had not been a sure caricature of myself, or if the material had not been mine, my life, I would have had a fine time, I imagine.

In shock I called Arthur and asked him about it.

"Oh, yeah, is that out now? How do you like it, kid?"

"Not much."

"Oh? Why not?"

I explained why, citing the intrusion, once again, into my private life.

"You're too sensitive, much too sensitive. Look, if you'll forgive me, no one knows you're alive. Besides, aren't you supposed to be writing a nonfiction book about the real life of Arthur Ziff? How do you think *he* feels, pal? Now here comes a story, a fictional piece about a young writer in the 1960s, which might as well be the 1860s, and you're up in arms about it. Aren't you, at the least, being a bit disingenuous?"

I was stopped in my tracks, suddenly stonewalled, and wondered why I had bothered to call. Because I was self-destructive as well as furious?

At last I got ahold of my thoughts. "But maybe I am not caricaturing Arthur Ziff in that biography, not mocking the writer protagonist, not imposing an overly simple satirical frame around a real and complex life."

"Nicely put. Maybe you're not. But, you know, a story is a story. What readers think about, and remember, is Mendy Katz and Josey McEvoy, fictional characters, not any real people. Have you forgotten, already, what fiction is all about?"

I paused. "*Why'd* you do it?"

"I'm a writer, so I write."

"Any other reason?"

He laughed slyly. "Sure, I know what you mean. For the money, that's right. They pay well."

I waited. "Okay, you win."

"Win? I don't win, or lose, actually. But I will let you know if you're interested, what the verdict is. I mean, how the readers vote. I've given out an 800 number, like *USA Today,* so they can call in and vote."

I nodded. "Sure, let me know. I'll be waiting. Well, thanks for giving me a straight answer."

"Oh, a straight answer he wants? How about a straight question instead: *Why do you think I wrote the story?*"

I nodded at his clever retort. "Oh, to give me another warning, another warning shot like the last story."

"Oh? A warning about what?"

"About what I'm writing, the project I'm engaged in, the possible consequences."

A moment of quiet. "You mean . . . I see. Well, you have to take it the way you see it, don't you? But it's too bad that you can't simply read the story as a story, and not as a political torpedo. That way you might want to interpret the stories within your own context, your 'literary biography,' right?" A laugh. "You know, your ninety days were up on that prostate material, and thus far I never even touched it. You take care now, and keep me posted about when you sight another Ziff piece. I'm interested in your reaction."

Checked beautifully in an endgame of exquisite maneuvering, I felt weak and helpless, my king alone without anywhere to move. At the same time, I couldn't help but admire my opponent's dexterity, his original moves. Consider the semihumorous gambit about the prostate! Here in life the fellow was a grand master, wasn't he?

I could do nothing but return to reread my completed manuscript pages, to the shape and substance I had given the Ziff life in my book, to my interpretation of his books, and his place in the culture. There, at least, on the printed-out pages, he was fixed and focused, a safe literary subject whom I could come to terms with, place, understand, interpret, criticize, admire, sympathize with, speculate about. Much more comforting, and maybe more knowable, altogether, than the real fellow.

Two days later, Becka came into my study, in a turmoil. "Don't go on with it, stop now, please! I mean, I can't take it anymore."

Unprepared, I stared at her and held out my palms, helpless. "What's wrong?"

"Wrong? Everything's wrong. You can't see what's been going on because you're in the center of it. It's a tornado around here daily, and it doesn't stop! The endless phone calls from magazines and strangers, the faxes from friends or enemies of Arthur, the urgent legal meetings and those *New Yorker* stories, the Jews who want you to hate him! It's crazy, it's made you crazy, and it's beginning to affect everyone in the house, especially me! Enough, please, enough!"

My heart began beating fast. "Did someone get to you, like write or call you?"

"You see, there you go. I say something to you about what's real, and you turn it around, *paranoid!* No one has called or written me, like you're imagining. It's just that this house, our home, has become a madhouse of . . . of wild comings and goings, a zoo of rings and beeps, and and . . ." Shuddering, she began to cry, and grew Italian beautiful in disheveled grief. "I don't know how much longer the boys and I can carry on this way! Maybe we should separate, if you decide to keep on going with this . . . it's not just another book, it's a . . . monster out of control!"

Touched, I stood up and held her, stroking her back. "Hey, it's going to be over soon, really."

She shook. "Oh? Is finished *over?* Won't things be just as bad later, maybe worse, during publication?"

I tried not to consider that. "Maybe, I don't really know."

"Well, right now it's awful, just awful, like living every day in a pressure cooker! Please, finish it up or give it up, for the sake of my sanity!"

Hers? What about mine?

Yet even as I tried to find out what had precipitated the scene—an intrusive phone call and a reporter visitor that morning—I knew she had made a good point: Things could indeed get worse, wilder later on.

"Think it over, please, you can give back the money, save the pages for a novel, and we can go back to being human again."

Being human, when you're writing? I rubbed her back, suggested a brisk walk for us, and mused what a trick that would be.

When the terrorist attack hit on September 11th, it reverberated up in the New Hampshire woods, too. I had taken my son to school, and on the way back heard the first reports on NPR, and for the next few weeks or so I was as stunned and stopped as the next person. No writing, no focusing on Ziff, just following the ghastly reports and trying to keep up with the daily news. In certain ways it was a relief to be away from the manuscript, the problems I was causing at home. But in other ways I felt as wounded as the next soul, as vulnerable, angry and helpless. Even in my boondocks the shock of those jets crashing into the Twin Towers hit my consciousness, ceasing all work, shifting my concentration.

twenty-five

In October, on a cool, overcast Monday, I drove down to the Boston area to take a brief tour of the old Jewish cemeteries cited so frequently in the Ziff novels. In West Roxbury I visited first the old Grove and Centre Street cemeteries, dating from the late nineteenth century, and a short distance away, bordering Newton, the Baker Street cemetery, dating from the 1930s, where Arthur's parents were buried. I strolled about the lot, shaped like a tall boot with the toes cut off, remembering the fantastic scene in *Goldfeld at Eighty* where Goldfeld goes to inspect his family plot, observes the graves of his two brothers, and faces his own approaching end. (Indeed, right there, by the two crooked tombstones in the Ostro Marsho plot, I recognized the site of the old man's long internal monologue, where, in the course of recalling his life, he curses his Jewish God with as much bile as Captain Ahab against his God, in part for taking Goldfeld's younger brothers before him. ("Death, be not undaunted, I'm coming, but I'm coming at you swinging, kicking, cursing! . . .")

Strolling about in the graveyard, I realized again how close to the real was Arthur's fiction, how hard it was to distinguish between the two in many of his scenes. And I recalled anew that dark, pressing detail from *G at 80,* as to why there were no really old Jewish cemeteries around Boston: Jews were not allowed to be buried in the old Boston of Puritans and Brahmins for the first few hundred years, so Jewish corpses had to be sent down to Newport, Rhode Island, to be laid to rest. Only Ziff would have landed a detail like that and found a fitting structure to set it in: Goldfeld's late "ninth-inning elegy." No platitudes or pieties there, just octogenarian anger, fiery emotion, resolute spite.

A fine drizzle was falling, and I was glad for my baseball cap and waterproof windbreaker. I was a boy again. And there among the dead, the anonymous ghosts, I felt curiously peaceful, respectful. A short walk on the sodden ground and I came to the Boylston Lodge plot, where I searched for and found the tombstones of the Ziffs, Judith and Morris. Modest stones, with names and dates ("In loving memory"), and a spare plot alongside; for Arthur? On my haunches, I sat and reflected. Despite all, the death of Ziff would be a personal loss for me, a close family member gone, a great old friend. You never had enough of those. Standing, I started to move off and away when my eye was caught by a tilting tombstone in the same row, bearing a very similar family name, Sieff, Gyorgy Paul "Pinchus" Sieff, with the birthplace Budapest, and the dates 1922–1966. But who was this? I wondered, startled. A distant relative, an uncle? . . . I had never heard his name mentioned anywhere. Was this a clue, in some (furtive) part, to Arthur's keen interest and steady involvement in Hungary? I jotted down the details, made a note to e-mail Éva, and ambled on.

Death flourished here; this was his stage and setting—Jewish death, specifically. The landscape was still, flat and gray, the light drizzle created a kind of bluish clarity, and it hit me as a fine place to think, to remember. I was beginning to understand why several recent Ziff protagonists returned here again and again, feeling it as a respite, a kind of second home, a site to retire to. Indeed, death had become a preoccupation in the last books, and the graveyard served well as a dark vacation home for the likes of those ardent realists, Goldfeld, Rosenthal, Raphael. Why not? Instead of Miami Beach or Scottsdale condos, the graveyard was closer, truer, for

Ziff's end-of-life loners. Soon even I, like the protagonists, was starting to feel the proximity of death as an alive presence, the ghosts as real as the tombstones, graves, iron railings. And it wasn't too bad after all, its pervasive gray presence, once you hung around the turf for a while.

Here they were, Moscowitz and Skolnick, Levine and Felstein, Fishbein and Tavel (*Tavel's Long Tenure?*), Greenberg and Gornick, on and on the names went, in the endless lineup. (If only a few voices could speak up, especially Gyorgy Pincus Ziff?) No sign of a caretaker, but the place was well maintained, groomed. The landscape of death was not so drab gray after a while, but rather quiet and clear; for some, like that pair of swallows diving about. Strangely calmed, I made my way out, wet, reflective.

And driving home, I thought how an anthology of great cemetery scenes in literature would make a unique book—starting with Gogol—and how Ziff's contribution would not be inconsiderable.

I e-mailed Éva that night, and received this the next day:

> *Never heard of your G.P.S. but it is intriguing. In the local phone book, I found these names, however: Gesa Ziffer, Ottö Ziffer, Ziffermayer, and a Cziffra. So Ziff has Hungary associations? Will check into all, and let you know. Éva.*

I wrote Arthur a note, too, citing the mysterious name, and waited. A few days later a postcard said: "No, I don't know of any rookie by that name playing for the Mets this year, but who knows?"

Ziff: A Life actually came out in winter 2002 after several stops and starts, and a legal scare.

[The legal scare sent shivers up my spine and exposed the spinelessness of the publishers and their lawyers. Indeed, I had to change publishers at the last minute, when they threatened to edit and/or expurgate whole sections of the book (despite the self-incriminating indemnity clause). What happened was that I was called in for a deposition by Ziff's legal team—for those interested, see the Appendix—a session lasting nearly two days, which had the effect of sending me away reeling, in a state of shock, and to bed for two more days, in a desperate frenzy that all was lost, the whole project doomed. In hiding, I cried on and off like a baby, for the bind I was in. The screws had been turned, good and tight, first by my own publisher's set of lawyers and then by Arthur's—obviously Larry T. was staying neutral—not to mention media predators. The pressure was tight, tight! I didn't succumb; I changed, deleted nothing. In any case, we luckily found a gutsy publisher who took the book over, and no suit was ever filed. Gerard stood by me, Pat felt awful and nearly cried about the whole situation and his loss of the book.

But I was at least entitled to a copy of the deposition, and, for the reader curious enough, I have enclosed a verbatim record of that awful inquiry. Because of its legal dryness and its somewhat tangential interest I have set this at the back of this account as a text separate unto itself.*]

Surprisingly enough (for me) *Ziff* was reviewed alongside Arthur's new Holocaust novel, *The Wallenberg Wars*. (In other words, the timing was ironically right—for one of us.) I read his book with eagerness—sent via his publisher—and had a mixed reaction. The first fifty to a hundred pages were fired by sections of brilliance and a design of stunning conceits, but the next three hundred did not live up to or fulfill that early promise. The portrait of Raoul Wallenberg was done with élan and style—the aristocratic voice handled convincingly, the Swedish/Hungarian material fleshed out with Ziff's special care for research. Raoul's secret Jewish girlfriend was sexy, smart. The use of counter-protagonists was audacious, two young Hungarian lads whom we follow to their different ends, modeled partly on Arthur's old Dorchester buddy (Siggy Goldberg). What was wrong, then? Much of the rest was too clever, too sensational—incredulous pyrotechnic scenes, juxtapositions of modern America and World War II Europe rather easy, melodramatic. As for great Holocaust moments, *TWW* tried too hard, revealing too much of the writer's machinery. (A notable exception: the long, detailed scene of the "Death March" of

*See page 397, in "Appendix."

Budapest Jews, via the town of Hegyashalom to the Austrian border.) In sum, *TWW* lagged behind the subtle works of other Holocaust story writers and novelists, Tadeus Borowski, Ida Fink, Ilona Carmel, (not to mention Primo Levi).

Predictably, however, *The Wallenberg Wars* went over big with the reviewers. After all, this was the Holocaust, this was America 2002, this was Arthur Ziff; sentimentality and the cultural fix were in. It was hailed as an "evocative masterpiece" (*New York Times*) and the "crowning work of A. Z.'s oeuvre" *(New York Review)*. Little doubt that *TWW* would be the cultural hit of the year, the National Book Awards, Book Expo, NJBA, *Irish Times* winner, the sequel to the Schindler blockbuster. The Culture Machine was at work.

For many critics, the timing, both books arriving more or less at once, was perfect, since my *Ziff: A Life* made for perfect fodder, while *The Wallenberg Wars* was hoisted up and up. The equation was easy, a Book of Calumny versus a Book of Virtue. For example, the *Sunday Times Book Review* held up the "terrific imaginative achievement" of Ziff, while doing a hatchet job on me. "Poor Danny Levitan," wrote the sly reviewer, an English writer, "always coming in second behind Ziff as the 'bad boy' of American litera- ture, as the creator of machismo protagonists, as the cultivator of a muscular and profane prose style. And now he comes in a poor second as the interpreter of his old friend—a second to Ziff him- self in his fiction and nonfiction in this misguided, envy-driven, scurrilous account of the modern American master." Whew. Right there in the *Times,* that poison language, that obscene indictment, stung, hurt, festered. So what if it wasn't true, any of it? So what if there was no evidence backing up those scurrilous charges? So what? Who cared—except for me?

The reviewer continued, "Sometimes the serendipitous timing of books is only too telling, and this is such an occasion. A cheap and nefarious biography appears alongside a heroic and towering novel by the very subject, revealing to us the lows and highs of literature. For his thinly disguised satiric work Mr. Levitan should be *condemned to no more publishing* for a long while, while for

Mr. Ziff the time is ripe to acknowledge that this writer is producing the one true ongoing oeuvre in tune with the pulse of our times. Read this *Wallenberg Wars* and you will understand the bleak, powerful workings of good and evil, and appreciate how the authenticity of one is tied ineluctably to the other. But to understand Mr. Ziff himself, we will have to wait for a more authentic and more generous book than the artificial and tendentious artifact produced out of greed by Mr. Levitan."

Ah, the clever Englishman, seeing right through me. Arthur had been right, as usual. He knew it, too, as his brief note indicated: "I warned you, pal, that you'd be fair game, and it's starting. I suggest you hide out, maybe Canada or Mexico, since this hunting season has targeted you and it's going to go on for several months, maybe longer. Too bad, huh? And bad luck, too, about the timing of my own novel coming out just now. . . . "

Brilliant, huh? He had had one last ace up his sleeve after all, and waited patiently to play it *(TWW)* at just the right moment.

And when *New York* magazine and *The New Republic* chipped in with long, dense attacks—while praising *TWW*—I knew he must be right again. My ethics, my sources, my prose, my manhood were held up for ridicule. On the map I searched out Regina, Moosejaw, Saint John, and, down south, Cuernavaca, Guadalajara, Oaxaca. . . .

I was thrown into a deep chasm, a quicksand of depression. Only those lonely survivors who have written a long book, endured three or four years of solitary effort and writer's strain, and then faced a hostile, unfair, mocking audience will understand the pain, the lacerating wound. An execution squad was neater, I surmised, far more merciful. I would gladly have accepted that alternative just then, I believe, had it been offered.

The injury, the despair left me so wounded, so isolated that finally one day Rebecca suggested it would be better if I left the house, since I was beginning to affect the boys. "What's wrong with Dad?" Jonathan had asked, she reported. "Why doesn't he snap out of it?" She wondered if I went on a trip for a while, a few weeks, or a few months, wouldn't be best? "Or you could stay in the area somewhere, rent a room and start seeing a doctor, maybe that'll do," she said, not without sympathy. "But you're not helping anyone around here this way, and you may hurt the boys seriously, permanently, if you keep this up."

Why not? She was right, too—again, just as Arthur had forewarned, in his first short story. So life was following art, and Arthur was making it happen. Maybe that Israeli writer was on the mark? Maybe he was a maker of miracles.

A week later, during a hard February month, I packed, and tried my best to say good-bye to the boys, sensing that this might be my very last one to them. "But why do you have to go so far away for so long?" cried Gaby. "I want to come with you! Please, Dad!" I kissed his scented face and felt his tears. Teenage Jon stood by his side, and when it was his turn, he said, "Yeah, Dad, why so long? Why not a week or two?" I hugged him, kissed his neck, felt my own tears, said, "We'll see, maybe it'll be only a week or two after all. I just need to get away for a while." He asked, "Is it because the reviews were not so good, Dad?" That sentence hurt as much as the leavetaking, but I only shrugged and said, "Oh, that's part of it, but not all. You guys take care of the house, of Mom, of Hobbes, okay?" Gave them one face-to-face look, a painful hug, and turned to Rebecca, to whom I had already given a reminder list of items to watch for—plumbing, snow weight on roof or leakage, icy drive-ways—along with phone numbers of helpers, and checks. Said the necessary "I'll be in touch," was advised to "take care, and get a good rest." Driving away on the dirt road in my Saab was as hard as anything, a little like watching the novel cross the finish line. An end to something. My just rewards.

twenty-six

Sitting in the shaded veranda of the Gran Hotel Costa Rica in downtown San José, I sipped my coffee and delicious soft roll, feeling the sultry air and taking in the outdoor scene about me.

Already I had established a little routine, ambling along the narrow streets from my small hotel to the large veranda of the majestic Gran, buying my *International Trib,* and taking my breakfast in the warm morning. Seventy-five feet away, in a small park, local Indians were hawking pineapple slices and bananas, students were sketching, and shoeshine boys tossed pennies, while surrounding me at the small tables were all sorts of hotel guests and travelers, Americans, worldly backpackers, German residents. (I could tell the latter from their semiformal dress, loud, confident talk in German, their switch to Spanish for ordering.)

This had been my ritual for five days now, resisting my strong nightly impulse to call the boys and hear their voices. I spent my days wandering about, seeing the handsome mixed faces of the Ticos and the baroque National Theater, the Gold Museum, the appealing side streets. Being bathed by the exotic atmosphere and the soft weather did me little good, however; I still felt the despair inside, like a knot hiding in the region of my stomach. I tried my best not to think about it, and focused instead on the sports news from the *Tribune,* the NCAA playoffs in basketball, baseball spring training. . . .

"Excuse me"—a fellow in a Hawaiian shirt leaned down—"but if I'm not mistaken, aren't you Jake Aarons from the Outfit?"

I shook my head, bewildered.

The craggy-faced fellow persisted: "Afghanistan, 1987 or '88, I think. Didn't we meet there?"

"Wrong fellow," I said, taken aback, wondering.

He gave me an odd glance, nodded skeptically, walked off.

I returned to my newspaper, my chest congesting at the mistake. A plant of some sort? . . . A few minutes later I smiled to myself. Maybe I was better off hiding out down here as "Jake Aarons" than as Danny Levitan? Certainly it made more sense. I had an impulse to follow the stranger, confirm his suspicion for him, and begin a new life. Aarons in Costa Rica, like (Malamud's) Levin in Oregon. . . .

I leaned back, and shook my head to no one. I felt the odd man out here, odd and estranged, when, under different circumstances,

I might have been having a grand time. This soft-weather country was so different, yet so civilized. Banks worked, drivers were sane, rooms were clean, citizens were helpful. But here I was, mourning my losses back home. What sort of losses—reviews, reputation, maybe family, that's all. Oh, well.

I returned to the scores of the previous night's games, happy to see Indiana knocked out again, especially by Princeton. The torch of Pete Carrill was still carried on by his successor, showing how the bounce pass and back-door cut could win; good for the college game.

Afterward I strolled down to the small park, past the vendors, toward a beckoning shoeshine boy.

"Sure," I said to his twelve- or thirteen-year-old smiling face. After his bright *"Buenos días, señor,"* he chattered on in Spanish, and I lifted my leather walking shoe onto his wooden box. As he applied his brushes and rags, I was taken back to my own childhood in Brooklyn, where, on the corner of Sutter and Ralph Avenues, I had had my own shoeshine beat. At age ten I was all set up, in front of Woolworth's, at 5:30 P.M., to catch the El crowd returning home from work on the New Lots IRT. The charge was a dime for a shine, and I hoped for a nickel tip. I had my own box, rags, brushes, and creams, plus dreams. After four or five shines, I'd feel like a prince, rich enough to go to the Sutter or Pitkin Theater for a movie, enjoy a charlotte russe, buy a pink spaldeen and a Captain Marvel or Batman comic, or save it for a bleacher seat at a Dodger game. What more could a boy ever want?

"Señor, iss okay?"

I looked down at the high-sheen shine—I preferred a flatter finish—but I nodded my approval and let him proceed. Childhood in Brownsville flooded me . . . playing our invented game of spaldeen baseball, throwing the pink rubber ball off the high side wall of Woolworth's and seeing if the opponent out in the street could catch it on the fly, and if not, on how many bounces—each bounce counting for another base—all the while dodging honking cars or charging buses. . . . Using that same wall to play Johnny on the Pony, with Ronnie K. or another chubby kid playing pillow up against the wall, while the rest of his four-man team lined up, backs bent over, awaiting the opposing team to run and leap on them in an attempt to collapse the pony. . . . The rush of ring-a-levio, either in Lincoln Terrace or there on Ralph Avenue, hiding out in the scary underground grease pits of the Flying Mobil station beneath the El. . . . Hanging out by the green upright metal mailbox on the Sutter Theater corner, a shifting pack of ten or twelve teenage boy cubs, pondering the evening plan, shadow-boxing, arm-wrestling, tossing a ball, mocking each other with the lowest slurs and curses or wise-cracking the young teenage girls strolling by, and winding up later at the corner luncheonette beneath the El for an egg cream or vanilla and chocolate frappé, squabbling over the Yankees and Dodgers, bantering with Al the owner's son. . . .

"Señor?" he called me back to see his finished performance; I nodded my approval and gave him an American dollar. His face lit up. Scraggly shorts, a stained T-shirt, small sandals. The hair jet black, thick, wild, the skin a dark olive.

Carefully, I leaned down to see what he carried in his bulging, battered sport bag. Grinning with pleasure, he displayed red and black string licorice, a plastic water bottle, a tattered gray soccer ball, a ragged fabric wallet, assorted pins with insignias, bottle tops, sports cards, string.

I smiled, he beamed, and I reached into my pocket for my key ring. Releasing the key to my house, I gave him the copper clasp, which was in the shape of an opera ticket, a little souvenir from the Sante Fe Opera House.

Amazed, he held it up in his hand as though it were gold. *"¡Muchas gracias!"*

I shook his hand firmly and meandered into the small park. The aromas from bougainvillea, honeysuckle, and oleander invaded my senses. I sat on a bench to finish my morning reading. Back then in 1950 Brooklyn, my two-hour shoeshine earnings shocked my Russian immigrant father, who spent his long days in a Manhattan sweatshop loft laboring over his embroidery machine for forty to forty-five dollars a week. (He had dropped out of college in his first year to get married and earn wages.) I took pride in my old wooden shoeshine box, which I had bought secondhand, keeping it clean and well organized, though I felt a certain ambivalence in impressing my father with the money I made. A greenhorn with ties to the old country, he never got to understand the America I knew, a place of fun and easy opportunity.

A Tico lady walked by with her child and nodded hello.

Ziff's father was a very different sort, a son of Bucovenia immigrants and a man more optimistic about the new country, a less severe personality, less arrogant, altogether more genial. I had met him during several Thanksgiving dinners at Arthur's house, among other occasions, and had gotten along with him well. He had a certain hard charm, a feisty determination. I admired the way Arthur had treated him in the fiction, with humor, sympathy, mild satire. And Samuel Ziff was an ardent supporter of his son, no matter what; when Jeanne L. became the girlfriend of record, he befriended her, even courted her in his persistent way (stage and movie star questions). And he viewed his place in Arthur's fiction (e.g., *Dorchester Boy*) as evidence of his importance and merit, regardless of the portrait. In *Ziff: A Life* I had done my best to convey his truculent charm, his amusing ferocity, his paternal determination. It was to Arthur's credit, I wrote, the way he kept his parents in his world of writing, from *DB* to *Judith: Dying Days*.

Samuel had grown used to his son's succession of gentile women, and grew bemused by them. Taking me by the arm one day, he explained, "Look, a good *shiksa* is far better than a bad Jewish *maidl*, right? And let's be thankful for small things, he never has had children with these *shiksas,* yeah?" He squeezed my arm. "Though it kills me that he's given me no grandchildren. 'Well, what can you do?' I only wish Judith was alive. He's a wonderful son, a real *mensch,* a famous American, he gives me plenty of *nachas,* you can't have everything, yeah? So, no *kinder,* big deal."

Seychl, common sense, he showed. I was truly fond of the seventy-five-year-old phenom who could tell you every single player on the old Boston Braves roster, his favorite being Sid

Gordon, of course, the slugger who came over from the Giants. "Imagine, a Jewish *bucher* who could hit home runs that way! No one except Greenberg could ever whack the ball like that!"

I sat down on a slatted bench, brimming with fine memory in the soft sun, before reverting to my dismal state of sorrow. Down and out in San José, in my condition, was every bit as bad as Orwell down and out in Paris and London.

Judith was another matter, I recalled, turning the large pages in the *Trib*. She—suddenly I came up short and found my heart pounding furiously. There, on the book review page, was a photo of myself, alongside one of Arthur, and a review of my book. Oh, my God. I swallowed hard, my breath coming fast. I closed the paper, felt my eyes beginning to tear. No, I couldn't take being trailed down here and punished anew. I had only bought the *Trib* to read the sports scores! It wasn't fair! I half cried out, standing up.

Ha, I mocked myself, *not fair.* That's pretty good. Sit down and take it like a man, Danny. You asked for it, you got it, *and were getting it, in spades.* Not fame, but infamy and calumny.

Holding the hot *Trib* in my hands, I surmised that maybe my breakdown was also the final result or payback of the many years of lonely toil, of my endless days of writing which had earned little public recognition in recent years, meaning, I had been a failure. You know, an unAmerican. But I hadn't fully understood or acknowledged that, and had gone on, unwaveringly, sitting at my desk day in day out, making up all sorts of illusory scenarios about why I had become obscure, in order to shield myself. Making up this or that reason for the victories and awards of other writers. But I thought now that maybe the accumulation of those lack of recognition years had created an invisible growth on my heart and psyche, pressing upon me, like some cancerous literary tumor.

Walking in sunny San Juan, I viewed myself sitting back home, on duty, at my birch desk, typing on the laptop or correcting with pencil the printed pages, and the portrait I observed was that of a brave but misguided soul, toiling on and on in a valiant but rather pointless effort. A portrait gray and sad, a *New*

Grub Street set in New Hampshire. Was this how it had truly been? I wondered. (Was this how Becka, and the world, had pictured me too?) Little wonder then that Danny L. had taken on the Ziff book, willing to chance exposing himself to public criticism and humiliation; for he was coming up for air, for the first time in years. And little wonder that such exposure and subsequent blows would then knock him flat, down, out. . . .

And yet, yet, the devotion had been worth it, the daily writing of four or five hours and two or three pages in the religious service to art. The solitary flying while sitting, the relentless pursuit of the imagination, the attempt to break free of the internal censor and the polite, the reach for the right scene, sentence, word—all this was a worthy labor of one's desire. So what if the hours, the months, the years, were not rewarded by the powerful world, by the literary society, those hours were reward in and of themselves. Danny Levitan was doing what he had wanted to do, he was working alone every day, in his small study, in the service of his vision, and maybe etching a little beauty and a few truths— maybe, maybe—and that effort buoyed the soul, like water bearing a boat. So what to others may have been a useless grind, a grand folly, was to himself a noble project.

For a minute I thought I heard the faraway music of Gabriel playing "The Swan" on his cello, and a recitation from the Odyssey, Book VI, by Jonathan, and I felt okay, felt able to sit down and take up the newspaper attack anew.

A long review, done by a guest reviewer who usually taught in the Buffalo area, a smart fellow who had never much taken to my fiction (with the exception of one book). Oh, well, at least it wouldn't be a hack attack.

Hardly ever in the history of American literature have we been offered a literary biography by one living writer on another living writer, both serious, in the manner of Gorky on Tolstoy, although we have had long essays, such as Henry James on Hawthorne or Howells on Twain. We have one now, and my report, much against the current of other reviews, is good. Danny Levitan, an interesting writer himself who has been down on his luck for the past decade, has not only written a fascinating account of his erstwhile friend and famous contemporary Arthur Ziff, but he has produced a book that raises new and valuable questions about the man behind the writer, the man behind the fictional masks. It will be the benchmark, I believe, for all future works on Mr. Ziff.

Now, the first thing to note perhaps about this *Ziff: A Life* is how so many of the easy traps and obvious pitfalls are avoided by Mr. Levitan, such as ravishing overpraise or vicious debasement. In other words, this is neither hagiography nor demonization. Rather, it is a surprisingly balanced account of a complex—perhaps super-complex—contemporary life. Second, and equally important, it is worth noting how in the end Mr. Levitan avoids concluding falsely and easily, or tying together too neatly, many of the hard dilemmas and real paradoxes of Arthur Ziff, as laid out in the book. That approach, while displeasing some and disconcerting others, satisfies this reviewer.

As one who has written at length on the works (and life) of Arthur Ziff, I will admit that I was quite surprised to read some of the biographical revelations, yet not at all dismayed by the repeated reservations, skeptical qualifications, and open questions presented along with those revelations. What others took to be veiled criticism by Mr. Levitan, criticism built on a bedrock of envy, I took to be quite otherwise—the deft uncovering of the vulnerabilities, the uncertainties, the wild risks of Mr. Ziff; this is not disingenuous satire, but reveals honest-to-goodness doubt and intellectual sympathy by the biographer. And as to the possible switching of personality by the novelist in the Old World—a life of saintly acts and uncommon virtues to the point of incredulity—I admire the way Mr. Levitan treats it, with a straightforwardness and "what-if contingency" sense that allows the reader to make up his own mind. Is this roguish disingenuity by Mr. Levitan, or rather, as I believe, frank authenticity?

I read on with such surprise and excitement that I hardly knew what I was reading. Two tears rolled down my cheeks, my heart was pounding, and the burning sun felt like a beatific heat splashing me. I slowed down my reading to a paragraph-at-a-time crawl.

I also must take issue with those critics who have taken Mr. Levitan to task for writing about Mr. Ziff's financial stakes. What they took as a vulgar research and intrusive burrowing, I took as an honest look at a famous but serious writer's fiscal fortunes in the contemporary world. Even more pertinent, however, is the link established between Mr. Ziff's money and the daring uses he has put it toward, in Budapest, Rome, Jerusalem. For without that crucial accounting I, for one, would not have believed possible those extraordinary acts of private generosity. Suddenly, the fabulous becomes practical, the unimaginable doable.

I felt redeemed. Indeed, I was actually pleased when I skipped to a paragraph of criticism and disagreement by the reviewer; it gave the long piece a sense of full plausibility, and for me, reality.

One of the things that is sadly missing here, of course, is a thoroughgoing research based on correspondence to and from Mr. Ziff. This was hardly possible, given Mr. Ziff's total noncooperation on the project. But this gives us cause to wonder about the many statements and judgments offered here, their potential for unreliability and narrowness. It also suggests other possible omissions,

which may only be discovered at some future date, by
someone who will have more access to all the letters,
papers, manuscripts, via Mr. Ziff or, afterward, his literary executor (not to mention other persons to be inter-
viewed, who may have refused because of Mr. Ziff's
refusal to participate). In other words, *Ziff*, valuable as it
is, is only the beginning.

Still, it is valuable indeed, and more than valuable,
vitally important for reevaluating the man and his
work. . . .

I paused, held up, cried slightly, blessed the fellow. Didn't
even mind the grand irony, that the gravest or grandest omission
of all was *in my hands but not in the book.* So what, right? Leave it
for posterity.

At that point I couldn't resist reaching into my wallet and
taking out the opening paragraphs from "A Fateful Affair"
which I had borne with me for the past eighteen months, for
verification, proof . . . that I wasn't mad, or had made it all up.
I unfolded the lined page, holding it up as though it were
Godel's proof or a leaf of Shakespearean folio, and read from the
second paragraph.

When I look back at that fateful affair that has stayed
with me for years and years, through my later life and
my friend's going on to a married life, I am struck by
how impotent I am to write about it, to remake the
"actual" thing into a coherent artful tale—which, after
all, is my trade—and thereby go on to another experience in my thinking and feeling. But this final solace,
the only real one I suppose for the likes of us, has eluded
me. Nevertheless, the affair, or the series of events that
made up the affair of those six years, presses upon me
today with all the urgency and immediacy of those days,
and therefore I shall go forward, though I realize I am
still lacking the underlying artifice, call it the necessary

structure, upon which I can reconstruct the material. So, abandoned by art here, I shall trek forward on my own as it were, propelled by memory, supported by desire. Are they enough? I wonder ruefully.

In all this I shall be guided by her full-featured face and dark, expressive eyes, by her swiftly mobile expressions and unrestrained interior ardor, by her sudden Yiddish inflections and phrases and low-pitched musical voice, by her passion to aspire to my expectation when, in fact, it was I who was trying to reach hers—in other words, by all the qualities I would have been sure to mock and dismiss in other accounts, including my own. Well, so be it, even here I circle, I suppose, so let me begin.

Enveloped by the scent of honeysuckle and by the aroma of the Ziff prose, I folded the page back into my wallet and returned to the *Trib*. Ah, the literary aroma, it was a fragrance all its own, and either you smelled it or you didn't. I paused to feel the thin paper and to slow the anticipation. I decided to take out a subscription to the *IHT* when I got back to my New Hampshire hill. Was any four-star French dish as ravishing as a good, intelligent review? I read on, and on.

The review and the sultry air and the wonderful flowers lifted me into the best mood I had been in for months, years. I'd be a fool to tempt my fate, and come up for air, return to real life, America. No, no, not now. Stay put, I figured, stay on this lucky little strip of land hugged by the Pacific and the Atlantic, where golden frogs cavort, giant turtles beach and birth, and exotic birds from north and south migrate and cross. Well, maybe Danny Levitan could join the crew, somehow, and find his own niche, and wait, read, wait. . . .

Why return?

At Monteverde Cloud Forest, a huge biological reserve, I stayed several days in a quaint hotel high on the mountain and toured the forest by day. Up there, on the continental divide, the clouds kissed the mountaintops, creating a kind of misty bluish sheen, and giving the place an eerie feeling. Huge crawling vines wound their way round trees ("strangler figs"), slowly choking them over the years. Loud gawking sounds erupted now and then, and tropical birds colored bright orange, canary yellow, and cobalt blue flitted by regularly. Wild orchids of delicate pink and mauve mingled with giant ferns and moss-hung trees. A realm of shimmering green, moist mountains, jungle forest flowing with ripeness. I expected Rama, W. H. Hudson's wild half-human creature in *Green Mansions,* to leap out from a tree.

Evenings I took my dinner at the spare inn, where a few other tables were occupied by biologists (from the University of Michigan) and foreign tourists. I stayed to myself, gazing out at the low clouds, reading my paperback *(The Red and the Black).* Julien Sorel up here was no stranger than Danny Levitan. If I hid out for six months, in this isle of clouds, I could get much reading done. Good reading. Get acquainted again with all the old friends whom I had known in youth but, later on, was too busy to meet up with again. Hans Castorp and von Aschenbach, Tess and Jude, Anna K., Ivan Ilych and Svidrigalov, Pip and Magwitch, on and on. Becka had been right to send me away. I was better off, it seemed, and happier, too.

"Excuse me, but aren't you Mr. Levitan, the author?" asked the fiftyish woman in an amiable voice. "I just read the review the other day in the *Tribune* and saw your photograph. I look forward to reading the book. Excuse me for bothering you."

"Not at all," I said. "You're a visitor here?"

"Oh, no, hardly." A slender, dignified woman, she smiled, embarrassed. "We came down nearly fifteen years ago. My husband passed away a year ago. My daughters and I live across the way, in the Quaker settlement. I come up here occasionally for dinner."

"Where'd you come from?" I asked, motioning her to sit.

"Upstate New York. New City. A group of us came for political reasons. Got tired of paying taxes to the Pentagon." Spoken merrily, not preachily. "It's worked out rather well. It's a very decent place. And I have much more time for reading!" She laughed mildly. "You've probably seen our cheese shop in the village, but have you visited the community yet?"

I shook my head.

"Well, you must, it's literally a stone's throw away from the reserve. Would you like to come tomorrow for lunch, or dinner?"

I thanked her and said maybe. "How large is the community?"

"Oh, twenty-five or thirty families. It fluctuates."

I took her phone number and said I'd call the next day.

She stood to leave. "You know, we've just ordered Mr. Ziff's new novel for our reading group—we're doing a Holocaust unit next month—and now maybe I will add your biography; it sounds fascinating. You won't happen to be around then, will you, to speak to us?"

"Oh, I don't know, but thanks."

She shook my hand and walked off. So the Holocaust had found its way down here, to a reading group in the clouds. Why not?

Later, back in my simple room, I sat in a rocker with my Stendahl, but my mind was wandering. Even in faraway Costa Rica, on a mountaintop reserve, amid the clouds and frogs, books landed. How curious, old-fashioned. The seventy-five-watt bulb illumined the plain wooden walls, a watercolor landscape. The stillness of the night in the modest hotel was satisfying. Here one could read, imagine, hike, discover, and—eventually go crazy. Maybe take up with a Tico woman, or even a Quaker widow, and start anew. But why?

I opened the door and saw the bubble of clouds hanging right there, waiting. Could I make out a message, a signal, in them?

Staring out at the gray sky. . . . That *Trib* review had given me a glimmer of hope at just the right moment. Now perhaps I could go home and take the next round of hits—the assault by the magazine bombardiers, the Quarterly tail gunners. The black flak that stayed around for a week, a month, in doctors' offices, on coffee tables, academic shelves.

Oh, forget it, I begged myself; it was small stuff. Focus on the boys, the energetic and aromatic boys.

And your life, your dimming life.

You gave it your best, pal. So you lost. You were warned. Get over it. Go up the coast and see the giant turtles come ashore, give birth. (Bring the boys down to see that, and let them have some real schooling, huh?) Call Arthur and tell him you understand now, you give in. Ha. Fat chance. Too late for that friendship now. The clouds moved slightly, parted for a minute, and revealed the shining, dark sky. Was that Orion gleaming there?

In Evelyn Randall's living room the next afternoon I took a tea, after my half-day hike through the magical forest. A tasteful house, with books, tapes, and old-style Danish furniture. Spare, comfortable, and sensible—a little like Evelyn herself.

"You see," she was saying, sitting in a Canadian rocker, "we got tired of paying the majority of our taxes for the armed services, their new weapons, little wars. There was little we could do to stop it, so Bob and I decided, when we heard about the community down here, to give it a try. And it's worked out well. Up in the States nothing much has changed from what I see—I go back up once a year or so—even when there is a Republican president. The Pentagon still rules like a fourth power, whereas down here"—she smiled beautifully—"there's still no real army. Along with the friendliness, the common decency, and the beauty, of course. Where do you live back home?"

As I answered, I thought how civilized Evelyn was, and her home. Not a bad situation, was it? Besides, she had very fine legs, I saw now, as she recrossed her legs and her skirt edged almost above her knee momentarily, before she tugged it down.

"Also I've learned a lot down here," she went on, "how narrow and prejudiced I've been, and judgmental. I used to judge people all the time, tacitly, as though I were morally superior, though I could never admit that aloud. No more. Now I take people as they come, for what they are, not for what their past or circumstances may suggest." She laughed. "Forgive me, I seem to be shooting my mouth off for no good reason—maybe I'm nervous from being in the company of a real live author?"

Not so real or alive, I wanted to say to that proper, decent woman. I observed her sitting there, graying hair handsome, slender figure and sitting posture erect, smooth-skinned face eager. Well, here was an opportunity, I thought; her remarks, and her lack of personal questioning, signaled something, didn't it? (Or was I going bonkers early?) Anyway, Danny Levitan among the Quakers had a certain ring to it. A new life indeed, my friend.

"This is unusual tea," I said, and, nodding, she expounded on the very special healing qualities of the local natural herb.

twenty-seven

I arrived back home in time for mud season, with the deep ruts and potholes of the dirt road a messy challenge for the Saab. Yet if I was able to keep at least one tire on high ground, I generally made it through. (Following the ruts, or moving over to the soft shoulder, was the danger.) Also, with the days sunny and above freezing, and the nights in the twenties, it was ideal temperature for sugaring. As we had done for the past few years, the boys and I hung the buckets from spigots we bored into half a dozen large sugar maples, and by late afternoon each day, they were filled with sap and ready to be gathered by the father-and-son team up the road, who boiled the sap in the Rube Goldberg evaporator in their sugar house. The sap was running well, and though it took some thirty-two gallons of the clear liquid sugar water to make one gallon of syrup, in a week they had made nearly a gallon for us.

Although I had been treated like a returning war hero by the family, I came back wounded, just as I had started out two weeks before. The surge from the review in the *Tribune* had slowly receded by the time I returned home. (After all, who read the *Trib* here, except maybe ex-CIA agents? Or, had it been syndicated from the *Washington Post?*) And the highs I had gotten from hiking the cloud forest and later viewing the giant turtles beaching, those, too, had evaporated. So I fell back to my starting ground more or less, subconsciously waiting for the next shot to be fired my way. Or was that to be the worst shot of all, silence, the stunning silence of indifference?

As for Arthur, who knew? It might be a very long time before I heard his voice again, if ever. . . .

After rearranging myself with the family, giving the boys their presents (painted oxcarts and T-shirts) and Rebecca hers (necklace, earrings), I settled in gradually with the mail, e-mail, and telephone messages. In the mail, letters from readers had already started coming in via the publisher, and I got around to these after several days. The first eight had come from a mix of friends, strangers, new foes.

Mme. Jeanne was short and not sweet:

> *You have betrayed my cause, my confidences, Daniel, and that is shameful. You present selections of my diary entries without a full context and explanation, and then worse, by deliberately avoiding comment on them, yet allowing Arthur the Fiend to counter, make it look as though you agree with him! With your role of 'neutrality,' you try to make yourself look like the Swiss—look at them now!—and make me come out appearing to be a sex maniac. Is that what you hoped for? Shame on you! You are either a coward or a liar, and shall pay dearly for the betrayal! Now it is CLEAR why you refused to send me the early ms.!*

Michelle from Boston was more moderate:

> *You have done a convincing job with Arthur's life, I must say, and my place in it. Though it is true that you make me seem a bit like Tuesday Weld in hot pants on roller wheels, it is also true that you write about me as a woman, not as slut, and that my place in Arthur's life has*

not been without its importance. On the other issue of my concern, that off-limits zone, The Wooing of the Princess, I was gratified to see, Major Problem Avoided. Honorable. (And smart.)

P.S.: There is more to A. Z.'s life than even I had imagined. What a surprising life. (Secretly virtuous??—I couldn't have invented that!)

P.P.S.: Dgter says you should come around for another drink. I agree.

From a well-known biographer in Cambridge, Massachusetts:

Mr. Levitan, did you really need to delve into the sexual and financial cubbyholes of your subject's life? As one who has written three major biographies, and who has won one NBA, among other prizes, I think not. Indeed, I think you are playing to the gallery, to the sensation-hungry public, not to the serious student and reader, and for that you do a dishonor to our profession.

A rabbi from Hartford, Connecticut, wrote:

What you have written is a shanda, *a complete* shanda! *How could you say this lifelong self-hating Jew would ever dream of helping his fellow Jews? Are you* meshugge? *Or simply a front man for this major anti-Semite? Or just a dangerous fool, an assimilated Jewgoy? I once had a conversation with the great I. B. Singer, and when Ziff's name came up, he shook his head in dismay and said, in America, a Jewish artist was no more than a common con artist, a merchant whose only Torah was the dollar bill! Do you think you know more than that great Jewish writer and* chochem???

From San Francisco, a note from an older, faded literary name:

> *As a writer who has been helped in past years by Arthur Ziff, let me commend you for your brave accounting of his life. I say 'brave,' because I know what it must have taken to lay out the truth, when much of it goes against the grain of the culture's image of him. I'm sorry you didn't get around to interviewing me, but, on the other hand, how could you have known about Arthur's largesse when he swore me to silence? Everyone knew only the daring writer but hardly anyone knew of the generous soul who performed acts of uncommon decency in quiet. In short, you got it just right.*

So there were comforts among the complaints, charges, threats. One or two comforts for every six to eight complaints was not too bad a percentage. Anyway, I answered what I thought appropriate. Locally, in the Upper Valley "family" newspaper, I had been reviewed harshly by the acerbic female reviewer, while the academic community, save for a few old friends, did their usual number, avoiding the book and me. Ah, that new American class, the tenured mediocre—apart from the Pentagon, was there ever a group upon whom was lavished and wasted more millions annually?

On April 10, with perfect New Hampshire predictability, we were hit with two days of snow, some fifteen inches, and we got out the skis and hit the trails. One day the boys went up on the slopes, downhilling at the Skiway, and the second day we went out cross-country skiing. Jon, near seventeen, was very good at it now, preferring to glide freestyle, and Gabriel, near eleven, was already better than me, from his downhill skills. We proceeded on the Cardigan trails, right up the road, starting out on the open meadows and moving through the thick woods, then out onto the lake, staying at the edge, Jon first, then Gaby, Becka, and me. The sun was out, the glare was brilliant, the tracks had been cut by a snowmobile, and the hour and a half were delicious, washing my mind clear. Great to see the boys so skilled and youthfully agile, and to feel my own legs strong enough to proceed. Who cared if I had failed out there, with literature? Not the trees or snow or boys, so I skied with glee down a small slope, feeling crazily that I was skiing for my freedom—until I crashed and just missed a tree.

Back home, on the answering machine, a voice spoke that was as shocking as the April snow. Arthur had called and asked me to phone him back.

With fear I did, and in a neutral voice he suggested we meet for dinner that weekend, when he was up from the city. We made a date for Sunday night and hung up.

Well, this is it, I figured, with dread. The big news, like bankruptcy, divorce, cancer. I could feel it in my bones. And it was easy to see, too, why he had waited for the book to come out, for the right words to appear in print, so he could then prove his case—malice with intent, demonstrated calumny, scenes of libel. Now he had all the evidence he needed. So what did he want from me now?

On Friday I received in the mail a copy of the *New Yorker,* and there, on the cover, was a foldout PR banner for one extended piece on Ziff and me, his new book and mine, titled, "Enemies: A Love Story." (Homage to Singer.) With grim determination and artificial calm I took it into my study with my coffee and bag of vegetable sticks (like our old days in Yaddo). Up went my No Entry sign, and I settled into my "stressless" (ha!) lounge chair. Written by the doyenne of Jewish letters, a woman whose essays were a combination of Kabbalistic study, nineteenth-century Lit. Crit., formal English philosophy, and Midrashic commentary, the present essay was huge, twenty-odd pages of long, winding sentences and dense paragraphs. Naomi Krasno was a kind of Dr. Johnson via Gershom Scholem. Arthur and I had nicknamed her, fondly, "The Great Krasno," after a breathtaking Russian circus performer.

Of the two most anticipated books of the year, I confess that I wish I had written one of them, and that I'm sorry about who wrote the second one. The first is the new novel by Arthur Ziff, *The Wallenberg Wars,* which is, to my mind, his greatest accomplishment and probably the most harrowing Holocaust novel ever written. No one will ever again question Mr. Ziff's seriousness or moral authority, and only fools will dare to tread upon the grounds of the Holocaust after *The Wallenberg Wars*. We should all be grateful that this living master has turned his unique attention to such sacred ground, for he has come up with a book so rich in its characters and scenes, so bold in its themes and original in technique and prose, that the heavily plowed fields of the Holocaust have been harvested like never before in fiction The result is a most complex and satisfying work, a kind of *Magic Mountain* of the Holocaust that requires the fullest of discussions, which I shall only begin later on in this essay.

But first let me deal with the second book under review, the so-called literary biography of Mr. Ziff (and his works) by his former friend Danny Levitan. I admit that I, along with many readers, had nothing less than great expectations for this work, since Mr. Levitan had been a good friend of Mr. Ziff's for years, had himself written a novel or two of some interest (and therefore understood the creative impulse), and finally, as a Jewish-American writer in the modern era, knew the peculiar territory of Ziff firsthand, up close, not as a tourist but as a resident. There were many reasons to hope for the best.

What went wrong, then? Why has he produced a book so woeful in conception, so meretricious in judgment, so disappointing in result?

[I stopped, took up my bag of raw carrots, and sat down to start chewing, maybe hoping for a broken tooth?]

It's of use perhaps to remember that we have come to understand certain complex Jews better through their fondest enemies, like Buber through Scholem, Ferenzy through Freud, Arendt through Bellow, to name just a

few pairs whose personalities and/or theories have col-
lided, for good and bad. So it was not a bad thing in itself
for Levitan to take on Ziff, his famous friend (and sometime rival). Now, in such clashes and arguments the first
requirement is honesty, sincerity, authenticity. And the
immediate problem here is the total lack of honesty on
Levitan's part; he acknowledges not at all his reservoir of
resentment of his friend and his long-standing envy.
Instead of citing that emotion, facing it squarely, and
even using it to serviceable ends in the tale of the famous
writer, Levitan mentions it once or twice and swiftly
skips away from the dilemma—as though it didn't exist,
as though it didn't color all his judgments. That stance of
denial, or act of cowardice, impedes insight, mars judgment, destroys credibility.

Could I go on? I let two tears roll down before restoring myself.
I found some celery to mix with the carrots, the attack.

Of equal failure in a different area is the pervasive lack
of knowledge of serious Jewish tradition, and the
attempt to glibly skim the surface. To understand the
riches that a life of Ziff offers, a Geniza discovery, you
would need to be familiar with a long line of radical
Jews, from Spinoza to Scholem and Singer, and their
resonant battles—the religious vs. the secular, the
sinful vs. the saintly, faith vs. assimilation. But Levitan
appears to have no knowledge whatsover of that three-
thousand-year-old world of philosophical antinomy and
tribal conflict. A glib voice, a few Yiddishisms, cannot
replace a grounding in Jewish tradition and history. (As
for the "discovery" of A. Z.'s private Midrash study, is
this supposed to be news to anyone who has read the
last several books?) Thus the powerful contradictions of
Ziff are never understood, let alone employed gainfully
within a larger context.

I refer here in part to a knowledge of a "collective Jewish memory" as discussed in the brilliant little book *Zakhor: Jewish History and Memory* by Yosef Yerushalmi. For instead of fumbling about with the many tensions in Arthur Ziff—the perverse and the pure, the erotic and the spiritual, the exiled and the rooted—Mr. Levitan would have recognized a recurrent Jewish prototype down through the ages, the insider-outsider rebel/hero of Jewish tradition which contains some of its greatest names and figures. And by so doing, he would have connected that complex life with the various dots on the torturous winding route of the Wandering Jew, from ancient catastrophe to (false) Enlightenment safety to modern catastrophe, from faith to idolatry to skepticism and (maybe) now back to faith. What a rich opportunity presented itself here to Danny Levitan, with the gorgeous facts before him, but how spectacularly he has missed it. For facts alone are not enough for interpretation. Ziff's secret life of Jewish virtue and knowledge only stunned and puzzled the myopic, ill-suited biographer; making little sense of it himself, he devised the disingenuous strategy of open judgment, as though his dearth of learning and bliss of bewilderment didn't count.

So we are left to piece together these odd, apparently unconnected parts of a life, and interpret for ourselves the whole Ziff in the long line of radical Jewish thinkers, artists, *chochems*. Only then might we see where and how Mr. Ziff's life fits, and where it transcends, or breaks new ground in that long, continuing tradition. And only then will we be able to make prudent and wise judgments about Mr. Ziff's role or place in the future of Jewish memory. If Mr. Levitan has done anything of use in his 445 pages, it is to give us a sense of the puzzle, however gross, however ignorant or disingenuous that sense may be, and we must thank him for that.

Oh, for the right Jewish prayer! Should I write Ms. Krasno and thank her for the generosity there at the end?

As for Naomi K., and others, knowing, that Ziff had been a student of Jewish texts, I was shocked but grateful—for that would give credibility to my speculations.

She proceeded to her "specifics" (just seven pages worth), but I could only reel off, chest heaving, starting a Kaddish for myself.

On Sunday toward evening I drove down Route 91 toward southern Vermont for my date with Arthur. Battered by Krasno, I knew I was in for it now, once and for all, a final knockout or at least a TKO. He had spoken to his friends (Éva, too?), and legal team, who now had all the hard evidence they needed, so, the question was what sort of deal was I going to be offered. In other words, was a plea bargain in the offing, or would it be jail, exile, a probation period (five years?)? Plus a full apology or writer's confession in the PEN newsletter or the NYRB (a native version of Breytenbach's ordeal?), maybe a signed pledge to write no more. Ever. Well, okay, I understood, I accepted, I was ready.

I had suffered enough under the weight of the book. Now . . .

Saxton's River village was tucked away some fifteen miles from the Interstate, in the southeastern corner of Vermont, nearly midway between our two homes. We met at the inn in the center of town, a gingerbread Victorian structure housing the restaurant. Ziff was already seated. He wore a tweed sport jacket and open-necked shirt, and greeted me with, "So I hear you tried to hide out in Central America. Why'd you come back, to catch spring training?"

I sat down and nodded.

"I ordered two dry vermouths with a touch of sweet. You used to like that, as I recall."

"Yeah, it was okay."

The waiter, seeing me, came over, set the drinks down, and gave us our menus.

I was nervous, and wished I could sign the papers immediately, whatever they were.

"*Salut!*"

"*L'hayim,*" I added, and sipped. "Look, before you say anything," I began, "I want you to know that in everything I wrote I tried for the truth. I'm not sure I always got it, but that's what I aimed for. No malice or harm intended, ever."

He sat quietly, staring at me.

"And it was a book I had to do, as it turned out. I mean, it just kept coming, it grabbed me up, and I felt as compelled in the writing, in the narrative, as with any novel. So I just went on."

I waited a moment to see a response, but he was sitting silently, not moving a muscle . . . maybe amazed? I couldn't tell.

The waiter returned, deposited cheese and bread. We gave him our orders (what?), and when he departed, I took up where I had left off.

"So I fucked up, I understand. You were right, again, and I was wrong, again. So it's the end for me, the career and all . . . the bit of reputation . . . but what now? I mean, is there something you want of me now?" Clumsy, so clumsy, my words, but what could I say and why had I spoken? My napkin had fallen from my lap, and I retrieved it.

He stared, and paused, to make sure, I believe, that my babbling had ended. More than usual he looked firm, resolved, Jewish-Bergmanish (von Sydow?), with the graying, nubbly hair, long, narrow face, exacting strip of half-moon beard; had he not turned into a version of Wallenberg himself?

"Aren't you exaggerating a little, Danny? After all, there's been some interest in what you wrote, though Krasno was tough the other day." He reached out, and I was sure he was simply going to slap my face, but instead he simply wiped a crumb from my sweater. "It's been lonely out there these past years, hasn't it, pal?"

I nodded.

"Literary lonely, right?"

I nodded.

"Watching all the second-raters, the ethnics, the cronies win the prizes, the awards, the fifty-grand fellowships. The 'cultural scene,' " his eyes widened—"as the *Times* calls it."

The waiter brought our salads, and half a bottle of wine.

He took two bites, using knife and fork European style, observing me. I felt a little like one of those rare butterflies caught, pinned, and set in a scrapbook for study by a collector. Glasses tinkled, conversation whispered in the large room.

After an interminable silence, a grave wait, in which my case was being considered (it seemed to me), my lepidopterist spoke:

"Well, Daniel, you did it, you proved me wrong, and yourself right, whatdya' know? You pulled it off, not so much for yourself, but for me. Amazing, huh?"

I was stunned; my chest began heaving. "I don't believe you. I don't know what you're saying."

"Yeah, really. It's a brilliant book, I just read it. Congratulations." A nod of begrudging approval.

I stared, couldn't swallow.

The waiter returned with two fish dishes and sides of pasta. Arthur nodded at his query, and he sprinkled fresh pepper.

"With one book," he spoke slowly, "you did what I couldn't do with twenty. What I'd *never be able to do*. You changed my image completely. What do you think of that? Loony? People have come up to me in Manhattan, mostly Jews, but not all by any means, and shaken my hand, saying, *they want to apologize, they never knew.* Can you believe it?"

I shook my head from side to side, not believing it or quite understanding the words.

"Do you see what I'm saying? Everything I couldn't do in forty-five fucking years, with stories, essays, novels, memoirs, you did with one book. You made me out to be a good guy. A friend of the Jews! Can you believe it? And even the reviews and spin on the new Wallenberg novel have been interpreted according to your book, consciously or unconsciously. Do you understand?" He smiled, "Can you?"

I tried to, but couldn't fathom it. I sat still, dumb.

He leaned forward slightly to impart a special word or two, the firm jaw jutted out. "And do you know *how* you managed it?"

Huh, *how?* I shook my head, again the pupil listening.

He spoke slowly, for emphasis. "You wrote a very clever novel, with brilliant patches in it, and called it 'a biography.' You did it so well, so smoothly, precisely because what you were doing was unbeknownst to you. Do you get it? You *thought* you were writing fact, when you were making things up, and this energized you. And after a while you had little idea which was which, yes? Your best novel in years, your most inventive, and you missed it. Nice irony."

I blew my nose, wiped my eyes, took in his words. Faced him and the famous stare, which radiated so authoritatively on magazine covers. Except now there was a touch of mirth at the corner of the mouth, irony and mirth.

He nodded. "Here, I brought you an invitation."

He handed me an envelope with an embossed card inside: the Star of David inscribed on an invitation to join Rabbi Scheerson at the Park Avenue Synagogue for a special evening "Honoring Arthur Ziff." I looked at it, him, puzzled.

"*It's because of you.* First time ever. They're giving me an evening of homage. Can you believe it? The same rabbi who said I was the lowest scum on the face of the earth, worse than a thousand anti-Semitic *goyim,* now is turned around. He wrote me a note and then called me '*personally, to apologize,*' and ask me if I would please attend." He moved back in his chair, the evidence set forth, delivered. "*You* did that."

I nodded, dumb still, trying to put it all together.

"He's going to call you and ask if you'll be one of the main speakers. Why not, huh? You deserve it, kid. It's going to be a big night. They've already booked Hertzberg, Krasno, Ted, among others. Who knows, maybe they'll get Wiesel?" Resisted the smirk. "You should do it. Big New York evening. It'll hit the *Times.*"

I took a bite of the fish and glanced at the well-appointed room with green embossed wallpaper and relaxed dinner guests, a sanity I could grasp, unlike these words.

"You know," he mused, "there's no end to where this might lead, don't you think?"

"Huh?" I looked at him.

"Think of it. My image over there in Europe, around the world."
Suddenly he burst out laughing. "Fucking unbelievable, right?"

I guess I laughed, too, weakly, then said, "Aren't you underes-
timating your own new book in all this? This new appreciation."

He nodded, nibbled on food. "Oh, that's a piece of it, maybe. But
you know what? Without the corroborating evidence of the life, *my
life,* as you told it," he shook his head, "it's just another novel by
me, *another made-up story by Moishe Pipik-Ziff,* which is about as
important as this salt shaker. No, what counts is, *my life for the Jews!
My life on the line!*" He drank his water. "And what made it so real,
so fucking convincing, are the vulgarities and obscenities you dug
for there, the dredging up of my financial accounts—you were *low*
by about 2.5 million by the way—and the sexual escapades, though
you missed a few cute ones, in Rome and Budapest. Mostly, though,
it was your total belief in the *truth* of your evidence, the *facts* had
me in stitches, laughing hard!" Remembering, "The stuff about my
'midrash,' oy gevalt!" And he was off on another jag! Heads turned.
When he finally ceased, he said, "Those moments maybe compen-
sated for the times when I got a little irritated, even angry. Like the
recalling of some of our real scenes together, say, where you put your
own spin on things. And I was impressed with what you managed
to get out of Michelle; I thought she'd be a little more distant about
me, you know." He sipped wine. "And you handled the *meshuggenah*
actress rather shrewdly, giving her enough diary rope to hang herself. Just right. Sure, certain things pissed me off at first, but after
thinking about it, I had a different take." He beamed. "Your use of
General Rommel as an analogy, well, at first that didn't go over too
well, but on reflection, I realized you could have used an American
military figure, Patton or MacArthur—as you mentioned in a footnote—and it would have been far nastier. Rommel did have a touch
of class, and I might have made a first-class strategist as a general,
so I grew to see your point. Though a few of the critics didn't, eh?
Where was it, *Commentary,* that you were called a neo-Nazi?
Anyway, you did all right, mixing in the reinvented with the wholly
imagined, while here and there touching up the fiction with the
real." He slipped a bite into his mouth.

Was it true, what he was saying now? Or something else . . . something again clever, masking? But what? I found my voice. "So Éva, for example, was merely putting me on, you're saying?"

"Oh, Éva, dearest Éva!" He emitted a fond laugh. "A special case, sure. She has great needs and fantasies, probably tied to her losses. Her view of reality is affected by all that, let's say."

I nodded. "Answer me straight, then, this one question: Did you not help her buy an apartment?"

He eyed me. "Okay, yes, I did. So what? All the work she had done for me . . . her own tragic life—she deserved it, sure."

"Then she did do work for you. Why then—"

Holding up one finger, he cut me off: "One question, remember?"

"But did you not help any of those Jews? Not in Rome or—"

He shook his head, smiled kindly. "You're over *one,* right? Your own limit. But you know what? I'm going to give you *two,* for old friends' day. Did I help Jews? Why not? If you prick them, do they not bleed?" Wry smile. "I'm a writer, with my special needs." I started to ask, but he held up two fingers. "Do you think I'm going to cooperate with you now, because a book is done? Don't go on being naive. My private life is my private life, period. Once upon a time, when we were good friends, I shared certain things with you." He nodded, "But now's now. You had your shot, did your best, and, in a curious twist of fate, your book had a surprising trajectory out in the big world. Hey, something wrong with the bluefish?"

"Huh?" I looked down, and noticed I hadn't yet eaten any. Feebly I lifted my fork and had a bite.

"There were, of course, a few other scenes that I read with interest, watching your distorted take. For example, I didn't appreciate your self-serving spin on our wanna-be movie-star waitress. And the citing of the possible Roman whores—Jesus, let me know the next time you're cruising the Via Veneto. Mine are not nearly as exotic, or talented—where is Eritrea, near Houston?" A grimace. "As for that little book-bidding scene, you should know better. That's an easy litigation, as my lawyer suggested."

And as he went on talking—no point in asking here about young Oriental girls—discussing this scene or revising that one; I had the sensation of my book curling back toward me like a boomerang I had sent flying that was now heading straight at me crazily! Dizzy, taking hits, I tried my best to stay clearheaded, to digest the full meaning and implications. It was hard, very hard.

"I understand you're having an auction for the paperback rights, by the way. You can put in anything you left out, maybe even this conversation. Or change the category to fiction." He gazed at me with a kindly irony. "You know, add something and jack up the price by a few hundred thousand."

My head was crammed and steaming; I leaned back, took yoga breaths, and noted his fit form, his relaxed, triumphant posture.

Involuntarily I said, "Well, it is true I left out certain . . . key material, intentionally."

He seemed to blink for the first time. "What do you mean?"

I swallowed. "The long-standing romance with the rabbi's daughter."

For about five seconds he stiffened, the tongue working its way against the cheek . . . in anxiety, or decision? Easing up, he smiled, shook his head. "Are you fantasizing about me once again? Haven't you done enough of that?"

Quietly I said, "And the short novel you wrote about it."

He set down his utensils and stared at me, fiercely. While the restaurant clinked and voices whispered, he said nothing but breathed hostility, folding his linen napkin into neat quarters.

"I don't think you know what you're talking about. If you had evidence about what you're saying, why didn't you write about it?"

I paused before answering. "Maybe I didn't want to chance it legally. Maybe I didn't see the point of dragging you, and me, through the gossip and rumors and questions. Maybe I couldn't produce enough evidence."

He nodded, scratched his neck with a forefinger. "But you must have had some evidence for your supposition, no?"

"Oh, yes, some."

"What might that be?"

He had turned very curious, surprisingly serious. "Well, I broke into your studio, searched for a manuscript, and found the short novel."

His nostrils flared. Containing himself, he shook his head. "I don't believe you. When, how?"

"The last time I was over, for that weekend visit, a few years ago. When your Swedish buddy was up for the weekend. That Friday night, after dinner. . . ." I went on, and described briefly my shenanigans.

"So you're a thief," he nodded. "An out-and-out criminal."

"Well, not really. I left everything intact. But breaking and entering, yes."

He shook his head in open disgust. "I don't believe you. You couldn't do that, even if you wanted to."

I reached into my jacket pocket, took out my wallet, and unfolded my page. I began reading, " 'When I look back at that fateful affair that has stayed with me for years and years, through my later life and my—' "

"Enough, enough!" His face was tense, dark eyes on fire. "What else? Go on, tell me!"

Now at that moment, feeling pushed by Arthur's taut demand and buttressed by my confession and reading, I bluffed: "I saw the letters, too." Had he not pressed me angrily, into a corner, I know that I would never have gambled with that sort of crazy lie. *"All of them."*

He clasped his hands and observed me. His lips pursed, he said nothing, but considered me. I was not that pinned butterfly now, but a ghastly predator, a tenacious, dangerous one perhaps.

Far from feeling triumphant, however, I felt demeaned, humiliated. Why'd you do it? I asked myself. Just when you were coming clean, and being clean, why'd you have to bluff and lie?!

"Did you take any of them? Copy any?"

I shook my head solemnly. My heart pounded as I understood the immediately rich result of my low action. "No."

He nodded, set the napkin down, drained his water. His Adam's apple was pronounced, revealing the pouch of aging skin.

His brown eyes never left me while he considered matters, my actions, my lowness, surprising me.

No restaurant or diners now, just his gathering wrath, his fierce stare, his powerful choices for reprimand, censure. Oh, I felt the moment expand into the one when Billy Budd tries to explain his actions to Captain Vere.

The waiter appeared, cutting the tension, but when he saw my nearly filled plate, he backed off politely.

"You shouldn't waste that fish," Arthur advised.

I nodded, took up my knife and fork, cut another bite.

"So you're a bit cleverer than even I thought," he observed at last, "more cunning." He caressed his trim beard, still deciding. "I give you credit."

I said, for no good reason, "Thanks."

He sat there, and I, sweating now, felt pressed to eat.

"Go slowly. You remember Elizabeth's note to Hal about his digestion? Take it to heart. . . . By the way, you did that scene very nicely."

I chewed more slowly, almost smiling.

After a pause, he said, "So you read the whole novella?"

I nodded.

"How'd you like it?"

"Good, awfully good." I added, "And new for you."

He nodded, in approval or agreement, and dabbed at his mouth with his napkin, gracefully.

At last I was beginning to taste my bluefish—

"You could go to jail for what you did, you know. Prison time."

That wouldn't have been too bad now, I figured, now pushing my plate away. "I guess so," I said, realizing how easy writing the book was next to this ordeal.

The waiter reappeared, removed our plates, and asked about coffee and dessert, citing several favorites. Arthur ordered a decaf espresso, and I took herbal tea.

I ventured forth. "If the Jews believe you've turned over a new leaf, or always had another secret leaf, who knows what the Gentiles will think, especially the Swedish ones, huh?"

It took him a split second of puzzlement before the mirth

returned to the corner of the mouth. "Very cute. Who knows? Stranger things have occurred."

The waiter brought us our tea and coffee.

"Well, if you do get an award, remember me in your speech."

He nodded. "I'll go one better, and maybe hire you to write it for me. I think you'd do a better job."

"Your ghostwriter, huh?" I restrained a smile.

"You know," he said, after sipping and reflecting, "I think we made a mistake. We should split one of those desserts after all, don't you think? How about the peach tart?" His eyes lit up. "You only live once." A pause. "Or twice, after a 'real' biography."

twenty-eight

Six weeks later, I was heading out to Omaha, Nebraska, for a two-day literary conference on the "Art of Arthur Ziff" at Creighton University. Sitting in the Manchester, New Hampshire airport, I checked my folder to make sure that, in my haste, I had packed the appropriate pages for my talk on "some recent Ziff protagonists." In their invitation for me to be the keynote speaker, the Creighton English Department had asked me to focus on the "life of Ziff" if possible, but I had decided to stick with the fiction. An easier, safer task.

Checking my calendar, I was taken aback to discover that during the fever of book excitement, I had agreed to speak at two more Ziff conferences in the next six months, in Edmund, Oklahoma, the other down in Albuquerque. What folly! Clearly, Arthur Ziff had become a hot property, and I had become the new certified expert! Well, a fitting irony, I thought, stuffing the talk back into my canvas briefcase, already bulging with small notebooks of jottings for my new novel. The splashy conference brochure tumbled out, and I read it, for the first time. Featured at the top, DANNY LEVITAN. What had I gotten into?! Far from being elated, I felt dismayed, especially as I skimmed the titles of Saturday morning talks. "The Metamorphosis of Postmodern Identity in *Raphael's Querulous Quartet* and

Mendelsohn's Meditations" (Chris Mews, University of Texas); "Joyce into Ziff: The Evolution of the Prose Soliloquy" (Shlomo Greenstein, UCLA); "Vagina-Envy: A Subtextual Theme in Late Ziff Fiction" (Pamela Messina, Wellesley College). Shaking my head, I felt congested, baffled. Why did I want to address such a dreary event, let alone attend one? Might I call in sick with the Asian flu? (Or better, go there to catch it?)

Was this to be my fate, I mused, to be delivered to sundry ports of call, those out-of-the-way stops in the sticks, to talk about Arthur Ziff? To become a shining star for the growing number of Ziff societies and chapters? Was this my reward for making it out alive, after spending the past three years digging down in the dark, elusive Ziff mines? A comic reward, no? Hadn't I already been rewarded with the crass reviews, the literary culture's disdain, my wife's growing estrangement, the lost friendship?

You see, several notes and two phone calls had gone unanswered, and it was clear enough that, as far as Arthur Ziff was concerned, I no longer was a friend, no longer had an existence. That testing, amusing dinner was a Last Supper, a final good-bye. And I found myself missing him, missing the friendship more than I had imagined. For while I was writing the book, Ziff had been with me, both as a hovering presence waiting to see what I was going to do, and also as an ongoing, developing literary character, growing new flesh and spirit by means of my text, my research, my invention— maybe more rounded and real in my book than in person. Now, with the writing done and the person gone, I was left alone, bereft, without the personal presence or the invention in words.

And also there was the burden of Rebecca's stony estrangement, the final consequence of months of public barbs and insults and my own mushrooming sadness, despair; yes, I was losing her, too. And losing myself as well, ironically enough; for while searching out the elusive Ziff in his/my work, I was also seeking out, in part, my own self, a firmer, more authentic self, as one does with books, especially personal books. But look what had happened. Why, even the boys . . .

I called Jonathan, as promised, to say good-bye.

"Hey, Dad, you're not going to miss my jazz band performance, are you?" he asked, his voice anxious, maybe resentful.

"Absolutely not," I said, wishing I had his youthful cheek to stroke. "I'll be back by Monday afternoon for sure."

"Oh, good." He said, placated. "Where are you going, anyway? Reading from a new novel?"

Feeling a pang in my heart for his stating my true desire, I said no, I was speaking on the works of Arthur Ziff.

"Oh, really," he said, his voice animated, probably remembering his bar mitzvah and his unique Ziff present. "That should be fun, huh? Will he be there to hear you?"

"I don't think so. Professors mostly, I imagine."

"Too bad. . . . Well, good luck, and see you Monday then."

"Hey, where's my hug?" I protested despite the folly of it.

"Well, next time wait till I get home from school before you take off."

"Good point," I said, miming his imitation of me and signing off. A cool kid, not emotional, like the little one. A teenager, but one with a mature sensibility and rich prose style. Was Arthur right about him being the writer in the family to watch?

Last call for boarding my flight, and I raced to the gate.

Soon enough, we were borne upward into the sky, arching forward and up into the heavens, nosing toward a bank of fluffy white clouds. The firm ground below receded, making the highways, river, buildings, and speeding cars look more and more like a Lego town. I relaxed, staring out the small window, seeing the long, silvery wing and the glancing reflection of the dying sun. Reluctantly, I opened the briefcase, found my manila folder filled with my endless notes on Ziff, and started in, once again, rehearsing my talk. A little like rehearsing my own bar mitzvah speech, I mused oddly, remembering that forty-nine-year-ago ordeal and wondering whether this time around my ceremonial talk would signify something else—my exit from manhood?

The stewardess was cautioning me to buckle up, and I obeyed.

One year after my *Ziff: A Life* came out, Arthur Ziff won the Nobel

Prize for literature, in 2003. To say that it was a surprise was to understate the matter, for practically everyone in the literary community had figured that he had been passed over, in great part because of the nature of his material—its explicit eroticism, its attacks on Judaism, its varieties of perversity. Plus the underlying, pervasive sense that Ziff himself was not a very wholesome character. And yet there it was, Ziff, at seventy, earning the highest prize. Rather remarkable.

It caused quite a stir, too, this awarding. Just as in earlier days, there was fierce controversy swirling, from rabbis to other public Ziff critics. For example, there were rabbis such as Arnold Weinstein of the Upper East Side and Nathan Finer, the rabbi of the Hebrew Institute of Riverdale, opining, "This is the greatest *shanda* in the history of the award. How and why would they give it to an anti-Semitic Jew like Arthur Ziff? Except to embarrass the Jewish people." And the veteran *Commentary* editor Irwin Shmuckler came out of retirement to write in the *New York Times*,

> We had always thought that the Nobel Prize had something to do with truth and morality in literature, but this award to Ziff fully exposes the hypocrisy of the current committee. Everyone knows that Arthur Ziff has earned his living and reputation by riding and flogging the backs of Jews, whether they be religious or secular, American suburbanites or Holocaust survivors. With this writer, there have been few if any boundaries of human civility or morals, historical or political veracity, that have not been deliberately violated for purposes of sensationalism and profit. The Nobel committee, its taste already in question in recent years, has permanently disgraced itself, tainted its original mission and philosophy, and should be written off as a group of hacks who are not fit to judge its own awards.

For its part, the Nobel committee stressed, in its statement, the growth of his career and the novels of his late career, a shrewd strategy. It cited his "powerful recording of the American experience from the 1950s through the new millennium," and his judicious weighing of the "era of moral ambiguity and culture in the post-Vietnam years." It admired Ziff as a "writer who confronted the major issues of the day, social, sexual, cultural, moral, with eyes wide open and skills fully honed." As for the Jewish realm, the committee observed, "Like other major twentieth-century writers scrutinizing their own peoples and ethnic manners, Joyce and the Irish Catholic or Faulkner and the American Southerner, Arthur Ziff has observed his Jewish brethren with a sharp eye and trenchant wit and criticism, but also has created a world of his own, with a dramatic power and wide perspective. We salute therefore not merely his skills and world, but also his courage and steadfastness."

I must confess that I was flattered, too, by the committee's citation of my own book in a line that read, "It may also be noted, though not as necessarily as a causal agent in the committee's judgment, that the recent biography of Mr. Ziff has revealed a man often misreported, misrepresented and even maligned by the general and literary public, and that this lengthy account, *Ziff: A Life*, has given us a much more rounded portrait of the man and the writer, one that suggests a far more complex life than anyone had imagined." In other words, you might say, he didn't merely resent and exploit Jews, use women and discard them, act crudely and selfishly, et cetera. No, Ziff was a man of parts. Yours truly, Danny Levitan, and his work had somehow, even if marginally, arrived to shore up the committee in its final judgment. Not bad and rather ironic, my work used to aid that noble purpose.

Yet something else began to stir in me, triggered by the committee's credit to my work . . . certain questions were emerging, turning into puzzles. For example Éva—who was she, how had she found me? . . . And Viking, hadn't they said they knew of my original proposal; but what proposal? That *New Yorker* editor, how did she discover my project? . . . Even Jeanne, how and why had she entered the scene? . . . My mind buzzed, heart fluttered . . . Could it be true, had I been played from the start? I shook my head, in disbelief. *Had Arthur wanted me to write the biography all along?* Me, not some fawning biographer, feminist foe, lightweight journalist, fact-hunting academician. Could it be?

But what about those sharp, threatening talks? Well, he knew his man, knew intimidation wouldn't deter me, but he had to make it look good, real good, for many reasons. And the short story attacks? Knew they would fire me up, keep me determinedly forward. Clever, oh so clever. Could it be true? Did he get his man, the right man, to write his biography, someone who knew him and wouldn't sell him short, someone literary who could appreciate his work, and put the finishing touches on the Complete Ziff? You know, get in all his virtuous deeds, the ten Ziffian rungs of *Tzedakah;* and even, timing-wise, leak out the news of the Wallenberg project! For this—a serious bio—was just what the Ziff career needed to take it over the edge for the Big One. . . . He was not going to win the Prize for his wild eroticism, harsh satiric portraits, comic adventures; no, he needed something big and international like Wallenberg, plus a high level biography. And Danny Levitan could produce that, with some extra creative topping! Oh Danny boy, even you, in your innocent biography, with its earnest purposes and high rhetoric, had underestimated his masterminding brilliance! . . . Could this just be more wild musings, or true? . . .

While this shocking reasoning, or hallucinating, was percolating, I received from Arthur a response, in answer to my fax of congratulations.

He wrote: "Well, old pal, your misnamed and mischievous 'biography' of collected fictions and half-truths about myself has been construed as a cloth of whole truths, virtuous ones no less, which is a fitting irony, don't you think? Suddenly in the space of a few years my whole corpus of fiction has been reinterpreted, and observed in a whole new light by your *Let's Pretend* type of narrative parading as truth-telling. Oh, it's rich, and will give me much to think about, and muse over, in my long flight to Stockholm. If I thought your Swedish was as good as your Yiddish, I'd invite you over as my private interpreter. But in any case I think I should bone up on your biography of me, so I will be fully prepared to answer any profound questions about my life."

Well, there you have it, a noble and honorable ending to it all—for Arthur, at least. It reminds me a little of a tale I heard last week on a local radio station, of a peregrine falcon pair that created a nest in New Hampshire that this spring hatched out the first baby produced here in some years. Yet the nest was not found on a white mountain peak in our glorious state but rather on the eleventh-floor rooftop of a Manchester office building, a truly unlikely setting for such a natural phenomenon. But some things were meant to be, let us say, some orders of nature are apparently unpredictable and mysterious until perhaps years and years later, when we discover a meaning for the event. Who knows? Maybe we'll look at Arthur Ziff's Nobel Prize in the same way one day. A quirk of nature that found its way into a surprising visibility, through unlikely means and patterns.

As for me, I'm more or less happy for my old friend. Warmed by it, even, like a moth near a flame. He got what he had worked for, and had earned, and had badly wanted, and that provides a measure of justice in our uneven world. And if it may be said that I had played a part-time role in helping along that Nobel effort—as a kind of big-bellied, short-legged practical Sancho Panza to his long, lean, idealist don—so be it. (Or was I getting the roles wrong again, in fact having played for a while no more than his bony nag Rocinanate?) Either way, let it be noted that I had been a role player to the elegant star, coming onstage for a few minutes in the second act, saying my lines, and departing on cue. One day I might be cited in one of those new biographies, the sort that chronicles what shirt and tie he wore on March 15, 1998, or his morning diet when writing *Mendelsohn's Meditations,* as an interesting footnote to Ziff's long and high career.

You know, Danny Levitan, to be found in footnote 46 in chapter three ("The Turbulent Years"), or maybe, see under "Rivalries."

As for my own career as a fiction writer, well, I'm in such demand now to talk about the Ziff legend or the great late books that I seem to have very little time to pursue my old path.

APPENDIX

Annotated bibliography of the works of Arthur Ziff from *Ziff: A Life* (2002) by Daniel Levitan

Dorchester Boy (Viking, 1957). A striking debut, at age twenty-six. A skillful novel about growing up in the Boston area in the 1950s. Detailed, textured, shrewdly ironic, DB signaled that a star is born.

That Time of Year (Viking, 1960). A restrained, sober look at the academy through the perspective of Jay Rothstein, a graduate student studying English—and high morality—at the University of Michigan. Though not a big seller, TTOY displays a writer in control of a firm prose style and literary voice, however flawed.

To Each According to His Needs (Viking, 1963). A close scrutiny of early '60s morality and social mores via two relationships, one ending in a conventional marriage and divorce, the second breaking up before marriage and sending the pair back onto independent paths. A further run on the track of social and psychological realism.

The Carnal Confessions of Rabbi Shmuel Siegel (Doubleday, 1966). A smashing send-up of official Judaism, a huge hit and savage satire, placing young Ziff dead center on the celebrity and infamy map.

Lustig's Last Game (Doubleday, 1969). A poignant-comic baseball romance focusing on a forty-two-year-old veteran player, now over the hill and in the minors, bewildered by the end of boyhood. Much baseball and national lore, a kind of grown-up Tunis. Underrated.

Mendele's Travels (Doubleday, 1967). A wild, picaresque journey through the towns of former Polish shtetls, centering on a native writer's obsession with the nineteenth-century Yiddish writer Mendele (Mokher Seforin), and his retracing of that writer's path. Eventually he metamorphoses into the original writer. A Gogolian tribute to the lost past of Yiddish life and literature.

Fucked (Grove, 1970). A brilliant tour de force of East European transgression, political and sexual, and its comic consequences, for an American writer. Darkly comic, politically exacting, erotically grotesque.

Judith: Dying Days (Knopf, 1973). The surprising nonfiction account of the last days of Judith Ziff, the writer's mother; nominated for the Pulitzer. A powerful, angry, resilient memoir, both an autopsy of the medical profession and a farewell meditation on filial love.

Rosenthal Subdued (Knopf, 1975). The first of a future trilogy wherein Aaron Rosenthal, young writer-to-be, learns about his craft by means of women, mentors, and crucifying mistakes. A studied work of the writing life, with several prominent roman à clef personalities appearing.

Rosenthal's Revenge (Houghton Mifflin, 1978). A fiery sequel, with a renewed distribution of energy in the prose, as Aaron R., hit hard by the critics and by the media, bounces back by means of his pen and his fury, composing a murderous satire of his enemies. An all-out counterattack.

Mendelsohn's Meditations (Harper & Row, 1982). Mel Mendelsohn, a professor of aesthetics at an Ivy League school and masturbatory addict, delivers huge monologues on the corrupt nature of the modern world, especially culture and colleges, via the four ex-wives and mistresses he revisits and dallies with. Comic, didactic, vitriolic, sometimes excessive, sometimes marvelously effective.

Reflections on Writing, Reading, Imagining, Lying (Harper & Row, 1984). Ostensibly a series of essays laying out favorite writers and readings, but also a cleverly designed assault on those critics who search for the real Ziff beneath the fictional masks.

Entropy and Kaos (Scribner, 1987). A Waugh-like comedy about two academics, Harry Entropy and Suzanne Kaos, who conduct vigorous public fights over texts while conducting a tumultuous affair across the coasts. Outrageous, clever, funny, right-on satire.

Goldfeld at Eighty (Scribner, 1990). A short novel about an aging professor on a journey to visit his dying friend in western Canada, who, on his train journey, revisits his life, only to be surprisingly dismayed and ultimately shocked. A Jewish Wild Strawberries in slow scenes and deliberate prose, with a forceful ending.

Raphael's Querulous Quartet (Warner Books, 1993). A rocking critique and roller coaster ride on the banks of the Hudson, with music as the all-terrain vehicle. Raphael G. is a musical genius and nihilistic dynamo, at home in classical salons, concert stages, and rock bars, who cuts a savage swath through Manhattan's elite, a little like Alex and his droogies in A Clockwork Orange.

A Countermemoir (Warner Books, 1995). A shrewd hide-and-seek fictional narrative, detailed at length with hard facts, about the so-called realistic life of the novelist. Gleefully obfuscating, bewildering, brilliant.

The Savage Yid (Hyperion, 1998). A return to the Blue Hills section of Boston in the 1950s, a portrait of anti-Semitism and witch-hunting in post–World War II Irish Boston. A scorching critique of the troubling times and abusive culture, and an admirable performance.

The Devils (Hyperion, 1999). A sharply conservative look at the radical Sixties by means of a portrait of a small group of university students, sons and daughters of middle-class parents, who commit devastating deeds on prominent Ivy League campuses and also ruin their parents' lives. A rather didactic political novel.

The Jewish Patient (Metropolitan, 2000). A somber narrative of the last years of Kafka's life, driven by meticulous detailing of place (Prague), and fervent inquiry into an artistic character. A portrait of the great Jewish master at once terrifying in its restrictiveness, comic in its procrastinations, emotional in its small dramas. A meditation on the tortured life, whose fear of the father rippled out to larger fears and paranoias.

The Wallenberg Wars (Metropolitan, 2002). A huge (645 pages) Holocaust novel set in World War II Hungary and contemporary Boston, which won for Ziff his fourth NBA award and a Pulitzer. A vast, sprawling canvas filled with harrowing scenes and memorable characters—especially the dashing Swede and his doomed Budapest Jewess—marred perhaps by high melodrama and postmodern trickery. A richly mixed bag, with the riches sounding a Nobel resonance.

Deposition

The Deposition of Daniel Levitan began on October 11, 2002 at 9:00 A.M. in the law offices of Meyers, Guttman, Rose, and Levy in Room 2124, 588 Madison Avenue, New York. The testimony itself lasted approximately nine and a half hours, over two days. In attendance were the lawyers for the plaintiff (Arthur Ziff), Martin Meyers and Stephen Levy; the lawyer for the deposed (Daniel Levitan), Stanley Leibowitz; the lawyers for the publisher (Emerson House), Chad Evans and John Williams; the literary agent for the deposed, Gerard Boucher; a legal secretary; and the deposed, Daniel Levitan.

What follows is a partial record of that deposition, as reported by the legal secretary, edited here for purposes of length. What is not fully recorded are the increasing stages of nervousness and anxiety experienced by the deposed, and his trembling collapse at one point near the end.

Plaintiff Atty. Meyers: Would you please give your name and address?

A. Danny Levitan, Rural Route 2, Mascoma, New Hampshire.

Q. Your age?

A. Sixty-two.

Q. Your occupation?

A. Writer.

Q. What sort?

A. Novelist, principally.

Q. You write made-up stories, fiction?

A. Yes.

Q. You do this for a living principally?

A. Yes, principally.

Q. How many books have you published?

A. Six to date.

Q. And they were all novels, all invented stories, yes?

A. Yes.

Q. Your entire career, then, has been in making up stories?

A. Well, you could say that, yes.

Q. Now, this new book, what is it called?

A. *Ziff: A Life*.

Q. This new book, *Ziff*, is it a novel, too, like your others?

A. No. It's a biography. You know that.

Q. Mr. Levitan, just answer the question. So this book is not made up, not an invention, not a fiction, like your other books?

A. That's right.

[Skipped text.]

Q. Now, Mr. Levitan, could you describe for us your mission or objective in this book?

A. Well, it's an attempt to tell or narrate the life and times of the writer Arthur Ziff. The literary times.

Q. But you do go beyond the literary times, don't you?

A. Well, yes, you could say that. Though I do try to see the life in terms of the literary life.

Q. Mr. Levitan, do you know Mr. Ziff personally?

A. Yes, I do.

Q. And for how long have you known Mr. Ziff?

A. Oh, twenty—no, thirty years or so.

Q. Beginning when?

A. Oh, the fall of 1968, I believe.

Q. And would you say you have been "good friends" during all that time?

A. [Pause for water] I'd say we were good friends for the first ten years or so.

Q. And after that?

A. Well, we were friendly through the next years, just not as close. And sometimes we were not so friendly, sure.

Q. Would you say you were hostile for any of those years?

A. Hostile? No; I'd say we grew apart, that's all, but never really directly hostile.

Q. Now, during the course of writing this so-called biography, did you have the full cooperation of Mr. Ziff?

A. No, not at all.

Q. Any cooperation?

A. None, really.

Q. How is that? Was he hostile, then, to this project?

A. Well, let's say he tried to persuade me not to write it, and then remained neutral, maybe indifferent.

Q. But if you were a friend, why did he choose not to cooperate? Did he say why?

A. He said it was my book and not his business.

Q. Did he think it was a good idea for you to write such a book?

A. No, not particularly. He thought I should stick to my trade, writing novels.

Q. Had you been trained at all in the art of biography?

A. No.

Q. So there was good reason, then, for him to be skeptical.

A. Perhaps so.

O. So when he tried to persuade you, as you say, he had good reason; but did he threaten you in any way?

A. Well, not directly, no.

Q. Oh, indirectly?

A. He did say the book could be subject to his lawyers' inquiry, possibly.

Q. You mean like this inquiry or testimony here now?

A. Yes, I suppose so.

Q. Well, that was not a threat then, but a prudent caution; would you not agree?

A. I suppose so.

Q. Do you feel threatened now?

A. A little, yes. It's a deposition, after all.

[Skipped text.]

Q. Now, regarding the work for this "biography," you've done lots of interviews, travel, library research, et cetera, yes?

A. Yes, that's right.

Q. And for this field research, you've taken copious notes, I take it, kept dates and precise data that can be corroborated if necessary, right?

A. Pretty much, I'd say, yes.

Q. 'Pretty much' means not everything?

A. Probably.

Q. Probably what?

A. Probably not everything.

Q. That's unfortunate. Would you say you are able to account in your notes for 80, 90 percent of the events, meetings?

A. Well, maybe 80 percent, yes.

Q. But apart from this field research, what else have you relied on for the basic facts of your book?

A. Well . . . I suppose our experiences together.

Q. Oh, you mean when you and Arthur were good friends?

A. Yes.

Q. So, you kept notes then of all the meetings and conversations and dinners and phone calls, especially those you referred to in your book?

A. [Pause for water.] Well, no, I didn't.

Q. But then how, or why, would you call such scenes in the book "factual"?

A. Well, I have a pretty good memory, first of all. And second, I don't pretend to get everything *just* right,

Q. Oh, a good memory, from so many years ago? Indeed, you do present scenes, which you're recalled from memory, and claim in the book to be factual?

A. Well, yes, a few scenes, where the gist of the matter is there, and also some details.

Q. Mr. Levitan, scenes from your memory of some thirty years ago, employed as factual without notes of any sort?

A. Well, some notes perhaps, but mostly . . . from memory, yes.

Q. And you present these as actual scenes that happened, as factual matter?

A. I've already told you, yes.

Q. Would you not acknowledge, Mr. Levitan, that your memory can be quite faulty, quite selective, after that long a time?

A. Well, sure, that's possible.

Q. And that Mr. Ziff may remember some scenes quite differently?

A. I suppose so.

Q. And that Mr. Ziff may even have a better memory at times?

A. Perhaps.

Q. So that those recollections of the scenes may come out very subjectively, and perhaps even biased, prejudiced—in your favor—against Mr. Ziff's memories, of how things happened. As his very well might, if he were writing a biography of you.

A. Well, I took special care not to show him in any unfavorable light, sir.

Q. Oh? [Consultation with Mr. Levy.] Let's take a specific scene, the scene in which you and Mr. Ziff are pretend moviemakers in Woodstock, New York, and the young waitress visits for a so-called audition. Do you think that Mr. Ziff is shown there in a "not unfavorable" light?

A. I tried to tell it, or write it, as it was.

Q. Precisely? Accurately? From memory, of thirty years ago?

A. As I said, the gist of it was there.

Q. But it's not how Mr. Ziff remembers it, the *gist* of it. He doesn't recall acting afraid, or looking foolish; in fact, if anything, you were the one frightened, and feeling a bit foolish.

A. Oh? Well, then he's got it wrong.

Q. But how do we know that it's not you who got it wrong? Unintentionally, or, perhaps, intentionally.

A. I guess you don't.

Q. But you called that scene in the manuscript a "fact from the past." Would you still stick by that label?

A. Yes, I would, with the modifications I put there.

Q. Would you not now want to call that biased scene a "made-up" one?

A. No, not chiefly.

[Plaintiff legal team consults.]

Q. We'll come back to that scene later. But for now let's take another scene, the one where you picture Mr. Ziff in business negotiations with his publisher of the time. Do you remember it? It's on pages—

A. Yes, of course. It happened in my apartment, in Cambridge.

Q. You do have your notes on that important scene, don't you?

A. [Pause.] Well no, I didn't take any, I don't think.

Q. And it occurred how long ago?

A. Oh, maybe in 1971 or '72.

Q. So you took no notes on a scene some thirty years ago, which you call factual. . . . Now, in the book, that negotiation took place in a room separate from where you were. Is this the way it happened?

A. Yes, that's true.

Q. Mr. Levitan, you want your readers to believe that your memory is keen enough, without notes, to record a conversation accurately from thirty years ago of a friend speaking in a room elsewhere from where you were sitting. Is this right?

A. Well, I do remember it.

Q. Especially a conversation wherein you draw Mr. Ziff as a mercenary wheeler-dealer, an agent of cunning business acumen? Is that what you mean by not painting him in an "unfavorable light"?

A. [Water pause.] I admired Mr. Ziff in that negotiation, admired his strength, his unique ability, and tried to convey that.

Q. Oh? I'm afraid you didn't succeed then, Mr. Levitan. Or else you're being disingenuous with us now.

Defense Atty. Leibowitz: Objection.

Plaintiff Atty. Meyers: Sure. Sorry. . . . So, Mr. Levitan, you seem to remember scenes in which Arthur Ziff doesn't come off so well to the common reader, but not other scenes in particular—

A. That's not true—

Q. Please, just answer my questions. Many of the scenes in question, which are at best of dubious value to Mr. Ziff and his image—at worst they are defaming—these are recalled quite differently by Mr. Ziff. So we may safely and prudently say that these scenes are subjectively viewed by you, yet presented as objectively factual. Why would you do this, Mr. Levitan?

A. It's the way I remembered them.

Q. Do you think now that you've made an error, a serious error, in presenting highly subjective material, which may even have been 60, 70 percent invented by you, as factual scenes, objectively observed?

A. No, I don't, because nothing that I say happened has been 60, 70 percent invented or nearly that.

Q. Do you think that it's possible that you, in one way or another, for one reason or another, were out to tarnish Mr. Ziff's image? Make him look ridiculous in private situations while making him look generous in larger frameworks?

A. No, I was not, and it's not possible.

[A half-hour lunch break suggested by defense is taken.]

Plaintiff Atty. Levy: Mr. Levitan, I want to pursue a different line of questioning, and I'd like to remind you again, you are under oath here, and you know what the penalties are for perjury.

Defense Atty. Leibowitz: Objection! Is this a useful reminder, or a subtle form of intimidation?

Plaintiff Atty. Levy: Not at all; and if you follow my line of questioning, I hope you'll see why I repeated the reminder. Now, Mr. Levitan, you've visited Mr. Ziff, and stayed over with him, at his home in the Berkshires, many times in the past. Is that right?

A. Yes.

Q. Let me cite here just a few of the visits in the recent years say, all right, sir? For example, in March, 1998, in September 1998, in January 1999, in June 1999, Thanksgiving 1999, and so on, yes?

A. Well, yes, I suppose so, I can't remember exactly.

Q. Of course, we understand. Now, during those and other visits Mr. Levitan surely there were times when you were left unattended, you know in a room by yourself and so on?

A: Probably, sure.

Q. Do you recall at any of those times perhaps touching a paper or a manuscript page of Mr. Ziff's?

A. Well, I don't know.

Q. Surely Mr. Levitan you can remember if, by chance or otherwise, you laid your hands on something that was not yours, that was private property of Mr. Ziff's, a letter perhaps? A note of some sort? A manuscript page or two?

Defense Atty. Leibowitz: This is just a fishing expedition.

A. (Mr. Levitan shakes his head.) I cannot really remember, perhaps I did touch a page sometime, for some reason?

Plaintiff Atty. Levy: Do you recall when? And anything more specific sir?

A. (A pause.) No, I don't think so.

Q. Please think carefully Danny, what it was that you may have laid your hands on that was not yours, but Mr. Ziff's, when he wasn't there?

A. I recall once opening a fan letter to Mr. Ziff, but it was only because Mr. Ziff had mentioned that he had received a very funny new batch concerning—

Q. Good. So you remember opening a letter addressed to him, without his permission. Okay sir. Now, can you recall any other invasion of Mr. Ziff's privacy?

A. (shakes his head.) I'm . . . not sure.

Q. What do you mean, not sure? Surely you can remember something else, especially since you have just recalled a small matter like the opening of a fan letter?

[Defense attorney Leibowitz consults with DL]

A. I may have, I, uh, can't recall anything specific.

Q. Mr. Levitan, I must remind you here that you are under oath here and subject to the statutes of—

Defense Atty. Leibowitz: Would you cut out that sort of obvious intimidation of my client! He understands the rules and laws here, and you've repeated them enough so that—

Plaintiff Atty. Levy: I'm sorry about that, I'm just trying to protect Mr. Levitan in case he has inadvertently forgotten to mention something pertinent—

Defense Atty. Leibowitz: Oh sure, thanks for the protection, counselor.

Plaintiff Atty. Levy:(shuffling some pages) Now Mr. Levitan, let us look at a few specific visits, let's look at the most recent visit say, in January 2000—no, there's a later one here, March 2000 you visited Mr. Ziff at his home yes?

A. (pause) I may have been there then.

Q. Well, we do have an affidavit here—which I am now showing you, Mr. Leibowitz—[affidavit handed to Defense]—by a friend of Mr. Ziff's, Ms. Bigan Swenson, which claims she fixed you dinner then, and you slept over as well.

A. (drinks water) Oh yeah, sure, I remember.

Q. Good. You were there for over 24 hours, I believe, is that right Mr. Levitan?

A. (nodding)

Q. Could you verbalize the answer, please.

A. Yes, that's right.

Q. Now Mr. Levitan, it was a pleasant time, a fine dinner, no fights or arguments, is that right?

A. Yeah, that's about right.

Q. Mr. Levitan, during those 48 hours were you alone at all? And when you were, did you happen to invade Mr. Ziff's privacy in any way. Think carefully. Touch or open anything you shouldn't have—that means, not given permission to look into, by Mr. Ziff? Which you then perhaps wanted to employ in your book? . . . Mr. Levitan, I see you shaking your head, could you please state aloud your answer? . . . Mr. Levitan, why the hesitation? Please sir answer the question.

A. No. And I'd like to take a break, use the bathroom.

Q. So soon? . . . Well, okay, go ahead.

[During this break the attys for the publisher get into an argument with the defendant's attys, which is finally broken up by the plaintiff's attys.]

[Some 10-15 minutes later D. L. resumes his testimony]

Plaintiff Atty. Levy: So, to take up where we left off sir, you answered that during the March 2000 visit you are unaware of disturbing any papers or violating any privacy of Mr. Ziff when you were alone in the house?

A. Yeah.

Q. Excuse me? Yeah, what? Mr. Levitan consider your answers here very carefully, remember you are—

Defense Atty. Leibowitz: I object to this constant badgering—he has already answered you. Now if you have evidence to the contrary—

Plaintiff Atty. Levy: I am merely trying to make sure the defendant understands the full scope of this question and line of inquiry. Furthermore, that he understands completely that it is against the law for him to have read without permission, purloined any papers from Mr. Ziff's possessions, and that he could even later be charged with breaking and entering if it were discovered—

Defense Atty. Leibowitz: Enough, enough! This it outrageous. You're not only badgering and trying to intimidate, but you are reading the law inadequately to my client. Reading a private correspondence is one thing, and breaking and entering, which you are implying, is quite another.

Plaintiff Atty. Levy: Fair enough. Mr. Levitan, did you at any time illegally enter a room or building of Mr. Ziff's, meaning without his permission, knowing he wouldn't have given you permission, while you stayed with him? You are under oath, sir.

Defense Atty. Leibowitz: My client knows well that he is under oath, Steve. And you've repeated that a dozen times.

Q. (to Mr. Levitan) Sir?

A. (a barely audible answer)

Q. Could you speak up?

A. Not that I know of.

Q. Well, that's a bit strange. But nevertheless, let me—

[At this point the publisher's attys request a brief consultation with the defendant's atty, and the defendant, but the consultation quickly turns into a shouting match between attorneys, and finally after some five to eight heated minutes the publisher's attys sit down again, arguing with each other.]

[Another ten minutes before the room is calm again and testimony resumes]

Plaintiff Atty. Levy: With all this interruption, Danny, let me come back to my line of questioning a little later, and for now turn you over to my colleague Atty Meyers, who would like to put some other questions to you sir.

DL: Must we? I mean . . . continue now? . . .

Plaintiff Atty. Meyers: Well, yes, I think we must. It's early yet.

Plaintiff Atty. Levy: Now, Mr. Levitan, you stated in your manuscript on page 268, if you wish to consult your copy, that you came to discover, via a conversation, that Mr. Ziff is "fond of young Asian girls who have been shipped to Rome on their way over to London, Los Angeles, Toronto, and other cities." I have several questions here: Do you have proof of this allegation? Do you intend to use it in your book, without proof? Do you realize that this is defaming Mr. Ziff's character, and in a particularly odious, if not racist way?

A. Well, I do intend to use it. I say very clearly how and whereby I came to that information, though I do not name names. And I call it pious, to say the least, your labeling it the way you do.

Q. So you don't have direct evidence of this charge, but you choose to use this defamatory hearsay anyway, Mr. Levitan?

A. Look, Mr. Jacobs, I'm not writing a biography of Florence Nightingale or Anne Frank. Mr. Ziff is a big boy, an adult who—

[At this point the attorneys for the publisher stand up and, interrupting the testimony, depart angrily from the room.]

Q. Well, let's continue. This is not the only place in the text, Mr. Levitan, where you cross the boundary of character analysis and trespass onto dubious even off-limits ground. But for now let's return to the two scenes we took up this morning and pursue them closely, in greater detail. Now, the young waitress—

[Deponent Levitan slumps over and collapses in his chair, knocking over his glass of water in a paroxysm of trembling and crying. The defense attorney asks for a break in the hearing until the next morning, which is at first contested by the plaintiff's attorneys but then is granted.]

[End of available document]

A Final Letter

About nine months later, after his grand award, I received a brief letter from Arthur. It read:

Dear Danny,

I recently visited Copenhagen, and learned from an American professor named Paul Levine, that you had delivered a paper there and also in Aarhus, on my recent work. And that you were off to Stockholm and Helsinki soon thereafter for conferences. Professor Levine, whom I quite liked, praised your paper highly. I'd be happy to read it, if you care to send it on. But also I had an idea for you: Why don't you think of contributing an essay now and then to the Travel Section of the Sunday Times, *on your various travels. The features editor there happens to be a friend of mine and I'd be happy to write her and give her your name. I'm sure they'd pay you decently, even well once you're a regular, and also that your travel pieces would add some lively words and thoughts to that rather unreadable section. Think about it, and let me know.*

Yours,
Arthur

P.S.: You do know you perjured yourself in that Deposition, don't you?

It was the last correspondence I had from Arthur, and as I have yet to answer him, or send him any paper, I don't suppose we will have any communication in the near future.

About the Author

Alan Lelchuk was born in Brooklyn. His education included serving intermittently as a deckhand on Norwegian freighters that sailed to Africa. He received his BA from Brooklyn College in 1960 and did his graduate work at Stanford University, with a research year at the University of London focusing on George Gissing. He received his Ph.D in 1965.

Lelchuk began teaching at Brandeis University in 1966, was Visiting Writer for two years at Amherst College, from 1982-1984, and has been a member of the Dartmouth College faculty since 1985. In 1986-1987 he was Fulbright Writer-in-Residence at Haifa University, Israel; in 1999-2000 he was the recipient of the Otto Salgo Chair in American Literature and Writing at Eotvos Lorand University (ELTE) in Budapest, Hungary. He has also served as a visiting professor at the University of Rome and New York's City College. In 1976-1977 he was a Guggenheim Fellow in Fiction, and a guest resident at Mishkenot Sha'Ananim in Jerusalem. In 1994 he co-founded Steerforth Press, and is a member of the independent publisher's editorial board.

His novels are *American Mischief* (1973) *Miriam at Thirty-four* (1974), *Shrinking* (1978), *Miriam In Her Forties* (1985), *Brooklyn Boy* (1990), and *Playing the Game* (1995). His work has been translated into half a dozen foreign languages. He co-edited *8 Great Hebrew Short Novels* (1983) and for young adults has written *On Home Ground* (1987).

Lelchuk lives with his family in New Hampshire.